THE BEAST CURSE

CALATINI TALES BOOK 6

KATHERINE DOTTERER

KatSpell Press

The Beast Curse

Cover by 100 Covers

Edited by Susan Bischoff, Lauralynn Elliott

A KatSpell Press Book

- ISBN 978-1-955614-22-1 (ebook)
- ISBN 978-1-955614-23-8 (trade paperback)

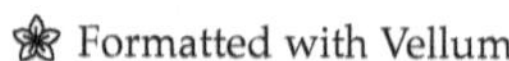 Formatted with Vellum

CONTENTS

ABOUT THE BEAST CURSE

*I*n the Regency-inspired kingdom of Calatini, enemies *can become lovers, and beauty can save the beast with her love... and powerful magic.*

All of court knows about the fierce enmity between Lady Juliet, the powerful royal witch, and the rakehell Duke of Oakmoor. What they don't know is that the two were once lovers—a mistake neither can forget. One Juliet vows never to repeat, no matter how her body longs for it, yet one Oakmoor would gladly repeat, if only to silence her sharp tongue.

But even Juliet doesn't know that in Oakmoor's youth, a jilted lover cursed him to transform into a hideous beast one day, and now that vindictive curse is finally about to manifest. Perhaps the royal witch could help him, but to ask Juliet would reveal—and risk—far too much. So Oakmoor consults a seer instead and discovers his curse can only be broken by true love.

Desperate, the cursed duke kidnaps an innocent young lady he believes can love him and break the evil spell. But that lady already loves another, so Juliet secretly takes her place. Trapped alone together until his curse is broken, Juliet and Oakmoor soon begin to feel more than enmity and unwanted desire. But getting to happily-ever-after isn't always as easy as breaking a curse...

IN *THE BEAST CURSE*, Beauty and the Beast are reimagined as the warring Beatrice and Benedick for the perfect low-spice enemies-to-lovers fantasy romance. Dive into this tale—or the other books in the Calatini Tales series—for cozy, heart-warming HEAs.

CHAPTER 1

Shortly before *Sea Vision* was due to dock, Oakmoor leapt from his carriage to await the Orandian ship's early morning arrival. As the Minister of Foreign Relations for Calatini, 'twas his duty to greet their first Orandian ambassador in a decade as soon as she arrived then escort her to the luxurious townhouse near the palace he'd secured for her and her delegation as their embassy. Hopefully, Lady Siobhan Driscoll was as clever and composed as she'd appeared in the letters and mirror calls they'd exchanged over the past two months. With everything else complicating his life at the moment, he didn't need a troublesome new ambassador adding to that.

He shoved aside his personal worries when the happily married Countess of Escana, who'd been assisting him at the Ministry of Foreign Relations for three years, joined him on the docks. She smiled at him with no hint of flirtation and briskly said, "I visited the Orandian's new embassy on my way here. The final repairs and decorating were finished yesterday, and the servants are preparing a breakfast feast to welcome the Orandians."

He nodded. Exactly like he'd specified. "Wonderful. Thanks for checking everything was ready."

Lady Escana calmly returned his nod. "Of course, your grace. What else are mere assistants for?"

Oakmoor couldn't help a chuckle. Lady Escana wasn't a mere anything, let alone a mere assistant. She was perceptive and engaging as well as diligent and poised, so she could assume his duties if he ever wanted to retire one day. Agreeing to allow her to become his assistant had been an excellent decision, although he'd initially been concerned her interest in assisting him had been a ploy to begin an affair, and he never trifled with committed ladies like wives or betrotheds despite his rakehell reputation. Thankfully, Lady Escana was devoted to her husband and had always treated him like an older brother. A refreshing change from most ladies at court, who adored his suave, rakish air and lusted after his title, wealth, and influence. Only one lady had truly disdained him for all that—the maddening royal witch who still pervaded his carnal dreams since their disturbingly intense night together nearly fourteen years ago. He dreamt of Juliet much too often, although his recent curse dreams had begun to eclipse the ones featuring her.

He was drawn back to the present when Lady Escana asked as *Sea Vision* started to dock, "Is Lady Driscoll a witch, do you think? I've heard that at least half of the people on the isle of Orandia are witches, like in Magehaven."

While the Orandian ship was secured, he shrugged. "She hasn't said, and prior Orandian ambassadors haven't been, but 'tis possible, and she might even be a Rhiannon descendant." Rhiannon, the founder of human magic, had eventually settled in Orandia, which was why so many in the island kingdom were witches or Rhiannon descendants, the most powerful of all witches who were descended from the early witches whose magical powers had been enhanced by Rhiannon through a blood-kith ceremony. The duchy of Magehaven only had as many witches as Orandia because it contained two of the three eminent witch academies in Calatini and was just south of the

Walle, the powerful magical wall that separated human kingdoms from the kingdoms of magical creatures.

Oakmoor frowned at Lady Escana. "But don't ask Lady Driscoll about her magical powers unless she mentions them first." Many witches, particularly Rhiannon descendants, didn't discuss their magical powers with ordinary humans to prevent jealousy and exploitation. 'Twas partly why he'd told no one when his erratic magic had inexplicably appeared on his forty-fifth natalday almost two years ago—thirty years late because most witches' magical powers finished developing when their bodies matured.

Lady Escana sniffed. "I know better than to be so rude as to pry about Lady Driscoll's magic."

Before the countess could grumble further, Lady Driscoll and an unknown gentleman strode down the gangplank. A mature couple around his age, they both wore the typical Orandian attire of tunics with long overcoats, although Lady Driscoll wore a long tunic, while her escort wore a knee-length one with boots. And both had reddish hair like many Orandians did, except hers was bright red and her escort's red-brown with flecks of gray.

When the Orandian ambassador and her escort reached them, Oakmoor swept a smooth bow while flashing a charming grin. He offered the archaic greeting common in Orandia, "Good morrow, Lady Driscoll and..."

Lady Driscoll grinned. In a lilting Orandian accent, she said, "Good morning, your grace." She squeezed the gentleman's arm still firmly entwined with hers. "This is Sir Lorcan Driscoll, my husband."

Oakmoor blinked. The Orandian ambassador had never mentioned having a husband while arranging her visit. Yet her being married, happily from the warmth between them, would eliminate romantic intrigue that he couldn't deal with right now. He smiled at Lady Driscoll's husband. "A pleasure, Sir Lorcan." He nodded at Lady Escana. "And this is the Countess of Escana, my assistant at the Ministry of Foreign Relations." Once everyone exchanged greetings, he gestured toward his carriage. "Shall we head to the embassy? Lady Escana shall handle transportation for the rest of your delegation."

After he'd settled in the backward seat across from Lady Driscoll and Sir Lorcan, Oakmoor asked them, "How was your voyage from Orandia?"

While the carriage rumbled forward, Lady Driscoll smiled and replied, "The three weeks were smooth, although I had to ensure Lorcan's nausea-healing charm was always fully charged."

Sir Lorcan shuddered. "Yes, even the calmest seas make me terribly ill. Why I married a sea witch, I don't know."

Oakmoor scrutinized the Orandian couple. No witch in Calatini so openly mentioned their magical powers. Perhaps they were more frank because many more people were witches in Orandia.

Lady Driscoll slanted her husband a laughing glance. "Maybe 'twas because my seven brothers threatened to kill you if you didn't."

Although there was an interesting story there, Oakmoor didn't ask them about it because he hated anyone prying into his own private matters, especially when they'd just met, so he tried to offer others the courtesy of not prying. Instead, he told Lady Driscoll and her husband about the plans to welcome them to Calatini.

Once he and Lady Escana ate the breakfast feast with Lady Driscoll and her delegation, he and his assistant left the Orandians to settle into their new embassy. He returned to Oakmoor House to check on the preparations for his soiree tomorrow to celebrate the Orandian ambassador's arrival. Everything was nearly ready, and he handled the last few matters requiring his attention before rejoining Lady Driscoll and Sir Lorcan to tour Ormas.

Following their tour, he hosted a sumptuous dinner for the Orandian couple at Oakmoor House, where they told him all about their family. He chuckled at their amusing stories about their four grown children back in Orandia, although his chest tightened somewhat too. If he'd married in his twenties like they had, he'd also have grown children. But love and commitment weren't for him, and having to remain faithful to one lady for the rest of his life had always made him shudder, so he never had. And now he never might. Given the curse dreams he'd begun suffering over six months ago, his obsessive first lover Elvaira's vindictive beast curse was surely close to manifesting, and that curse would destroy any chance of happiness or a normal life.

After dinner, Oakmoor showed Lady Driscoll and Sir Lorcan his ballroom's renowned stained-glass ceiling created by his duchy's fantastic artisans and made unbreakable by magic. Both were fascinated and asked to perform probing spells to study the stained-glass ceiling's magic, and he agreed so long as their spells didn't touch it. Glass shattering on them would be unpleasant, and repairing the ceiling would be near impossible.

The next morning following an early breakfast, he met with Lady Escana to discuss the Orandians' arrival before heading to the embassy to escort Lady Driscoll and Sir Lorcan to the palace to meet King Devon and Queen Kiera. Like most, the Orandians exclaimed at the sprawling white castle that had been home to Calatini's kings since the kingdom's founding. And rightly so —'twas a stunning and exquisite palace that possessed no equal.

Once Oakmoor ushered the Orandians into the vast throne room and introduced them, King Devon, who was crownless like usual, smiled at them from the left-hand throne. "Welcome to Calatini, Lady Driscoll, Sir Lorcan. I'm glad we can reestablish relations between our kingdoms after so many years."

Also crownless and seated on the other throne on the dais, Queen Kiera beamed at the Orandians. "I hope you don't mind we met you here rather than in more intimate surroundings, but

Calatini's first Orandian ambassador in a decade was too momentous not to."

Lady Driscoll grinned. "Of course." She waved toward the white velvet curtain wafting behind the two thrones despite there being no breeze. "And meeting in the throne room allows us the opportunity to see the legendary Mirror of Wisdom."

Oakmoor stiffened and eyed Lady Driscoll and her husband askance. To boldly mention the powerful and perilous enchanted mirror must mean they were interested in using it. Yet although the Mirror of Wisdom could show the watcher the answer to any question, using it could be deadly. Years ago, the Mirror of Wisdom had killed King Devon's mother and induced the king's premature birth, making the entire kingdom fear the Vireni line would end. Oakmoor swallowed. Even he had never been tempted to risk using the Mirror of Wisdom to discover how to break the nearly thirty-year-old curse that would soon turn him into a hideous beast.

Sir Lorcan nodded and leaned forward. "We've heard the Mirror of Wisdom was bathed in water from our seer's divination pool. Such a wondrous tool to help your reign. We'd greatly love to see it."

King Devon and Queen Kiera traded a lengthy glance. Then King Devon murmured, "We can show you as long as you swear not to use it."

Lady Driscoll smiled and inclined her head. "Of course. Enchanted tools frequently lose their effectiveness if used too often."

At that nonchalant reply, King Devon and Queen Kiera exchanged another glance, and Oakmoor almost shook his head. The Orandians evidently didn't consider the mirror perilous, probably because they were accustomed to using enchanted items on their magical isle. A mistake. But not satisfying their curiosity could hamper relations between Calatini and Orandia, and Lady Driscoll *had* sworn they'd not use the mirror.

After a moment, King Devon returned Lady Driscoll's nod then gestured for a royal guard to draw aside the curtain.

Oakmoor exhaled. Despite having been at court for nearly three decades, he'd never seen the Mirror of Wisdom because King Sarastor had covered it and forbade its use after it had killed Queen Mynee. When the mirror was revealed, his neck prickled at the power emanating from the massive mirror with a mahogany frame of crescent moon faces and flowing vines. The mirror and its frame gleamed with a peculiar opalescent sheen which betrayed its magical nature too. Definitely eerie and powerful. Even ordinary humans without the least magic could sense that.

While he suppressed a shudder, Lady Driscoll hummed, her eyes bright. She chirped, "You can cover the Mirror of Wisdom again now."

His gaze gleaming too, Sir Lorcan tugged on his long overcoat while a royal guard covered the mirror and said to King Devon, "Your mother commissioned *quite* the faegift for your father, your majesty. You must use it often."

King Devon's mouth tightened as Queen Kiera shivered, and he grasped her hand. Both were doubtless remembering the mirror's deadly legacy.

To distract them, Oakmoor drawled, "Queen Mynee was in love, and people in love are mad I've found." He winked at the royal couple. "Some even obsessively hunt for a mysterious mermaid they knew all of one night then marry her, for instance. Makes me glad I've never suffered such madness. I enjoy my freedom too much."

At the description of their courtship, King Devon smiled, and Queen Kiera chuckled then replied, "'Tis apparent from your rakehell ways, your grace." Queen Kiera turned back to the Orandian ambassador and Sir Lorcan. "We'll let you begin your tour of the palace so that you'll have time to rest before the Duke of Oakmoor's soiree tonight. I remember how draining court introductions can be."

. . .

THAT EVENING, Oakmoor, Lady Driscoll, and Sir Lorcan greeted his many guests while Lady Escana ensured his soiree ran smoothly. His drawing room was extremely crowded tonight. *All* of court was in Ormas this year because the social season had started three weeks ago on Plantfete with King Devon and Queen Kiera's wedding ceremony and her coronation. Plus, everyone wanted to gawk at Calatini's new Orandian ambassador.

Not long after they'd greeted King Devon and Queen Kiera, Juliet glided into the drawing room wearing a modish ballgown of deep-amethyst satin. Tingling heat flooded him like it always did when the royal witch was near. Goddess, why must Juliet's exotic beauty and powerful air bewitch him so? Despite all his experience with women, he became as desperate as a lusty satyr who'd not fornicated in years whenever she was around. After their long ago night together when their mutual hunger had taken her unexpected innocence, he'd ensured they were never alone and kept their public interactions brief and restricted to council affairs. On the one occasion he hadn't, in Childes House's garden seven and a half months ago, their explosive passion had consumed them, and they'd nearly ravished each other against an alcove wall before she'd slapped him and vanished with a jump travel spell. And since that passionate encounter, he'd been unable to settle on another lover. Juliet had cursed him as surely as Elvaira had, damn her.

Yet when Juliet paused to greet them, he gritted a smooth smile. No one must guess his primal hunger for her, especially not the lady herself. He said, "Lady Driscoll, Sir Lorcan, allow me to introduce Lady Juliet, the royal witch. Lady Juliet, this is our new Orandian ambassador and her husband."

Like always, Juliet returned his smile with a cool one that didn't touch her gorgeous dark-brown eyes. Then she turned toward the Orandians, her smile warming and becoming genuine. "A pleasure, Lady Driscoll, Sir Lorcan."

Lady Driscoll grinned back. "Likewise, Lady Juliet. We've been eager to meet the most illustrious witch in Calatini. Your reputation for intricate and innovative spellwork is impressive, and we'd love to swap spells sometime. I'm a sea witch, while my husband is a lore witch."

Juliet's dark brows quirked. Clearly she was as surprised by the Orandians' openness about their magical powers as he'd been and couldn't imagine revealing her own so quickly. Like him, she'd always been discreet. Juliet was his only lover who'd not told anyone about their night together, so it had thankfully remained secret because he never overtly seduced his lovers in public or discussed them afterward. Juliet also rarely mentioned her past, and all she revealed was that she'd traveled with gypsies before settling in Calatini. Yet she'd obviously been born a lady from her perfect manners and ease at court, albeit not from Calatini given her luscious olive skin and intense dark-brown hair and eyes.

As more guests approached, Juliet said to Lady Driscoll, "I'd enjoy swapping spells too. Good evening." Then without acknowledging him, she swept into the crowd. The maddening witch was never so disdainful in her letters.

Aching to chase after Juliet to transform her cool disdain to fervid desire with fierce kisses, he made himself unclench his jaw and grin as he turned to his next guests, Lord and Lady Ravenstone, who'd shocked court three months ago by convincing their parents to accept their marriage, thus ending the centuries-long Greysnowe-Ravenstone feud. And from the frequent heated glances between the couple, Lord Ravenstone had truly thawed the beauteous "Lady Snow", which was almost as shocking as their families' feud ending. Not that Oakmoor resented the count's success, despite having briefly attempted to court the lady himself over six months ago.

He swallowed a sigh while greeting the next couple, Sir Ellis and Lady Campbell. He'd only attempted to court Lady Ravenstone because, once his curse dreams began, he'd known he wouldn't remain human much longer, and the responsible cousin who should have inherited his duchy had recently died in a tragic fire. His responsible cousin's younger brother would ruin the duchy in under a decade with his spendthrift ways, drunken stupors, and countless greedy women. To prevent that degenerate cousin from inheriting, he needed to sire an heir while he still could, even though he'd never desired marriage. An ice-perfect lady like the former "Lady Snow" had seemed ideal since she'd not miss him after his beast curse manifested. Yet when her parents had dissuaded his courtship, he'd moved on without regret to the fashionable Countess of Blaine. He'd been about to propose to the sultry yet strong countess when she'd mysteriously disappeared on Longnight. In the four months since, he'd begun courting various eligible ladies, but none held his interest for longer than three weeks. They were all so *young* and bland, and he couldn't even summon the desire to kiss them thanks to Juliet.

He tensed when he greeted the elderly Duke of Osbourne, a fellow councilor, along with the duke's youngest daughter, Lady Georgiana Laurent—the eligible lady he'd been courting for the last three weeks. Despite her youth, she'd seemed a suitable choice at first since she was steely behind her sweet smiles and understood his duties thanks to growing up with her father. Plus, with her dark hair and brown eyes, Lady Georgiana was his type except for her pale skin. Yet her coy giggles and feigned fragility had begun to grate. He couldn't possibly marry her and suffer those for the brief time he'd left as human. No, he must end their courtship, although not during his soiree for the Orandian ambassador.

After everyone finally finished arriving, Oakmoor left the Orandians engrossed in conversation with the royal couple and the Ravenstones before circulating and entertaining his guests with stories about Orandia as well as Lady Driscoll and her husband. Then he frowned mid-sentence when an ancient woman in a servant's dress climbed atop a chair near the wall by the garden. *Who* was that? She clearly didn't possess an invitation to an exclusive court event. Was she here to gawk at or assault the Orandian ambassador for some reason? He'd better handle her at once. Excusing himself, he began striding through the crowd toward the interloper.

CHAPTER 2

After escaping Oakmoor, Juliet swept straight to the refreshments table for a flute of sparkling wine to settle her treacherous body's inevitable tingling in his presence. Why must she always react so to that unrepentant rakehell? 'Twas unfair that Oakmoor was even more handsome now than when they'd first met fourteen years ago. The distinguished touch of gray at the temples of his almond-brown hair only enhanced the masculine allure of his strong features and still fit body.

She sighed as she took some sparkling wine. Her susceptibility to Oakmoor could so easily make her abandon her ambitions and identity to suit his whims like she'd been raised to do as a Varkhoran lady. They'd known each other less than a month when she'd let him seduce away her innocence after a few feeble protests. Then she'd nearly succumbed again thirteen years later when he'd kissed her for the next time in Childes House's garden. And she'd not been shyly hesitant during either encounter because somehow Oakmoor possessed the power to turn her into a ravaging venus. Yet she'd striven too hard for the influence, respect, and renown she'd earned at court as Calatini's royal witch to surrender that for any *man*.

Her lips twisted while she sipped her sparkling wine. If he

was even alive at the ancient age of seventy-two, Father—the Duke of Appenninos, the most prominent duke in Varkhora—would never credit all she'd achieved here in Calatini. But like most men from the warrior kingdom of Varkhora, Father believed women should be subservient and belonged to their male relatives. He'd doubtless raged when she'd run away with a gypsy family after he'd attempted to force her to marry his royal cousin's bullying son, the now deceased King Cesare—his attempt to advantageously dispose of the teenage daughter made worthless by his healthy toddler son and heir, her adorable brother Giovanni.

Juliet grimaced into her glass flute. Both Father and King Cesare had surely pursued revenge for years following her disappearance. Which was why she'd done all she could to disappear completely. To avoid being found, she'd fled in the middle of the night, met the gypsies half a day's distance from court, never contacted Mother or Giovanni despite aching to, and concealed herself with a tracing-ward spell until recently. And to avoid betraying her heritage, she'd abandoned her sweet faebird Gentian, quit using her full name and changed it from its Varkhoran form, refused to return to Varkhora, never dared mention her past before traveling with the gypsies, and worn a glamour spell for years that prevented anyone from recognizing her ethnicity.

She buried her pointless reflections as she joined Lord and Lady Islaye, Dowager Lady Ravenstone, and Lord and Lady Greysnowe. All five were acknowledged witches from Magehaven and Wildewall, the most magical duchies in Calatini, although Magehaven possessed more witches thanks to its witch academies. A powerful witch but not a Rhiannon descendant like herself, the studious Lord Islaye served on the council with Oakmoor as the Minister of Magic and represented Magehaven. His wife Lady Islaye was a minor witch who wasn't truly a hearth witch, even though she mostly used spells that tended households and kitchens like they did. Residents of Wildewall,

Dowager Lady Ravenstone and the Greysnowes had been ancestral enemies until the dowager's son and the Greysnowes' daughter had become soulbound and fallen in love, activating an ancient curse that she herself had helped break. Ever since then, the trio were effusively cordial toward her, and the two mothers had become the best of friends and were often together, which still shocked court.

Juliet smiled at the five Calatinian witches while they exchanged polite greetings. Despite being acknowledged witches like her, they were merely friendly acquaintances rather than close friends. She couldn't risk sharing her true identity with them, and royal witches must remain somewhat apart to serve their kingdom and royal family properly. Plus, none of the five witches truly shared her deep fascination with magic and hunger for creating innovative spells. After their greetings ended, she arched her brows over her flute of sparkling wine. "What did you think of the Orandian ambassador and her husband?"

Lady Islaye grinned. "I was amazed at how open they were about their magical powers. Even in Magehaven where at least half of us are witches like in Orandia, we're more cautious about that."

Juliet nodded and tapped her flute against her lip. She'd been surprised by the Orandian's openness too. As Calatini's royal witch, she'd shown she was a powerful Rhiannon descendant on occasion, but she never outright admitted that unless necessary. Doing so could make matters difficult.

Lord Islaye rubbed his chin. "I'm surprised Orandia sent us a pair of witches this time. Orandians are rather insular, with only those who aren't witches traveling to mainland Damensea. I remember our previous Orandian ambassador didn't have the slightest magical powers."

Juliet hummed. "True, he didn't. But no doubt their seer sent us witches for a reason. The Orandian seer is supposedly the most prescient in Damensea." Except possibly for the dratted veiled witch, the incredibly powerful Rhiannon-descendant seer who owned a witch shop near the docks and whose powers eclipsed her own like the sun eclipsed the moon. "Hopefully, it doesn't mean trouble is headed for Calatini."

They all traded frowns, then Dowager Lady Ravenstone said, "We should attempt to find out why their seer sent Lady Driscoll and Sir Lorcan so that we can be ready to resolve whatever trouble is approaching."

Lady Greysnowe sighed. "'Tis fortunate we've ended the ridiculous feud between our families. We'll need all the witches in Calatini united if trouble is imminent."

As Lord Greysnowe nodded to echo his wife, Juliet drained her sparkling wine. Especially Rhiannon-descendant witches like the Ravenstones and the Greysnowes. Dowager Lady Ravenstone and Lord Ravenstone were both particularly powerful nature witches with abilities most didn't possess. And while Lady Greysnowe was an ordinary witch, Lord Greysnowe's family was descended from the legendary Esme the Great and bore soul healers like her every few generations. Soul healers were extremely rare female witch healers who could heal nearly anything, and although very few knew it, the Greysnowes' daughter was one. She'd used her secret powers to save Lord Ravenstone after her brother had nearly killed him in a duel, which had created their life-changing soulbond. The new Lady Ravenstone's secret powers might be crucial in times of trouble.

Juliet exhaled and waved her empty glass flute. "I need more sparkling wine; excuse me."

She was heading to the refreshments table when Oakmoor strode through the crowd, pulling an ancient maid behind him by her wrist. Although tingling anew at his nearness, she stared at him like his surrounding guests. The suave duke was never so heavy-handed, particularly in public. And why was he approaching *her*? Since their upsettingly intense night together, he'd avoided her as much as possible, and she did likewise. Their unwanted hunger for each other was too irresistible and too explosive—as their feverish kisses at the Duchess of Childes's fete for her first grandchild over seven months ago had proved. They'd nearly ravaged each other against the garden wall. Thankfully, she'd managed to recall herself before they had and escaped with a jump travel spell.

Oakmoor halted before her and gritted, "This crone here claims to be Lady Blaine under an illusion."

Juliet pursed her lips. *That* explained the crowd's staring even more than Oakmoor's unusual behavior did. The fashionable Countess of Blaine's mysterious disappearance on Longnight had been gossiped about the past four months, and for the sultry beauty to appear like an ancient maid made it even more gossip-worthy. Juliet narrowly eyed Oakmoor, her stomach hardening. And no wonder he'd been so heavy-handed. An elderly maid claiming to be the first eligible lady he'd ever seriously courted must have upset him. It also explained why he'd approached *her*. He'd no magical powers to verify the lady's claim himself. She swallowed then drawled, "I suppose you wish me to check for you." When both Oakmoor and the lady glowered at her, she sighed. "Very well, I'll perform a probing spell."

She gathered her will, squinted at the possible Lady Blaine, and silently cast her probing spell. Although using her will required more magical energy than using another order of magic, like an incantation, doing so was best when discretion or secrecy was needed. The ancient lady almost shimmered for a moment, but no white glow indicating active magic surrounded her. Juliet tsked. "There's something peculiar about the lady, but I can't sense an illusion spell glowing about her."

As Oakmoor humphed, the elderly lady stiffened then said in a young voice that didn't match her appearance, "'Tis a spell from the Goddess, so only priests or seers can sense it. However, if you can read my aura, you'd recognize me as Lady Blaine."

Juliet blinked. Spells from the Goddess were *exceedingly* rare, even more than soul healers were. How had a fashionable Cala-tinian countess received one? And why? Yet she doubtless wasn't lying because such blasphemy could cost Lady Blaine her life and soul.

Oakmoor glared at the ancient-appearing Lady Blaine. "Spin your lies for someone more gullible."

Juliet raised her eyes skyward. Distrustful idiot. "If the lady *is* under a holy spell, she's correct that I'd be unable to sense it." She hummed and studied Lady Blaine. Too bad she couldn't help prove the countess's identity to the overly suspicious duke. "I could read your aura if I wished, but 'twouldn't help since I don't know Lady Blaine's. Only seers, soul healers, and most magical creatures instinctively read auras. For the rest of us, 'tis difficult and considered an intrusion, so we rarely do so."

Lady Blaine sagged. "Please, just let me speak with Lady Ravenstone."

As Juliet began to frown, Oakmoor glared and asked what she was thinking, "Why do you need to see *her*?"

Straightening, Lady Blaine tugged on her captured wrist and glared back. "I can't explain, but someone direly needs Lady Ravenstone's help."

Juliet inhaled a sharp breath. Somehow Lady Blaine knew about Lady Ravenstone's secret powers. And for someone to direly need the soul healer's help meant they were dying. "I think you'd better release the lady, Oakmoor."

Still gripping Lady Blaine's wrist, Oakmoor whirled to scowl at Juliet.

But before he could speak, Lady Ravenstone's serene voice interrupted them, "Lady Blaine? What happened to you?"

While Oakmoor gaped at the elderly-appearing lady he held, Juliet relaxed and nearly smiled. As a soul healer, Lady Ravenstone always saw auras and would recognize Lady Blaine's, proving the elderly-appearing lady's identity. And the dying person Lady Blaine was here to save could get the healing they needed.

Lady Blaine wrenched her wrist free and faced Lady Ravenstone, who was on her husband's arm with King Devon and

Queen Kiera beside them. Lady Blaine said, "Never mind what happened to me. Wren needs you. She's in childbirth and likely dying."

Juliet gaped as Oakmoor had earlier. Although Wren, more properly known as Lady Beza Hawke, was close friends with both Queen Kiera and Lady Ravenstone, she and Lady Blaine had never been friends. Indeed, Lady Blaine had gleefully told all of court that the other lady had fallen pregnant without being married. Fortunately for the former Miss Keyes, much of the scandal had quieted after her swift yet happy marriage to Lord Beza Hawke, the reformed rakehell responsible for her pregnancy, who was a cousin of King Devon's and the youngest son of the influential Duke and Duchess of Childes.

At hearing their friend's peril, Queen Kiera and Lady Ravenstone turned white, and Queen Kiera gasped, "What?!"

Then Lady Ravenstone surged forward without her typical grace. "I'll go at once. I hope the carriage is fast enough."

The wizened Lady Blaine gulped a breath and grabbed Lady Ravenstone's arm. "I've a flying carpet in the garden that shall get us there faster."

Juliet blinked again. More surprising magic from Lady Blaine. Flying carpets were expensive, conspicuous, and not at all common in Calatini. But if Lady Beza Hawke was dying, 'twas goddess-sent.

While Lady Ravenstone and Lady Blaine bolted through the still gawking crowd, Queen Kiera called after them, "We'll fetch Wren and Hawke's families then follow you in our carriages."

As King Devon, Queen Kiera, and Lord Ravenstone rushed off too, Juliet and Oakmoor turned toward one another. He no longer appeared upset about Lady Blaine, just wryly amused. Her heart quickening once more, damn his allure, she managed a cool smile. "Well, *that* was interesting."

Oakmoor grimaced. "I expect gossip about Lady Blaine and Lady Ravenstone shall surpass that about our new Orandian ambassador. Much more titillating."

She inhaled and gripped Oakmoor's arm. "We mustn't let gossip about Lady Ravenstone spread." 'Twould endanger the soul healer if everyone knew about her powers. Thankfully, she was soulbound to Lord Ravenstone, so she couldn't be coerced into forming another, but soul healers were coveted and often exploited if they were known. And they were especially vulnerable because they could only perform their special magic, which didn't include defense spells.

His hazel eyes darkening with the same desire she was suffering at their nearness, Oakmoor shifted even closer. "And why not? She's always been gossiped about for her ice-perfect beauty and her family's ridiculous feud."

As Oakmoor's earthy sandalwood scent surrounded her, Juliet shivered and forced herself not to sway toward him. Goddess, how she burned to kiss him again. But she'd lose herself if she did. She glared at him. "Trust me; 'tis important."

Oakmoor quirked a brow then laid his hand over hers on his arm. "You know I trust no woman."

Her pulse flaring at his touch, she glared harder. Flippant beast. "And no woman can trust *you*." She leaned nearer despite her unruly pulse. "I swear King Devon and Queen Kiera shan't be pleased for this gossip to spread about their close friend."

His gaze never leaving hers, Oakmoor caressed her hand with his thumb, only increasing the tingling heat coursing through her. He rumbled, "Then we'd better ensure court forgets about her involvement and only gossips about Lady Blaine's ancient appearance, hadn't we?"

Juliet stared up at him without moving. If she shifted slightly closer, her aching body would finally enjoy his hardness again, and she could easily seize his mouth in a deep kiss.

Oakmoor smirked. "Unless you'd rather I drag you into the garden to couple against an alcove wall first. I'm willing—as long as this time you swear not to slap me, shock me with an energy spell, or disappear with a jump travel spell before we consummate our passion."

Although hunger throbbed in her veins as heated images of them entwined flashed before her, she jerked back and fisted her hands in the deep-amethyst satin skirt of her favorite ballgown. "Don't you dare, you disgusting rakehell."

Oakmoor chuckled and shifted closer again. "Why not? We both want it, and I might get some restful sleep for once if we ravish each other senseless."

Juliet flushed. Surely the rakehell duke didn't suffer the same disturbingly carnal dreams she did. He was never without a lover, while she'd solely ever desired him. If only she didn't. She made herself grit a cold smile. "No. Now go divert the gossip from Lady Ravenstone. I'll begin near the refreshments table." She desperately needed another flute of sparkling wine.

After fetching her sparkling wine, she circulated about the opposite end of the drawing room from Oakmoor, talking about Lady Blaine's elderly appearance without mentioning Lady Ravenstone, and everyone she talked to was soon doing the same. Good. She finished her rounds with the Orandian ambassador and her husband.

Her freckled face almost impish, Lady Driscoll grinned at Juliet and said in a lilting voice, "Interesting bit of drama earlier. I was surprised to see the charming Duke of Oakmoor act so rough. What was that all about?"

Juliet managed a light shrug to trivialize the incident. "The duke didn't believe the lady was who she claimed to be. Normally, she's a young and beautiful court lady, but she's under an illusion from the Goddess."

Lady Driscoll and Sir Lorcan traded wide glances, then they both nodded. Sir Lorcan leaned toward her and said, "Excellent probing spell, by the way. Since you cast it with will alone, you're clearly a Rhiannon descendant, unlike us. I assume you're responsible for the potent protection charms both King Devon and Queen Kiera wear about their left wrists?"

Juliet smiled and inclined her head. Those intricate and powerful charms were some of her best spellwork. Powered by the love Calatini felt for King Devon and Queen Kiera, the gold bracelets had four strands that each served a different purpose without interactions between them. Three were fused together to strengthen them: the one that defended against enchantments, the one that defended against poisons, and the one that served as the token for their secret bloodbinding. The fourth strand, which they'd quit wearing after their public wedding ceremony, was a detachable contraceptive charm. Like many spells, the powerful protection charm must be renewed every year, and as the spell's creator, she was the only witch who could do so without destroying the delicate balance between its different parts. She suppressed a grimace. Except for possibly the veiled witch. No doubt such a gifted Rhiannon-descendant seer could manage it.

Shoving that aside, she explained, "Yes, after consulting the Mirror of Wisdom, King Devon's father King Sarastor hired me as Calatini's royal witch fourteen years ago to create that special protection charm for his son's sixteenth natalday. Then after Queen Kiera arrived at court," and was nearly poisoned by the treasonous Lady Morwynne, "King Devon requested I create one for her too."

Lady Driscoll fingered the edge of her open white overcoat atop her long indigo tunic. "How interesting that King Sarastor trusted a foreigner to create such a crucial spell."

Juliet almost grimaced again. Not surprising the newly arrived Orandians recognized she wasn't from Calatini. Her olive skin was darker than most Calatinians, and she'd dropped her glamour spell that prevented anyone from recognizing she was Varkhoran after King Cesare had died three years ago. She'd been so established in Calatini by then that no one at court thought of her as anything but their royal witch, and the new king of Varkhora, King Cesare's younger brother Alessandro, had no reason to pursue revenge. In fact, she and Sandro had been close growing up since they were both misfits in Varkhoran society—he for being a crippled gentleman, and she for being a driven lady. Yet she'd not dropped the tracing-ward spell that prevented anyone from locating her using magic until after Queen Kiera's coronation. From what King Sarastor had seen in the Mirror of Wisdom, she'd *had* to remain in Calatini until then, and Father might still be alive and pursuing revenge for ruining his ambition to be father to Varkhora's queen. But now she could leave if necessary, and always maintaining such a spell was draining.

Sir Lorcan rubbed his jaw as he answered his wife, "I suspect the Mirror of Wisdom showed King Sarastor that Lady Juliet was the witch needed to create his special protection charm. 'Twas bathed in water from our seer's divination pool, after all. Such a wondrous tool."

Her mouth quirking, Juliet nodded. Of course a lore witch immediately guessed the details the mirror had shown. "It did." Although the Mirror of Wisdom was more perilous than wondrous.

But before she could say as much, Lady Driscoll glanced about the ballroom and asked, "I assume that magical fabric Queen Kiera and some of the other ladies are wearing is another of your innovative spells? Its residual magic is most intriguing— I can't tell what it does, and I've never seen anything like it during all our travels in Orandia."

Juliet followed Lady Driscoll's gaze to the nearby Lady Farson and Miss Philippa Hawke, who were both wearing arachne silk ballgowns. Lady Farson's was decorated with horses, while Miss Hawke's with suns. Most appropriate. Lady Farson's husband was the councilor who represented the horse-mad duchy of Golddell, where the horse-like nightmara also lived. And Miss Hawke, who'd been courting Lady Farson's serious twin Lord Blaine for months, was always so radiantly cheerful that she'd resemble a sun nymph if not for her chestnut hair.

Smiling, Juliet shook her head as she told Lady Driscoll, "I'm afraid that magical fabric isn't one of my spells. Arachne silk is woven by the arachne on Mist Isle and can become any color or pattern imaginable using a drop of blood but without any other magical cost. Lord Beza Hawke—who's a cousin of King Devon's as well as those two ladies—and his merchant partner began importing it into Calatini last season."

As Sir Lorcan rubbed his jaw, Lady Driscoll grinned and said, "How fascinating. I must speak with Lord Beza Hawke about this arachne silk. Where is he?"

Juliet stilled. "Lord Beza Hawke rarely attends court events since his marriage." And 'twas his wife Lady Ravenstone had left to save. To distract the Orandians from asking more about the Hawkes, she said, "Come visit my workroom in a week. I'd invite you sooner, but I'm sure you require time to settle in. I remember how long it takes to become adjusted to a new court."

Lady Driscoll and Sir Lorcan beamed at her, and Lady Driscoll replied, "We'd love that, thank you."

After saying goodbye to the Orandian couple, Juliet began heading toward the door. Other guests were beginning to leave, and she daren't be Oakmoor's final guest. The one time that had happened almost fourteen years ago, she let him seduce her.

She'd almost escaped when his smooth voice drawled behind her, "Leaving without a farewell to your host? How rude. And shouldn't we discuss our progress diverting the gossip?"

Tingling flooding her once more, she turned to face Oakmoor and cocked a sardonic brow. "Why bother? I did my part, and you're more charming than a courtesan wearing a seduction spell, so I'm certain you did too."

CHAPTER 3

His pulse surging at Juliet's barb, Oakmoor sauntered closer to the maddening witch. Juliet was always so polite in her letters, yet never to his face. But somehow her biting tongue bewitched him as much as her exotic beauty and powerful air. Not that he could reveal the depths of his desire for her. So he asked in a dangerously silky voice only she could hear, "Calling me a talented whore again?" Like she had the morning after their night together.

Juliet sniffed. "If the griffin cloak fits, wear it." Griffins were renowned for inspiring truth in addition to taking lifelong mates, so cloaks made from their fur and feathers could only be worn by those true to their heart.

He almost shuddered. And the unmated that wore griffin cloaks often found love and commitment, which were for mad fools. Wanting both had made his first lover Elvaira, a seductive Rhiannon-descendant gypsy witch, become obsessed with him then curse him to turn into a hideous beast one day because he'd ended their affair. And Father had been unable to live without his beloved after Mother had died in a carriage accident, so he'd committed suicide despite still having a four-year-old son to raise. Oakmoor made himself smirk. "No self-respecting rakehell would ever wear a griffin cloak. We enjoy our freedom too much."

Juliet's lush lips twisted in an echoing smirk. "Really? But from your dogged pursuit of every eligible young lady at court these past several months, you're clearly seeking a wife at last. Yet for *some* reason, no young lady has deigned to accept you. Didn't you tell me that even in your dotage you'd remember how to excite a woman? Apparently not."

His blood heating, Oakmoor stepped forward until Juliet's deep-amethyst skirt brushed his legs. A thorough kiss would stop her disdainful mouth. And he might finally get relief from the primal hunger tormenting him. As her eyes turned black and lips parted, he began lowering his head. Goddess, her spicy gingyr scent was more bewitching than any seduction spell. "I'll show you excitement."

"Your grace, what are you doing?" Lady Georgiana's light voice trilled from behind him.

He stilled. Yes, what *was* he doing? He always kept his flirting light in public, sticking to charming banter, dancing slightly too close, and kissing hands. He *never* truly kissed ladies at court events, even if alone with them, much less before all of court. Even for the greatest rakehell in Ormas, being so indiscreet could have dire consequences—namely marriage. Damn Juliet for bewitching him so much that he forgot.

He stepped away from Juliet and faced the duke's daughter with a smooth smile. "Lady Juliet and I were merely discussing a private council matter."

Despite her flushed cheeks, Juliet glowered at him and said, "Yes, 'twas too sensitive for others to overhear. Unfortunately." She smiled at Lady Georgiana. "Good evening, my lady," not glancing at him, she muttered, "your grace." Then she turned and glided from the drawing room.

Not letting himself stare after Juliet, Oakmoor nodded at Lady Georgiana. They mustn't remain together since he meant to end their courtship. "I should see how Lady Driscoll and Sir Lorcan are faring."

Before he could escape, Lady Georgiana fluttered her lashes and clung to his arm. "Stay and talk with me first. You've been so busy with your duties that we've barely spoken all evening, and your soiree is nearly over."

Lady Georgiana still clinging to him, he hastened across the drawing room toward her father. "Yes, and I've still more duties to attend. I'll call on you tomorrow, and we'll talk then." Although she'd not like the result. When they reached the Duke of Osbourne, Oakmoor managed to extract his arm then nodded at his fellow councilor and swept a bow toward Lady Georgiana before striding away.

He grinned as he joined the Orandian ambassador and her husband. "How have you enjoyed your introduction to court?"

Nestled against Sir Lorcan, Lady Driscoll smiled and replied, "Everyone has been wonderfully welcoming." Her smile turned impish. "And the drama you provided was most entertaining—first with that elderly-looking lady then with Lady Juliet."

Oakmoor nearly winced. Then with? Hopefully Lady Driscoll just meant with. After all, he'd only approached Juliet because of Lady Blaine—he'd needed her to verify Lady Blaine's unlikely story. Even if he could trust his erratic magical powers to work properly, he couldn't perform a probing spell in public without revealing them. He made himself drawl, "It has been an eventful evening, hasn't it? I hope you don't mind that your arrival has been eclipsed by court drama."

Sir Lorcan chuckled. "Only fitting that a lady under an illusion from the Goddess eclipses us. Such holy spells are rarer than an opal faebird's teeth. I could hardly believe it when Lady Juliet told us. Too bad I didn't get to talk with Lady Blaine before she left."

Lady Driscoll squeezed her husband's arm. "You're such a lore witch." She twinkled at Oakmoor. "*I* found your and Lady Juliet's almost kiss more entertaining."

He stiffened as his neck heated. Why must newcomers have the clearest vision? He quirked his brows and refuted, "We were discussing a private court matter, not almost kissing. The royal witch and I have always disliked one another."

Lady Driscoll and Sir Lorcan traded smiles, then she murmured, "I see."

Oakmoor swallowed a sigh. The Orandians obviously weren't convinced, but if he protested further, they'd *definitely* not believe him. He'd better distract them. "Where would you like to ride tomorrow? Along the ocean or to a forest?"

Sir Lorcan leaned forward, his eyes gleaming. "We'd love to ride to the royal forest if King Devon and Queen Kiera would allow it. We've heard Esme the Great's melissae hive is extraordinary."

Oakmoor hummed. Of course the Orandians wanted to see another perilous magical item. Although probably less perilous than the Mirror of Wisdom, the massive hive could be deadly if the bee-like melissae were angered, so the royal forest had been created to protect the legendary melissae hive as well as the unwary from the melissae. And already showing foreigners a second of Calatini's magical secrets mightn't be wise. Besides, riding on royal lands required permission from King Devon or Queen Kiera, and they'd left when Lady Blaine had told them that Lady Beza Hawke was dying. Oakmoor shook his head. "The royal forest is too far; you just arrived in Ormas yesterday. Another time, perhaps. However, we could have a picnic on the shore where we hold kelpie races throughout the season."

Lady Driscoll inclined her head. "I'd enjoy that."

He grinned. "Excellent. I'll arrange it then." And if he paid enough, he could hire a few kelpies and their riders to race for them. Lady Driscoll being a sea witch would help too.

After that, the Orandians said farewell, and he spent the rest of his soiree talking to his now rapidly departing guests. The last to leave were Lord and Lady Escana. Once they discussed how the soiree had gone, him carefully not mentioning Juliet or Lady

Ravenstone, he invited the couple to tomorrow's ride. His assistant and her husband enjoyed riding, often with their beloved children and hounds, although he made them promise not to bring their pets to avoid disturbing the kelpies.

THE FOLLOWING morning after hiring some kelpies and requesting a picnic luncheon, Oakmoor headed to Osbourne House to call on Lady Georgiana. Thankfully, given all his experience ending affairs, he should be able to end their courtship without upsetting her too much. When her family's butler showed him into the morning room, he bowed with a charming grin then sat on the sofa across from her.

Her silver dress perfectly matching the morning room's elegant furnishings, Lady Georgiana responded with a sweet smile and asked, "No kiss this morning, your grace? And why are you sitting so far away?"

He let his grin turn wry. How surprisingly direct. "Neither would be appropriate, given what I'm here to discuss."

Lady Georgiana's eyes narrowed briefly before flaring wide like a curious child. "Whatever do you mean?"

He nearly chuckled at the innocent picture Lady Georgiana made. The wily Duke of Osbourne, who'd served on the council as the Minister of Intelligence for almost five decades and excelled at intrigue, had taught his youngest daughter well.

Oakmoor arched a brow. "I think you know." He resumed his warmly charming smile as he shared the part of the truth that would convince her to release him, "While talking with the Orandian ambassador and her husband, I realized that I could have grown children your age and tying you to me would be unfair to you, Lady Georgiana. You deserve to find a husband near your own age."

Her gaze transforming from innocent to sultry, Lady Georgiana leaned forward. "But age and experience can be *extremely* attractive to young ladies."

He inclined a nod. "Perhaps, but you also deserve a husband who can love you." And she didn't deserve to be tied to a gentleman who'd soon turn into a hideous beast.

Lady Georgiana's brows rose. "I didn't take you for a romantic, your grace."

Oakmoor couldn't help a snorted laugh. Ever since he'd tangled with Elvaira, romantic was the *last* thing he was. "For myself, no. But young ladies like you deserve the chance to have what they dream about." Even if they were mad fools for doing so.

Lady Georgiana flashed another sweet smile. "Not all young ladies dream of love. Some of us are more practical." When he simply shook his head, she eyed him for several heartbeats then sighed. The sweet smile draining from her face, she said, "But you've made your decision to end our courtship, haven't you, your grace?"

He nodded again as his chest eased. "I have."

Lady Georgiana pursed her lips. "Then I shan't press you further. A shame because we could have been an excellent team. We're both from ducal families, and thanks to growing up with Father, I understand your duties as a councilor."

Oakmoor smiled. At last he was seeing the steely lady behind Lady Georgiana's sweet smiles. So much less bland. Yet ending their courtship was still for the best. He leaned forward. "Tell me, why do you conceal your true self?"

Lady Georgiana snorted and tossed her head. "Because most gentlemen are intimidated by strong ladies."

Chuckling, he rose. Only if they were weak. He himself had always preferred strong ladies—'twas why Juliet, one of the strongest ladies he'd ever met, bewitched him so. He gave Lady Georgiana a deep bow. "Strong ladies don't intimidate the gentlemen worthy of them. Good day, my lady."

On the carriage ride back to Oakmoor House, he drummed his fingers against his thigh. His endless courting of various eligible young ladies had to stop. Although he needed an heir, he clearly couldn't manage to settle on any of them, not even when they quit being bland. If only he could break Elvaira's beast curse. Then there'd be no pressure to wed immediately, and he could focus better on the young ladies without the curse looming over him. Yet powerful curses cast by Rhiannon-descendant black witches were only visible to seers and often grueling to break. So how could he begin to unravel Elvaira's vindictive curse?

AFTER A SUCCESSFUL RIDE with the Orandians and the Escanas— the kelpies had given their all to impress Lady Driscoll— Oakmoor headed to his study to handle the correspondence he'd neglected since the Orandians' arrival. Due to long practice, he swiftly addressed the large pile of letters involving court events, business matters, former lovers, and foreign affairs. Then he leaned back in his chair and eyed the carved walnut transport box on his desk. He was a day late writing his weekly letter to Juliet, but he'd been too busy with the Orandians and his soiree.

He'd begun writing Juliet almost two years ago, two months after his erratic magical powers had appeared, because he'd made little progress learning how to control them from books. He could have hired a witch to instruct him, but he couldn't trust a strange witch with his secrets. And hiring someone would have caused gossip about his inexplicably late powers, and having constantly fluctuating magic that he couldn't control would damage his suave reputation at court. Besides, Juliet was the most illustrious witch in Calatini, so she was the best instructor he could find.

His lips twisted as he penned his usual greeting to Juliet. But given their past, he'd not dared openly approach her about instructing him. Even if she'd agreed, which wouldn't have been likely, they'd have ended up quarreling then ravishing each other more than they'd have discussed magic. So he'd written her instead, and to conceal his identity, he'd pretended to be a young witch from the town closest to Oakmoor Castle. He'd mentioned two neglectful mentors since having two mentors was rare and would intrigue Juliet enough to answer the unknown witch who'd written her. And he'd signed his letters as Mordred Thyme—his first and middle names that no one remembered since he'd become Oakmoor so young. Even *he* barely remembered his given names.

After waiting a full month to reply, Juliet had sent a succinct letter which had thoroughly answered his question, so he'd continued writing her with all his magic questions. For the first year, they'd exchanged one or two letters a month using Calatini's magical transport system for letters and small parcels run by the Ministry of Health and Community. But longing to hear from Juliet more frequently, he'd enchanted a pair of transport boxes to send their letters directly, and in the over eight months since, they'd begun writing weekly.

Oakmoor tapped his pen on the desk. What should he write about today? Once he'd learned the basics of magic, he'd asked Juliet about topics inspired by recent events, allowing him to learn magic he never would have thought of otherwise. He grimaced. Too bad he couldn't risk asking her about curses again. He'd written Juliet about them on his last natalday, the twenty-ninth anniversary of Elvaira cursing him, and Juliet had been clearly concerned in her reply. If he asked again, she might use a scrying or tracing spell to find him.

He sighed, then after a moment, he jotted a brief question about flying carpets since Lady Blaine had arrived at his soiree on one. Flying carpets were uncommon in Calatini, so he knew little about them, and their magic was no doubt fascinating. He smiled as he signed his letter before sealing it and placing it in the transport box. Juliet's reply was sure to be interesting and insightful. Reading her letters was often the best part of his week.

He grinned when he opened his transport box three mornings later and found Juliet's reply. He tore open her letter then froze at her opening line about the curious coincidence that they both had acquaintances who recently traveled by flying carpet. He swore and dropped her letter as if scorched. How could he have forgotten that such a coincidence might make Juliet suspect who Mordred Thyme truly was? She'd never write him again if she did. And probably slap him or shock him with an energy spell when she next saw him.

Oakmoor inhaled then forced himself to pick up Juliet's letter and read the rest of it. Thank the Goddess, no hint of suspicion tainted her detailed reply. He'd not inadvertently revealed his secret identity through a slip of the pen. But to ensure she forgot, he'd not write his next letter for a while, and he'd select a topic she didn't know involved him. Please let that be enough to save the letters he'd come to love.

CHAPTER 4

$\mathcal{W}$hen Juliet swept into the council room five days after Oakmoor's soiree, she almost stilled as her pulse quickened. Oakmoor was talking to Lord Treyvan, directly across from her seat beside the head of the table where the royal couple always sat. Why couldn't Oakmoor be in his usual seat down near the foot of the table? 'Twas the farthest apart they could get—one of the reasons she sat where she did. The other was that as Calatini's royal witch, her place was beside the king and queen when she attended, which she only did when magic would be a focus or spells were needed. Although it might have been more politic to attend every council meeting, attending meetings where she'd nothing to do was not only pointless but painful as well.

As she settled in her seat, she murmured greetings to the Duchess of Wildewall beside her, but she was truly listening to Oakmoor's conversation with King Devon's cousin and best friend Lord Treyvan, who was the fair-minded eldest son of the Duke and Duchess of Childes and had become nearly as influential as his parents since he'd joined the council three years ago.

His smile smooth as glass, Oakmoor was saying, "Twins? How remarkable. I'm glad Lady Beza Hawke is well again, and I imagine your brother is too with *two* infants to raise. And congratulations on your middle brother's recent betrothal. Somehow I wasn't terribly astonished that Priest Melchior and Lady Blaine decided to wed. Whenever I saw them together, there was an energy between them."

Juliet inhaled and eyed Oakmoor, her stomach hardening. Lady Blaine was the first lady he'd ever seriously courted, although he'd not seemed to care when she'd disappeared at Longnight or when she'd left his soiree the other day. And he appeared unruffled to hear that she'd chosen another. But Lady Blaine had been the only lady he'd courted for longer than three weeks, so she must have been special to him.

Lord Treyvan chuckled. "Yes, Mother and Father weren't astonished either. And Mother is ecstatic to see the last of her sons finally settled."

Oakmoor chuckled too, his smile becoming a grin. "I could tell from the Duchess of Childes's invitation I received yesterday to her fete next month celebrating their betrothal. Your ballroom shall be even more crowded than usual to see the elderly-appearing Countess of Blaine and her unfashionable priest betrothed."

Nodding at whatever the Duchess of Wildewall had just said, Juliet swallowed as her stomach eased. From Oakmoor's chuckle and ready grin, his former lady choosing another didn't matter to him at all. She suppressed a snort. Given his inveterate rakehell ways, she should have known. But his sudden determination to marry several months ago while completely concealing his current lovers had made her wonder if he'd changed. Yet a basilisk never lost his spots, even when shedding his skin.

The Duchess of Wildewall touched her arm. "Lady Juliet, are you well? You seem distracted."

She made herself turn toward the temperate duchess, who served as the Minister of Justice and was observant after decades managing the formerly feuding Greysnowes and Ravenstones.

Juliet forced a faint smile. "I apologize; I was gathering my thoughts about the Orandian ambassador and her husband." The Orandians were the focus of today's council meeting, and she was attending to provide magical perspective since the isle of Orandia possessed much more magic and witches than other human kingdoms.

The duchess grinned and nodded. "They *are* fascinating, aren't they?"

But before the duchess could continue, King Devon and Queen Kiera strode into the council room, and all twelve councilors, including Oakmoor, took their usual seats. After King Devon and Queen Kiera opened the council meeting, King Devon turned to Oakmoor and said, "Tell us how the Orandians' arrival has gone so far, your grace."

Oakmoor inclined his head with a charming smile. "Very well, I think. Lady Driscoll and her husband have been genial and eager to experience Calatini." His smile quirked. "Particularly our magic."

King Devon and Queen Kiera traded glances, then King Devon grimaced and replied, "Yes, I remember how interested they were in the Mirror of Wisdom when we first met them."

Juliet blinked. The Orandians had already asked King Devon and Queen Kiera about the powerful and perilous enchanted mirror? Lady Driscoll and Sir Lorcan were remarkably open about magic and had mentioned the Mirror of Wisdom to her, but to ask about one of Calatini's magical secrets upon first meeting the king and queen was... *bold.*

Queen Kiera tilted her head. "Have they said why their seer sent them? I understand most Orandian witches remain on the isle."

Still smiling, Oakmoor shrugged. "Not yet, your majesty."

Lord Islaye shifted in his seat. "Lady Juliet and I were discussing that at your soiree, and we worry that the Orandian seer might have sent them because trouble is approaching Calatini."

Murmurs swept the council room as Juliet and the others all frowned.

Then the elderly Duke of Osbourne, the longtime Minister of Intelligence, creaked, "We must discover why they're here at once. I'll ask the spies I placed in their embassy."

Lady Ducharme—the farsighted Minister of Defense despite being a lady, which would *never* happen in Varkhora—leaned forward and asked, "But what if your spies know nothing? They mustn't be blatant and reveal themselves. We daren't risk offending the Orandians and sparking a war."

Juliet almost shuddered. Although Orandia was a quarter the size of Calatini, the island kingdom was led by a powerful seer and possessed much more magic, so a war between the two kingdoms could be as catastrophic as the Stone Wars between humans and magical creatures over a millennium ago. She tapped the table before her. "Also, Lady Driscoll and Sir Lorcan mightn't even know why the Orandian seer sent them. Seers must be careful how and what they reveal because people knowing too much can change the future from how it should be."

More murmurs swept the council room, then Lord Islaye said, "Perhaps we should consult the veiled witch. She's a seer too, and her prophecy led to the dangerous Magehaven ore being neutralized. Surely she'd help us again."

As many of the councilors nodded, although Oakmoor merely narrowed his eyes, King Devon and Queen Kiera exchanged glances but remained silent.

Juliet gripped her hands in her lap. "I don't think we should approach the veiled witch just yet." Constantly consulting that dratted seer would give her too much influence. "We should see what the Duke of Osbourne's spies know first. And the Driscolls are visiting my workroom the day after tomorrow, so I should be able to learn more from them, witch to witch."

The Duchess of Wildewall eyed her. "You almost sound as if you don't trust the veiled witch for some reason."

Juliet nearly winced as her neck heated. "'Tisn't that. We simply know so little about her." And with her incredibly powerful magic, the veiled witch could easily usurp the royal position that Juliet had striven so hard to achieve, which would leave her with nothing.

Oakmoor smirked at her from the far end of the table, clearly recognizing her jealous insecurity. "We could say the same about *you*, Lady Juliet."

She glared at Oakmoor, fire flaring through her. Insufferable beast. "Except *I* swore an oath to serve Calatini when King Sarastor hired me as the royal witch—just like all of you did when you assumed your titles and when you became councilors. Plus, I've faithfully served the kingdom for the past *fourteen* years. The veiled witch has done neither."

King Devon raised his hand. "Your loyalty isn't in question, Lady Juliet."

Queen Kiera beamed at her. "We all—Devon and I, especially —know how loyal you are to Calatini."

Juliet inhaled a calming breath. So they did. After all, they'd asked *her*, not the veiled witch, to protect Queen Kiera and unearth her treasonous poisoner back when the then-future queen had arrived at court. Plus, they'd trusted her to create the tokens for their secret bloodbinding, which no one else besides their close family and friends knew about because of the ramifications. Bloodbound couples could only have children together and often died at the same time, and if King Devon and Queen Kiera never produced an heir or both died before their heir was old enough to rule, it could be devastating to Calatini, which had been happily ruled by the Vireni family since its founding. She smiled at the royal couple then inclined her head. "Thank you, your majesties. And I agree that the veiled witch could be helpful to consult, but only if necessary. We don't wish to become dependent on her."

Queen Kiera nodding beside him, King Devon said, "I agree. So we'll wait to decide if we consult the veiled witch until after you and the Duke of Osbourne share your findings at the next council meeting." He turned to Oakmoor again. "Anything further to report about the Orandians?"

Oakmoor hummed. "Not particularly, but like I mentioned, they're eager to experience our magic. Sir Lorcan already asked to visit the royal forest to see Esme the Great's melissae hive."

King Devon frowned and took Queen Kiera's hand as she paled. He ordered, "Distract them from that. The melissae are too deadly when angered."

Juliet swallowed. A swarm of irate melissae could kill even the most massive roc within moments, and their stings were said to be excruciating. And only soul healers like Lady Ravenstone could successfully communicate with them. She herself had ridden to the royal forest to see the melissae on occasion—Esme the Great's melissae hive *was* an extraordinary sight—but she'd taken great care not to upset them.

Still somewhat pale, Queen Kiera glanced at Oakmoor. "Perhaps talk to High Priest Theodag about the Orandians seeing the Great Temple's magical endeavors instead. None of Orandia's temples are near as magnificent as our Great Temple."

When Oakmoor nodded, King Devon asked the rest of the council if they'd other matters to discuss, and the council meeting shifted from the Orandians before ending soon after. Then Juliet hurried from the council room before she and Oakmoor could clash again. Such quarrels were much too revealing and dangerously exciting.

TWO MORNINGS LATER, Juliet scanned her bright and airy workroom while waiting for Lady Driscoll and Sir Lorcan to arrive. As usual, her workroom almost sparkled, and all her magical accoutrements and spell ingredients were meticulously arranged. In Varkhora, women were trained in the domestic arts from a young age and expected to keep everything immaculate, so having the archetypal cluttered witch's workroom made her skin twitch. Hiring an excellent maid had been one of the first things she'd done after moving into the royal witch's wing, and she paid that maid and her successors extremely well.

Soon, her current maid Lara ushered Lady Driscoll and Sir Lorcan into the workroom. Then the little maid in starched livery bobbed a curtsy. "Shall you be requiring anything else, Lady Juliet?"

Juliet glanced at the Orandians. "Would you care for tea or kahve?" Hopefully, they chose tea. She couldn't serve them proper Varkhoran kahve, a concentrated brew served in tiny cups, without betraying her true heritage, and the weaker kahve served in Calatini always disappointed her. When she was alone, she often used an adapting spell to transform it into proper kahve.

Once Lady Driscoll and Sir Lorcan shook their heads, she turned back to Lara with a smile. "That will be all; thank you, Lara."

After the little maid left, Lady Driscoll grinned. "Your workroom is stunning."

Sir Lorcan peered at the large enchanted cabinet in the corner that contained her more dangerous or confidential magical items and could only be opened with her magic. "With your special accoutrements locked away using a magic-key spell, I presume. Sensible."

As Juliet nodded, Lady Driscoll tilted her head and asked, "Given how tidy everything is, are you a hearth witch?"

Juliet stiffened. "No, I'm an ordinary witch." Although Father and Mother had always wished she'd been a powerful hearth witch like her gentle maternal cousin Aurora, who'd married Sandro and eventually became queen three years ago. But nearly all female witches in Varkhora trained as hearth witches since Varkhorans considered other magic the purview of men. Indeed, the hearth witch who'd trained her had refused to teach her any magic outside of that for households and kitchens. She'd had to sneak into the library at night to learn other types of spells, which would have infuriated her parents if they'd ever discovered it. Thankfully, Ceija Lovari, the grandmotherly head of the gypsy family she'd traveled with after fleeing Varkhora, had greatly broadened her magical education by teaching her all the spells the Lovaris knew. And she'd continued expanding her knowledge by reading all the magical tomes she could find. Then she took that knowledge to create new spells, like King Devon's and Queen Kiera's protection charms.

She managed a bright smile. "I simply prefer being tidy. Now, would you like me to demonstrate some magic or perhaps swap spells? I've never visited Orandia, so I'd love to learn more Orandian spells." Visiting the magical island kingdom would have been thrilling, but she'd worried the excess magic there would disrupt the tracing-ward spell hiding her. Plus, although she'd traveled widely with them, the Lovaris preferred to remain on mainland Damensea. So sadly she'd never traveled to the resting place of Rhiannon, the founder of human magic.

Lady Driscoll slanting him a fond smile, Sir Lorcan grinned and replied, "Swap spells, please!"

Juliet and the two Orandians sat around her worktable and spent the morning exchanging spells. As a sea witch, Lady Driscoll knew mostly spells about the ocean and its denizens, while as a lore witch, Sir Lorcan knew an *impressive* variety of spells. And both shared her deep fascination with magic and innovative spells, although neither were Rhiannon descendants or created spells themselves. She'd not met such likeminded souls since her days with Ceija and Ceija's grandson Shandor.

The hours passed swiftly, and the three witches only quit discussing magic when their stomachs rumbled like starved manticores. Then they adjourned to her small dining room and fell upon the luncheon Lara brought them.

Lady Driscoll beamed at Juliet over her cream of spinach soup. "I feel as if we all know each other so well now."

Juliet nodded. How true. After many years remaining somewhat apart at Calatini's court, she'd never imagined she'd meet such close friends. Perhaps it helped that Lady Driscoll and Sir Lorcan were foreigners too, in addition to being fascinated by magic.

Lady Driscoll beamed brighter while she continued, "Please call us Siobhan and Lorcan."

Her heart warm, Juliet returned Siobhan's smile. "As long as you call me Juliet. This morning was delightful. I've not learned so many new spells since I first traveled with the gypsies."

Lorcan leaned forward, his roll only half-buttered. "That must have been fascinating."

Juliet hummed as she sipped her white wine. "It was. Although after years of travel, settling in Calatini's court was a relief." Especially since she'd grown up in Varkhora's court and had never really felt comfortable with the gypsies' rough and informal life. To encourage Siobhan and Lorcan to reveal why their seer had sent them, she added, "I chose Calatini because women are equals to men here due to their longstanding treaty with the matriarchal horse-like nightmara. Plus, there's a variety of magic and magical creatures here due to Calatini's size and location. Why did you two choose to travel here? I know most Orandian witches remain on the isle."

Siobhan smiled as she began cutting her honey-glazed salmon. "Once your Magehaven ore crisis was resolved, our seer declared we must send an ambassador again. And Lorcan has always wanted to travel, so we volunteered."

Juliet eyed the Orandians. Perhaps them being witches wasn't relevant, but with a seer involved, who could say? Yet if there was a purpose behind them coming to Calatini, Siobhan and Lorcan obviously didn't know it. She arched a brow. "Why isn't Lorcan the ambassador if he's the one who wanted to travel?"

Siobhan chuckled. "Because my lore-witch husband only wants to discuss magic, and everything else bores him, especially politics."

His smile wry, Lorcan tsked. "Be fair, love. I adore discussing our children too."

Juliet stilled as a pang pierced her, her fork of sauteed sparrow grass before her lips. Siobhan and Lorcan were married and between her and Oakmoor's age, so them having children wasn't surprising. Yet she'd not heard that any children were with the Orandian delegation. Surely they wouldn't have left beloved children behind. She lowered her fork. "Children?"

Siobhan grinned and cleared her plate. "Yes, we've four grown children. Two girls—Aine is twenty-two, Cara twenty-one. And twin boys, Rian and Aden, who just turned twenty."

Lorcan nodded while serving his wife more mashed cauliflower. "We miss the scamps dearly, but they've their own lives now and couldn't join us, although we made them promise to make weekly mirror calls."

Juliet swallowed, the ache in her chest deepening. She'd never enjoyed such a loving relationship with her father, and since she'd never trusted any man enough to marry him, she'd no children to love like that. And at a year and a half shy of forty, she likely never would. But at least she'd achieved the influence, respect, and renown she'd dreamt of as a powerless girl trapped in Varkhora. Love and marriage might endanger all she'd achieved. Even here in Calatini where women were equals, 'twas too easy for them to lose themselves to suit their husband. Particularly for her, given she'd been raised to do precisely that. Remaining strong and independent but alone and childless was much better.

Siobhan leaned toward her. "So what's happening between you and the suave Duke of Oakmoor? You two almost kissed at his soiree the other day."

A blush warming her neck, Juliet managed to shrug while she used Oakmoor's excuse for their madness, "It may have appeared like that, but we were merely discussing a private council matter."

Siobhan and Lorcan traded smiles, then Siobhan murmured,

"So the duke said, but your discussion appeared too intimate for it to be just that."

Her blush now scorching, Juliet waved a dismissive hand. "The Duke of Oakmoor is a rakehell who flirts with anyone in a skirt, that's all." She pointedly glanced at Lorcan's traditional Orandian garb. "Lorcan is fortunate that the duke doesn't consider tunics on gentlemen skirts." Then to distract her new friends from Oakmoor, she asked, "Tell me more about your children—are they all witches too?" Although the children of witches were often witches, they weren't always or could have different powers than their parents because magic was unpredictable.

Juliet spent the rest of luncheon with Siobhan and Lorcan discussing their children. Once the Orandians left, she headed to her study to address her correspondence and mirror messages like she did throughout the day. As Calatini's royal witch, she never knew when she'd receive one that she must handle immediately.

That done, she checked the carved walnut transport box on her desk, even though Mordred's next letter shouldn't arrive until tomorrow. In the nearly two years they'd been corresponding, she'd become eager to read the charming letters from the younger witch who lived on the other side of Calatini. He was curious about everything regarding magic—definitely a like-minded soul like Siobhan and Lorcan, the closest she'd found in Calatini until them, although she'd never met him in person and doubtless never would. And unlike the overly suave duke who headed his duchy, Mordred was always straightforward and wryly modest.

Juliet sighed at the empty transport box. She'd check again tomorrow morning. There'd probably be a letter then, or by the day after at the latest. Since sending her the transport box over eight months ago, Mordred had only been late sending his weekly letters a few times.

CHAPTER 5

On the carriage ride to the Duke of Osbourne's card party three days after the council meeting, Lady Driscoll eyed Oakmoor with a frown. "Are you well, your grace? You appear tired."

He resisted the urge to yawn and rub his face. He *was* tired thanks to poor sleep the past few nights. His curse dreams were getting worse: more vivid, more complicated, more lengthy. Whenever he jerked awake among his tangled sheets, which was often, they lingered in his mind as his pulse and breath slowed. Grotesque images of fornicating goats mounting anything that moved, backbiting snakes striking all they passed, and mauling lions attacking everyone who approached. The three creatures Elvaira had cursed him to become as a beast. Just like a chimera —the monstrous three-headed hybrid of a ravening lion, venomous snake, and fire-breathing goat—who often left destruction in its wake, especially when crazed with rage. And in his dreams, the three types of beasts destroyed everything they touched, until nothing remained. He almost grimaced. The curse dreams had become so unremitting that he no longer dreamt his disturbingly carnal ones about Juliet, which awoke him for a far different reason.

He gritted a smooth smile for the Orandian ambassador and her husband seated across from him. "I'm fine. Too many late evenings. I'm getting old, I suppose."

His arm about his wife, Sir Lorcan sighed and nodded. "We all are. As a lad, I could remain awake for days to read a fascinating tome on magic, but now I'm tired for days if I stay up late one evening finishing a chapter."

An impish grin danced across Lady Driscoll's freckled face. "I doubt 'twas books that kept the duke awake, unlike you, love. Given his reputation, 'twas likely a lady."

Oakmoor waggled his brows then winked to play his familiar role as the greatest rakehell in Ormas. Not that he had been since those damned kisses with Juliet in Childes House's garden. The costly strong-magic contraceptive charm about his neck was dusty from disuse. "I'm too much of a gentleman to say, Lady Driscoll."

The Orandian ambassador chuckled. "One who's also much too charming for his own good."

He clung to his rakish smile. But charm allowed him to entertain everyone without encouraging them to pry into his private matters. "There's no such thing as too much charm."

Lady Driscoll hummed. "Except it prevents sensible ladies like Juliet from taking you seriously."

Oakmoor tensed. Why must Lady Driscoll keep mentioning Juliet? So much for his hope that the Orandian ambassador being married would eliminate romantic intrigue. He arched a brow. "And why would I wish any lady to take me seriously?"

Sir Lorcan smiled and squeezed Lady Driscoll's shoulders. "Because finding your mate and knowing she's always there for you—no matter what her seven fearsome brothers say—is a glorious thing."

As a beaming Lady Driscoll kissed Sir Lorcan's cheek, Oakmoor shifted in his seat. Except relying on another like that was mad. Goddess knew when they'd betray you or die.

Thankfully, before Lady Driscoll and Sir Lorcan could further harp on the glories of love and commitment, the carriage halted at Osbourne House, and he ushered them to the drawing room. Of course, as soon as they'd greeted their host, the Orandians headed straight for Juliet, who'd just finished talking with Lord and Lady Islaye.

Lady Driscoll grinned at Juliet. "Have you a partner yet? You could partner with the duke and join us at our table. Fellow foreigners should unite when playing card games everyone else grew up with, and we could discuss magic more."

Juliet's lips tightened briefly before warmly curving for the Orandians. Without glancing at him, she drawled, "I'm certain the duke already has a partner in mind."

Despite Lady Driscoll's unwanted and blatant matchmaking, Oakmoor shifted closer to Juliet. That cold disdain and biting tongue of hers drove him mad. Especially given the uncontrollable hunger between them and her warm wit in her letters. He gave Juliet his most seductive smolder. "No, I don't have a partner this evening."

Juliet turned to face him at last, her gorgeous eyes narrow. "What about Lady Georgiana Laurent?"

He held Juliet's gaze, not bothering to look for the duke's daughter he'd once courted. "I believe she's found another partner."

Juliet inhaled then flashed a smirk. "Lost another eligible young lady, did you? One who lasted three weeks too—the longest they ever do now. What a pity."

His skin heating, Oakmoor gritted an echoing smirk as he stepped even closer to Juliet. Maddening witch. "I didn't lose Lady Georgiana. I released her to find a husband who could love her."

Juliet sniffed. "How unexpectedly *noble*."

He glowered and was about to retort when Lady Driscoll coughed a laugh and said, "As amusing as your truculent flirting is, I believe the card games are starting now."

Oakmoor and Juliet jerked apart, both flushing. How could

he have forgotten they were in public yet again? Another moment and he would have surely kissed her to silence her biting disdain. He must resume avoiding her like he usually did or all of court would realize their well-known dislike was actually thwarted desire.

Lady Driscoll chuckled and added, "And everyone seems to have paired up, so you'll have to be partners."

Not daring to touch Juliet, Oakmoor escorted her to the last empty card table. As he bent to help her into her chair, his body tightened at the spicy gingyr scent wafting from her kahve-colored hair. Why must she wear the exotic, aromatic root originally from the Tsarkan Empire south of Calatini that he'd always adored? To calm his unruly body, he made himself recall his curse dreams while he sat beside her.

As Oakmoor shuffled the cards, Sir Lorcan peered at the round table and said, "I assume the spell glowing about the table and cards is to prevent cheating."

Oakmoor smiled. "Yes. The Duke of Osbourne is serious about his cards. Only play against him if you're prepared to lose." The wily old duke rarely lost and preferred playing wild arcana, a lengthy game with intricate rules. "What game shall we play?"

Lady Driscoll hummed. "Trick six? We learned that from a Calatinian bard years ago."

Oakmoor nodded as he swiftly dealt. The trick taking card game for two pairs of partners where tricks of six or greater each earned a point was one of the most popular in Calatini. Once everyone had their sixteen cards, he revealed the last two which would set the trump arcana. Then Sir Lorcan on his left began the first trick.

As they played, Juliet and the Orandians talked with cordial ease while he interjected random comments. Clearly, the three witches had become friends during Lady Driscoll and Sir Lorcan's visit to Juliet's workroom yesterday. Wonderful. 'Twould make avoiding her impossible while he was helping the

Orandians settle in Ormas. And when they discussed magic, as they had four times during their first game, he must remember he wasn't an acknowledged witch and stifle the magical knowledge he shouldn't possess, much of which he'd learned from Juliet's letters to Mordred.

After he and Juliet resoundingly won the first game, Lady Driscoll turned to him with an apologetic smile while Sir Lorcan dealt their second one. "I hope our magic talk hasn't bored you, your grace. My dear husband can't resist discussing it."

Oakmoor chuckled. Most lore witches couldn't. He grinned at the Orandian ambassador. "I don't mind. We often discuss magic on the council, so I'm accustomed to it." Although he had to force himself not to eye Juliet hungrily during those council meetings. Thank the Goddess she rarely attended the ones where they didn't discuss magic.

Sir Lorcan leaned toward him. "As a councilor, you must know the details behind the neutralization of the Magehaven ore."

Oakmoor suppressed another laugh. Sir Lorcan must be keen to discuss magic to ask *him* about the Magehaven ore when the royal witch right beside him would obviously know much more.

Rubbing his jaw, Sir Lorcan played a card. "I suppose King Devon and Queen Kiera used the Mirror of Wisdom to unearth the ore's secrets."

While Lady Driscoll nodded and Juliet's brow furrowed, Oakmoor sobered and shook his head. Using the perilous Mirror of Wisdom wouldn't have been wise, even during such a crisis. "No, King Devon and Queen Kiera needn't bother using *that*. They had Lady Juliet, Lord Islaye, and Lord Nolan handle the crisis, although the veiled witch's prophecy helped."

As Juliet stiffened like always at the mention of the veiled witch, Lady Driscoll and Sir Lorcan traded a wide glance, then Lady Driscoll asked, "The veiled witch? Is he or she a seer?"

Oakmoor shrugged and began the next trick then glanced toward Juliet, who should answer that as Calatini's royal witch.

Yet she remained silent, her face tight. She'd never approved of the veiled witch. Because she was jealous of such a powerful rival or because the veiled witch wasn't trustworthy? He'd pressed Juliet about the veiled witch at the last council meeting to determine which, although her response hadn't proved either one. She was definitely hesitant to consult the veiled witch but would if forced to. So he still wasn't certain if he should risk consulting the veiled witch about breaking Elvaira's beast curse even though the seer should be able to see it, unlike most witches.

After a moment, he turned back to the Orandians. "I believe the veiled witch is a seer, although I've never met her."

Lady Driscoll nudged her husband to play a card as she arched her brows at Juliet. "Have you?"

Juliet sighed. "I have."

Sir Lorcan plucked a card and tossed it on the table without glancing at it. He leaned toward Juliet and blurted, "What do you know about this veiled witch?"

Oakmoor studied the Orandians. Although Sir Lorcan was apparently always curious about magic, he appeared desperate to hear about the veiled witch. And since she failed to play her card after making her husband do so, Lady Driscoll was just as desperate. Why?

Juliet pursed her lips. "I don't know much. Her black veils conceal all but her eyes, which are dark. And she never offers her name. All I really know is that she's a Rhiannon-descendant seer who opened a witch shop in a poorer area of Ormas eleven years ago, although I didn't know of her until recently. She's proven helpful to King Devon and his family over the past few months, but I don't know why, other than her being paid for her help."

As Lady Driscoll and Sir Lorcan exchanged another wide glance, Oakmoor hummed and tapped the table. No wonder Juliet was so hesitant to consult the veiled witch. 'Twas impossible to guess the veiled witch's motives from what little she revealed, and a witch who so thoroughly concealed her name and appearance doubtless prevented her magical signature from being traced. And likely also ensured her blood or hair was never taken to be used against her, as he had since Elvaira's curse. All that meant Juliet couldn't perform an effective scrying spell to discover more about the veiled witch. How the clever and skilled royal witch must hate not knowing and being unable to address it.

Lady Driscoll smoothed her tunic beneath her overcoat. "Our seer wears similar concealing veils, although they're white rather than black. Do you think the veiled witch is Orandian too?"

Oakmoor blinked. *That* explained Lady Driscoll and Sir Lorcan's desperate interest in the veiled witch.

Juliet grimaced and blew a sigh. "Perhaps, but knowledgeable witches are aware that the Orandian seer wears veils. 'Twould be too obvious for the veiled witch to be Orandian. She's probably just emulating your seer since the Orandian seer is always the most prescient in Damensea." She smiled. "Siobhan, shall you play your next card now?"

Lady Driscoll glanced down at her cards as if she'd never seen them. Then she laughed. "I'd better if we ever want to finish this game."

During that second game and the two that followed—all of which he and Juliet won like they had the first—Juliet kept their conversation on court gossip, like today's sudden arrival of the once-fashionable Countess of Blaine's scandalous and secret family, who were wealthy Dracwyn smugglers. Clearly Juliet didn't wish to discuss the veiled witch further. Once King Devon and Queen Kiera left early as had become their wont, Juliet smiled and rose while he began shuffling the deck for another game. Her gaze firmly on the Orandians, she said, "I must go as well. Shall I see you at the Islayes' illusion evening tomorrow? I believe Lord Islaye has prepared some illusions of Orandia in your honor."

Lady Driscoll nodded. "We're looking forward to it, particularly Lorcan."

Sir Lorcan flashed a wry smile. "Observing other witches' spellwork is fascinating."

Refusing to watch Juliet as she glided from the drawing room, Oakmoor grinned at Lady Driscoll and Sir Lorcan. "Shall we play another game, or would you prefer to circulate?"

Lady Driscoll took her husband's arm and rose. "We're rubbish at cards, as we demonstrated by not winning a single game. Let's find Lord and Lady Islaye to quiz them about their illusions for tomorrow."

As Sir Lorcan brightened, Oakmoor set down the deck and led the Orandians across the room to the Islayes. With Juliet gone, the evening would be much easier to manage.

AFTER ANOTHER DRAINING night full of curse dreams, Oakmoor took Lady Driscoll and Sir Lorcan to Islaye House for dinner before the Islayes' illusion evening. If only the Orandians would want to leave early. He was so exhausted that maintaining his usual charming smiles and smooth conversation was a struggle.

He grimaced when they entered the Islayes' drawing room. Of course, the Islayes had invited Juliet to even the numbers. And since the happily married couples would likely prefer to remain paired, he'd be forced to escort her to dinner. Why couldn't they have invited Lord Islaye's childhood friend Dowager Lady Ravenstone instead?

Once the others left them behind as expected, he sighed and offered Juliet his arm. She sniffed when she accepted it, barely resting her fingers on his evening coat. Yet even that light touch made his pulse quicken, damn her.

Juliet raked him with a narrow glance. "You look dreadful, Oakmoor. Your current lover must be demanding."

His jaw tightened. Except he'd no current lover thanks to Juliet. Just Elvaira's curse dreams. He made himself smile at Juliet then rumbled, "No more than you were."

Juliet inhaled and flushed while glancing at the two couples several steps ahead of them. She hissed, "I wasn't."

He eyed Juliet's parted lips like a lusty satyr about to pounce. How spicy and sweet and hot she'd tasted. His body hardened. And if he dragged her to the nearest room and locked the door, he could taste her again outside of his carnal dreams about her. He halted. "You were. I've never enjoyed such explosive passion —before or since."

Her exotic skin flushing deeper, Juliet dropped his arm. "Quit attempting to seduce me. I'll not succumb to your disgusting rakehell ways again."

Oakmoor grasped Juliet's wrist to prevent her from escaping. Staring into her dark-brown eyes, he kissed her palm like he would her tempting mouth as soon as he found that room. "Won't you?"

Juliet jerked her hand free and fisted it, obviously about to hit him.

But before she could, Lady Driscoll called from the door of the dining room, "Come along, you two. Our food shall get cold."

As Juliet replied they'd be there shortly, Oakmoor shuddered a cleansing breath. What was he *doing*? He never seduced ladies in open halls directly before dinner when they'd be missed. His exhaustion and recent celibacy had destroyed his control.

When he offered his arm again, Juliet glared. *"Don't touch me."*

He swallowed. Probably wise. His body was still aching, so he'd drag her to the nearest room if they resumed touching, regardless of the consequences.

He and Juliet joined the others for dinner then spent most of the lively and delicious meal ignoring each other. He didn't even glance at her while serving her the various courses. As the evening progressed, his head began to throb in time with his heart. No doubt due to his exhaustion, forced charm, and suppressing his uncontrollable desire for Juliet.

By the time the rest of court—except for King Devon and his family who were celebrating his cousin Philippa Hawke's natalday—began filling the Islayes' ballroom, he could barely smile, and talking was near impossible, so he resorted to something he never did. He retreated to the outskirts and pretended to sip his sparkling wine rather than talk to anyone. Thankfully, Juliet was entertaining Lady Driscoll and Sir Lorcan by speculating about the upcoming illusions, so the Orandians didn't notice his withdrawal. Although she did from the narrow glances she slanted his way every so often.

Eventually, Lord and Lady Islaye swept to the front of the ballroom, then Lord Islaye said, "Welcome, everyone. We hope you enjoy our first illusion, one honoring Lady Driscoll and Sir Lorcan."

The studious count raised a hand and chanted the final words to activate the first illusion. As a white glow, visible only to other witches, burst along the front wall, the blazing witchlights dimmed, and the many chattering guests hushed. The isle of Orandia appeared on the wall as if the ballroom was a ship approaching it.

While Orandia grew near enough that the massive white-and-silver marble seer's tower at the heart of the isle became distinct, a dizzying wave of intense heat swamped Oakmoor. What the...? He swayed and dropped his flute of sparkling wine, which shattered with a tinkling crash. Fortunately, the other guests were too engrossed in the Islayes' illusion of Orandia to notice.

His chest heaving but still dizzy from lack of breath and the heat coursing through him, he staggered into the anteroom directly behind him. Then the heat flared into boiling agony— the same he'd suffered when Elvaira had cursed him nearly thirty years ago. He collapsed and bit his lip until it bled to stifle his scream as his heart raced, bones broke, and skin melted.

When the agony stopped, he shuddered at his new hands. Tipped with a lion's sharp claws and covered by a snake's rough scales, they definitely belonged to a beast. He frantically explored his still burning face with his beast hands. More scales covered his face, and a goat's curved horns throbbed in his forehead, while a lion's heavy mane brushed his shoulders. His feet felt odd too, although his shoes concealed why. Elvaira's curse had manifested at last. And Goddess, 'twas as hideous as she'd promised.

Then with another flare of boiling agony, he transformed back to his human self. Gulping air, he stared at his once-more ordinary hands. He'd been a beast for less than a minute. Surely that couldn't be the extent of Elvaira's vindictive curse. No, that excruciating transformation was merely the beginning.

Oakmoor lurched upright. Now that his beast curse had manifested, he *must* risk consulting the veiled witch about breaking it, and soon—before it became permanent. Even though the veiled witch was too secretive to fully trust and Juliet was hesitant to consult her.

He'd just finished casting a minor healing spell on his lip and a grooming spell on his evening clothes so he could rejoin everyone when Juliet burst into the anteroom. After flinging a listening-ward spell along the walls, she scowled and demanded, "Oakmoor, *what* is going on?"

CHAPTER 6

*H*is face pale and haggard, Oakmoor gritted a tight smile that barely resembled his usual charming grins as she used her will to cast a probing spell to check him for active magic. He replied, "Nothing. I just wanted to escape the crowd."

Juliet snorted and strode across the anteroom toward Oakmoor. Although her probing spell revealed nothing unusual, something was clearly going on. He'd appeared tired recently, but tonight he looked downright dreadful, and he'd hardly talked to anyone all evening before dropping his sparkling wine and slipping away alone. Such unsociability and clumsiness wasn't at all like the social and suave duke. She fisted her hands on her hips. "Since when do *you* want to escape a crowd? Are you ill?"

Oakmoor glared at her. "Of course not."

She snorted again. "Well, you look it." And the idiot man would never admit to feeling ill, especially to her. Her chest tightened. She was no healer, but she could manage a decent enough healing-sight spell to check if Oakmoor was lying. She swiftly gathered her will once more and did so, yet all she could sense was exhaustion from poor sleep and a slightly too fast pulse, both of which could be caused by almost anything. In Oakmoor's case, probably his current lover. Her fists clenching, she leaned toward him. "You should retire early tonight instead of cavorting with your current lover."

Oakmoor quirked a brow as his normal color returned. "My dear Lady Juliet, are you perhaps jealous?"

A blush heating her neck, she glowered at the insufferable duke. "Don't be ridiculous."

Oakmoor shifted closer until they almost touched. "Because I'd gladly *cavort* with you instead of my current lover."

Juliet swallowed to control the ache flooding her at Oakmoor's nearness. Goddess, why must his hard body and earthy sandalwood scent always be so tempting? Before she could succumb and kiss him, she jerked backward even though that hinted at her hateful hunger for him. "I told you to quit attempting to seduce me."

Oakmoor smirked. "Only if you quit acting like you want me to."

Fire flared and supplanted the desire coursing through her veins. She snapped, "I do no such thing."

Oakmoor stepped closer once more and caressed her lower lip with his thumb. "I could prove you a liar with one kiss, darling witch."

Juliet shuddered as her earlier desire returned like a repelled curse on its caster. Damn Oakmoor for making her so weak. She raised a hand to drive him away.

Before her hand landed, Oakmoor grasped her wrist, yanked her against him, and seized her mouth in a punishing kiss.

Feverish emptiness swamping her, she whimpered and fiercely returned Oakmoor's kiss while wrenching at his evening clothes. She needed him—now. At his groaned laugh, she froze. *What* was she *doing*? She shoved his chest then wrested herself free and staggered across the anteroom. Panting, she leaned on the wall. "Stay away from me, you rakehell."

His skin flushed and hazel eyes black, Oakmoor smirked

again as he repaired his destroyed cravat. "A rakehell you can't help but desire, my lying wanton."

Juliet winced at that shameful truth. Yet she straightened and slashed Oakmoor a disdainful glare before removing her listening-ward spell and gliding out of the anteroom. If only she could run. But 'twould betray her vulnerability to him as well as attract the attention of court.

When she rejoined Siobhan and Lorcan, Siobhan murmured without removing her gaze from a dazzling illusion of two firebirds' mating flight, "What made you disappear?"

Juliet managed a shrug. Keeping her voice light, she replied, "I required a moment alone."

An impish grin darted across Siobhan's freckled face as she glanced toward the back of the ballroom. "A moment alone with the Duke of Oakmoor."

Juliet tensed. How had Siobhan realized that? She'd kept the Orandians' attention from Oakmoor's peculiar behavior since they'd entered the ballroom, hence they'd not seen him slip away. She lifted her chin. "I didn't—"

Siobhan interrupted dryly, "The duke just emerged from the anteroom you disappeared into, so I know you did."

Heat suffusing her skin, Juliet swallowed and resolutely inspected the firebirds' vivid orange, red, and yellow feathers that emitted sparks as they flew intertwined. "We'd that private council matter to discuss."

Siobhan chuckled. "Of course you did."

Juliet blushed harder at her friend's clear disbelief. Unlike Calatini's court, Siobhan plainly recognized the unwanted attraction between her and Oakmoor. Protesting further would just convince Siobhan they were involved. Thankfully, Siobhan fell silent when the mating firebirds faded and a merfolk's underwater ballroom took their place.

While she clapped with the other guests, Juliet nearly frowned. Although not a council matter, she'd followed Oakmoor to discover what was causing his peculiar behavior tonight. Yet they'd barely discussed it before he'd threatened to seduce her then kissed her. Tingling flooded her as that wild kiss echoed through her. She'd practically ravaged Oakmoor like a starving venus—just like she always did when he kissed her, damn him. Whereas he, despite initiating the kiss and his obvious arousal, hadn't bothered to loosen her bodice or lift her skirt to touch her more intimately, unlike when he'd kissed her before. She inhaled a sharp breath. He'd only kissed her to distract her. That beast!

Her teeth clenching, she forced herself to remain still. Charging after Oakmoor and attacking him would just engender gossip. Instead, she turned her mind back to when she'd entered the anteroom. What did Oakmoor not want her to discover? When she'd entered, he'd appeared ill, but the air had felt peculiar too—heavy and charged and musky. She pursed her lips. Almost as if a powerful spell had just been cast. Yet *that* was impossible since Oakmoor didn't possess the slightest magical powers and he'd been alone. Plus, the only white glow of active magic about him had been his contraceptive charm beneath his cravat. So *what* was going on?

Juliet hummed as paired merfolk swam around their ballroom, their hair and tails glowing. If Oakmoor was involved in some sort of magic, 'twas her duty as Calatini's royal witch to discover what. One of the king's councilors being embroiled in magic he wasn't equipped to handle could be dangerous for Calatini. Her eyes narrowed as she glanced at Siobhan and Lorcan beside her. And it happening now, during the arrival of the first Orandian ambassador in a decade, was odd to say the least. Not that her candid friends were intentionally involved. But the prescient Orandian seer had sent them for some unknown reason. Could that reason involve Oakmoor?

She studied Oakmoor, still lingering along the back wall with a fresh flute of sparkling wine, although he was no longer haggard. She was going to need to keep an eye on him to discover what magic he was embroiled in. She swallowed a groan. Yet by doing that, not only would she be near him more, which would mean she'd suffer her unwanted desire more, but she'd also encourage Siobhan's belief about their involvement. Wonderful.

So after Lord Islaye cast his final illusion and brightened the witchlights again, Juliet escorted Siobhan and Lorcan across the ballroom to Oakmoor. The duke had brought them in his carriage, and he must return them to their embassy anyway.

His gaze coolly flicking over her before turning to the Orandians, Oakmoor flashed a smooth smile, nothing like his gritted one in the anteroom earlier. "Which illusion was your favorite?"

As Juliet used her will to cast an aura spell on Oakmoor to check him for remnants of inactive magic even though doing so was an intrusion and took all her magical strength, Siobhan chuckled and replied, "The first illusion, of course, since 'twas of Orandia."

Juliet relaxed when her spell revealed Oakmoor's yellow aura undimmed by ill health or dangerous magic. She stilled. Yet were there a few ivory motes indicating magical powers inside his aura? Surely not. Oakmoor wasn't a witch, so it must be a trick of the light. Yellow and ivory were similar shades after all.

While she released her aura spell, which was already draining her, Lorcan nodded and continued after his wife, "Did you know our seer's tower is the tallest building in Damensea and was built by Rhiannon herself soon after she settled on the isle? Lord Islaye's illusion of it was exactly right too—his detailed accuracy was most impressive. Scrying Orandia can be difficult due to the excess magic there. Did he perhaps use the Mirror of Wisdom? Such a wondrous tool would have no trouble scrying there."

Juliet discreetly gulped a steadying breath to recover from her aura spell. Fortunately, since only Rhiannon descendants could cast that difficult spell, and most couldn't manage it using will alone, neither Siobhan nor Lorcan appeared to notice her silent spellwork. Oakmoor, however, was narrowly eyeing her, but only because she'd been eyeing him. She gave him a superior smile as she replied to Lorcan, "Of course Lord Islaye didn't use the Mirror of Wisdom. When he and his wife decided to host an illusion evening for you, he requested my help creating a scrying spell he could maintain on Orandia."

As Oakmoor waved over a servant and muttered in his ear, Lorcan asked her, "How did you manage that? Especially when outside Orandia, the excess magic there often blinds witches' magical sight and swamps their scrying spells."

Juliet shrugged to minimize her achievement. "The simplest way imaginable. I weaved that excess magic into the scrying spell, which powered it as well."

Siobhan and Lorcan stared at her, then Siobhan murmured, "Only the most powerful of Rhiannon descendants can manipulate Orandia's potent magic like that."

While Juliet shrugged again and blushed, Oakmoor smirked then passed her the full plate the servant had just brought him. He drawled, "Lady Juliet is known as the most illustrious witch in Calatini for a reason."

Her stomach rumbling, she slowly accepted the plate. How had Oakmoor known she'd needed it? Could he have sensed her aura spell somehow? Impossible. Perhaps she just looked pale, and the too charming duke was always astute. She inclined her head and managed a polite smile. "Thank you for your kind words, your grace."

As she devoured the full plate and her energy trickled back, she and the Orandians discussed Lord Islaye's other illusions with Oakmoor interjecting a few bland comments. Then Siobhan said they should leave, and Oakmoor escorted Siobhan and Lorcan to the Islayes to say farewell.

Juliet scrutinized Oakmoor while he and her friends left. Yes, for all that her earlier spells revealed nothing, something odd was definitely going on with him. Yet if she kept observing Oakmoor, she'd discover the problem and handle it before it impacted Calatini. Hopefully, it didn't involve one of his jealous former lovers.

OVER THE NEXT FEW DAYS, Juliet watched Oakmoor at every court event they both attended and silently cast healing-sight spells or probing spells on him once she was close enough. However, she detected no illness or unusual magic about him, although he continued to appear tired, but never pale and haggard like in the anteroom at Islaye House. Despite sensing nothing odd with her other spells, she didn't risk casting another aura spell since doing so had noticeably drained her, enough that even Oakmoor, who'd no magical powers, had noticed. Yet although she'd not discovered his problem, she *knew* there was one. Along with always appearing tired, Oakmoor had quit pursuing young ladies and barely flirted anymore. Granted, he was forever escorting Siobhan and Lorcan around Ormas, but his duties as the Minister of Foreign Relations had never prevented his rakehell ways before.

In addition to her concern about Oakmoor, she began to fret about Mordred. His weekly letter *still* hadn't arrived and was now several days late, later than he'd ever been since sending her the transport box. Had something terrible happened to the curious young witch? His last letter about flying carpets had seemed innocuous enough, but the topics he'd chosen had varied over the past few months, so the next one to interest him could have been dangerous. She considered casting a tracing spell using the magical signature on his transport box, although she soon decided against doing that without more proof something terrible had happened. She and Mordred had rarely touched on personal matters in their letters, so he'd doubtless consider a tracing spell a meddlesome invasion and might quit sending his charming letters if she used one to find him. Instead, she started checking the carved walnut transport box on her desk several times a day for his letters, although 'twas always empty.

On her way to the next council meeting, four days after the Islayes' illusion evening, Juliet checked the transport box for the second time that morning and grimaced at the still empty interior. What was delaying Mordred's letter? She sighed then strode from the royal wing, burying her concern for the young witch. She must focus on sharing her findings about Siobhan and Lorcan with King Devon, Queen Kiera, and the council.

When she entered the council room, Oakmoor was thankfully in his usual seat down near the foot of the table. She almost frowned. He appeared more tired than ever and wasn't bothering to speak with anyone. *Very* unusual.

Not long after she'd sat at the opposite end of the table like always, King Devon and Queen Kiera arrived and opened the council meeting. Then King Devon turned to her and asked, "What did you discover about the Orandians since our last meeting?"

Juliet inclined her head and smiled at King Devon and Queen Kiera. "As I suspected, neither Lady Driscoll nor Sir Lorcan know why their seer sent them, although it might involve the Magehaven ore crisis. Also, them being witches may be irrelevant. They volunteered to come to Calatini since they've always wanted to travel."

King Devon and Queen Kiera traded glances, then Queen Kiera arched her brows at the Duke of Osbourne and asked, "Does that match what your spies told you?"

The elderly duke nodded. "It does." He tapped the table. "And the Orandians are so open about themselves and magic that I doubt they're concealing any secrets about why they're here."

Oakmoor echoed his fellow duke's nod, his face sober for once. "I agree. Sir Lorcan is particularly transparent about magic, and both Lady Driscoll and Sir Lorcan are enamored with Lady Juliet and her magical prowess, so they doubtless would have told her anything they knew."

She eyed Oakmoor and almost frowned. He'd said that

without smirking at her like he normally would. He really was off today. Not that she could cast spells to check him here. Even though she excelled at casting spells with will alone, Lord Islaye might sense her spellwork, especially since he was familiar with her magical signature. She'd have to talk with Oakmoor alone after the council meeting. She gripped her hands as her treacherous heart quickened at being alone with Oakmoor again.

Lord Islaye leaned forward. "Should we consult the veiled witch to see she can tell us?"

Juliet stiffened and pursed her lips. Not the veiled witch again. "I doubt we'd learn anything. If the Orandian seer couldn't reveal her reasons to avoid changing the future, the veiled witch likely shan't be able to reveal more."

After King Devon and Queen Kiera exchanged another glance, Queen Kiera nodded and said, "We should wait until we truly need the veiled witch to consult her. She'll tell us more then."

King Devon added dryly, "Although it shall probably be cryptic." As Queen Kiera slanted her husband a tender smile, he turned the discussion to other matters.

As soon as the council meeting adjourned, Oakmoor left without speaking to anyone, although everyone else remained about the table talking. He *never* did that. Definitely off.

So even though the Duchess of Wildewall was leaning toward her to say something, Juliet nodded farewell and hurried after Oakmoor. Once they were out of earshot of the royal guards flanking the door, she called, "Oakmoor, wait."

CHAPTER 7

At Juliet's call, Oakmoor stiffened but halted. No doubt she was about to use her will to silently cast another spell on him that he must pretend he couldn't sense. She'd been doing that whenever she saw him ever since she'd found him after his transformation at Islaye House four days ago. Clearly, she'd realized something had happened that night, but she couldn't tell what because Elvaira's curse was visible only to seers. Yet despite her repeated lack of success, she kept casting her spells. The illustrious and skilled royal witch wasn't accustomed to her magic failing, so he'd have to continue enduring her spells until he transformed into a hideous beast before her. Not that he intended to let *that* ever happen. She'd either smirk or pity him, and even Juliet couldn't break a curse she couldn't see. His only hope for that was the veiled witch, although he'd be unable to visit the mysterious seer for a while yet. His duties with the Orandians currently kept him too busy. Of course Elvaira's vindictive curse had manifested when he hadn't time to address it.

He inhaled then turned to face Juliet and arched a brow. "Yes?"

Juliet narrowly eyed him. "Why are you so unsociable today?"

He gritted a bland smile as Juliet's spell flared about him. Although he couldn't tell exactly what spell she'd cast without analyzing it using a probing spell, her spells invariably pricked his skin like a swarm of curious flying blood-ants. If only he could cast a sight-ward spell to block her magical sight, but 'twould reveal his erratic magical powers. Another secret he didn't intend for her to discover since his inability to control his magic would amuse and disgust her. Plus, she might begin to suspect he was the Mordred who'd written her all those letters. "Am I being unsociable?"

Juliet snorted. "Yes, you barely spoke to anyone in the council room, and you're unusually sober. You didn't even smirk when you complimented me."

Oakmoor exhaled when Juliet's itchy spell faded. Then he managed the smirk she'd obviously missed. "I'm sorry that you feel neglected."

Her gaze narrowing further, Juliet glared at him. "I do *not* feel neglected."

He caressed Juliet's lower lip with his thumb like he had in the Islayes' anteroom, and his body hardened with painful hunger. Goddess, he needed to kiss the maddening witch again. He'd kissed her then to distract her, but he'd been about to tumble her to the floor and take her when she'd wrenched herself free. Her wild passion at his kisses along with her spicy and sweet taste were as bewitching and addictive as ever. How had he not kissed her for eight months? He leaned toward her and rumbled, "*I* feel neglected."

Juliet's lush lips parted as she inhaled a shuddering breath. "Oakmoor, I..."

His blood surged. She was *his*. Neither of them could deny or control the passion burning between them. He began bending his head to seize her mouth in the fierce kiss they both needed.

"Your grace, Lady Juliet, there you are. I must speak with

you," the Duchess of Wildewall said from several steps behind Juliet.

As Juliet whirled to face the temperate duchess, Oakmoor swallowed a groan. He'd almost kissed Juliet in an open hall again. He really must start taking her somewhere private first. Otherwise, they'd keep getting interrupted, and all of court would discover their uncontrollable desire. But being near Juliet made him forget every trick he'd ever learned as a rakehell. Fortunately for them both, the Duchess of Wildewall's easy smile revealed she'd not been close enough to notice he'd been almost kissing Juliet.

He forced himself to return the duchess's smile. "Speak to us about what?"

The Duchess of Wildewall replied, "I'd like to host an intimate garden party for Lady Driscoll and her husband, inviting the witch families at court." She cocked her head, the frost in her auburn hair shimmering. "I thought such an event would thrill the Orandians as well as build rapport between them and our witches."

He hummed. Lady Driscoll and Sir Lorcan had already met many of court's witch families but likely hadn't known they possessed magical powers since most witches in Calatini refused to discuss magic in mixed company. Even longtime members of court without acknowledged magic like himself weren't certain which families had witches. There were often rumors but nothing definite because magic and possessing it were unpredictable. Having a witch ancestor didn't guarantee possessing magical powers, and as he proved, families without magic could bear witches. But the Duchess of Wildewall should know whom to invite thanks to her lore-witch husband, one of the few witches at court who'd always been open about his magical powers even though he didn't have duties requiring that.

Oakmoor leaned forward. "An excellent idea. When?"

The duchess pursed her lips. "Five afternoons from today, I think. No other court events are planned then, and the only major court event that night is the Westons' musical evening." She glanced at him. "Even though you're not a witch, you should still attend since you're currently escorting Lady Driscoll and Sir Lorcan everywhere."

He suppressed a grimace but nodded. He'd planned to visit the veiled witch that afternoon, but his duties outweighed his private concerns. And the Orandians building rapport with Calatini's witches *was* important, especially if trouble was approaching like they'd discussed at the council meeting before last.

The Duchess of Wildewall continued, "I'll personally invite everyone to avoid creating gossip among those without magic at court." She turned to Juliet. "I'd like to consult with you and Lord Islaye to ensure I don't miss inviting any witch families."

Juliet smiled. "Of course."

The duchess took Juliet's arm. "Come, the three of us can discuss my guests over luncheon at Wildewall House." The duchess gave him a smiling nod as she drew Juliet away. Juliet, however, didn't glance at him again, probably upset over their almost kiss.

Oakmoor exhaled and strode from the palace too. 'Twas just as well that the duchess had interrupted them. Rekindling his affair with Juliet wouldn't be at all sensible. She'd surely curse him if they did, and he couldn't handle *another* curse from a Rhiannon-descendant witch. Plus, he was tired from his recurring curse dreams and constantly waiting to transform into a hideous beast again. At the first hints of that, he must conceal himself so no one discovered his curse.

Back at Oakmoor House, he headed to his study to handle correspondence before meeting the Orandians for dinner and the Campbells' ball afterward. Too bad he couldn't fit in a visit to the veiled witch this afternoon, but her witch shop was across Ormas and consulting her could be lengthy. He reviewed his upcoming schedule and frowned. The Duchess of Wildewall had taken his only available afternoon for the next several weeks.

Great. He couldn't visit the veiled witch with the Orandians along, although they'd both doubtless love meeting her, and 'twould be rude to abandon them for an afternoon while they were getting settled. Hopefully, delaying his visit to the veiled witch wouldn't cause problems.

AFTER LUNCHEON FIVE DAYS LATER, Oakmoor sighed and rubbed his aching head as he took his carriage to collect Lady Driscoll and Sir Lorcan for the Duchess of Wildewall's garden party. Dear Goddess, he was exhausted—more so every day. It had been nine days since his first transformation, and he'd not transformed into a beast again, but constantly remaining vigilant about that was draining. And what little sleep he got was poor thanks to his damned curse dreams. Thankfully, only Juliet appeared to notice the depths of his exhaustion. He'd managed to divert everyone else from it, including the observant Lady Driscoll and Sir Lorcan, with charming smiles and deft talk.

Before long, his carriage halted at the Orandians' embassy, and he straightened then leapt out to collect Lady Driscoll and her husband.

Once they'd settled in the forward seat across from him, Lady Driscoll smiled at him and said, "I hope you shan't feel bored or excluded at today's garden party, your grace."

He flashed a bright grin. "I enjoy conversing with anyone, so I'll be fine." Besides, discovering the witch families at court would be interesting as well as potentially useful. And none of them could be Rhiannon-descendant seers who could see his curse. Seers weren't common, and Rhiannon-descendant ones even less so. Besides, if any were at court, they'd have reacted to his curse long ago.

Lady Driscoll chuckled. "At the very least, you and Juliet can be together again." Fingering the edge of her overcoat atop her tunic, she slanted him an impish smile. "For people who apparently dislike each other, you two can never keep apart."

His headache sharpening, Oakmoor made himself shrug. "Only because we're socializing with you and Sir Lorcan." And Juliet was curious about what had happened at Islaye House. "Before then, we both avoided each other." Since neither wanted to inflame their primal attraction.

Lady Driscoll and Sir Lorcan traded grins, then Lady Driscoll murmured, "Did you now? How interesting."

He exhaled when the carriage halted before the Orandians could continue quizzing him about Juliet. Then he escorted them to the Duchess of Wildewall.

The duchess greeted them with a warm smile then said, "Everyone except the most reclusive witches at court accepted my invitation, and they're eager to speak with you about magic. Go enjoy yourselves."

As he and the Orandians entered the Duchess of Wildewall's vibrant garden, he scanned the other guests. There were a lot fewer than at an ordinary court event, which wasn't surprising since less than a quarter of humans were witches. Two-thirds of the Magehaven families were here, nearly half of the Wildewall families, and a few families from each of the other duchies. Two families were from Oakmoor—the Merryweathers from central Oakmoor who were known for their musical talents and the Serles from near Golddell whose castle crafted the perfect armor. Interesting. Despite being their duke, he'd not known either family had witches.

Juliet joined them near the refreshments table, and he almost winced as another of her silent spells pricked his skin and made his head pound worse. Thankfully, her spell soon faded, and she turned to Lady Driscoll and Sir Lorcan with a smile and said, "An excellent turnout today. Who did you want to speak with first?"

Sir Lorcan grinned at her and leaned forward. "The nearest guests so we've time to speak with everyone before they leave."

As Juliet chuckled at that, Oakmoor smiled into his teacup

despite his lingering headache. Sir Lorcan's thirst to discuss magic was truly rapacious.

Lady Driscoll arched a brow at her husband and drawled, "Remember, casting a trap spell on the duchess's garden to ensure we speak to everyone would be unspeakably rude and likely spark a war between Orandia and Calatini."

Sir Lorcan sighed. "I know."

Oakmoor's mouth twitched. Otherwise, Sir Lorcan would clearly risk casting such a spell. Lore witches.

Juliet escorted them to the Islayes and Dowager Lady Ravenstone while the Greysnowes drifted to the refreshments table. Sir Lorcan immediately began quizzing the three remaining witches on their magic. After the Islayes talked about their recent spells, Dowager Lady Ravenstone grimaced and said, "I've mostly been gathering my natural energy. I'm a nature witch, you see."

Oakmoor hummed. Being a nature witch certainly explained why Dowager Lady Ravenstone had never attended court until her son had nearly been killed last Summerday in a duel with Lord Alexander Greysnowe, their family's then ancestral enemy and her son's now brother-in-law. Nature witches despised living in cities because it separated them from nature too much.

Lady Driscoll beamed at Dowager Lady Ravenstone. "I'm a sea witch, so our magic is quite similar. Sea witches are the nautical version of nature witches, after all. We must arrange an afternoon to swap spells."

Once Lady Driscoll and Dowager Lady Ravenstone arranged that, Juliet escorted Oakmoor and the Orandians to the next nearest group, Lord and Lady Merryweather and their youngest daughter. After a lively conversation about music spells, they continued to the next group, High Priest Theodag, Elder Priestess Letitia, and Elder Priest Sidney, who all rarely attended court events thanks to their many duties at the Great Temple. Yet their discussion about holy magic and healing magic was fascinating. Too bad neither type of magic could help break his curse.

Oakmoor, Juliet, and the Orandians soon resumed circulating, and midway through, they joined Lord and Lady Ravenstone and her brother Lord Alexander.

Lady Driscoll grinned at Lord Ravenstone. "Are you a nature witch like your mother?" When the rugged count nodded, she added, "Then you must join us when we swap spells at Ravenstone House in a few weeks."

As Lord Ravenstone nodded again, Sir Lorcan turned to Lady Ravenstone and Lord Alexander, blurting, "You Greysnowes are descended from Esme the Great, I believe. How often does your family bear soul healers like her?"

Oakmoor blinked when Lady Ravenstone stilled as Lord Ravenstone and Lord Alexander shifted infinitesimally closer to her. Why?

Juliet chuckled and shook her head at Sir Lorcan. "Lord and Lady Ravenstone don't wish to discuss soul healers, Lorcan. One forming an inappropriate soulbond started the centuries-long feud between their families that only ended with their marriage."

While Sir Lorcan murmured apologies, Oakmoor eyed Juliet. She obviously knew why Lady Ravenstone's husband and brother were acting protective. And from her behavior here and at his soiree, she felt protective of Lady Ravenstone too. Casting his mind back to that evening, he sipped his tea then almost choked. Lady Blaine had fetched Lady Ravenstone because Lady Beza Hawke had been dying, yet Lady Beza had been completely well a few days later. Lady Ravenstone must be a soul healer like her legendary ancestress. His blood pounding in his aching head, he stared at the ice-perfect beauty he'd briefly courted. No wonder Juliet, Lord Ravenstone, and Lord Alexander were protective of her. The extremely rare female witch healers were coveted for their powerful healing magic and often exploited because they couldn't protect themselves with ordinary spells.

He swallowed. Could Lady Ravenstone break his curse? A regular witch healer couldn't because his curse wasn't a true ailment. Yet soul healers could heal nearly anything, so maybe she could manage it. He glanced at Lord Ravenstone and Lord Alexander flanking her. Their protectiveness would make asking Lady Ravenstone difficult, and both were known for being skilled swordsmen. He'd better consult with the veiled witch first. *She'd* not have protective relatives prepared to challenge him to a duel for approaching her about her special powers.

After Sir Lorcan finished apologizing to the Ravenstones and Lord Alexander, Juliet whisked them away to talk with the Count and Countess of Mythacre from Magehaven. Then she kept her friends away from Lady Ravenstone for the rest of the afternoon, but she did it so subtly that neither Lady Driscoll nor Sir Lorcan appeared to notice. Adroit witch.

The Orandians insisted on circulating until the last of the guests left. By then, Oakmoor's lingering headache had transformed into an agonizing one. He blew a relieved sigh when he, Juliet, and the Orandians finally approached their hostess to bid her farewell. He needed some quiet in a dark room to recover before the Westons' musical evening tonight.

The Duchess of Wildewall grinned at Lady Driscoll and Sir Lorcan. "Did you enjoy yourselves?"

Lady Driscoll grinned back. "Very much. We spoke to all the guests about their magic."

Sir Lorcan leaned toward the duchess. "Except you, your grace."

Oakmoor quirked a smile despite his throbbing head. And him and Lady Ravenstone.

The Duchess of Wildewall waved a hand. "Oh, I'm not a witch, although I'm aware of most of the witch families at court since my husband Niall is a lore witch like you." Her brown eyes flickered. "He's disappointed not to meet you, but since our daughter Sionna was born, he's preferred to remain in Wildewall to take care of her."

Oakmoor eyed the duchess. It *was* odd that her husband hadn't returned to Ormas to meet the Orandians. Like Sir Lorcan, the Duke of Wildewall loved discussing magic with everyone, and he'd often assisted Lord Islaye with his duties as the Minister of Magic despite possessing no official position himself, so meeting witches from the most magical isle in Damensea would thrill him. He and the duchess must have decided their daughter remaining in Wildewall was more important, although the duke and their daughter had visited Ormas this past Longnight season when the duchess and the other councilors couldn't leave with the Nightmara-Calatini Treaty unrenewed. But the duchess had mentioned their caravan travel spell had made her husband and daughter dreadfully ill, so perhaps that explained the duke's absence now.

Sir Lorcan beamed. "Another lore witch? You must give me his communication mirror's call signature."

The duchess laughed and did so then added, "Niall shall be thrilled to hear from you."

Oakmoor, Juliet, and the Orandians finished saying farewell then left the duchess's garden. When they reached the carriages, intense heat swamped him, and he almost staggered. Oh, Goddess. His lingering headache wasn't due to mere exhaustion —it had been a harbinger of his second transformation.

He gulped air to steady himself. Last time, he'd transformed moments after the heat had swamped him. He must escape the others at once. Fortunately, Juliet could escort the Orandians back to their embassy. He gritted a blinding smile at Lady Driscoll and Sir Lorcan. "I just recollected I've a private matter to handle before the Westons' musical evening tonight. Please excuse me. I'll see you at dinner."

While Juliet and the Orandians gaped at him, Oakmoor vaulted into his carriage, banged on the ceiling to signal the driver to start, then yanked down the curtains. And not a moment too soon because a heartbeat later, the heat coursing through him flared into boiling agony as his body transformed. A transformation that somehow felt even longer and more excruciating the second time, though it wasn't since the carriage was still gathering speed when his transformation ended.

As he stared at his beast hands, more boiling agony flared, and he transformed back to human again. He swallowed the blood filling his mouth from him biting his tongue to stifle his screams during his excruciating transformations. He must consult with the veiled witch about his curse before he endured another. But not today. He was too exhausted, and he must arrange for Lady Escana to escort the Orandians in his absence. Somehow he must find the energy to attend the Westons' musical evening like he'd promised. He sighed. 'Twould be grueling, but at least he could speak with Lady Escana there. Then he could visit the veiled witch tomorrow.

CHAPTER 8

$\mathcal{A}$s a flushed yet haggard Oakmoor leapt into his carriage, Juliet gaped after him and used her will to silently cast a healing-sight spell at his back despite Siobhan and Lorcan standing beside her. Oakmoor looked even worse than he had at Islaye House, and for him to abandon his companions so clumsily wasn't like him at all. Yet same as before, all she could sense was exhaustion and a racing pulse. She frowned while his carriage rumbled down the street. She should have cast a probing spell to examine the active magic around him, but he'd looked so dreadful that she'd instinctively cast a healing-sight spell. And she hadn't time to cast a second spell before he'd bolted, so she was no closer to discovering what magic Oakmoor was embroiled in.

She started when Lorcan murmured, "The Duke of Oakmoor's private matter must be serious indeed for him to be abrupt."

Shoving aside her concern for Oakmoor, Juliet sniffed and pursed a sardonic smirk. "Knowing Oakmoor, he probably arranged to meet two jealous lovers at the same time or some such." She smiled at Siobhan and Lorcan. "But since he's abandoned you, I'll take you back to your embassy."

Once they'd settled in the carriage, Siobhan frowned as she nestled against Lorcan. "I think you've misjudged the Duke of Oakmoor, Juliet. Whatever's going on clearly upset him. He looked almost ill."

Juliet made herself shrug and keep smiling. Oakmoor would hate Siobhan and Lorcan analyzing him. Despite his many lovers and charming manner, he kept everyone at a distance and never discussed his private matters. For him to even hint at one revealed his desperation to escape. Yet his desire for privacy was understandable. She was much the same, particularly about her past in Varkhora. So to divert her friends from Oakmoor, she asked, "With your duties representing Orandia, shall you be able to manage all those meetings you arranged to further discuss people's magic?"

Siobhan chuckled and squeezed her husband's tunic-covered knee. "Oh, yes. Lorcan can *always* manage to fit in discussing magic, and those meetings are part of our duties to Orandia."

Lorcan grinned. "The best part." He glanced at Siobhan. "Do you think I've time for a mirror call with the Duke of Wildewall before dinner? 'Tis been years since I spoke with another lore witch."

Juliet swallowed a laugh. Lorcan appeared as excited as a little boy on Longnight morning with all his gifts before him.

Siobhan arched her brows at her husband. "As long as you swear to end the call when I fetch you for dinner. We've a court event afterward."

Lorcan sighed but nodded. "Like always."

Juliet's lips twitched. Now Lorcan was frowning like a little boy denied a sweet. Men. "The Westons' musical evening, right?"

Siobhan inclined her head. "Yes, and I'm looking forward to it. Lorcan was too, until he discovered another lore witch. We both love music."

Juliet echoed Siobhan's nod. "Then you'll definitely enjoy tonight. Music lovers say the Westons' musical evenings are superb, especially since they never permit talking during the performances." She tapped her knee. Since she cared little about music, she rarely attended musical evenings, but doing so tonight would allow her to check on Oakmoor. She grinned at Siobhan and Lorcan. "I must hear your opinions afterward."

After she'd dropped her friends at their embassy, she let her grin drain from her face. Oakmoor's magic troubles were beginning to impact his duties. And that could cause kingdom-wide problems given his position as the Minister of Foreign Relations. She'd better discover what was going on soon so she could handle it before it exploded.

As soon as she finished dinner, she headed to Weston House and was one of the first to arrive. Only Lord and Lady Beza Hawke were already there, talking with the two granddaughters they'd helped the Westons discover last summer. Neither girl was out yet, so Juliet had never met them, but the younger girl looked about six or seven, while the elder one appeared around a decade older and oddly familiar. Juliet eyed the teenage girl. Where had they met before? She sharply inhaled. In the veiled witch's garden on Longnight when helping break the ancient curse killing Lord and Lady Ravenstone. The girl was the veiled witch's apprentice Cassandra. She hummed. She'd not realized Cassandra was also the Westons' newfound granddaughter. Too bad she hadn't. She'd have told the Duchess of Wildewall to invite Cassandra this afternoon if she had.

Beside Cassandra, her little sister was bouncing before Lord and Lady Beza and saying, "I thought you'd bring the twins with you, Miss Wren. I wanted to meet them."

Lady Beza chuckled. "They're less than a month old, Amaranth. They're not up for musical evenings yet."

Slowly crossing the room, Juliet turned her gaze from Cassandra to scrutinize the smiling Lady Beza, who showed no signs of illness despite nearly dying in childbirth two and a half weeks ago. Not surprising since soul-healing immediately restored people to perfect health. Lady Ravenstone's magical powers were truly amazing.

As Cassandra laid her hands on Amaranth's shoulders, Lord Beza tweaked the little girl's nose and added, "And we can't leave Kestrel and Peregrine for long, so we only stopped by to say hello since we'd promised we'd attend tonight."

Lady Weston tsked. "You should have brought them along. We could have settled them in the nursery for the evening."

While Juliet joined them, Lady Beza slanted her husband a wry grin as he shuddered. Lady Beza replied to Lady Weston, "Thanks, but we *finally* got the twins to sleep an hour ago, and if we disturbed them, they'd be awake until dawn. Just like after Pippa's natalday celebration last week."

Lord and Lady Weston turned to Juliet, then Lady Weston beamed at her and said, "Lady Juliet, how nice to see you tonight. We've some magical surprises in honor of the Orandians that you'll enjoy." She beckoned her granddaughters. "I don't believe you've met our granddaughters, Cassandra and Amaranth."

Juliet smiled at the two girls. "A pleasure." Then she sharply inhaled when they fully faced her. Cassandra had mulberry eyes —just like Ceija Lovari. She'd not noticed that when they'd met on Longnight since she'd been too absorbed in meeting the veiled witch for the first time. She exhaled as she studied Cassandra's unusual yet familiar eyes. The only others she'd ever seen with that eye color besides Ceija were Ceija's grandson Shandor and his toddler daughter. But his daughter would be nearly seventeen now, and his wife Anne *had* been the daughter of prejudiced Calatinian nobles who'd refused to allow her marriage to a gypsy traveler, even though he was a powerful Rhiannon-descendant bard witch.

Juliet leaned toward the teenage girl. "Cassandra Lovari?"

Cassandra stilled and almost frowned. "I go by Weston now. 'Tis less confusing for people at court. How did you know my true surname?"

An ache flooded Juliet's chest. That meant Shandor and Anne were dead. The Westons had found their granddaughters in

Queen Kiera's former orphanage. Juliet gulped a steadying breath. Discovering that Shandor and his wife were dead was heartrending. A loving and trustworthy man, Shandor Lovari had been the second gentleman she'd ever trusted—her crippled cousin Sandro had been the first. Although they'd lost contact, she'd always imagined Shandor and his family happily living in Pruzirias, a small kingdom on the other side of the D'vark Mountains from Calatini. Yet he and Anne had died in Calatini last year. How could she not have known?

Burying her aching grief for her dead friend and his wife, Juliet smiled warmly at their two daughters. "Before I settled in Calatini, I traveled with the Lovaris for years. Your father became a dear friend and was the best bard witch I ever met. We spent many afternoons discussing magic and life and music, despite me possessing no musical abilities whatsoever."

As Cassandra and the others stared at Juliet, Amaranth gripped Juliet's sapphire skirt with tears shimmering in her dark eyes. "You knew Papa?"

Her chest aching again, Juliet grinned at the little girl and smoothed the loose, brown curls which Amaranth and her sister had inherited from Lady Weston. Anne's hair had been just the same. "Yes, and I knew your mother too, although not as well as your father since she only traveled with the gypsies for a year before she and your father settled in Pruzirias. But your parents adored each other and were so happy together."

While Amaranth buried her face in Juliet's skirt and Cassandra blinked back tears, Lord and Lady Weston traded a solemn glance, and Lady Weston murmured, "We'd greatly appreciate it if you could visit again and tell the girls more about Anne and Shandor's life together."

Juliet scrutinized the older couple. Although they'd been too prejudiced to allow their daughter to marry a poor gypsy, their grief after Anne had run away had pervaded their lives according to court gossip and doubtless changed them. The Westons certainly spoke of Shandor now without rancor, and their love for their half-gypsy granddaughters was apparent. Her throat tightened. If only Father had changed likewise after she'd run away. But Varkhorans didn't value daughters like Calatinians did, and he surely despised her for ruining his ambition to be the queen's father instead of just a prominent duke. She swallowed to ease her tight throat. And Father still had her now twenty-two-year-old brother Giovanni to console him.

A pang slicing through her at the adorable toddler she'd left behind when she'd fled Varkhora, Juliet answered Lady Weston, "Of course I'll visit and tell you about Shandor and Anne's life, although we lost contact once I settled at court as the royal witch." Likely because Shandor hadn't wanted to risk word of them reaching the Westons. He'd been determined not to let his beloved Anne be hurt by her parents again. Not that they would have given their current behavior. The Westons probably would have joyfully welcomed Anne and Shandor back if they'd ever contacted them.

Lady Beza Hawke and her husband both grinning, Lady Beza extracted Amaranth from about Juliet and embraced the little girl. Lady Beza said, "What an exciting development. Unfortunately, we must return home now. We'll invite you and Cassandra to visit the twins in a week or two, Amaranth." Then she embraced Cassandra before smiling at Juliet and the Westons.

As Lord and Lady Beza left, other guests started arriving, and Juliet slid her arm through Cassandra's. They should talk before too many others were around to overhear. "Could we take a turn about the room?"

At Cassandra's nod, they began walking along the wall. Juliet slanted the teenage girl a considering glance. "I should have recognized you as Shandor's daughter when we met before, but the last I'd heard from him, your family was still living in Pruzirias. I'd no inkling you'd returned to Calatini. I wish I had. Then I could have helped when your parents died." She sighed as grief flooded her chest once more and Cassandra's mulberry eyes darkened. To distract them both, she smiled and asked, "So how did you become the veiled witch's apprentice?"

Cassandra lifted a shoulder. "Wren introduced me eight months ago, and Tihdseare has been teaching me since then."

Juliet nodded. Ah yes, Lady Beza Hawke *had* purchased her glamour spell for the king's masquerade last year from the veiled witch. And although Cassandra called the veiled witch "Tihdseare", that couldn't be the veiled witch's true name since it simply meant "teacher" in the witch's tongue. Juliet arched her brows at Cassandra. "I'm not surprised the veiled witch agreed to teach you. Even when you were small, you showed signs you'd grow into a powerful witch. Are you a bard witch like Shandor?"

Cassandra smiled and shook her head. "I'm an ordinary witch, although Amaranth may be one. She doesn't have magical powers yet, but her voice is celestial, and she can play practically any instrument."

Juliet winked at the younger witch to reassure her. "Being an ordinary witch isn't a shortcoming. I'm one as well. And so were many influential witches of the past."

Before she could ask Cassandra about what she'd learned from the veiled witch so far, Oakmoor arrived with Siobhan and Lorcan. No longer flushed, he still looked dreadful. She gathered her will and silently cast a probing spell but sensed nothing again. How vexing.

When Oakmoor left Siobhan and Lorcan to join his assistant Lady Escana and her husband near the refreshments table, Juliet almost pursed her lips. Overhearing their conversation might reveal something that would help her discover whatever magic he was embroiled in. But she couldn't just abandon Cassandra. She smiled at the teenage girl. "Come, let me introduce you to the Orandian ambassador and her husband. Both are witches too, and they'll love meeting you."

Juliet did, and Siobhan and Lorcan were soon eagerly quizzing Cassandra about what gypsy spells she knew. As

Cassandra began describing the ones Shandor had taught her, Juliet murmured, "I need some sparkling wine; excuse me." After fetching that, she drifted close enough to overhear Oakmoor and the Escanas.

Oakmoor was saying to Lady Escana, "I'm relieved you're free tomorrow. Could you accompany Lady Driscoll and Sir Lorcan to Serle House for me? The Serles are showing them samples of armor created by their castle's artisan witches."

Her tone revealing her surprise, Lady Escana murmured, "Yes, of course. But shan't the Serles be offended that their duke chose not to attend their display? Especially since you've escorted the Orandians everywhere else so far."

Oakmoor sighed. "I'd attend if I could, but unfortunately I've another commitment. I'll write the Serles tonight to explain."

Juliet suppressed a frown. No doubt Oakmoor's "commitment" involved his magic troubles. But what was it?

Lady Escana chuckled. "The Serles shall likely be so charmed by your letter, your grace, that they'll thank you for not attending." She paused. "It looks like the music is about to start."

As Lady Escana and her husband headed toward the seats, Juliet surged before Oakmoor. She narrowed her eyes at him. "We must talk."

Oakmoor arched a brow. "Now?"

Resisting the urge to fist her hands on her hips, she leaned toward Oakmoor. "Yes, now."

Oakmoor sighed but strode into the nearest anteroom. She followed and flung her hand toward the door to cast a listening-ward spell about the anteroom to keep their conversation private, but she remained across the room. Every time she and Oakmoor got too close, they ended up kissing or almost kissing. Damned unwanted desire.

Oakmoor flashed a smoldering smile then rumbled, "Attempting to seduce me again? 'Twould be simpler if you just visited Oakmoor House one night. I'll gladly accommodate you."

She glared at Oakmoor and clenched her flute of sparkling

wine. Unrepentant rakehell. "Don't be disgusting. We must talk because 'tis clear that you've become embroiled in some sort of magic, and as Calatini's royal witch, I must handle it before it explodes."

His charming mask fading for once, Oakmoor straightened and glared back at her. "Given your suspicions, I'm sure you've cast countless probing spells and the like on me, royal witch. Have you sensed any magic about me?"

Juliet huffed then set down her glass flute before she snapped it. "No, but I *know* 'tis there. Otherwise, why else would you be abandoning your duties? Especially now, when you're escorting the first Orandian ambassador in a decade."

CHAPTER 9

Oakmoor stiffened at Juliet's perceptive accusation. Why must the meddlesome witch keep prying? 'Twasn't as if she could help break the beast curse afflicting him. She'd just confirmed that she couldn't even sense it. He inhaled and leaned toward Juliet to appear earnest. "I'm *not* abandoning my duties—I'm delegating."

Her lush lips tight, Juliet huffed again. "*Delegating*? Oh, please."

Hunger surged through him as he eyed Juliet's disdainful mouth. He could so easily stride across the anteroom, yank her into his arms, and kiss her until she purred. Yet he'd probably not stop at a kiss if he did, and anyone could stumble across them here. Besides, distracting her with their explosive passion had only provided a temporary reprieve before. He *must* get Juliet to quit prying, otherwise she'd eventually witness one of his excruciating transformations. And he couldn't betray such a vulnerability to her.

He gritted a cold grin. "How I handle my duties is no concern of yours. And neither are my private matters. Quit prying, or I'll retaliate in the way that'll hurt you to the quick."

Juliet lifted her chin. "You can't hurt me."

Oakmoor smirked at Juliet. "No? Not even if I ensure everyone knows about our past affair? Being known as a discarded lover of the greatest rakehell in Ormas would tarnish your reputation as Calatini's most illustrious witch." Her fierce pride would *hate* that, as would his if reversed. Not that he'd ever actually carry out his threat. 'Twould simply encourage court to pry, which was even worse than Juliet prying.

Juliet's luscious olive skin paled. "You beast."

His chest squeezing at her upset, he nevertheless smiled and sauntered past the bewitching royal witch toward the door. "Only if you force me to be. Stay out of my private matters, Juliet."

He rejoined the Orandians and settled in the empty seat beside Sir Lorcan, leaving the one beside Lady Driscoll for Juliet. Then he pretended not to notice when she joined them several moments later, her skin no longer pale but her lips still some-what tight as she ignored him as thoroughly as he was ignoring her. His threat had definitely upset her. But he'd had to get the stubborn witch to quit prying somehow.

He fixed a smooth smile to his face while enduring the lengthy musical evening. He was still exhausted, so remaining awake was a battle, especially during the more soothing songs. Yet somehow he managed it and escorted the Orandians back to their embassy. Afterward, he collapsed into slumber as soon as he returned home, although his sleep was as unrestful as ever because of his grotesque curse dreams.

Oakmoor staggered from bed early the following morning and downed three cups of bitter kahve with his breakfast—two more than he usually drank. But as his exhaustion grew, so did his need for the energizing brew. Then he took his carriage to the poor neighborhood near the docks to visit Rhiannon's Veils.

He frowned at the witch shop's weathered red door, which suited its shabby surroundings. If Juliet hadn't confirmed that the veiled witch was a Rhiannon-descendant seer, he'd never believe it from the veiled witch's unprepossessing shop. He inhaled then strode inside and nearly sneezed at the pervasive incense in the dim, empty chamber.

Glass beads tinkling behind her, a woman concealed by black veils and possessing the strongest air of magic he'd ever seen—the veiled witch obviously—sashayed through the door along the rear wall. She immediately stilled, her exotically lined eyes widening. "I can guess why you've come to see me. 'Tis *quite* a nasty curse you're suffering."

As the veiled witch waved for him to sit at the wooden table, her bracelets and tiny bells jingling, Oakmoor forced a charming grin and sat in the chair she'd indicated. "A gift from a vindictive former lover, I'm afraid."

The veiled witch set a large quartz bowl on the table and added crystalline water from an opalescent leather flask. No doubt to perform a scrying spell. Such a spell would further enhance her keen-eyed seer vision that encompassed hindsight, nowsight, and foresight, allowing her to see everything about anything. Hopefully, she'd keep her prying to his curse. The veiled witch sat, extracted a needle, and reached for him. "Your full name and your hand, please."

He clung to his smile despite the chill skittering across his skin at giving the veiled witch his blood. Since Elvaira had cursed him, he'd not let anyone use his hair or blood and always ensured any discarded were destroyed so that no one could create a magical link to him. Yet the veiled witch couldn't see everything about him without it, and he *needed* her magical insight to break his curse. So he slowly offered his hand and drawled, "Mordred Thyme Tremblay, the Duke of Oakmoor."

The veiled witch hummed then pricked his finger and shook three drops of blood into the large quartz bowl. She peered into the now pink water, and as her potent powers flared, the dim chamber hushed like the hours after midnight when inky silence lay heavy on the land. His neck prickled. Goddess, the veiled witch's magic was so powerful that she made Juliet seem nothing but a minor witch, and Juliet was the most illustrious witch in Calatini.

Eventually, the veiled witch returned her gaze to him, her dark eyes probing yet gleaming with amusement. "A nasty curse indeed. It shall take a great deal to break it. As well as a special lady."

He exhaled as energy burst through him. Yet Elvaira's beast curse *could* be broken. Thank the Goddess. He leaned toward the veiled witch. "A special lady like a soul healer, perhaps?"

A chuckle undulated the veiled witch's black veils. "Not unless she was the lady meant to break your curse. And your lady isn't a soul healer."

Oakmoor drummed his fingers on the wooden table. Seers were always so damned cryptic. "Then who *is* the lady meant to break my curse?"

The veiled witch shook her head. "I can't tell you her name. If I did, 'twould change the future from how it should be, and you'd likely never break your curse." As his shoulders sagged, she added, "But I can provide you with a prophecy to help find her, along with wards to keep you together until your curse is broken."

He straightened. A prophecy and a spell to help were better than nothing and much more than he'd had before. Smoothly smiling at the veiled witch, he waved for her to continue. "Very well."

The veiled witch intoned, "To break your beast curse, a special lady you must find. Cousin to royalty most wise she'll be. Dark of hair and eye with the power to brighten any room. Possessing love so strong and true that she'd agree to marry a chimera-like beast and can reverse your past lover's bitter hatred. But be warned, you must find your lady before your natalday when your curse becomes complete, and she'll have from then until your next natalday to break it, or you'll remain a beast forever."

Oakmoor stiffened. So to break Elvaira's curse, he must find a lady to fall in love with him and agree to marry him despite being a hideous beast. Made sense considering what Elvaira had said when she'd cursed him. He frowned. Since brown hair and eyes weren't uncommon, being a cousin to royalty was the most useful clue to determine the right lady, although doubtless the connection wasn't obvious considering 'twas part of a seer's prophecy. He'd need to begin courting the eligible young ladies at court again, hunting for that royal connection. Wonderful. And he only had until his natalday in three weeks to unearth the lady meant to break his curse.

Her power flaring again, the veiled witch circled her hand over the large quartz bowl, and his drops of blood rose from the once-again crystalline water, ending her scrying spell. Then the veiled witch flicked her fingers, and his blood vanished. Impressive.

The veiled witch rose. "Return tomorrow after luncheon for your wards. It shall take me a day to create the type you require."

He nodded and tossed the veiled witch two bags of gold coins as he rose too. In addition to needing time, the veiled witch likely preferred to perform her powerful magic without another witch analyzing her spellwork. From her witch shop's ambience and her attire, she clearly reveled in appearing eerie and mysterious. He flashed another charming smile. "Until then, madam witch."

He returned to Oakmoor House and headed to his study. He immediately wrote out the veiled witch's prophecy to ensure he'd remember it accurately later. Then he studied his smooth script and pondered every line. Over the next three weeks, he must allow Lady Escana to escort the Orandians more often so that he could court young ladies instead. His assistant doing that would also prepare her for fully assuming his duties in three weeks when he permanently transformed into a beast on his natalday. And she'd probably need to act as the Minister of Foreign Relations for nearly a year because 'twould take that long for the lady meant to break his curse to fall in love with him as a hideous beast. But the engaging yet poised Countess of Escana could handle it, no doubt so well that some might regret his eventual return.

That evening at the Reids' rout party, once the Orandians and Juliet left to fetch sparkling wine, he asked Lady Escana, "How was the visit to Serle House?"

His assistant smiled. "Fascinating. I never realized how much craftsmanship and magic went into creating their perfect armor. Lady Driscoll and Sir Lorcan were fascinated as well, especially Sir Lorcan. I suspect he'd still be there discussing magic if his wife hadn't reminded him about tonight."

Oakmoor almost laughed. Typical. He grinned. "I'm glad the visit went well. Now that Lady Driscoll and Sir Lorcan are fairly settled in Ormas, I'd like you to begin escorting them more often. It shall be excellent experience for you. Could you accompany them to Mythacre House tomorrow afternoon?"

Her husband blinking beside her, Lady Escana arched her brows and replied, "Of course. I assume you'll explain the change in escorts to Lady Driscoll and Sir Lorcan like you did the Serles."

He nodded. Although he must wait until Juliet wasn't around. His threat yesterday had been utterly useless—Juliet had cast yet another spell on him when she'd arrived tonight. She was obviously still determined to discover what magic he was embroiled in. And she probably knew that his desperate threat had been toothless. Stubborn, insightful witch. She'd doubtless also realize that Lady Escana assuming his duties was because of his magic troubles and become twice as suspicious. Then she'd pry even more and definitely witness his next transformation.

But Juliet remained with her friends the entire evening, so he wasn't alone with Lady Driscoll and Sir Lorcan until the carriage ride back to their embassy. He grinned at the Orandians as the carriage rumbled forward. "I heard your visit to Serle House with Lady Escana was a success. Unless you object, I'd like her to begin escorting you more so that she gains experience."

Lady Driscoll and Sir Lorcan traded a glance, then Lady Driscoll pursed her lips and murmured, "Is that really why? Or are you just attempting to avoid Juliet? You both looked strained when you rejoined us at Weston House yesterday, so 'twas apparent you'd just had another bitter quarrel." Lady Driscoll tsked. "You two can't avoid your feelings for each other forever."

Oakmoor clenched his jaw. *Feelings*? Lady Driscoll clearly meant love. What nonsense. The only feelings he and Juliet had for each other were dislike and aggravation, both fueled by their uncontrollable desire that neither of them wanted. He managed a cool smile. "I've no reason to avoid Lady Juliet. The private matter I mentioned the other day simply requires my attention right now."

The Orandians glanced at one another again, then Lady Driscoll hummed and said, "We shan't mind Lady Escana escorting us. If you've no reason to avoid Juliet, you should ask for her help with your private matter. She'd be even more help than the Mirror of Wisdom. She's excellent at developing solutions as well as creating intricate and innovative spells to solve any problem. I'm sure Juliet could help with your private matter even if it doesn't involve magic."

Despite Lady Driscoll's blatant matchmaking, he made himself incline his head and reply, "Perhaps I might." Nagas, the half-serpent enemies of the half-bird harpies, would fly first. Then he smiled and turned their conversation to Lady Driscoll and Sir Lorcan's upcoming visit to Mythacre House without him.

While Lady Escana escorted the Orandians on that visit for him the following afternoon, Oakmoor returned to Rhiannon's Veils for his wards. The dim witch shop was empty again when he arrived, but the veiled witch sashayed inside a heartbeat later carrying a canvas sack.

The veiled witch said, "At six hours to midnight once you have your lady at Oakmoor House, you'll begin setting these wards to prevent anyone from entering or leaving your townhouse until your curse is broken. I've written out instructions and the incantations, but let me review the basics now since the spell is intricate."

He nodded. A good idea since he'd no formal training and had only performed fairly simple spells until now. The most complicated he'd done had been creating the transport boxes for him and Juliet, which were surely nothing compared to the veiled witch's wards.

The veiled witch continued, "First, you'll walk the outer perimeter of your townhouse and cleanse it with the cleansing incantation." She extracted a gold gargoyle statuette that blazed with magic from the sack. "Then while chanting the ward incantation, place thirty of these statuettes along the outside of your townhouse's walls, spacing them at equal distances and alternating between gold, silver, and iron. Next, you'll place the final six statuettes along the perimeter of your ballroom, using the same incantation and configuration as for the outer ones. Finally, you'll repeat the ward incantation twelve times from the heart of the ballroom to finish setting the wards." She dropped the gargoyle statuette back into the sack. "Make sure you're done at precisely midnight. Any questions?"

Oakmoor shook his head as he accepted the sack from the veiled witch. An intricate spell indeed. Please let him be able to manage it. "I'll review your instructions tonight, and if I've any questions, I'll return tomorrow. My thanks, madam witch."

Her dark eyes gleaming, the veiled witch chuckled. "I was pleased to be of service to you and your lady, your grace. Good luck breaking your curse." Then she turned and sashayed through her door of glass beads at the rear of the witch shop.

He headed back to his study at Oakmoor House and spent the rest of the afternoon reviewing the veiled witch's detailed instructions and practicing the unfamiliar incantations, which were in an ancient form of witch's tongue that he'd never seen before despite having taught himself the modern form. His head and tongue were both aching when he left to escort Lady Driscoll and Sir Lorcan to the latest illusion play at The Nightingale, but he'd no questions for the veiled witch about setting her intricate wards.

Oakmoor drummed his fingers on his knee when Juliet joined them and the Escanas in his box. However, he'd like to learn what she knew about wards. 'Twould help him understand the theory behind the veiled witch's spell, which should make it easier to cast. It had been nearly three weeks since he'd written as Mordred, so surely Juliet had forgotten the inadvertent hints to his identity in his last letter. He'd write to her as soon as he returned home.

CHAPTER 10

$\mathcal{A}$s an illusion of a bucolic meadow appeared onstage and a lovely shepherdess entered to begin the play, Juliet slanted Oakmoor a probing glance without turning her head from the stage. He'd continued "delegating" his duties since their quarrel two days ago, and every time they met, he still looked weary and somewhat pale. Because of his threat, she'd quit confronting him about his magic troubles, but she'd kept casting spells to discover them. Despite all his arguments to the contrary, 'twas still her duty as Calatini's royal witch to handle his magic troubles before they caused kingdom-wide problems.

She gathered her will and silently cast a probing spell then a healing-sight spell in swift succession, but like always, neither revealed anything unusual. Whatever magic Oakmoor was embroiled in must only be active when he was alone. Perhaps she should ask a royal agent to obtain some of his hair or blood so she could cast a scrying spell on him. As long as he wasn't under a sight-ward spell—which he wasn't because the spells she'd just cast worked on him even though they revealed nothing—she could use a scrying spell to see any moment from his past or present, although not his future since she wasn't a seer like the veiled witch. Performing hindsight and nowsight on him would be an intrusion, but nothing else had succeeded so far. She'd arrange it tomorrow. She exhaled and turned her attention back to the stage.

During intermission, Siobhan leaned toward Juliet while her husband began extolling the illusion play to Oakmoor and the Escanas. Siobhan murmured, "The Duke of Oakmoor looks tired, don't you think? Has he asked for your help with the private matter upsetting him yet?"

Her lips twisting, Juliet almost snorted. A Varkhoran woman would own property and live independently of their male relatives first. "No."

Siobhan hummed and eyed Oakmoor. "He said that he would. But since he's still avoiding you, I wonder if his private matter involves you."

Juliet froze. Why would Oakmoor's magic troubles involve *her*? Yet since she couldn't reveal to a foreign ambassador that Calatini's Minister of Foreign Relation's private matter was troublesome magic that might explode into kingdom-wide problems, she simply replied, "I doubt it. He probably impregnated one of his many lovers or something. Deciding whether to marry to give his child a name would be traumatic for an unrepentant rakehell like Oakmoor." Not that he'd actually refuse to marry if that ever happened, although he'd resent his poor wife forever.

Siobhan tsked then shook her head. "I'm sure you've misjudged the duke again, Juliet. Despite his rakehell ways, he's never seemed less than honorable. Why do you always act so bitter toward him? A secret affair, perhaps?"

Juliet stiffened as if struck. "I'm not bitter toward Oakmoor." Her barbs were out of vexation.

An impish smile danced across Siobhan's freckled face. "I notice you didn't deny the affair."

After checking to make sure Oakmoor and the others couldn't overhear, Juliet leaned closer to Siobhan and hissed,

"Oakmoor and I aren't having an affair." One night nearly fourteen years ago then a few recent kisses hardly counted.

Siobhan arched her brows. "No? You act either like a lady scorned or one concealing her *true* feelings."

Juliet sniffed. "Don't be ridiculous. My only true feeling for Oakmoor is dislike." Caused in part by his masculine allure, damn him.

Siobhan opened her mouth to reply, but thankfully before she could, Lord and Lady Weston glided into Oakmoor's box and straight toward them. After they exchanged good evenings, Lady Weston smiled at Juliet and asked, "Could you join us for luncheon tomorrow? Both Cassandra and Amaranth are eager to hear more about Anne and Shandor's life together."

Juliet returned Lady Weston's smile. Not surprising. Fortunately, she should be free for luncheon. There was a council meeting tomorrow morning, but since 'twasn't focused on magic, she'd not planned to attend. Plus, 'twould be good to talk with Cassandra more about her magical education. "Of course."

Lord Weston grinned. "Thank you, Lady Juliet. The girls shall be ecstatic when we tell them tomorrow." He chuckled. "If we told them tonight, they'd never fall asleep. Not that Amaranth shall be awake when we return, and she'd be upset if we told Cassandra without her."

The witchlights dimmed indicating the end of intermission, so the Westons hurriedly said farewell and left. Then the stage curtains opened and the illusion play resumed before Siobhan could quiz Juliet about Oakmoor again. Thank the Goddess.

AFTER BREAKFAST THE FOLLOWING MORNING, Juliet summoned a royal agent to her study. When he entered, she studied the brown-haired man, utterly nondescript except for his long, ratlike nose—the perfect person for clandestine tasks. She folded her hands on her desk. "I need you to obtain some hair or blood from the Duke of Oakmoor without him knowing."

The royal agent's long nose twitched. "Of course, my lady."

At that sardonic twitch, she straightened and flashed her most superior smile. The agent clearly assumed her request was for personal reasons. How insulting. Yet explaining the truth would be indiscreet and likely wouldn't convince him. So she only said, "You may go."

Once the royal agent left, Juliet sagged back in her chair. Why must *everyone* keep assuming she felt something for Oakmoor? She didn't. She was just attempting to perform her duties as Calatini's royal witch.

She huffed then absently flipped open Mordred's walnut transport box like she'd done every morning for the past fourteen days even though she no longer expected to see a letter from the young witch. She glanced inside and stilled. Mordred had written at last! She tore open his letter then frowned. All he wrote to excuse his delay was that he'd been busy with his studies. *That* was why he'd quit writing for weeks? She'd been worried that something terrible had happened to him.

Juliet pursed her lips. Then following that paltry excuse, Mordred inquired about wards without mentioning why he wanted to know. Him asking about defense spells after an unusual and lengthy silence was suspicious. Something terrible *must* have happened, and Mordred was either unable, too diffident, or too embarrassed to reveal it. But perhaps he would if she wrote how worried she'd been at his silence.

Pulling out some paper, she stared at the blank page and tapped her pen on the desk. How to convey her concern without nettling Mordred's masculine pride? Eventually, she just admitted her concern, accepted his excuse, then offered her assistance if he ever needed it before explaining all about wards and requesting he write again soon. Please let that encourage Mordred to reveal what was truly going on.

Once she placed her letter in the transport box, Juliet glanced at the clock on the mantel and winced. She'd been so engrossed in writing Mordred that she was late for luncheon at Weston House. She leapt upright then rushed from the palace out to her carriage that she'd asked Lara at breakfast to have prepared.

As soon as she entered the Westons' drawing room, she said, "I apologize for being late. I got engrossed in some duties."

Her husband smiling beside her, Lady Weston grinned and replied, "You were only a little late. We'd not even noticed yet."

Amaranth bounced like an excited sprite. "I did! But I'm glad you're here now and didn't forget."

As Juliet swallowed her laugh at the little girl's energetic excitement, Cassandra laid a restraining hand on her sister's head and drawled, "Stop bouncing. You'll make Lady Juliet dizzy."

While Amaranth frowned at Cassandra but stopped bouncing, Lord Weston chuckled then asked, "Shall we head to luncheon?"

Juliet spent the lively luncheon regaling the Westons and their granddaughters about Shandor and Anne—from how their duets always earned them heaps of coin and applause, to how Shandor insisted they settle in Pruzirias when Anne's pregnancy made her too ill to travel despite his lifelong love of traveling. The Westons shared related tales from Anne's childhood as well as a few about Shandor from when he'd been Anne's fiddle tutor. Laughter, smiles, and tears suffused the entire meal.

Following luncheon, Amaranth sang several ballads and accompanied herself on the keyharp. Cassandra was right about Amaranth's voice and musical talents. The little girl would definitely grow into a bard witch like her father. Shandor and Anne would be delighted if they knew. But perhaps they'd suspected before they'd died. And at least they'd known that Cassandra had inherited the Lovari's strong magical powers.

A pang pierced Juliet as she watched the two girls. They were both delightful—lively, sweet, and gifted. What would it be like to have such children to love and carry on after her? She'd likely never know. Shandor and Anne had been fortunate in that and the sincere love they'd shared. How terribly sad they'd died so young. If only they hadn't.

After her performance, Amaranth was exhausted from all the excitement, so Lady Weston took her upstairs to the nursery for a nap regardless of the little girl's protests.

Juliet arched her brows at Lord Weston. "Do you mind if Cassandra and I discuss magic now?" Since the baron wasn't a witch, such a conversation would doubtless bore him.

His eyes crinkling, Lord Weston waved toward a sofa across the room. "Enjoy yourselves. I'll read until Emily returns."

Once they sat on the sofa, Juliet asked Cassandra about what she'd learned from the veiled witch so far. Then her brows rose and her stomach stiffened as the girl listed everything. The dratted seer was as incredible at teaching as she was at seeing the future. Of course she was. Juliet inhaled and made herself say after Cassandra finally finished, "Quite a thorough education. The veiled witch is obviously an excellent teacher."

Cassandra nodded then glanced at her grandparents, who'd been quietly talking since Lady Weston returned from the nursery. Cassandra leaned toward Juliet then murmured, "Do you know how to contact Father's family? We lost touch after Father and Mother were killed. I'd like to see them again, and I'm sure they've gypsy spells to teach me too."

Juliet blew a sigh. If only she could. "I haven't heard from the Lovaris since your great-grandmother Ceija died nine years ago. She and Shandor were the only ones I was close to, and most gypsies aren't comfortable being friendly with those in authority because they don't wish their movements and activities to be controlled."

Cassandra sagged. "I should have realized that."

Juliet arched her brows. "You could always use a kin spell to trace them—as long as the Lovaris haven't concealed themselves with a tracing-ward spell. And I can't imagine why they would." *They* didn't have bitter relatives seeking revenge. Plus, constantly maintaining such a spell was draining, and the Lovaris needed their magic for other tasks. That magical drain was why she'd quit maintaining hers once she could leave Calatini if necessary. She smiled at Cassandra. "After you have their location, you can use a transportation spell to send them a letter. The veiled witch could easily teach you how to perform both spells, or I could show you now if you like." Teaching Shandor's daughter would probably be the closest she'd ever get to nurturing her own child. And although the veiled witch's powers eclipsed hers, she'd still make as excellent a teacher.

Cassandra grinned and leapt upright. "Grandmother, Grandfather—Lady Juliet is going to show me how to perform some spells in my workroom. We'll return shortly." Cassandra beamed at her as they left the drawing room. "Thanks for offering to show me. I'd like to attempt the spells soon."

After Cassandra ushered her into a large, cluttered workroom, Juliet concealed her grimace as her fingers itched to organize the various piles. Yet since the teenage girl wouldn't want advice about that, she simply began describing how to perform a kin spell using maps, blood, a scrying bowl, knotweed, ground amber, clary oil, unicorn water, and an incantation in the witch's tongue. Once Cassandra repeated all that back to her, Juliet described how to perform a transportation spell using will and a brief incantation. Cassandra recited that with few stumbles too. She was a quick learner, much like her father.

Juliet and Cassandra returned to the drawing room, and they talked with the Westons for another half an hour before Juliet said farewell. She'd some duties to attend to before dinner and attending the Nolans' ball tonight. However, she offered to return another afternoon next month. Visiting the Westons and their granddaughters had been delightful and made her almost feel part of a family again. An impossible dream for her.

• • •

When Juliet arrived at Nolan House that evening, she joined Siobhan and Lorcan, who were with the Escanas rather than Oakmoor tonight. He was "delegating" his duties again. And although speaking to her friends without enduring the rakehell duke's vexing presence should have relieved her, she tensed and glanced about the ballroom. What was Oakmoor doing? Did it involve his magic troubles? Her jaw tightened when she eventually spotted him flirting near a garden alcove with the blonde, coquettish Miss Landry and her two brunette best friends, the plump Miss James and the slender Miss St. Claire. He'd not flirted like that since Siobhan and Lorcan had arrived three weeks ago.

Siobhan followed her gaze. "I suspect we're seeing the rakehell Duke of Oakmoor in action for the first time tonight. After saying good evening to us, he began flirting with every eligible lady he passed."

Her stomach hardening, Juliet forced a cool smirk as she used her will to silently fling a probing spell at Oakmoor. Same as ever, no unusual magic shone around him. She drawled, "Until several months ago, Oakmoor stuck to flirting with every *ineligible* lady he passed. Yet he must have finally realized he needed a wife to produce an heir, so he began doggedly pursuing eligible ones instead. Your arrival paused his hunt, but he must believe you're settled enough for him to resume it."

As Lady Escana and her husband traded wry smiles, Lorcan tugged on his long brown overcoat and frowned at Oakmoor then asked, "Aren't those ladies a bit young for the Duke of Oakmoor? They're not much older than our daughters, if that."

Juliet smirked harder and tossed her head. "I suspect that's why his hunt has been unsuccessful so far despite all his wealth, influence, and supposed charm. 'Tis hard for most young ladies to be interested in marrying a gentleman a generation older." Served him right for claiming he could excite women even in his dotage. "Oakmoor *really* shouldn't have waited so long to seek a wife."

Siobhan slanted her a sidelong glance. "Or perhaps his hunt has been unsuccessful because he's not interested in those young ladies. But the lady he truly wants pretends to dislike him, so he can't pursue her."

A blush scorching her skin, Juliet stiffened. Ridiculous. Oakmoor would never want *her* as his wife. Not that she wanted him to. She smoothed her emerald-green skirt. And how could Siobhan hint at the unwanted attraction between her and Oakmoor in front of others, especially an observant couple like Lord and Lady Escana?

Luckily, the beginning strains of the first waltz echoed through the ballroom and distracted everyone. Juliet smiled as Lorcan and Lord Escana led their wives onto the floor. Then she couldn't help glancing toward Oakmoor. He'd chosen the plump brunette Miss James as his partner. How curious. Her slender brunette friend Miss St. Claire or her coquettish friend Miss Landry seemed more likely choices.

Although Juliet didn't dance the first waltz, she danced many of the others. Oakmoor danced every single one, but always with a different brunette as his partner. Yet most of his previous lovers had been ladies with dark hair, so that wasn't unusual at least.

Over the following few days, Oakmoor continued pursuing eligible young ladies and neglecting Siobhan and Lorcan. Juliet kept casting probing and healing-sight spells on him whenever she first saw him because the royal agent had no success obtaining his hair or blood. Apparently, Oakmoor only trusted servants that were from his own duchy and had been working for him for years, and he had his valet burn the discarded hair in his brush and from barbering every morning, so 'twas none to steal. Most people in Calatini weren't that fanatical about destroying items that could create magical links to them. Why was Oakmoor?

Then five days after Mordred's last letter, she received another from him about trap spells. Why was the young witch writing again so soon after his lengthy silence? And for him to ask about wards *then* trap spells meant something must be happening with him. Yet he'd ignored her invitation in her last reply to share his problems. She worried her lip as she read Mordred's letter yet again. She'd write her reply tomorrow morning. 'Twould allow her time to ponder how to encourage the thickheaded man to trust and confide in her.

CHAPTER 11

Two days after Oakmoor had sent his letter about trap spells to Juliet, he headed to his study directly after breakfast to handle his correspondence even though his head still ached from last night's poor sleep despite gulping four cups of kahve earlier. First, he flicked open his carved walnut transport box to check if she'd replied. Nothing yet. He sighed and rubbed his aching brow. He needed that information about trap spells so he could continue planning his confinement with the lady meant to break his curse. While practicing how to cast the veiled witch's wards the other day, he'd realized that since the wards would take six hours to set, he'd require a spell to keep his lady with him while he set them—hence the trap spell.

He frowned as he swiftly sorted the invitations and letters he'd received over the past few days. He'd also realized that 'twould be cruel to keep more than himself and his unknown lady confined to Oakmoor House for the year she'd need to break his curse. So he'd slowly begun arranging for all his long-time servants to have paid respites back home in Oakmoor, using the excuse that they needed to go see their families. After all, none of them had returned home since before last season because the council had remained in session throughout the usual break. He was also sending his horses back to Oakmoor along with his grooms since he and his lady would be unable to leave the townhouse.

He quirked an almost smile. Fortunately, unlike most gentlemen, he knew how to live without servants thanks to the elderly paternal cousin who'd been his guardian. Bedivere hadn't cared what his young ward had done so long as it never disturbed him. So the servants at Oakmoor Castle—particularly the grandmotherly head cook Millie, the mother of Oakmoor's valet Miles and his current head cook Martha—had taken Oakmoor under their wing and taught him how to care for himself. His lips twisted. During their confinement alone together, his unknown lady would simply have to make do with him as the only servant.

Once he discarded all the invitations on his natalday or later, he shut his eyes and leaned back in his chair, massaging his now throbbing head. If only he'd as much success finding the lady meant to break his curse as he'd had sending away his servants. Over the past week, he'd danced and flirted with every eligible young lady possessing brown hair and eyes unless they were almost betrothed. But, Goddess, they were all so bland that they blurred together, and none of his deft probing had revealed a royal connection.

He snorted. Given his lack of success and the vindictiveness of Elvaira's curse, he'd probably not unearth his unknown lady until the evening before his natalday. Then he'd have no chance to woo her as a human, so 'twould take her *ages* to fall in love with him. And he'd probably need to kidnap her too. No young lady would consent to visiting an unwed gentleman's townhouse alone, even if he hadn't permanently transformed into a hideous beast yet.

Oakmoor sighed again. Yet none of those problems mattered unless he unearthed the lady in the veiled witch's prophecy. He rose to change for the Landrys' tea party. With less than two weeks before his natalday, he must attend every court event possible—even if his head throbbed and the events would be as dull as a ponderous tome on an obscure philosophy.

But suddenly, intense heat swamped him, and he dropped back into his chair. That heat flaring to boiling agony, he groaned as his body broke and melted into a beast for the third time. After his excruciating transformation finished, he gulped air and rested his throbbing head on his desk with his beast hands gripping the wood on either side. Then boiling agony flared once more, and his claws gouged the desk before his body transformed back to human again.

Panting, he lurched upright despite his trembling exhaustion. He *had* to attend that tea party. So he staggered upstairs to his chambers then dismissed Miles's concern at his haggard appearance and insisted his valet help him dress. Since that had taken all his energy, he collapsed in his carriage and dozed, only rousing when the carriage halted at Landry House. He rubbed his face then headed into the dull tea party that would only strengthen his desire for sleep. As he did, he pursed a wry smile. At least with his transformations nine days apart, he'd only have to suffer three more: another temporary one, the permanent one on his natalday, and when his lady broke his curse at last. Thank the Goddess for that.

Since the Orandians were visiting Elliot House to swap spells instead of attending the Landrys' tea party, Oakmoor immediately began pursuing the eligible young brunettes. Yet he could barely stifle his yawns because the afternoon event was as dull as he'd expected. Typical. And by the end of it, he was no closer to unearthing the lady meant to break his curse. Still drained from his excruciating transformation, he dozed on the carriage ride back to Oakmoor House then napped before dinner, which provided him just enough energy to attend the St. Claires' ball that evening.

At St. Claire House, he forced himself to dance every waltz with a different young lady. He only managed to do so without stumbling or yawning thanks to decades of practice attending balls. But his conversation wasn't as lively or deft as usual. Not that his partners noticed anything amiss. They were all too awed by his wealth, influence, suave manner, and quite possibly his greater age.

Yet when he fetched some sparkling wine between waltzes near the end of the ball, Juliet joined him at the refreshments table with a narrow-eyed frown. One of her spells pricking his skin, she drawled, "You look dreadful again. When did you last sleep?"

Oakmoor straightened and glowered at Juliet over his sparkling wine. Of course, *she'd* noticed his exhaustion. Unlike his young partners, she'd never been awed or even impressed by him. Maddening witch. His pulse quickening, he leaned toward her. "Still prying into my private matters? Need I remind you how I'll retaliate if you do?"

Juliet sniffed while exchanging her empty flute of sparkling wine for a fresh one. "If you collapse in the middle of the floor during a court ball and give one of those little girls you're dancing with an apoplexy, 'tis no longer a *private* matter. Now, tell me what magic is troubling you so I can handle it before that happens."

He sipped his sparkling wine through clenched teeth. How dare Juliet suggest that he was about to collapse? Her disdainfully biting barb had gone too far this time. He was *fine*. He smirked and retorted with words sure to provoke her, "Perhaps if you possessed the powers of the veiled witch, I might."

Juliet glared but leaned toward him. "So you admit there's magic troubling you."

Oakmoor stiffened. Damn his weary tongue. He was never so indiscreet. "I didn't. Simply that I wouldn't bother asking you for help since you couldn't possibly provide it."

Juliet strode closer, until her topaz-yellow skirt brushed his legs. Her gorgeous dark-brown eyes almost black, she hissed, "Just because I'm not an incredibly powerful seer doesn't mean

I'm useless. I could resolve whatever magic troubles you've embroiled yourself in perfectly well."

He stilled as Juliet's spicy gingyr scent surrounded him. 'Twould be so easy to yank her closer and kiss her. But *she* wasn't the lady from the veiled witch's prophecy. Although her coloring fit, nothing else did. So instead, he cocked a sardonic brow. "Are you about to attack me? I shan't even need to tell anyone at court about our past affair then. They'd all guess."

Juliet inhaled and stepped back, still glaring at him. "What I *should* do is quit attempting to help you. But unfortunately for me, my duty as Calatini's royal witch prevents that. Until later, Oakmoor." Then she turned and swept across the ballroom.

Despite Juliet's predictions, Oakmoor managed to finish the remaining waltzes at the St. Claire's ball without collapsing. However, he did collapse in bed and succumb to slumber as soon as he returned to Oakmoor House. And after a night of vividly gruesome curse dreams, he awoke close to noon the following morning. He downed five cups of kahve in quick succession but waved away the breakfast Miles had brought. He'd wait until luncheon to eat. His stomach wasn't awake anyway.

He strode down to his study and opened his transport box then smiled at the letter inside. He tore open Juliet's letter and devoured her insights into trap spells. From what she'd written, his trap spell should be set on a specific room. His best guest bedchamber should do. Plus, 'twas in the opposite wing from his own, so the lady meant to break his curse would feel safer at first. He'd purchase the spell ingredients he'd need this afternoon.

Oakmoor placed Juliet's letter in the locked desk drawer where he kept all her replies. Then he drummed his fingers on his desk and frowned at his transport box. Given her prying and request for a mirror call at the end, he couldn't risk writing Juliet again. She was becoming too suspicious. To avoid the temptation to write again regardless, he placed his transport box in the drawer with her replies. He sighed as he locked the drawer. How he'd miss Juliet's interesting and insightful letters.

After luncheon, he visited various witch shops for the magical supplies he'd require to kidnap his lady and for their confinement. He also purchased some dresses and other items she'd need during her stay. 'Twould be simple enough to resize her attire with magic once he knew who she was—much easier than creating everything with magic alone.

When he returned to Oakmoor House, he requested his servants take his magical purchases to his study and the rest to his best guest bedchamber, but he instructed them to leave everything wrapped. He'd rather not start gossip among his servants that he was preparing for a lady's arrival.

As he strode up his front steps, he frowned at Miles talking outside with an unfamiliar groom possessing a long, rat-like nose. Who was that? All of his servants were from Oakmoor and had served his family for years. Why was an unfamiliar groom around when his beast curse was about to permanently manifest and he was preparing to kidnap the lady meant to break it? And why was his valet talking with an outdoor servant anyway?

So he asked Miles about the unfamiliar groom while Miles helped him dress for the Duke and Duchess of Merrilea's rout party that evening. He relaxed when his valet said the groom had recently begun serving at Rushworth House next door and was smitten with Martha. Unfortunately for him, Miles's sister was still devoted to her husband who'd died two years ago.

At Merrilea House, Oakmoor greeted his hosts then the Orandians before resuming his pursuit of the eligible young ladies who might be the one in the veiled witch's prophecy. However, he ensured he stayed across the drawing room from Juliet to prevent her prying and another quarrel. He must remain focused. Juliet and his primal hunger for her were distractions he couldn't afford. He'd only eleven days to find the lady meant to break his curse.

The next morning, he continued his preparations despite his continued lack of success unearthing that lady. He sent several more servants back to Oakmoor before the council meeting. During that, he realized he must disclose the full truth about his beast curse to King Devon and Queen Kiera before his confinement, in case his unknown lady failed to break his curse. They'd need to appoint his replacement on the council for the remaining two years of the current term as well as contact his degenerate cousin to become the next Duke of Oakmoor. He'd send them a letter once he'd his lady at Oakmoor House. He suppressed a grimace. No doubt the king and queen would share it with the royal witch. Juliet would be smug that she'd been right about him being embroiled in magic. But at least he'd not be there to see her smug smirks.

He kept up his preparations and pursuit of his unknown lady so vigorously that his head ached with fatigue when he attended the Greysnowe's ball the following evening. But thankfully, his headache couldn't be a harbinger of his fourth transformation since that wasn't due for another six days.

Oakmoor greeted Lord and Lady Greysnowe with a charming smile in spite of his throbbing head. "Quite a crowd this evening." Which meant he might encounter eligible young ladies he didn't often see. Perhaps one of them was the lady meant to break his curse. That could explain why he'd not unearthed her yet.

Lady Greysnowe grinned. "All of court is still shocked by the warmth between me and Daphne, so they've attended to gawk."

Oakmoor almost chuckled. Because the friendship between Lady Greysnowe and Dowager Lady Ravenstone *was* shocking after centuries of strife.

Lord Greysnowe drawled, "Or they're hoping that we erupt like we did during our ridiculous ancestral feud. Court always enjoyed those."

Oakmoor did chuckle at that truth. He arched a brow. "I expect you'll deny court the pleasure. Lord and Lady Ravenstone wouldn't like it." And the Greysnowes wouldn't wish to upset their soul-healer daughter.

After the Greysnowes ruefully nodded, he threaded through the crowd toward the Orandians and the Escanas. He greeted them then asked Lady Driscoll and Sir Lorcan, "How was your visit to the magic marshals with Lord Islaye?" Magic marshals were the agents who policed magical crimes for the Ministry of Magic.

Lady Driscoll smiled. "Fascinating. We met a Magic Marshal Thurston, and he showed us his current cases."

Sir Lorcan leaned forward. "As well as told us all about the capture of the black witch Lord Treyvan helped him find three years ago."

While the lore witch spoke, intense heat swamped Oakmoor, and he locked his muscles to remain still. Dear Goddess, was he transforming already? 'Twas almost a week too soon.

Lady Driscoll frowned at him. "Are you feeling well, your grace? You appear flushed."

He gritted a bright smile. Damn Elvaira's curse for manifesting again in front of the observant Orandians and equally perceptive Escanas. "Just overheated from the crowd. Excuse me."

Before the others could reply, he turned and rushed out the garden door just behind them. The cool evening air not easing his boiling agony, he panted as he staggered into the nearest alcove. Then he fell to his knees and bit back his screams as his fourth transformation ripped through him.

CHAPTER 12

When Juliet glided into their ballroom, Lord and Lady Greysnowe both beamed, then Lady Greysnowe squeezed her hands and said, "Lady Juliet, how wonderful to see you."

Juliet smiled back and nodded. She was about to respond to the Greysnowes' cordial greeting when her gaze caught on Oakmoor bolting out the garden door across the ballroom. If she hurried, she might witness the magic troubling him. She briefly returned Lady Greysnowe's squeeze then freed her hands. "I'm glad to be here. Your balls are always exciting." Particularly their last one when they'd announced their daughter's marriage to Lord Ravenstone.

After leaving the Greysnowes, Juliet flicked her fingers and whispered the incantation to cast an ignore spell about herself before darting through the crowd and out the garden door after Oakmoor. Releasing her spell, she glanced about the garden then frowned when she spotted him in the nearest alcove. Oakmoor was kneeling on the ground in a hunched ball like a gored furbull, the massive furry bovine from the Tsarkan grasslands. Dear Goddess, *what* had happened to him?

She surged into the alcove and used her will to silently fling a healing-sight spell then a probing spell on Oakmoor. Yet although the air was heavy and charged and musky like at Islaye House, she still sensed no unusual magic about him. She was too late again, damn it. She scowled and fisted her hands on her hips. "Oakmoor, would you quit being such an obstinate fool and tell me what's going on? 'Tis clearly more than you can handle alone."

Oakmoor glanced up at her, his eyes black holes amid his white and haggard face. He rasped in a voice containing none of his usual smooth charm, "Go *away*, Juliet. I've told you my private matters aren't your concern."

She snorted. Idiot man. "And I've told you they are. As Cala-tini's royal witch, I can't allow your magic troubles to cause king-dom-wide problems. Which they doubtless shall soon."

Oakmoor glared at her. "Nonsense. I don't need your help." Gulping air, he lurched upright then paled even further and swayed.

She slid beneath Oakmoor's arm and helped him stagger across the alcove. Tingling flooded her as their bodies met and his earthy sandalwood scent swamped her. When they collapsed together on the stone bench, she was trembling almost as much as Oakmoor, both from desire and exertion. He was strongly built, so supporting him took all her strength.

Unable to make herself pull away from Oakmoor, Juliet poked his chest. "Don't need my help, do you?"

Oakmoor's growl vibrated against her and further fueled her tingling. He rumbled, "I could have managed on my own."

She tsked. "Right..."

Oakmoor growled once more, and she nearly shivered. She *had* to pull away before she kissed him or he kissed her. 'Twould be disastrous to succumb to that explosive desire again. She inhaled. *Unless* she used it to steal some hair for her scrying spell. The royal agent had yet to succeed at that and likely never would.

Her heart surging, she slid her hands up Oakmoor's chest

and about his neck to thread her fingers through his almond-brown hair. "You're truly the most vexing man." Then she drew his head down and pressed her mouth against his.

Oakmoor stilled for a heartbeat before yanking her closer and deepening their kiss. She moaned as their tongues dueled and feverish hunger consumed them both. She pressed against him and gripped his hair even fiercer. Wait... his hair. She needed his hair. Still wildly kissing him, she pinched a lock of his hair and gathered her will to cut it.

But before she could, Oakmoor jerked back and gripped her wrists then tore her hands from his hair. Panting, he snarled, "*What* are you doing?"

Panting too, Juliet licked her swollen lips. "I should think the greatest rakehell in Ormas would know the answer to that."

Oakmoor gripped her wrists tighter. "But you've never initiated our kisses before. Why now? And what were you doing with my hair?"

She flushed. How had Oakmoor noticed that amid their passionate kisses? She tugged on her captured wrists to deflect him. "Release me. You're hurting my wrists."

His eyes narrowing, Oakmoor loosened his grip but didn't release her. "Were you attempting to distract me with kisses to steal some of my hair for a spell?"

Juliet flushed deeper and wrenched her wrists again. She must escape. *Now.*

Oakmoor glared. "You were! Treacherous witch."

She huffed while returning Oakmoor's glare. "Don't act so outraged, you hypocrite. You use kisses to distract me whenever I say words you don't like or ask questions you don't wish to answer."

Oakmoor shook her wrists. "Simply to silence you, not to *steal* something that can create a magical link to you."

Juliet pursed her lips. Oakmoor truly was fanatical about people creating magical links to him. "I wasn't attempting to harm you, merely discover what magic you're embroiled in."

Oakmoor snapped, "How many times must I tell you to stay out of my private matters?"

She almost snorted. They'd just discussed this. "And how many times must I tell you 'tis my duty to help you?"

Oakmoor yanked her against him using her captured wrists. "'Tis only one way you can help me, you maddening witch."

Juliet whimpered as he seized her mouth in another ravaging kiss. Oh, Goddess, so good.

A sudden cough pierced the alcove, and a deep voice said, "You may want to continue this in another alcove, your grace, Lady Juliet. This one is too close to the ballroom door. Anyone seeking some air could stumble across you."

Fire flaring beneath her skin, Juliet pulled away from Oakmoor at last and whirled to face a smiling Lord and Lady Ravenstone. How embarrassing to be caught kissing the greatest rakehell in Ormas. She should have cast an illusion and a listening-ward spell about the garden alcove to ensure their privacy, but she'd been too worried about Oakmoor when she'd arrived. But at least the Ravenstones were invariably discreet. They had to be, particularly Lady Ravenstone. Not only did Lady Ravenstone have to conceal being a soul healer to prevent people from exploiting her rare magical powers, but she also had to conceal her special insights that reading everyone's auras gave her.

Although still haggard, Oakmoor rose with a suave grin. "We've no need to continue. 'Twas a mistake to even start. I've young ladies to dance with; excuse me."

As Oakmoor strode back into the ballroom, Juliet fisted her hands in her ebony skirt adorned with silver swirls. How dare that insufferable beast practically ravage her then return to those little girls as if nothing had happened? She'd curse him with a terrible spell he'd *never* forget if she was a black witch. She exhaled and relaxed her fists. Although if she did, she'd simply have to undo it along with whatever other magic was troubling him.

She smiled at the Ravenstones then rose and smoothed the

wrinkles from her skirt with a grooming spell. "'Twas fortunate for the duke that you arrived when you did. I was about to attack him." If only that was true. "Shall we return to the ballroom?"

Lord and Lady Ravenstone traded a glance but nodded.

While they headed inside, Juliet eyed Lady Ravenstone. Perhaps she should ask the soul healer if she'd noticed anything amiss with Oakmoor. Even though the aura spell she herself had used three weeks ago hadn't revealed anything unusual, she'd not been able to hold the difficult spell for long, and she'd not risked another because of how it had drained her. Besides, she wasn't accustomed to reading auras like Lady Ravenstone was.

She stiffened as they entered the ballroom. Oakmoor was twirling with Lady Georgiana Laurent, the last young lady he'd seriously courted before "releasing" her when his duties welcoming Siobhan and Lorcan had claimed his time. Yet despite resuming his attempts to find a wife over a week ago, he'd not approached Lady Georgiana again until tonight. Juliet swallowed and resolutely turned toward Lady Ravenstone. "Tell me, do—"

Before she could finish asking about Oakmoor, Siobhan swept over with Lorcan and the Escanas. "Juliet, there you are. And with Lord and Lady Ravenstone too." She grinned at the Ravenstones. "Lorcan and I can hardly wait for our visit to your townhouse next week. Shall you be joining us, Lady Ravenstone?"

Lord Ravenstone stilling beside her, Lady Ravenstone shook her head with a cool smile. "Discussions about magic shall bore me." Likely because she couldn't perform anything they'd discuss. Plus, she wouldn't want to risk revealing her secret powers. "But I'll join you afterward and coax my mated faebirds to sing for you, even though Rain is territorial right now since Aria is brooding."

As Lorcan began quizzing Lady Ravenstone about her faebirds, Juliet inhaled to ease the pang darting through her.

She'd suspected Lady Ravenstone had faebirds from the long, jewel-colored feathers Lady Ravenstone sometimes wore, but she'd never dared mention it. Discussing faebirds only reminded her of Gentian, who'd surely pined when she'd abandoned her in Varkhora. Not that she'd had any choice but to abandon Gentian. Faebirds were too fragile to withstand a gypsy's traveling life, and she'd known Mother would care for Gentian along with her own faebird. Plus, Gentian would have hated living in a cage, and carrying a faebird on her shoulder would betray she was a Varkhoran lady because Varkhora's court was the only one where ladies always carried faebirds and gentlemen draklizards. Training them to endure that calmly took rigorous effort, but the warrior kingdom prided itself on such grit, and draklizards especially could be useful weapons.

She murmured excuses and slipped away to fetch some sparkling wine. Then she spent the rest of the Greysnowes' ball watching Oakmoor dance every waltz with a different dark-haired young lady. Yet he appeared weary and didn't flirt as much as usual. How was he even remaining upright after whatever magic had drained him in the garden earlier? Obviously, he was desperate to find a wife to exert himself so. Could his magic troubles be why? *What* had Oakmoor gotten himself embroiled in? She really must discover and resolve it soon.

WHEN JULIET ARRIVED at Dracwyn House the following evening for their card party, she greeted the Duke and Duchess of Dracwyn then glanced about the drawing room for Oakmoor and tensed. He was across the room with Lady Georgiana again. Radiant tonight in her silver arachne silk gown, the Duke of Osbourne's daughter was holding Oakmoor's arm and standing much too close while her father beside her narrowly eyed them. Oakmoor was never indiscreet with ladies in public, so he was definitely desperate for a wife to risk inflaming a father's protective wrath that way, especially if said father was the wily duke who'd served as the Minister of Intelligence for nearly five decades.

After checking Oakmoor with another probing spell that revealed nothing, Juliet joined her friends and the Escanas along the opposite wall. She grinned at Siobhan and Lorcan. "Ready to play some card games?"

Siobhan straightened her cream overcoat atop her long green tunic. "Not particularly. You know we're rubbish at cards. We'd have attended something else if the Dracwyns weren't a duke and duchess and he wasn't a councilor."

Lorcan sighed. "Yes, the Merryweathers are hosting a musical evening tonight."

Juliet inclined her head. A musical evening hosted by a witch family known for their musical talents *would* be much more to her friends' taste.

Siobhan twinkled at the Escanas. "But at least we shan't inflict our rubbish card skills on anyone serious about them. Lord and Lady Escana have agreed to be our opposing partners."

Lady Escana smiled. "Anthony and I don't care much for cards either, although we'd prefer to be attending the kelpie races tonight. Ah, the sacrifices we make to promote peace between Calatini and other kingdoms."

Siobhan arched her brows at Juliet. "So you'll be free to join another table." She nodded toward Oakmoor. "Perhaps you should rescue the Duke of Oakmoor from Lady Georgiana. She's been clinging to him since he arrived."

Her stomach hardening, Juliet snorted. "Oakmoor is capable of rescuing himself if he so chooses. Clearly he doesn't wish to. Perhaps he's found the young lady he wants as his wife at last."

Still studying Oakmoor, Siobhan tilted her head. "I doubt it. Now, go rescue him."

Juliet almost winced as the Escanas traded glances. She'd better go before Siobhan began referring to her supposed feelings for Oakmoor in front of the observant Lord and Lady Escana again. "Oh, very well. But only to please you."

She glided across the drawing room to Oakmoor, Lady Georgiana, and the Duke of Osbourne. Then she stiffened when Oakmoor's brows quirked as she greeted them. She'd not sought him out because she wanted to. Arrogant rakehell. She scoured him with a narrow glance. "You look better than when we spoke last night—more like a man than a gored fur-bull."

Oakmoor's jaw tightened, then he smirked. "And you look less flushed and trembling—more like a golem imitating a woman than an actual one."

She inhaled, heat scorching her cheeks. How could Oakmoor allude to their kisses before others, particularly another councilor and a young lady interested in marrying him? *And* call her a magical construct made of mud that could only imitate humans without magic? Insufferable. She raised a hand and let sparks swirl about her fingers. "A golem, am I? Even you must know that no golem, regardless how well enchanted, can perform magic of its own."

As the sparks about her fingers faded, Oakmoor smirked harder and drawled, "Among other things."

Juliet blushed. Of course a rakehell like Oakmoor would also know that golems couldn't achieve release like living creatures did.

The Duke of Osbourne cleared his throat. He doubtless didn't like such a suggestive remark being said before his unwed youngest daughter. "I believe the card games are about to begin. Would you be my partner, Lady Juliet? Then we can form a table with Georgiana and the Duke of Oakmoor."

No longer blushing, Juliet beamed at the elderly duke. "I'd be delighted. A master like yourself shall be an improvement over the last card partner I was forced to accept."

Oakmoor cocked a brow while they settled at the nearest table with Lady Georgiana and the Duke of Osbourne between them. "As I recall, we won every game we played together."

Juliet sniffed. "Only because we played against Siobhan and Lorcan, who aren't familiar with Calatinian card games."

Deftly shuffling the cards, Lady Georgiana interjected, "Shall we make our games of wild arcana more interesting? If the duke and I win the majority, we dance the first and last waltzes together at the Duchess of Childes's fete tomorrow celebrating Priest Melchior Hawke and Lady Blaine's betrothal. If Father and Lady Juliet do, she wins that pleasure."

Juliet tensed and eyed the younger lady. Despite being less than half Oakmoor's age, Lady Georgiana truly wished to marry him and saw *her* as a rival. Ridiculous. She accepted her cards. "Such a prize shall only encourage me to lose."

Oakmoor smirked at her over his cards. "How about I agree to answer your questions instead?"

Juliet inhaled. Then she'd *finally* discover the magic troubling Oakmoor. And she could resolve it at last. "Agreed."

She and the others played three lengthy games of wild arcana in silence. She and the Duke of Osbourne won the first by a mere six points. Oakmoor and Lady Georgiana the second by two. Then Oakmoor and Lady Georgiana won the third with an unexpected good fortune, a hand containing the five strongest cards in the white arcana that was impossible to beat.

His jaw tight, Oakmoor gathered the cards after their third game. "It seems you won your waltzes, Lady Georgiana. We haven't time for another two games."

Juliet blinked at Oakmoor. Why didn't he appear eager about that? He'd been desperately pursuing Lady Georgiana and other young ladies like her for the past eleven days. But now that he'd managed to find one that wanted him, he didn't seem to want *her*. Then she suppressed a snort. Such inconstancy was typical of the rakehell who changed his lovers more than most gentlemen changed their clothes. Despite his apparent desperation to marry, Oakmoor would never settle on just one lady until he *was* in his dotage.

CHAPTER 13

Oakmoor suppressed a grimace when Lady Georgiana captured his arm as soon as he arrived at the Duchess of Childes's fete celebrating Priest Melchior Hawke and Lady Blaine's betrothal. He never should have danced with Lady Georgiana at the Greysnowes' ball the other day, but after his explosive passion with Juliet, he'd been desperate to have a partner before she'd returned to the ballroom. Plus, his unexpected fourth transformation had drained him, and Lady Georgiana had been the first eligible young lady he'd encountered. So he'd asked her to dance even though he'd known she couldn't be the lady in the veiled witch's prophecy since she'd no connection to royalty. Having courted her before and after serving with her father on the council for over two decades, he knew her family well enough to be certain of that.

Unfortunately, asking Lady Georgiana to dance had made her believe he wished to resume their courtship, and she'd been relentlessly pursuing him since then, which had prevented his hunt for the lady meant to break his curse. And since he'd barely a week before his natalday, he must evade Lady Georgiana's pursuit. At the Dracwyns' card party, he proposed that wager to Juliet hoping her determination to discover his magic troubles and the Duke of Osbourne's skill at cards would ensure they won so he needn't dance with Lady Georgiana tonight. Although he should avoid Juliet, answering her questions with deft evasions would have been much better than Lady Georgiana continuing to monopolize him when he needed to unearth his unknown lady. However, he'd not expected Lady Georgiana's skill at cards to rival her father's nor for them to draw a good fortune.

Since he couldn't free his arm from Lady Georgiana's firm grip without offending her and causing a scene, he simply nodded with a smooth smile. "Good evening, my lady."

Lady Georgiana grinned. "I'm so looking forward to our two waltzes tonight. I know we can't dance together more than that without engendering gossip, but I thought we could remain together throughout the fete like other couples do."

Oakmoor almost winced. Which would again make his hunt for his unknown lady impossible. Somehow he must divert Lady Georgiana. He glanced about the ballroom, his gaze stilling on a somber Lord Morwynne and a grinning Lord Alexander Greysnowe talking nearby. Although slightly younger than Lady Georgiana, both gentlemen were extremely eligible and always affable, and Lord Morwynne was a fellow councilor while Lord Alexander possessed an amusingly witty manner. Surely both gentlemen would ask Lady Georgiana to dance, and she couldn't refuse them without appearing rude.

As he began escorting Lady Georgiana toward the younger gentlemen, another of Juliet's spells pricked his skin. She must have just entered the ballroom, although he refused to glance about to find her in the growing crowd. The maddening witch would only distract him and make him burn to kiss her rather than hunt for his lady. Instead, he paused beside Lord Morwynne and Lord Alexander to further his plan to divert Lady Georgiana, and like expected, the younger gentlemen requested her second and third dances. When Lady Georgiana arched her brows at him, obviously hoping he'd claim her company the entire evening, he smiled and remained silent. After a moment, Lady Georgiana sighed then graciously agreed to dance with Lord Morwynne and Lord Alexander.

Before he could find more gentlemen to ask Lady Georgiana to dance, the Duke and Duchess of Childes opened the fete by announcing Priest Melchior and Lady Blaine. He and the other guests stared when the couple glided from an anteroom. Unlike at his soiree a month ago, Lady Blaine no longer appeared ancient—and she wore novice priest robes over her ballgown. Despite her unsurprising decision to wed Priest Melchior, the once-fashionable Countess of Blaine also deciding to become a priestess and give up her influence at court *was* surprising. Her time as a crone had truly changed the sultry lady he'd once thought to marry. And from her glowing grin, Lady Blaine was happier than she'd ever been. Remarkable.

Soon the first waltz began, so Oakmoor escorted Lady Georgiana onto the floor, joining Priest Melchior and Lady Blaine along with various other couples.

While they twirled, Lady Georgiana eyed him. "Why did you maneuver my dances with Lord Morwynne and Lord Alexander Greysnowe?"

He smiled. "Because you deserve to dance with gentlemen besides myself." And when her relentless pursuit came to nothing, she'd have suitors to comfort her pride.

Lady Georgiana's gaze narrowed. "Why so determined to avoid courting me again? Perhaps a strong lady intimidates you after all."

His jaw tightening, Oakmoor spun Lady Georgiana in a complicated twirl. "Or perhaps I prefer to do the pursuing. Most gentlemen do."

Lady Georgiana hummed. "Yes, but gentlemen often don't know what's best for them. You, for instance, are determined to pursue young ladies too weak to truly interest you, which is why you dance every waltz with a new partner."

He nearly grimaced. The eligible ladies he'd been pursuing

recently *were* too bland and young to interest him, yet since one of them was the unknown lady in the veiled witch's prophecy, he must continue pursuing them. And avoid Juliet, who invariably distracted him from that.

Lady Georgiana continued, "What you need is a lady strong and clever enough to force you to pay attention to her for longer than a waltz."

Oakmoor sighed as the waltz ended and he bowed while Lady Georgiana curtsied. Clearly Lady Georgiana considered herself that lady. But she wasn't the one meant to break his curse. And she wasn't exotic or mature enough to hold his interest much longer than the other young ladies at court did. Unlike Juliet, damn her. *She* definitely wasn't his unknown lady either.

He left Lady Georgiana with Lord Morwynne then excused himself to greet the guests of honor. Delaying that might make court believe he resented Priest Melchior for winning Lady Blaine, which he assuredly didn't. Lady Blaine's indifference during their courtship and her eventual rejection had never troubled him. Their near betrothal had been a fashionable alliance with no bothersome love on either side, although they'd have remained faithful after speaking their vows.

He strolled over to the radiant couple, who were discussing with her stepson Lord Blaine and Priest Melchior's cousin Miss Philippa Hawke the charities tonight's entertainment would support. He smiled when Lady Blaine said Goddess's Refuge was one of the two. Of course it was.

Joining them, he said, "You've always favored supporting that family refuge, haven't you? You chose it as the cause for my Longnight charity luncheon." He studied Priest Melchior and Lady Blaine. Perhaps her becoming a priestess *wasn't* so surprising. "Congratulations on your betrothal. You two make a splendid couple." He grinned. "Would you favor me with the next waltz, Lady Blaine?" Although she wasn't the lady in the veiled witch's prophecy, dancing with Lady Blaine would allow him to scan the ladies who might be without missing a waltz.

Doing that would only encourage Lady Georgiana's futile pursuit.

Her face glowing, Lady Blaine smiled at Priest Melchior, who grinned back. She murmured, "I'm afraid Mel has claimed all my dances tonight, except for those with family. Excuse us."

Oakmoor quirked a wry smile as the couple glided back to the center of the ballroom. Lady Blaine had definitely changed to refuse a waltz with a wealthy and influential councilor. He turned to Miss Hawke and Lord Blaine. Although the bubbly young lady's coloring matched the veiled witch's prophecy, he'd not bothered to pursue her because she and Lord Blaine had been seriously courting for months, so she couldn't be the lady meant to break his curse. Yet dancing with her would provide the same benefits as with Lady Blaine. He let his smile warm. "Shall you oblige me instead, Miss Hawke?"

Lord Blaine stiffening beside her, Miss Hawke stilled then inclined her head. "Very well, your grace."

Oakmoor swallowed a laugh while he swept Miss Hawke onto the floor. Neither Lord Blaine nor Miss Hawke appeared pleased for her to dance with another. Well, he'd return her to Lord Blaine soon enough. He glanced about the ballroom, scanning the eligible young brunettes. Who hadn't he quizzed about a possible royal connection? Then he chuckled when his gaze fell on their beaming hostess. In his decades at court, he'd rarely seen her so smug. "The Duchess of Childes looks more smug than a sphinx with an unanswerable riddle."

Miss Hawke smiled. "The duchess is pleased to see all her sons so happily settled."

He chuckled again. How true. Yet what would the managing Duchess of Childes do now that her sons were all settled? He arched a brow. "Doubtless she'll soon turn her formidable attention to her unwed relatives, like you or Lord Blaine."

Miss Hawke beamed, her gaze demurely lowered. "I suppose."

Oakmoor inhaled. Although too young and sweet for him,

Miss Hawke had the most radiant smile—radiant enough to brighten any room. Just like his unknown lady's would according to the veiled witch's prophecy. Not that Miss Hawke could be her since she was already devoted to Lord Blaine and wasn't free to fall in love with him. He hummed. "Your father shall probably be grateful for the Duchess of Childes's assistance, considering how rarely he attends court events. Is he here tonight?"

Miss Hawke's mouth tightened. "Father is too busy with his magical experiments to attend most court events."

Oakmoor blinked at Miss Hawke. Magical experiments? Sir Julian must be a witch despite not attending the Duchess of Wildewall's garden party for court's witch families. The eccentric baronet was likely one of the reclusive witches who hadn't accepted the Duchess of Wildewall's invitation. His pulse leapt. If Sir Julian was a witch, his daughter could be one too. She might *literally* have the power to brighten any room. Just like she was literally King Devon's cousin. Perhaps the royal connection in the veiled witch's prophecy *was* obvious. The sole part of the prophecy that Miss Hawke didn't match was being able to love him. Yet maybe the courtship between her and Lord Blaine wasn't as serious as he'd believed—after all, they'd been courting nearly a year, and they'd not announced a betrothal yet.

To confirm his suspicions, he asked, "Magical experiments? What kind?"

Miss Hawke pursed her lips. "Attempting to determine the nature of faedust and thereby magic itself."

He whistled. For Miss Hawke to be so familiar with her father's magical experiments, she must be a witch too. She *had* to be the lady meant to break his curse. "Impressive."

Miss Hawke shrugged as their waltz ended. Once they'd exchanged a bow and a curtsy, she asked, "Could you escort me back to Lord Blaine? I believe he's fetched a flute of sparkling wine for me."

Oakmoor muffled his sigh as he nodded and obeyed Miss

Hawke's request. Clearly Miss Hawke possessed some affection for Lord Blaine even though their courtship wasn't serious. Winning her love wouldn't be easy, especially as a hideous beast. Yet since she was the lady in the veiled witch's prophecy, somehow he must do so. But once he set the veiled witch's wards, neither of them would be able to leave Oakmoor House, so they'd have plenty of time alone for him to win her love.

When they reached Lord Blaine, Oakmoor bowed again and kissed Miss Hawke's hand then rumbled, "I greatly enjoyed our waltz, Miss Hawke. Until later."

Releasing Miss Hawke, he turned and strode through the crowd. Now that he'd unearthed his unknown lady at last, he no longer needed to bother dancing with other eligible young ladies. And he must leave to prepare for kidnapping Miss Hawke and their confinement together. Yet he should greet the Orandians before he left the fete because he'd not see them again until after Miss Hawke broke his curse. Even though Juliet was with them like always.

Not glancing at Juliet, he joined her, the Orandians, and the Escanas. He mustn't let Juliet distract him now. Although Miss Hawke hadn't broke his curse yet, she would, and they'd be married when he next met Juliet. No more explosive kisses for him and Juliet ever again. He flashed a smooth smile at the Orandians. "Enjoying yourselves?"

Lady Driscoll nodded and sipped her sparkling wine. "I'm most intrigued by the charity-themed entertainments the Duchess of Childes has planned. Most unusual for a betrothal fete, although fitting for one celebrating a match between a priest and a future priestess."

Sir Lorcan eyed Priest Melchior and Lady Blaine amid the twirling dancers and sighed. "Although I wish the two of them would quit dancing so I can ask Lady Blaine how she broke that illusion from the Goddess."

Oakmoor exchanged grins with Lady Escana and her husband. Such a typical comment from the lore witch.

As Lady Driscoll tsked at her husband, Juliet drawled, "Somehow I doubt Priest Melchior and Lady Blaine shall quit dancing during their betrothal fete, especially given how in love they seem."

His pulse quickening, Oakmoor couldn't resist facing the bewitching witch he mustn't want. He was committed elsewhere. No matter how much Juliet's exotic beauty and bold strength bewitched him.

Juliet smirked back at him. "I've never seen Lady Blaine look so besotted, have you, your grace?"

He inhaled as hunger flared in his veins at Juliet's delightfully biting barb. If only he could kiss her again. But he couldn't. His kisses belonged to Miss Hawke now. Not only would she be his wife, but she'd also be the lady who saved him from Elvaira's vindictive curse with her love. And although he'd no intention of returning that love, he'd always treat Miss Hawke with the warmth and respect she deserved.

He inclined his head and replied to Juliet, "No, Lady Blaine wasn't the least besotted during our brief courtship, although her attraction to Priest Melchior was apparent even then. 'Tis fortunate they're marrying." He turned to the Orandians. "If you wish to discuss Lady Blaine's illusion from the Goddess, Lady Escana can arrange a visit with her in the next week or two."

Lady Driscoll grinned at his assistant. "I'm sure she can. Lady Escana has proved an excellent escort over the past two weeks."

Oakmoor nodded. He'd known she would. He echoed Lady Driscoll's grin at Lady Escana. "Then I shall leave you in her excellent hands." As the third waltz began to fade, he gave the Orandians a slight bow. "I must go. Good evening."

He hurried from the ballroom to ensure he left before Lady Georgiana convinced Lord Alexander to return her to him. Then he tensed when another of Juliet's spells hit his back. His unusually early departure had made her even more suspicious. Not that it mattered now. He and Miss Hawke would be confined at Oakmoor House after tomorrow, and Juliet would hear the truth of his magic troubles soon after from King Devon and Queen Kiera.

IN THE STILL HOURS AFTER midnight, Oakmoor slipped out to his stables and saddled a sturdy yet placid gelding then rode to Miss Hawke's townhouse. He tied the gelding to the railing near the window he'd identified was hers using a scrying spell in his study earlier. Then he activated the levitation charm he'd prepared to reach Miss Hawke's bedchamber.

At her window, he pressed the glass and was about to chant an opening spell when it flung open and Miss Hawke gaped at him. As she moved to shut it, he shoved his way inside, and she stumbled backward. He flashed a charming smile to reassure the surely panicking lady. "Good evening, or morning rather, Miss Hawke."

Miss Hawke straightened and glared at him. "W-what are you doing here?"

He eyed Miss Hawke, who wasn't panicking at all. No doubt why she was the lady meant to break his curse. He grimaced as he answered her defiant question, "Kidnapping you, I'm afraid."

Miss Hawke gasped. "No!" Then she fiercely punched his stomach.

Oakmoor wheezed and bent over but gripped Miss Hawke's wrist to prevent her escape. He'd better subdue her before she broke free or screamed and roused her family. "None of that, my darling."

He flicked the fingers of his free hand at Miss Hawke and crooned a sleep spell. She yanked on her captured wrist then swayed and collapsed in his arms as his spell overpowered her. Too bad he was forced to be so draconian.

He activated the ignore charm he'd prepared to prevent anyone from noticing them. Then he carried Miss Hawke to the window and descended to the ground using the alighting charm he'd also prepared. He hoisted her onto the saddle then untied his gelding and climbed before her, tying her arms about his waist to prevent her from sliding off as they rode.

Back at Oakmoor House, he unsaddled his gelding then carried Miss Hawke to his best guest bedchamber and laid her on the bed. After setting the trap spell about her bedchamber, he returned to his own and fell into bed. Drained from all the spells he'd cast tonight, he soon succumbed to the first dreamless sleep he'd enjoyed in months.

Oakmoor rose early and devoured a hearty breakfast since he'd be too busy to eat later. Afterward, he went to his study and wrote a brief letter to Lady Escana requesting she assume his duties during his absence and a longer one to King Devon and Queen Kiera explaining everything, which he enclosed in Lady Escana's letter for her to deliver tomorrow. Although he locked his letter to royal couple with a time-key spell in case Lady Escana delivered it early. He couldn't have King Devon attempting to rescue his cousin until after the veiled witch's wards were in place.

Then he gathered all his remaining servants and instructed them to return to Oakmoor for their paid respites. Once the others left, Miles and Martha fiercely argued against leaving him alone at Oakmoor House, and his head ached by the time he convinced his longtime valet and head cook to depart too and deliver his letter to Lady Escana on their way home.

By early afternoon, Oakmoor House was hauntingly empty. He checked on Miss Hawke, and she was still sleeping, so after using magic to resize the attire he'd purchased for his unknown lady, he left without disturbing her. Since he couldn't start setting the veiled witch's wards until six hours before midnight, he prepared their dinner instead, although struggling to recall his half-forgotten cooking lessons made his headache worse. He arranged their meal on a tray and added a deep-red rose as a romantic token. Ladies always loved receiving roses, especially the ones representing passionate love. Then he returned to Miss Hawke's bedchamber. Fortunately, she was awake at last. "Good evening, my darling. I cooked you some dinner."

Miss Hawke stared at him. "*You* cooked me dinner?"

He nodded, almost chuckling at Miss Hawke's blatant surprise despite his growing headache. "I sent away all my servants, so I had to." He set the laden tray on the tea table with a warm grin to reassure her. "And I'll even share it with you, so you know 'tisn't drugged."

Once Miss Hawke sat, he filled their plates while she poured their tea. She murmured as they began eating, "Why have you kidnapped me, your grace?"

He studied Miss Hawke and hummed. She was once again remarkably composed, so she was strong enough to handle the truth. He replied, "To marry you. I require a lady like you to fall in love with me and agree to marry me in order to break the curse about to befall me."

Her eyes widening, Miss Hawke blinked at him then gave a brilliant smile. "I'm afraid you'll need to find another lady to break your curse. I'm already in love and betrothed to Edouard."

Oakmoor nearly winced. Yes, winning Miss Hawke's love wouldn't be easy. Thank the Goddess the veiled witch said he'd an entire year before his beast curse became permanent. He arched his brows. "There's been no announcement about your betrothal to Lord Blaine."

Miss Hawke sighed and held his gaze. "Father insisted we wait until after Mel and Kit's betrothal fete. We're announcing our betrothal at Elise's rout party tonight."

He scrutinized Miss Hawke, his chest tightening. Not any more they weren't.

Suddenly, intense heat swamped him, and he stiffened. Damnation, he couldn't transform *now*. He was attempting to reassure Miss Hawke. But the heat soon flared into boiling agony, and he groaned as his body transformed for the fifth excruciating time.

After he was human again, he lurched upright and almost

swayed. Goddess, so tired. He managed to smile at Miss Hawke, who was white and rigid against the back of her chair. His transformation to a hideous beast had plainly horrified her. "Despite your unannounced betrothal to Lord Blaine, regrettably I can't let you go, Miss Hawke." If only he could, but he couldn't remain a beast forever.

He inhaled a steadying breath then continued, "You match the veiled witch's prophecy about breaking my curse, and I'm certain you'll learn to love me and agree to marry in time. Now, please excuse me. Since 'tis finally six hours to midnight, I must begin setting the wards the veiled witch provided me to prevent anyone from entering or leaving Oakmoor House until my curse is broken."

Oakmoor left, resetting the trap spell behind him before striding downstairs to set the wards. Once Miss Hawke could no longer flee his horrifying beast curse, he could reassure her further then get to know her and win her love. Although that must all wait until after he'd slept because setting the veiled witch's intricate wards would consume the meager energy he'd remaining following his transformation.

CHAPTER 14

The day after Oakmoor's suspiciously early departure from Childes House, Juliet glided into Golddell House for the Farsons' rout party and glanced about for the vexing duke. She almost frowned when she didn't spot him. Oakmoor should be here since 'twas a fellow councilor's court event. Perhaps whatever had made him leave early yesterday had delayed him today. Doubtless it involved the troublesome magic he was embroiled in.

Shoving that aside, she greeted Lord and Lady Farson along with their ward the young Duke of Golddell. They all appeared somewhat tense. Odd—the Farsons hadn't been that tense at the duke's first court event last summer to celebrate the nightmara's arrival. So why would they be at tonight's simple rout party?

Juliet joined Siobhan and Lorcan near the refreshments table. They were alone for once, most unusual. "Evening. Where are Lord and Lady Escana?"

Siobhan hummed. "Talking with King Devon and Queen Kiera. I suspect about the Duke of Oakmoor's sudden absence from court."

A faint chill prickling her neck, Juliet stilled and eyed her friend. "Absence?"

Siobhan nodded, her freckled brow furrowed. "Yes, the duke wrote to Lady Escana this afternoon and made her the acting Minister of Foreign Relations because he had to leave to handle a private matter."

Juliet stiffened. Oakmoor's magic troubles had *definitely* exploded at last. Why hadn't the obstinate fool let her help him before they had?

Lorcan tugged on his tan overcoat. "The Duke of Oakmoor also sent Lady Escana a letter for King Devon and Queen Kiera, although apparently 'tis locked with a time-key spell until tomorrow. Shall they use the Mirror of Wisdom to discover its contents, do you think?"

Juliet frowned and stiffened further. Oakmoor had hired a witch to lock his letter to the king and queen? Why? And why did her friends keep mentioning people using the Mirror of Wisdom? 'Twas a perilous risk best avoided. "Of course King Devon and Queen Kiera shan't use the Mirror of Wisdom. It helped kill his mother."

Siobhan grimaced. "Only because she used it too often and she'd no magical powers to control it. They'd be fine if they used it sparingly."

Lorcan inclined his head. "Yes, 'tis a waste not to use such a wondrous enchanted tool. We've plenty of them in Orandia, and they can be incredibly useful."

Juliet leaned toward her friends. "The Mirror of Wisdom is no mere tool."

But before she could elaborate, Lord Blaine joined them, his smile tight. He appeared just as tense as his sister and her family did. He nodded and said, "Good evening, Lady Juliet. Could we talk for a moment?"

She arched her brows. The count had little interest in politics or magic and had never requested to speak with her before. His reason tonight must be serious—as much as Oakmoor's absence was. She could finish warning Siobhan and Lorcan about the Mirror of Wisdom after she'd helped Lord Blaine. She returned his nod. "Of course, Lord Blaine." She smiled at her friends. "Until later, Siobhan, Lorcan."

Once Lord Blaine began escorting her toward the door, she eyed him and said, "I'm surprised that Miss Hawke isn't with you." The two had been courting for months and were rarely apart.

Lord Blaine's smile tightened further. "'Tis why I wished to talk with you." He glanced about then murmured, "Pippa went missing this morning, and I need a tracing spell to find her."

Juliet inhaled, her eyes widening. No wonder Lord Blaine and his family appeared tense and he'd asked to speak with her. "I see."

Lord Blaine touched the pocket above his heart. "I've Pippa's hair in a charmed locket to cast the spell."

Juliet pursed her lips. Too bad Lord Blaine didn't have unenchanted hair. "Since 'tis already enchanted, I may not be able to use it for another spell. Could I see the locket?"

Lord Blaine glanced about again then nodded. "Of course, but not here."

She studied the other guests nearby. 'Twouldn't do for Miss Hawke's disappearance to be overheard and gossiped about at court. Juliet swiftly cast an ignore spell about them. "No one shall notice our departure now, Lord Blaine, unless they already know of Miss Hawke's disappearance."

Exhaling, Lord Blaine swept her from the drawing room. "Thank you."

While they hurried down the hall, she accepted the gold locket Lord Blaine handed her then stiffened. The magical signature glowing about the locket was irritatingly familiar. "This is the veiled witch's work. Why didn't you ask *her* for a tracing spell?"

Lord Blaine glowered. "I would have, but her witch shop's door was locked."

Juliet frowned as another chill prickled her neck. An incredibly powerful Rhiannon-descendant seer like the veiled witch had to know when her magical gift would be needed, so why hadn't she been there? And the veiled witch was the third person mysteriously missing today. *What* was going on?

She murmured, "Peculiar," then sighed and returned the charmed locket to Lord Blaine once they neared the front door. "Very well, I'll see if I can create your tracing spell, but we must head to my workroom at the palace."

Lord Blaine nodded as they strode outside. "I assumed as much." He mounted a brown-dun stallion and pulled her behind him, and they galloped to the palace then hurried to her wing upstairs.

When they entered her workroom, her maid Lara whirled from the shelves she was stacking to face them. "Lady Juliet, why are you back so early?"

Juliet smiled at Lara to convince her that everything was fine. Not the truth, but the little maid could do nothing to help and would only fret. "Lord Blaine requested a small spell for Miss Hawke." She waved toward the door. "Go retire for the evening. You can finish stacking in the morning. Thank you, Lara."

After her maid bobbed a curtsy and left, she turned to Lord Blaine. "Give me the veiled witch's charmed locket then sit on the sofa by the door while I create your tracing spell."

Once he did, she set the charmed locket on her worktable before whisking to her enchanted cabinet. She crooned the incantation and weaved the pattern of light to unlock the cabinet's magic-key spell then extracted the scrying hand mirror Mother had given her on her sixteenth natalday. Although she rarely let others see it because its purple gentians betrayed her Varkhoran heritage, she'd need it to carry her tracing spell from her workroom.

She relocked her enchanted cabinet then gathered the other magical supplies she'd need for her tracing spell from her shelves—her massive scrying bowl, unicorn water, eyebright, mandrake, sandalwood, and colloidal silver. She added all the ingredients except Miss Hawke's hair into her scrying bowl. As the magical mixture began to emit a redolent icy steam, she flipped open the charmed locket to add Miss Hawke's hair and set the focus of the tracing spell.

She frowned when Lord Blaine burst from the sofa and peered at the charmed locket. His hovering would interfere with her spellwork. "What are you doing, Lord Blaine? I've not even begun casting your tracing spell."

Lord Blaine offered a contrite smile. "Sorry for distracting you. The veiled witch enchanted the moving portrait to mirror Pippa's actual movements, so I wanted to see if she was well."

Juliet blinked and eyed the charmed locket. "Actual movements? Impressive." Creating such an enchantment would be complicated and beyond most witches. But of course the veiled witch could. She must study the veiled witch's technique when she removed Miss Hawke's hair. "Too bad that removing the hair shall destroy the enchantment."

His mouth firming, Lord Blaine straightened. "I don't care as long as we find Pippa."

Juliet smiled and patted the count's arm to encourage him. "We shall. Now, please sit so I can concentrate."

As Lord Blaine returned to the sofa, she scrutinized the enchantment behind the moving portrait. The veiled witch had used the hair to connect to the truth of Miss Hawke, allowing the moving portrait to reflect her ever-changing present instead of a set moment like most did. Complicated indeed, which likely meant the veiled witch's enchantment had consumed the hair's magical link to Miss Hawke. Juliet suppressed a grimace and extracted Miss Hawke's hair from the locket anyway. Then her brows rose as she eyed it. The hair's magical link was untouched. *How* had the veiled witch managed that? She said to reassure Lord Blaine, "Even more impressive—the veiled witch managed to set her enchantment to not consume the hair's magical link to Miss Hawke like most similar charms would. Creating a tracing spell with it shan't be a problem."

She dropped Miss Hawke's hair into the tracing spell mixture and stirred, making the icy steam thicken as the focus set. She swirled her hand over the bowl while chanting the incantation to complete the tracing spell. Then she leaned over and peered into her scrying bowl to locate Miss Hawke.

The icy steam coalesced into ghostly images that sharpened and turned vibrant until a clear vision appeared of Miss Hawke calmly sitting in a plush chair inside a luxurious bedchamber. Why wasn't she attempting escape? Juliet expanded the vision to encompass the entire room. Ah, a trap spell glowed along the bedchamber's walls. Now where exactly was that bedchamber? She expanded the vision further to show the building then inhaled. 'Twas Oakmoor House! Oakmoor and Miss Hawke were both missing because he'd *kidnapped* her. Why? He'd never seemed interested in the bubbly young lady already devoted to Lord Blaine. Had his magic troubles driven him mad?

Lightheaded from her intense spell, she shuddered and glanced at Lord Blaine. "Miss Hawke is at Oakmoor House, locked in a bedchamber with a trap spell. Let me scry her surroundings before we leave to rescue her."

She bent into the steam again then steered the vision through Oakmoor House, starting with the rooms closest to Miss Hawke. The luxurious townhouse was empty and still, with Oakmoor outside along the left wall. What was he doing there? As she narrowed in on the duke, she told Lord Blaine, "The townhouse appears empty except for Miss Hawke in that bespelled bedchamber. The duke is outside along the left wall."

Then she gasped as Oakmoor placed an iron gargoyle statuette against the wall while chanting a lengthy incantation. "Is Oakmoor setting *wards*?" Impossible. He was no witch. "Since when does *he* have magical powers?" She'd have seen them in his aura when she'd read it. Unless those few ivory motes amid his yellow aura hadn't been a trick of the light after all.

Lord Blaine leapt from the sofa. "How long until the Duke of Oakmoor finishes setting his wards?"

Juliet humphed while she examined the wards' construction.

"Several hours at least. His wards appear intricate and incredibly powerful." How was Oakmoor even setting them? The few motes in his aura had been faint, indicating weak magical powers. She leaned closer to her scrying bowl. The veiled witch's magical signature shone throughout the wards. Of course that dratted seer was involved too. "Not that he created the wards himself—the veiled witch did." And had probably constructed them so that a minor witch could set them.

Lord Blaine strode toward her worktable. "Have you scried enough yet?"

She straightened and tossed Lord Blaine his destroyed charmed locket. The count was clearly desperate to rescue his beloved. But she'd some preparations to make first. "For now. Let me transfer the tracing spell to my scrying mirror."

She held her scrying hand mirror face down over her scrying bowl then swirled her other hand over both to draw the tracing spell into the mirror. The icy steam sucked into the scrying mirror until all the magical mixture in her scrying bowl had evaporated. That done, she began gathering the magical supplies she might need. First, she snatched her enchanted satchel that could hold the contents of an entire room. She swept everything on her shelves inside before unlocking her enchanted cabinet and adding several magical tomes, a gold ritual dagger, a silver potion chalice, and a copper divining pendant. Then she gathered her will to cast a transportation spell to fetch Mordred's transport box from her study and added it too. Finally, after relocking her enchanted cabinet to protect the few magical items remaining, she stuffed her massive scrying bowl inside her enchanted satchel.

Panting and her pulse swift from her rapid spells, she slung her bulging satchel over her shoulder and grasped her scrying mirror in her free hand. Now she was ready to rescue Miss Hawke. She glanced at Lord Blaine. "Shall we go?"

As they rushed out, the count asked, "Why did you pack all those magical accoutrements?"

Juliet grimaced. "I wanted to ensure I'd have anything I needed. Considering Oakmoor's inexplicable magic and the veiled witch's involvement, matters could be complicated." Plus, she must resolve Oakmoor's magic troubles as well.

The bells tolling two hours to midnight, Lord Blaine pulled her behind him on his stallion, and they galloped to Oakmoor House. She swiftly used her will to cast an ignore spell about them again even though her head whirled. Goddess, she was going to be drained before the night was through.

While Lord Blaine tied his stallion to a railing, she peered at the tracing spell on her scrying mirror to check on Miss Hawke and Oakmoor. The young lady was still locked inside the bespelled bedchamber, while Oakmoor was now along the back wall. She told Lord Blaine, "Everything looks the same as before. Come along."

She and Lord Blaine slipped inside Oakmoor House through the servants' entrance then crept upstairs. When they reached the third bedchamber that held Miss Hawke, she raised a hand to halt him. Although Oakmoor was doubtless still outside setting his wards, she whispered, "This is it. Now be quiet while I weave an opening in the trap spell."

After sliding her scrying mirror into her enchanted satchel, she extracted a glittering skein of electrum thread. Half gold and half silver, her electrum thread equally contained gold's protective powers and silver's sight powers, making it ideal to create an opening in Oakmoor's trap spell without alerting him. She began humming an incantation as she tossed the skein and it hovered at the center of the door. Still humming, she waved her hand to unravel the skein in an ever-widening spiral. When it covered the entire door, she spread her hands to form a massive ring framing the door.

Her vision blurry, she smiled and nodded at her opening in the trap spell. "It should be safe to enter now."

Lord Blaine surged forward and flung open the door.

She smiled as she collected her satchel and followed the

eager count inside. By the time she did, he and Miss Hawke were already passionately kissing. To give them privacy, Juliet turned and shut the door then began drawing her electrum ring through the wall. Even though Oakmoor should be engrossed in setting his wards, 'twould be better to not leave her opening in his trap spell visible in the hall.

When Juliet was midway through, Miss Hawke suddenly gasped and said, "Edouard, we must escape at once. If the Duke of Oakmoor finishes setting his wards, we shan't be able to leave until I fall in love with him and agree to marry him to break the curse transforming him into a chimera-like beast. And since that shall never happen, we'll be trapped here forever."

Juliet almost gasped too. Oakmoor's troublesome magic was a curse transforming him into a beast? Yet she'd sensed no such curse despite her many probing spells, so it must have been cast by a Rhiannon-descendant black witch. Their curses were visible only to seers and grueling to break. The veiled witch *must* have seen his curse when he'd purchased his wards from her. Why hadn't she simply broken it instead of providing him a spell to trap an innocent young lady with him?

Lord Blaine growled, "The duke kidnapped you to force you to *marry* him to break some curse?" He paused then said in a lighter tone, "Let's go."

Her electrum ring now inside the bedchamber and her entire body heavy, Juliet turned and cleared her throat. Simply fleeing would be disastrous. "Not so fast, Lord Blaine. If Miss Hawke leaves now, the trap spell shall alert Oakmoor, and he'll thwart your escape." She smiled at the young couple to hearten them. "But if I shift the focus of the trap spell to myself, you can escape with him none the wiser."

Miss Hawke inhaled. "You'd do that? But you'll be unable to leave until you break his terrible beast curse by falling in love with the duke and agreeing to marry him."

Juliet sniffed. Oakmoor had surely misunderstood how to break his curse. As an unacknowledged witch, he'd probably received little training. And breaking curses, especially ones cast by a Rhiannon descendant, were advanced magic. She extracted her scrying hand mirror and her scrying bowl from her enchanted satchel at her feet. She'd need both to free Miss Hawke. She drawled, "I'm sure I can break Oakmoor's curse without resorting to falling in love and marrying him." Even the most powerful magic couldn't make her do either.

As Lord Blaine and Miss Hawke exchanged wide glances, Juliet snapped her fingers over her scrying mirror to expel the tracing spell. Steam poured from the scrying mirror and condensed into the tracing spell mixture inside the scrying bowl. Feigning vigor, she retrieved her gold ritual dagger and approached Miss Hawke. "Before I shift the focus of the trap spell, I'll assume your appearance, and we'll trade garments. Give me your hand."

Lord Blaine stiff beside her, Miss Hawke swallowed but did so.

Juliet pricked Miss Hawke's finger and shook three drops of blood onto the face of her scrying mirror. Then she waved her hand over the mirror while chanting an incantation that created an illusion of Miss Hawke using her blood. The scrying mirror began glowing like the sun, and the glow soon flared and engulfed Juliet. When it vanished, she appeared exactly like Miss Hawke. Hopefully, she could act enough like the bubbly young lady to fool Oakmoor until she discovered how to break his curse. If she revealed herself, he'd complain at her outmaneuvering him then constantly attempt to seduce her, and she was never good at resisting him. Being innocent Miss Hawke would protect her from all that.

Her heart racing after casting her illusion, she twirled her hand at Lord Blaine. "Turn around, Lord Blaine, so Miss Hawke and I can trade garments."

Once the count whirled away, she doffed her silver gown and donned Miss Hawke's nightgown and dressing gown. Thankfully, both fit due to their loose cut, even though she was curvier and half a hand taller than the younger lady. Not that she seemed to be while under her illusion. She murmured, "You can turn back around now, Lord Blaine." She smiled at Miss Hawke. "Your hand again, please, Miss Hawke."

While Lord Blaine recaptured Miss Hawke's other arm, Juliet pricked Miss Hawke's finger again and shook four drops of blood onto the face of her scrying mirror, which contained no remnants of her illusion spell. Then she pricked her own finger and added four drops of her blood to Miss Hawke's. Forcing herself to not stagger, she waved her hand over her scrying mirror while chanting an incantation and walking along the bedchamber walls to shift the focus of the trap spell from Miss Hawke to herself.

She smiled at Lord Blaine and Miss Hawke after she'd finished even though she almost trembled with exhaustion. "I've shifted the focus of the trap spell. Hurry and leave—I suspect Oakmoor shall finish setting his wards at midnight in half an hour."

Miss Hawke tightly embraced her then swept a curtsy. "My deepest thanks for helping rescue me and taking my place, Lady Juliet."

Lord Blaine bowed as well and flashed a warm smile. "Mine too."

Juliet waved the young couple toward the door. They'd little time for pleasantries. "Of course. Now go." Then she inhaled. She'd not informed King Devon and Queen Kiera in her rush to rescue Miss Hawke, and she couldn't do so now and still be able to prepare for her confinement with Oakmoor. So she asked Lord Blaine and Miss Hawke, "Could you inform King Devon and Queen Kiera where I am? I may be unable to once Oakmoor sets his wards." As a witch, he might sense her contacting them.

Lord Blaine and Miss Hawke both nodded before they hurried from the bedchamber. As soon as the young couple left, Juliet allowed her shoulders to sag. Dear Goddess, so tired.

Please let her have enough magical energy to cast her final spells.

Since she couldn't leave any sign that she possessed magical powers unlike Miss Hawke, she hummed and waved her hands at her electrum ring to close the opening in the trap spell. The ring spun with her movements and unraveled into a skein hovering before the door again.

Black shading the edges of her vision, she slid the electrum skein in her enchanted satchel then used her scrying hand mirror to check on Oakmoor. He was setting wards in the ballroom now and would likely finish soon. She sighed and returned her scrying mirror to her satchel.

Juliet sank to the floor and gulped a bracing breath. Then she used her will to cast a cleansing spell on the tracing spell mixture to leave only pure unicorn water behind. She might need that to help break Oakmoor's curse later. Chilled and shaking, she added the unicorn water and scrying bowl to her satchel also.

With the final bit of her magic, she flicked her fingers and whispered an incantation to conjure fruit-nut bars drizzled with ambrosia. After all her spellwork, she required that to recover her physical energy. Too bad 'twould take her days to recharge her magical energy from her surroundings. She'd not drained herself like this in years.

She devoured her fruit-nut bars and remained on the floor until she'd enough energy to shove her bulging satchel beneath the bed and stagger upright. Then she collapsed on the bed and dragged the covers atop herself before succumbing to slumber.

Juliet jerked awake hours later at a loud knock on her door. She whimpered and rubbed her face. What time was it? She glanced at the clock on the mantel and whimpered again. Almost noon. She never slept so late. Yet her body still felt heavy and sluggish.

Then she gasped when Oakmoor strode inside her bedchamber as the trap spell broke. How rude. She glared at him. "Go *away*. I was sleeping."

His brows rising, Oakmoor smiled and set his tray laden with food, kahve, and three deep-red roses on the tea table. "So I see. A bit late, isn't it?"

She glared harder. Impudent beast. "Well, what else have I to do locked in this bedchamber?"

Oakmoor chuckled as he sat at the tea table. "You're delightfully biting today, my darling. Hunger, no doubt. Come eat the breakfast I made for us."

Juliet almost winced. She wasn't acting at all like the bubbly Miss Hawke. Oakmoor would realize her identity if she wasn't careful. Then he'd yank her into his arms and kiss her, and she'd hungrily kiss him back like she always did. Damned irresistible rakehell. She swallowed then forced herself to rise and join Oakmoor at the tea table. Her cheeks warmed as he eyed her disheveled hair and nightclothes. 'Twas nearly as bad as after their long ago night together. Although at least this time she wasn't naked.

Her stomach rumbling, she silently began devouring the eggs, bacon, tubers, toast, and kahve Oakmoor had brought while he did likewise. 'Twas delicious despite the kahve not being proper Varkhoran kahve, and her physical energy returned with every bite. A breakfast he must have cooked since no servants were left in Oakmoor House. A curious skill for a wealthy duke to possess.

When they'd both cleared their plates, Oakmoor flashed his annoyingly smooth smile. "You *were* hungry, weren't you? I've never seen a lady devour so much."

She drained the last of her weak Calatinian kahve. "Not even after—" She snapped her mouth shut to silence the rest of her retort. Innocent Miss Hawke would never say it.

Oakmoor chuckled again and arched a brow. "Not even after?"

Juliet blushed. After a wild night in his bed. She managed a sweet smile. "Nothing." She said to distract Oakmoor, "Tell me about your beast curse and why *I'm* the lady to break it."

His amusement fading, Oakmoor sighed but nodded. "I suppose I should. I was cursed nearly thirty—"

Suddenly, Oakmoor groaned, a rictus contorting his face. No magic glowing about him but the air turning heavy and charged and musky, he transformed into a beast with a lion's mane and claws, a goat's horns, and a snake's face. Yet his hazel eyes remained unchanged, which somehow made the rest of his transformation more horrible.

She swallowed, her heart pounding. A chimera-like beast exactly like Miss Hawke had said. And definitely a curse from a Rhiannon-descendant black witch since she could sense no magic even during his agonizing transformation, which obviously wasn't the first he'd suffered since she'd witnessed that air about him at Islaye House and Greysnowe House.

She shuddered then lifted her chin. Somehow she was going to break Oakmoor's curse. 'Twas her duty as Calatini's royal witch, and she'd handled complicated magic before. She just needed him to tell her everything about his curse.

So once Oakmoor transformed back into his human self, Juliet flashed Miss Hawke's sweet smile again and said, "Quite nasty, this curse of yours. So, nearly thirty?"

CHAPTER 15

Gulping air to steady himself, Oakmoor studied Miss Hawke, who appeared less horrified at this transformation than at the first she'd witnessed. Not rigid against the back of her chair today, she was merely somewhat pale with her defiantly raised chin belying her sweet smile. Undeniably strong enough to break Elvaira's vindictive curse. Despite his whirling head after his draining transformation, he straightened and returned Miss Hawke's smile with a wry grimace. "Thirty years ago on my natalday next week, I was cursed by my first lover to turn into a chimera-like beast one day."

Her eyes narrowing, Miss Hawke brightened her smile. "What did you do to inspire such vindictive spite?"

He almost grinned at Miss Hawke's continued biting remarks. Perhaps she wasn't all sweetness and light. So much more interesting, and 'twould make being married easier. She'd be his equal rather than a lady he must coddle. Like Juliet was. Suppressing all thought of the bewitching witch he could no longer have, he held Miss Hawke's narrow gaze and replied, "I chose the wrong woman to be my first lover. She was obsessed with me and a Rhiannon-descendant gypsy witch. I ended our affair when she said I belonged to her after one time together, perhaps not the most gracefully since I was only sixteen. So she returned eight months later and cursed me, sealing it with her life."

Miss Hawke paled. "She *killed* herself to curse you?" At his nod, she shuddered. "You definitely chose the wrong woman."

Oakmoor sighed and inclined another nod. "Yes, I was a young fool led astray by too much wine, newfound independence, and lust for an exotic, older woman intent on seducing me."

Miss Hawke hummed. "No wonder you trust no woman. I'm surprised you even believe one can break your curse."

He managed to shrug even though his shoulders were heavy and sluggish. "Not all women are mad like Elvaira." And he was desperate. "Besides, that prophecy from the veiled witch I mentioned states I need a special lady to break Elvaira's curse—you."

Her mouth tightening, Miss Hawke drummed her fingers on the tea table. "How do you know 'tis me? What else does this *marvelous* prophecy say?"

Oakmoor arched his brows. Sarcasm about a Rhiannon-descendant seer's prophecy from Miss Hawke? How unexpected. And refreshing. "Enough to know that you're the lady meant to break my curse. You're cousin to royalty, have brown hair and eyes, and can brighten any room. And to break my curse, you must fall in love with me and agree to marry me within a year of when I permanently transform into a beast on my natalday."

Miss Hawke frowned. "You must have misunderstood. I'm not the only lady that matches those requirements, and why would falling in love be enough to break a powerful curse cast by a Rhiannon-descendant black witch, especially one that took thirty years to manifest?"

He snorted a bitter laugh. "Because doubtless Elvaira created it that way. When she cast her curse, she made it clear that no one would ever love such a hideous beast, therefore breaking the curse would be impossible." He made himself give Miss Hawke a warm smile. "But she was too spiteful to understand a sweet lady like you who loves with her entire being and cares nothing for appearances."

Miss Hawke sniffed and shook her head. "Except you kidnapped a sweet lady already in love with someone else. There must be another way to break your curse."

Oakmoor sagged back in his chair. If only there was. Marrying a lady who loved him whose love he could never return would make for a life full of guilt and awkwardness. But he'd no choice unless he wanted to remain a beast forever, which would be an even worse life. He straightened. "There isn't another way." When Miss Hawke opened her mouth to protest again, he added, "I wrote out the veiled witch's prophecy word for word. I'll let you read it. You'll see then."

Miss Hawke leaned forward, her face tight. "Could I read that prophecy now?"

He examined Miss Hawke. The bubbly young lady never looked so serious. 'Twas as if she was desperate to find a loophole in the prophecy. Not that there was one. But even if there was, 'twouldn't alter her situation. Neither of them could escape until she broke his curse thanks to the veiled witch's wards. And after living alone with him for Goddess-knew how long, she'd *have* to marry him regardless of whether she loved him or not. Yet reminding her of all that would upset Miss Hawke. So he simply said, "Later, my darling. You must recover from your ordeal first."

Miss Hawke pursed her lips. "You mean the ordeal of you kidnapping me and locking me in a strange bedchamber?"

His gaze fixed on Miss Hawke's newly saucy mouth, and a zing darted through him. What would it be like to kiss her? He inhaled. He'd not imagined kissing anyone other than Juliet for months, and now he was wondering about kissing the young and innocent Miss Hawke? Perhaps knowing she was his future wife made the difference, although her unexpected strength and biting remarks certainly helped. She almost sounded like Juliet sometimes. He stiffened. He was thinking about that maddening witch again, damn her. He *had* to stop. Miss Hawke deserved his thoughts now.

He made himself flash a charming grin at his future wife. "Yes, I do mean the ordeal of being kidnapped. But your bedchamber is no longer locked unless you wish it."

Miss Hawke returned his grin with another sweet smile. "What good would locking my door do? You're a witch, so you could easily unlock it with a spell."

His pulse leapt at yet another biting remark from Miss Hawke. So stimulating. To reassure her, Oakmoor laid his hand over his heart and replied, "Yes, but I swear upon my honor as a gentleman that I shan't unlock your bedchamber door."

Miss Hawke's eyes narrowed. "And just how much honor does a kidnapping rakehell possess?"

He couldn't help a laugh. Young Miss Hawke was turning out to be delightful, and kissing her was becoming more and more tempting. "How about I swear upon my life then? I want you to be comfortable here. You may go wherever you like in Oakmoor House, including the garden. I would recommend you not visit my chambers, however." A room he never wanted ladies in anyway. Only Juliet had ever been there during their one night together—a terrible mistake. Burying that unbidden memory, he clung to his smile for his future wife.

A blush darkening her cheeks at him mentioning his chambers, Miss Hawke tossed her head. "I've no desire to visit there *ever*, your grace." She huffed. "And your offer is no better than fool's gold, considering the wards you set to trap us here."

Oakmoor grimaced. "Preventing anyone from entering or leaving the townhouse until my curse is broken was a regrettable necessity, I'm afraid. We need time alone for you to fall in love with me." He began stacking the dishes on the tray he'd brought, leaving behind the vase of roses to remind her of him. "If you've finished eating, I'll let you amuse yourself this afternoon. I must rest before I cook dinner."

Miss Hawke blinked at him. "Rest, why?"

He exhaled a heavy sigh then admitted, "My transformations are draining." He shook his head. "I'll be almost grateful when I permanently transform into a beast in a few days."

Miss Hawke's brow furrowed. "How often do you transform?"

Oakmoor scrutinized Miss Hawke. Was that concern furrowing her brow? He lifted a shoulder. "I'm not certain. At first, my transformations were every nine days, but now they're daily, and I suspect I'll suffer them even more frequently closer to my natalday."

Her eyes darkening, Miss Hawke bit her lip. Definitely concern. So tenderhearted—surely why she was the lady meant to break his curse. She murmured, "Your transformation looked agonizing." At his involuntary shudder, she frowned. "That first lover of yours was truly a cruel, vindictive witch."

He grasped the tray and stood. And he'd been a damned fool for succumbing to Elvaira's seductive wiles in the first place. "Yes, she was. A mad one too." After all, she'd killed herself to curse him. To distract himself and Miss Hawke, he nodded at the large wardrobe near the dressing table and said, "There's attire for you in that wardrobe. Everything should fit and is in simple styles that shan't require a maid's assistance."

Miss Hawke arched her brows. "The veiled witch's prophecy included my measurements too? How *remarkable*."

Oakmoor almost grinned. Such lovely continued sarcasm about the veiled witch's prophecy. Yes, Miss Hawke was definitely much more than he'd imagined when he'd kidnapped her. Thank the Goddess. He smiled at his future wife. "Of course not. I resized everything with magic while you slept yesterday."

A grimace flickered across Miss Hawke's face. "I see."

He warmed his smile to ease her disquiet over his intrusion when she'd been helpless. Although he'd kidnapped Miss

Hawke because he needed her to break his curse, he'd never harm her, or any woman for that matter. "Join me for dinner in the family dining room in six hours. Any special food you'd like?"

Miss Hawke gaped at him, then a hint of a smirk curved her lips. "Pastry-wrapped beefsteak."

Oakmoor laughed. Miss Hawke had clearly selected the difficult recipe to poke at him. "I doubt my culinary skills can manage that, you demanding girl. How about grilled beefsteak instead?"

With that, he strode from Miss Hawke's bedchamber and returned the tray to the kitchen. Then he forced himself to wash the dishes before staggering up to his chambers and collapsing into slumber. He jerked awake several hours later and returned to the kitchen to cook dinner.

He'd just placed dessert in the cold pantry to set when Miss Hawke swept into the kitchen. He blinked. He'd not expected her to join him until dinner. "It should be another hour before dinner is ready."

Miss Hawke's gaze flicked over the marinating beefsteak and other food on the counter then the soup simmering on the stove. "Sounds good. Could I help?"

Oakmoor blinked at Miss Hawke again. She wanted to help? Most ladies only stepped into the kitchen to speak with their cook, if that. "Have you ever cooked before?"

Miss Hawke stilled, her gaze remaining on the food. "Ladies aren't taught to cook. But I spent the afternoon exploring the townhouse, and I've nothing better to do."

He handed Miss Hawke a rinsed tuber and a knife. "You can help me peel the tubers. Like so." He demonstrated slicing off the skin then watched as she repeated him. She was deft for someone who'd never cooked before. "Excellent job."

They were mostly finished peeling the tubers when Miss Hawke said, "I'm surprised that you chose to cook rather than conjure our meal. And that you even know how."

Ignoring the second indirect question since the answer was too revealing, Oakmoor shrugged and replied, "As you said, there's little else to do while we're confined to the townhouse." Although he would need to conjure fresh ingredients once they consumed the ones Martha left behind. He winked at Miss Hawke. "Besides, I thought meals cooked by my own two hands would impress you more."

Miss Hawke sniffed as he placed the tubers on the stove to boil. "That depends on how good of a cook you are."

He chuckled. If Miss Hawke kept up her biting remarks, he'd kiss her before the evening was through. Probably not the best idea since such passion would shock the innocent young lady. He'd better restrain himself. Too bad she wasn't mature and experienced like Juliet. Then he'd not need to. He suppressed a scowl. He was thinking about that damned witch again. He shoved Juliet from his mind once more.

He and Miss Hawke finished cooking dinner, and after he cast a preservation spell on the main course to keep it hot, he carried the creamy rhubarb soup and the red wine to the family dining room, while Miss Hawke carried the rolls. Once they sat at the table he'd decorated with a fresh vase of deep-red roses, he asked about her explorations of the townhouse, and they discussed that throughout dinner, except when they fetched the main course of grilled beefsteak, mashed tubers, and sauteed sparrow grass.

When she finished her last bite of beefsteak, Miss Hawke leaned back in her chair with a sigh. "An excellent meal, your grace. I'm impressed with your cooking after all."

Oakmoor arched a brow then drawled to tease Miss Hawke, "Even though I didn't cook pastry-wrapped beefsteak?"

Miss Hawke laughed. "Even though you didn't cook that. How did you learn to cook so well?"

He nearly grimaced. 'Twould be rude to ignore a direct question, and being rude wouldn't help him woo Miss Hawke. So he shrugged and replied, "The head cook at Oakmoor Castle taught me as a boy." When Miss Hawke opened her mouth, no doubt to ask why a servant would teach a duke to cook, he rose with a smooth smile. What with telling her about Elvaira and his curse, he'd already told Miss Hawke enough about his private matters today. "I'll fetch dessert."

Once he placed her dessert plate before her, Miss Hawke studied the tawny-brown squares and asked, "What's this?"

Oakmoor grinned as he sat beside Miss Hawke. Hopefully, she loved it too. "Triple gingyr fudge."

Miss Hawke tilted her head. "I've never heard of it. An interesting choice of dessert."

He devoured his first piece, humming as the sweet and spicy fudge melted in his mouth. He swallowed then replied, "Not for me. 'Tis my favorite dessert. I adore anything with gingyr."

A blush darkening her cheeks, Miss Hawke lowered her gaze. "Oh."

Oakmoor eyed Miss Hawke. Why would his love of gingyr make her blush?

Miss Hawke nibbled on a piece of gingyr fudge then beamed at him. "You're right. 'Tis delicious."

After dinner, Miss Hawke offered to help with the dishes, so he washed them and handed them to her to dry. Whenever their fingers met, his pulse would quicken, and her cheeks would flush. Yet somehow he managed not to kiss her despite the attraction between them. And he didn't follow her when she muttered good night and fled to her bedchamber once the dishes were done.

THAT DAY SET the pattern for their next few together. He cooked for them, often with Miss Hawke helping him. Although they focused on their tasks when cooking, they talked throughout their simple meals, but they both kept their conversations away from private matters. To woo her while he was still human, he flirted using banter, smoldering smiles, and more deep-red roses, but he never let himself succumb to temptation and kiss her, even though she invariably responded to his flirting with saucy barbs that further bewitched him.

As he'd expected, the frequency of his transformations increased as his natalday approached. Three per day during the next two days, then nine during the last two days before his natalday. His transformations remained as excruciating and draining as ever, so at the first hint of one, he'd retreat to his chambers to suffer in private and rest afterward. During those times, Miss Hawke either wandered the townhouse or read in the library, but her concern for him darkened her gaze more often as the days passed, although her tongue remained as delightfully biting as ever.

At dinner the evening before his natalday, they were just finishing their spice cake when the intense heat of his eighth transformation of the day swamped him. Halting his anecdote about his first soiree mid-sentence, he surged upright, muttered his excuses, then fled to his chambers. He'd barely made it inside before his transformation tore his body apart.

Once human again, Oakmoor panted in a hunched ball before the door for several heartbeats then crawled to the nearest chair and dragged himself onto it. Thank the Goddess these transformations would end tomorrow. His eyes drifting shut, he dozed until a firm knock sounded.

Miss Hawke called through the door, "Open up, your grace. I've brought you tea and sweet biscuits to help you recover."

He sighed. Although he drank tea to be polite, 'twasn't spicy enough for him to actually like it. And he still didn't particularly want Miss Hawke in his chambers. Yet he couldn't spurn her tender concern. He staggered to the door and opened it with a faint smile. "My thanks."

Miss Hawke swept inside and set her laden tray on the tea table. "Sit before you fall down." Once he returned to his chair, she handed him a steaming teacup. "Drink."

He did then smiled at the sweet yet unexpectedly spicy brew.

"Gingyr tea with honey; how well you know me, Miss Hawke." He took another sip. "'Tis spicier than I remember."

Miss Hawke shrugged. "I added a bit of red pepper. I thought you'd enjoy the extra kick."

Oakmoor drank more of Miss Hawke's spicy gingyr tea. He definitely did. She truly knew him well.

Before he could reply, Miss Hawke passed him a full plate. "Have some gingyr sweet biscuits."

He blinked as he took the plate. Odd. "Where did you find these? I don't recall making them."

Her eyes flickering, Miss Hawke stilled. "Your cook must have before she left. Finish your refreshments—you need the energy."

Oakmoor swiftly did so, and his exhaustion eased. Once he set his empty dishes on the tray, he drawled to tease Miss Hawke, "I thought you'd no desire to ever visit my chambers? Yet here you are." The second lady he'd allowed inside.

While he banished Juliet from his mind yet again, Miss Hawke blushed but tsked and collected the tray. "Only because you were unwell. Not for any other reason."

He chuckled. Miss Hawke hadn't glanced at his bed her entire visit. Determined lady. He rose and followed her to the door. "I must thank you for your tender concern." With a tray between them, their passion couldn't go too far and shock her. "In the traditional manner between gentlemen and ladies."

He bent forward and kissed Miss Hawke. He'd intended a gentle kiss, but heat flared in his veins when their lips met. He began devouring her mouth instead, and she whimpered as she returned his kiss with equal hunger. He grasped her shoulders and yanked her closer, grunting when the tray hit his chest. Dear Goddess, what was he doing? He couldn't kiss an innocent young lady so wildly. Yet somehow explosive passion had consumed him like when he kissed Juliet. His nine months of celibacy was surely responsible. Damn Juliet for cursing him to that. Such voracious kisses would shock his innocent future wife. He jerked backward.

Her gaze dark and hazy, Miss Hawke stared at him. Then she gasped, and her cheeks flushed scarlet. Not dropping the tray, she slapped him with such force that the tang of blood filled his mouth. "How *dare* you ravage an innocent girl, you disgusting rakehell?"

Oakmoor rubbed his stinging cheek while Miss Hawke stormed down the hall. She was the second woman who'd ever slapped him—Juliet had been the first in Childes House's garden nine months ago. And Miss Hawke slapped even more fiercely than she punched. Kissing her had definitely been a mistake. She'd no doubt be furious with him for what little time he'd left as human. He must win her forgiveness before his final transformation tomorrow. Being a hideous beast would make it much harder to inspire tender feelings like forgiveness or love. Although he would eventually since Miss Hawke was the lady meant to break his curse.

CHAPTER 16

*J*uliet hurtled downstairs to the kitchen, the empty dishes on her tray clattering. That insufferable beast! He'd spent the past few days constantly flirting with a lady he believed was an innocent. One who was young enough to be his daughter. And then he'd *kissed* her in his chambers when she'd brought him refreshments to help him recover. Apparently, anyone in a skirt would do to satisfy his rapacious masculine lust—even a girl devoted to another.

She growled while she began washing the dishes. Not that she'd done well at pretending to be Miss Hawke. Forever maintaining the younger lady's sweet smiles had been impossible, and barbs kept slipping past her lips, although she'd silenced her more disdainful and knowing ones. But even so, she'd not encouraged Oakmoor to kiss her. She shivered when her treacherous body tingled anew. Despite how much she'd ached for that whenever they were close.

Juliet grimaced as she put away the clean dishes. She never should have brought Oakmoor refreshments even though he'd needed some to help him recover from his draining and agonizing transformation. And she definitely shouldn't have conjured sweet biscuits she'd known he'd like. Not only had he recognized he'd not made them, but he also didn't deserve her wasting her magic on him so frivolously. After days of gathering magical energy from her surroundings and performing no spells except for maintaining her illusion of Miss Hawke, her powers were finally at full strength again. And she'd require every bit of her magical powers to break Oakmoor's beast curse.

She humphed while striding from the kitchen. Although the rakehell duke didn't deserve her help with that either. But she was trapped with him until she broke his curse, and she'd her duty as Calatini's royal witch to consider. She shuddered. His beast curse was truly cruel and not something she'd want her fiercest enemy to endure. Elvaira had clearly wanted Oakmoor to suffer as much as possible for spurning her.

Juliet pursed her lips as she entered her bedchamber and locked the door behind her. Oakmoor's disgraceful behavior toward women made sense given his obsessive first lover had cursed him. He couldn't trust any woman, but he was too passionate to avoid them entirely. So he took lovers, but he never let them close and disposed of them before they'd the power to hurt him.

She began pacing about her luxurious bedchamber. Yet his past didn't excuse Oakmoor ruthlessly kidnapping young Miss Hawke and trapping her with him then devoting himself to charming her. Over the past few days, he'd treated "Miss Hawke" with gentle consideration, entertained her with engaging conversation, cooked delicious meals for her, and always brought her deep-red roses representing passionate love. Oakmoor had never wooed *her* like that. Instead, the disgusting rakehell had given her knowing smirks, fiercely clashed with her, then ravaged her whenever they were alone. Probably because he didn't truly want a lady like her as his wife.

Her chest twisting, she lifted her chin. Not that she wanted to be Oakmoor's wife anyway. Besides, his charm and roses were simply a rakehell's seductive tricks with no love behind them. Oakmoor merely wanted to make her love him so that she could break his curse by agreeing to marry him. She snorted. Yet love and marriage weren't the answer. A curse cast by a vindictive Rhiannon-descendant black witch couldn't be broken by such a simple solution. He *must* have misunderstood the veiled witch's prophecy about that and the lady meant to break his curse.

Juliet hummed. Now that her magical powers were fully recharged, she should examine Oakmoor's copy of the veiled witch's prophecy for insight. She'd hunted for it on her first afternoon trapped in Oakmoor House. Unfortunately, because she'd no magical energy then, she'd been unable to unlock his desk drawers where he surely kept it. And she'd wanted all of her magic back before she'd begun striving to break his curse, so she'd not returned to his study. He'd be suspicious if he caught her prying there. She'd visit tomorrow once he was resting after permanently transforming into a beast.

She opened her wardrobe to change into a nightgown then sighed. Although first, she must resize the attire Oakmoor had provided. To avoid draining her recovering magical energy, she'd used her rusty sewing skills to lengthen and loosen the pieces she'd worn, which had taken ages. After donning her nightgown, she dragged her enchanted satchel out from beneath the bed then gathered the mentha, yarrow, lymongrass oil, and powdered opal for an adapting spell. Mixing everything in a tin bowl, she chanted the singsong incantation until the mixture evaporated into a sparkling mist. Still chanting, she pointed at the open wardrobe, and the mist swept across the bedchamber and engulfed the clothes. Once the mist sank into the fabric, everything shimmered then grew to the proper size.

Not at all lightheaded from her spell, Juliet smiled and returned her bowl to her satchel before shoving it back beneath the bed. Since she'd used a potion and an incantation rather than will to cast her adapting spell, she'd recover what little magical energy she'd used by tomorrow. She slipped into bed and drifted to sleep.

The following morning, she woke refreshed and ready to

begin unraveling Oakmoor's curse. She surged from bed then pulled out her enchanted satchel. She must create an opening charm before she joined him for breakfast. She collected ground peridot, thyme, nettle, a white river stone, and an iron bowl. Gesturing over the bowl and murmuring the incantation, she combined the spell ingredients in the bowl until it became a vivid green. Then she dropped the stone into the bowl, and the magical potion wicked into it, turning it green.

After concealing her satchel beneath the bed once more, Juliet changed into a demure ivory dress, suitable for the girl she was pretending to be but so bland. If 'twouldn't have betrayed her identity, she'd have made her attire more vibrant and modish when resizing them yesterday. She slipped her opening charm into her pocket and headed down to the breakfast room.

When she joined Oakmoor, she gave him her iciest stare to deter his habitual flirting and another kiss. She couldn't risk more of that. She was here to break his curse not to let him seduce her. Yet thanks to her hateful hunger for him, she might succumb if he kissed her again like he had yesterday. Why must she find him so alluring?

His gaze steady over the customary vase of three deep-red roses between them, Oakmoor quirked a rueful smile while he handed her a cup of kahve and a full plate, both glowing with the remnants of a preservation spell to keep them warm until she arrived. "I must apologize for my rakish behavior last night. I never meant for our kisses to explode like that."

Juliet huffed as she stirred a spoonful of sugar into her weak Calatinian kahve. Kisses between them always exploded. Not that she could say as much since she was pretending to be Miss Hawke. Her jaw tightened. And he'd kissed her believing her to be the younger lady, damn him.

Oakmoor sighed. "I'm sorry for upsetting you. And I'm glad you joined me for breakfast. I feared you might hide in your bedchamber the entire day."

She gulped some kahve then began her eggs and bacon. "I

was too hungry to hide." Especially after her spellwork yesterday and today. "Otherwise I might have."

Oakmoor flashed a smooth grin. "Thank the Goddess for your hunger then." He sipped his kahve. "We require time together to talk and settle matters. Although I'm transforming into a beast, I'm not a monster. I want you to be comfortable with me."

Juliet glared at Oakmoor over her forkful of eggs and bacon. He'd never shown such consideration for her as herself. "You expect me to be comfortable with my kidnapper? Especially one who forces his kisses on me when he *knows* I'm devoted to another."

His eyes flickering, Oakmoor studied her. "Again, I apologize." He began his own food. "Please allow me to atone for upsetting you."

She bit into her buttered toast then swallowed and arched a brow. "How? With another kiss? After all, you claimed yesterday they were traditional between gentlemen and ladies." Impudent rakehell.

Oakmoor leaned closer and drawled, "Would you like another kiss?"

Treacherous tingling flooding her, she jerked back and glared harder. "What? No!"

Oakmoor smiled. "Then how about a boon of your choosing? Given enough time, I can find a spell to provide whatever you wish. So ask me for anything, and 'tis yours."

She clenched her fork. Oakmoor's faintly smug smile made her burn to slap him again, even harder than she had last night. And she could perform her own spells. She gritted Miss Hawke's sweet grin. "I'd like my freedom please, your grace."

His vexing smile fading, Oakmoor sipped his kahve. "Anything except that sadly. I'm sorry."

Juliet sniffed as she resumed eating. "So much for your *boon*. And a gentleman actually capable of feeling sorry would never have resorted to kidnapping an innocent young lady and trapping her with him."

Oakmoor's mouth tightened. "I do regret that, but I *had* to. How else am I supposed to break my curse?"

She glared at the obstinate fool. "You could have asked someone much more knowledgeable about magic for help breaking it. The royal witch, perhaps?"

Oakmoor stiffened. "Lady Juliet would never help me. Besides, the veiled witch's prophecy made it clear she wasn't the lady meant to break my curse."

Juliet almost snorted. Not hardly. She matched the requirements Oakmoor had listed even better than Miss Hawke. He just didn't realize it since she'd ensured that no one knew she was Sandro's and Aurora's runaway cousin. She narrowed her eyes at him as she finished her eggs and bacon. "Why wouldn't the royal witch help you?"

Oakmoor cleared his throat. "She just wouldn't. All of court knows how much we dislike each other."

She drained her weak Calatinian kahve and set down her cup with a thunk. She could disregard their mutual dislike and vexing attraction for someone she was honor bound to help. "You're a duke and a royal councilor, so she'd be obliged to help you break your curse."

Oakmoor grunted as he cleared his plate. "Lady Juliet would doubtless say my curse was fitting and refuse to help despite her duty."

Juliet inhaled and clenched her hands in her lap to avoid attacking Oakmoor. How dare he malign her so? "You're an insufferable *idiot*, your grace."

Oakmoor frowned at her. "Why are you so angry at my refusal to consult the royal witch?"

She hissed a steadying breath. If she didn't take care, she'd reveal her identity. Oakmoor was astute, and she'd not been acting much like Miss Hawke. She leaned toward him. "Because your refusal led to you kidnapping me away from the gentleman I love and want to marry."

Oakmoor stared at her for several lengthy moments then sighed. "For both our sakes, you must learn to forget Lord Blaine, my darling."

Her pulse flaring at Oakmoor's continued condescension, Juliet surged to her feet. "I'm not your darling and never will be. *Stop* calling me that."

As she began leaving, Oakmoor leapt upright and grasped her elbow. "Don't go, Miss Hawke. Please. I apologize for upsetting you once again." He sighed. "I owe you an even greater boon now."

Unwanted tingling darting up her arm, she wrenched her elbow free and whirled to face the too suave duke.

But before she could reply, Oakmoor gasped and hunched as if struck, his skin flushing. Then he fell to his knees with a moan as the air became heavy and charged and musky.

Juliet swallowed, and her chest tightened. Oakmoor's final transformation, no doubt.

His body slowly morphing from human to beast, Oakmoor's moans turned to screams while he writhed with tears coursing down his contorted face.

She fisted her hands at her sides to not touch Oakmoor. She could do nothing to help his curse's final manifestation. But, Goddess, his agony was horrible to witness. And this final transformation was much more lengthy than the previous one she'd seen. Damn Elvaira's vindictive cruelty.

Eventually, Oakmoor's transformation ended, and he quieted and quit writhing but remained on the ground panting—now a chimera-like beast with a lion's rugged mane and claws, a goat's curving horns, and a snake's face with human eyes currently clenched shut.

Unable to help herself, Juliet touched his trembling shoulder. "Oakmoor..."

The beast duke winced away. "Don't." Gulping air, he lurched upright then swayed.

She darted beneath Oakmoor's arm before the idiot man could collapse. "You'll never make it up to your chambers without help. You can count letting me help you as my boon, you obstinate fool."

Oakmoor grunted but sagged against her. "Fine."

Juliet helped Oakmoor stagger from the breakfast room. She was panting and trembling from exertion as badly as he was when they reached the stairs. So much further than across a garden alcove, and he weighed the same as a beast as he had before. Plus, his earthy sandalwood scent was making her dizzy. 'Twas stronger than ever with a hint of animal musk beneath it now.

Somehow, she managed to help Oakmoor into his chambers and drop him onto his bed. Then she trod to the kitchen and brewed him some gingyr tea. Gathering her will, she conjured ambrosia to sweeten it. The bee-like melissae's ambrosia could cure any ill and would help him recover faster. She returned to his chambers and poured the restorative tea down his throat despite his grumbled protests.

Juliet left Oakmoor to rest and headed to her bedchamber for a nap of her own. Her stomach rumbling, she woke around noon and leapt from bed. After checking on Oakmoor, who was still slumbering, she hurried to the kitchen and prepared herself a simple luncheon of Varkhoran kahve and rolls stuffed with meat and cheese.

No longer ravenous, she strode to Oakmoor's study to find the veiled witch's prophecy. She sat behind the desk and fingered the deep gouges marring the warm-brown walnut. Oakmoor had clearly suffered a transformation here at least once.

She extracted her opening charm and placed it against the keyhole of the locked drawer. With a click, the drawer unlocked, and she pulled it open. She grinned at the top sheet of paper covered with an oddly familiar smooth script that began, "To break your beast curse..."

Juliet grabbed the veiled witch's prophecy, but before reading it, she glanced at the rest of the locked drawer then froze. Like Oakmoor's handwriting, that carved walnut box was familiar. Extremely familiar. She'd its twin in her enchanted satchel upstairs.

Numbness suffusing her chest, she dropped the prophecy on the desk and seized the walnut box instead. She gasped at her many letters concealed beneath it.

Oakmoor was *Mordred*!

Juliet hissed a breath as fire flared beneath her skin. That, that... devious beast! For nearly two years, he'd deceived her by pretending to be a curious young witch from his duchy. How Oakmoor must have laughed. Especially when she'd expressed sincere concern for him in her recent letters.

His transport box clenched in her fists, she surged upright and hurtled upstairs. Forget about breaking his beast curse. She was going to kill him instead.

CHAPTER 17

Oakmoor was dozing halfway between asleep and awake when his door slammed open and jolted him fully conscious. What?! He jerked upright and gaped at Miss Hawke bursting into his chambers with his transport box gripped in her hands.

Her skin flushed and gaze black, Miss Hawke flung the transport box on the bed beside him. "Care to explain this, *Mordred*?"

He rose and frowned at Miss Hawke. His transport box had been locked inside his desk. She must have used magic to unlock it. And she'd read Juliet's letters too since she knew his given name. His frown darkened. Even Miss Hawke being his future wife didn't permit her to pry into his private matters like that. Or burst into his chambers. Resisting the urge to growl, he asked, "Why were you prying in my desk? You'd no right to read my private correspondence."

Miss Hawke scowled at him. "No right? How dare you say that to *me*? You're a devious rakehell who resorted to kidnapping an innocent young lady."

Oakmoor clenched his hands, wincing when his claws pricked his palms. "'Twas necessary to break my beast curse."

Miss Hawke snorted. "Was it? And was it *necessary* to pretend to be a young witch from your duchy for nearly two years?"

He blinked and scrutinized Miss Hawke. Why did his letters to Juliet infuriate the bubbly young lady so? "Yes, because Lady Juliet never would have replied otherwise, and I needed her help to learn about magic."

Her eyes narrowing to slits, Miss Hawke hissed like a boiling kettle. "You deceiving beast! I should curse you myself. All the hours I spent on those letters."

Oakmoor stiffened. The hours *she* spent? But that meant... His jaw spasmed. No wonder "Miss Hawke" had kept sounding like Juliet. And why he'd imagined kissing her. *And* why his gentle thank-you kiss had exploded. He swallowed a bitter laugh. He should have known that he couldn't desire innocent Miss Hawke like that. Only Juliet bewitched him so. He inhaled. But how and when had she taken Miss Hawke's place? And why? She'd never love and marry him, even to break a vindictive curse. His thoughts still awhirl, he rasped, "Juliet?!"

The maddening witch wearing Miss Hawke's face stilled. Then she huffed. "I suppose 'tis little point in maintaining my illusion. I wasn't good at pretending to be Miss Hawke anyway." She flicked her fingers while muttering an incantation, and the illusion which had allowed her to take Miss Hawke's place vanished.

He glared at Juliet and tightened his fists to remain still. If he moved, he'd strangle the meddling witch. "And you dare complain about *my* deceit? I was just seeking knowledge. You destroyed my only chance to break my curse."

Returning his glare, Juliet clenched her hands on her hips. "I did no such thing. I simply rescued the poor girl you never should have kidnapped. Someone had to protect the innocent Miss Hawke from an unrepentant rakehell like you."

Oakmoor glared harder. What was Juliet implying? "I'd no intention of harming Miss Hawke. I was going to marry her."

Juliet smirked and drawled, "An *honor* to be sure." She leaned toward him. "Kidnapping Miss Hawke was harm enough. She's not the lady you need. If I'd not taken her place, the two of you would be trapped here forever."

His pulse stirred. Instead, he was now trapped here with the biting and bewitching Juliet forever. An equal he didn't need to coddle—a much more stimulating prospect. And he could quit suppressing his uncontrollable hunger for her since he wasn't marrying another. Except she'd not want a hideous beast kissing her. Shoving all that aside, he snapped, "Not hardly. We'd have been free as soon as Miss Hawke broke my curse."

Juliet's smirk sharpened. "Which would never happen. Miss Hawke isn't even a witch, so she could never break a Rhiannon descendant's curse."

He straightened. "Of course Miss Hawke is a witch." He'd ascertained that at the Duchess of Childes's last fete. "Her father is one, and she was familiar with his magical experiments."

Juliet shook her head. "Because Sir Julian Hawke talks about them constantly, not because she's a witch. None of the baronet's children inherited his weak magical powers."

Oakmoor exhaled but set his jaw. Perhaps the power to brighten any room hadn't been literal then. "Magical powers aren't truly needed to break my curse. Miss Hawke just had to fall in love with me and agree to marry me."

Juliet raised her eyes skyward. "Even if love and marriage could break your curse—which I *doubt*—Miss Hawke couldn't help there either. She's already in love with Lord Blaine and would never agree to marry you no matter how long you trapped her here."

He winced then glowered at Juliet. "She'd be more likely to fall in love with me than *you*." Like him, Juliet had always resented their uncontrollable attraction. Not that she'd feel attraction for him now.

Her lips twisting, Juliet tsked. "Why are you obsessed with love and marriage breaking your curse? They'd never be enough to break a powerful curse cast by a Rhiannon descendant. You need a lady who understands magic, which I do."

Oakmoor stalked toward Juliet. Must she be forever so certain she was right? "You may understand magic, but you're *not* the lady in the veiled witch's prophecy." He halted a handbreadth away and scowled down at her. "You don't match her requirements, particularly the one about being a cousin to royalty."

Despite his intimidating scowl, Juliet smirked and arched a brow. "Actually, I do. I'm cousin to both the king *and* queen in the kingdom of my birth."

He inhaled, his scowl fading. From the moment Juliet had arrived in Calatini, her perfect manners and ease at court had made it obvious she'd been born a lady, but cousin to royalty? "Why aren't you the royal witch in your birth kingdom then? And why did their ambassadors in Calatini not recognize you?"

Juliet's face tightened. "'Tis irrelevant."

An ache pierced him. Leaving her birth kingdom had clearly hurt Juliet. No wonder she rarely mentioned her past.

Juliet lifted her chin. "Shall we return to what *is* relevant... breaking your curse?"

Oakmoor nodded but studied Juliet. Despite everything, she appeared sincere. "I'm surprised you're willing to help the deceiving and disgusting rakehell you despise."

Juliet humphed. "If you recall, I've been attempting to help you for the past month. As I've repeatedly told you, 'tis my duty as Calatini's royal witch to help you, no matter how little you deserve it and regardless of how you vex me."

He swallowed as warmth eased his chest. Juliet was invariably so determined and dedicated. "But how can you help? You'll never love and agree to marry me."

Her eyes narrowing, Juliet poked him. "Goddess, why are you such an obstinate fool? I've already told you love and marriage shan't break your curse. No, understanding it shall."

Oakmoor almost growled. He wasn't the only obstinate one.

"And how can you possibly understand a curse you can't even see?"

Juliet pursed her lips. "That does make it more difficult. But the veiled witch's prophecy should provide some insight. And I can scry to see how Elvaira cast her curse. That should be enough for me to unravel it... eventually."

His gaze fixed on Juliet's tempting mouth, and his heart quickened. He could kiss her if he simply bent his head. He tensed. Except his kisses would disgust her now instead of arouse her. He made himself step back and drop into the nearest chair. Weariness swamped him, and his leaden shoulders sagged. "You only have a year before my curse is permanent according to the veiled witch's prophecy."

Juliet frowned. "I hope breaking your curse doesn't take so long. We might kill each other if we're trapped together for an entire year."

Oakmoor couldn't help a wry laugh. True, especially since ravishing each other senseless was no longer a possibility.

Juliet tilted her head and examined him. "We'll discuss this further tomorrow. You look dreadful."

He snorted another laugh, a bitter one this time. "Not surprising. I'm a hideous beast."

Juliet sighed. "Don't be so sensitive. 'Tisn't what I meant. You look exhausted still. Rest for the remainder of the day. I'll bring you dinner later." She smirked at him. "Another reason 'tis good I'm here rather than Miss Hawke. Unlike a sheltered lady like her, I know how to cook thanks to my years traveling with gypsies." With that, she turned and swept from his chambers.

Oakmoor smiled and leaned his heavy head on his chair. Trust Juliet to have the last word. He slowly exhaled. Before she'd left, she'd mentioned how and why she'd taken Miss Hawke's place, but she'd never said exactly when. He shut his eyes as he thought back. Doubtless during the six hours he was setting the veiled witch's intricate wards. At dinner before then, Miss Hawke had been more horrified and less biting. He grimaced. And he'd not imagined kissing her then. He really should have realized that she was Juliet once he had. The real Miss Hawke was too sweet and innocent to attract him, unlike the exotic and spicy witch who did. He suddenly snorted. So Juliet remained the only lady he'd allowed inside his chambers. Damned witch.

As JULIET HAD COMMANDED, Oakmoor spent the remainder of the day resting and devoured the hearty dinner she brought him before returning to bed. The following morning, he awoke around his usual hour, completely refreshed for the first time in eight months. He'd not suffered his curse dreams, probably because Elvaira's curse had fully manifested at last.

He rose and inspected how his body had changed as a chimera-like beast. He'd a lion's heavy mane and sharp claws, although his hands were otherwise human-shaped. He'd a snake's face except for his still-human eyes, and his skin on his face, neck, hands, forearms, and lower legs was scaled too. Finally, he'd a goat's horns curving from his forehead, and his feet were now cloven hooves, which made wearing shoes impossible. Apart from all that, his body was the same as before his transformation, including his size and coloring, down to the touch of gray at his temples.

Shuddering, he turned away from his reflection in the cheval mirror. He dressed like he normally would except without stockings and shoes then headed to the kitchen to cook breakfast.

He was halfway done when Juliet strode into the kitchen. Eyeing him, she said, "Morning. You look better today."

As Juliet deftly retrieved clean dishes, he almost snorted. He really should have suspected "Miss Hawke's" deftness in the kitchen. A lady who'd never cooked before wouldn't have shown that. But Juliet had that experience with the gypsies that she'd mentioned. Shaking his head at his blindness, he poured eggs into the sizzling pan and answered Juliet's unspoken question, "I got my first restful sleep in ages. I'd been suffering curse dreams for months, but they stopped now that I'm fully a beast."

Juliet hummed while placing a basket of rolls on a tray. "Curse dreams?"

Grimacing at the vivid, grotesque images from his recent curse dreams, Oakmoor added a third of the tubers and bacon to her plate then the rest to his. "I dreamt about the evildoing of the creatures Elvaira had cursed me to become as a beast—goats, snakes, and lions. The dreams grew worse the closer I got to my final transformation."

Juliet nodded and set their kahve on her tray. "When exactly did your curse dreams start?"

He added their eggs to their plates. "Eight months ago." He blinked at a sudden realization. "Thirty years to the day since Elvaira seduced me."

Juliet nodded while he carried their plates and she her tray from the kitchen. "Not surprising. Linking the curse to your shared past would strengthen its power. As would the many years it took to manifest." She sighed. "Your beast curse shan't be easy to break."

His stomach tightening, Oakmoor sat beside Juliet in the breakfast room, which he'd not bothered decorating with a vase of deep-red roses today. Juliet wouldn't want flowers representing passionate love from him. "Are you saying you can't? Quite a change from yesterday."

Juliet glared at him while stirring sugar into her kahve. "No, just that it shall require time for me to unravel." She sipped her kahve, a faint frown flickering across her face. "While you were resting yesterday, I reviewed the veiled witch's prophecy. We can discuss my initial thoughts after breakfast."

He frowned as he began his eggs and bacon. Once again the meddling witch had pried without permission and was commanding him about. He exhaled, his frown fading. Yet she'd done both to help him, a rakehell beast she despised. And the sooner they discussed his curse, the sooner she could break it. So he drawled, "Why wait?"

Juliet shook her head. "I want to refer to specific phrases in the prophecy, and I left your copy in your study." She glanced at him. "Do you have a magical workroom? I'll need one while unraveling your curse."

Oakmoor grimaced into his kahve. Made sense, except he'd never set up a magical workroom. "No, I used my study instead. I couldn't risk any gossip spreading about my magical powers."

Her brow furrowing, Juliet eyed him. "Why? Even the most secretive of witches have workrooms in their own homes."

He jerked a shrug. Juliet would smirk at this. "Because my powers appeared thirty years late two years ago, and I couldn't control my constantly fluctuating powers."

Juliet blinked over a forkful of tubers. "*Thirty* years late? No doubt Elvaira's curse was responsible for that too. She probably cast her curse to use your magical powers as fuel."

Oakmoor stilled, his shoulders easing. Juliet wasn't smirking. How unexpected. "I'd never considered that. I didn't possess magic before Elvaira cursed me."

Juliet arched her brows at him. "Were you raised among other witches?" When he shook his head, she continued, "Then 'tis likely you missed the signs of your budding magical powers since you didn't know what to look for and neither did those around you." She shrugged. "We'll know if Elvaira's curse consumed your powers if they stabilize now that 'tis complete."

He smiled and nodded as he finished his eggs and bacon. "I hope they do. 'Tis been frustrating not being able to rely on them." And embarrassing.

Nodding too, Juliet drained her kahve. "I can imagine. Although from what I've seen, you've mastered your magical powers quite well despite their unreliability. You set the veiled witch's intricate wards without any difficulty, and you've performed small magic like preservation spells every day during our confinement."

Oakmoor stared at Juliet. Had she just *complimented* him? Perhaps because he no longer attracted her, she could relax, so her defensive disdain had softened. A pang darted through his chest at Juliet always being civil to him. Her biting barbs were invariably delightful.

Juliet rose and began loading her tray. "Shall we handle the dishes then head to your study?"

He inclined his head and followed Juliet into the kitchen. Once they'd finished the dishes, he said, "Let me show you a potential workroom on the way to my study." He led her to a large room on the ground floor toward the back then waved her inside. "The ancestor who commissioned the ballroom's stained-glass ceiling had this room constructed as well. He enjoyed dabbling with glass."

Her eyes wide, Juliet studied the dome furnace at the center of the large room then the metal tables along the walls and the massive windows. "That explains the glass furnace and metal tables. This shall make an excellent workroom, thank you. Plenty of space, light, and fresh air."

Oakmoor smiled as he escorted Juliet down the hall. "I'm glad. 'Tis been generations since anyone has used it. If you require anything changed to better suit you, let me know."

In his study, he sat beside Juliet before his desk so they could review the veiled witch's prophecy together rather than taking his usual seat. Then he asked, "Your initial thoughts?"

Juliet pointed at the beginning of the prophecy. "The first three sentences—'To break your beast curse, a special lady you must find. Cousin to royalty most wise she'll be. Dark of hair and eye with the power to brighten any room.'—are meant to identify the lady you need to break your curse." She smirked at him. "And I clearly match all that better than young Miss Hawke. My hair and eyes are darker, I actually possess magic, and I'm cousin to more members of royalty."

He gripped his knees to remain still, his claws digging into him. If only he could kiss the smug smirk from Juliet's lips. But he was a beast now. "Fine. You're the *perfect* lady I need. Quit belaboring it."

Juliet chuckled and pointed at the end of the prophecy. "The final sentence—'But be warned, you must find your lady before your natalday when your curse becomes complete, and she'll have from then until your next natalday to break it, or you'll remain a beast forever.'—is about the timing of your curse: when you needed to find me and how long I have to break it. We've fulfilled that so far, and I'll definitely break your curse within a year."

Oakmoor grunted. At least Juliet was confident of that. "And what about the middle sentence? 'Possessing love so strong and true that she'd agree to marry a chimera-like beast and can reverse your past lover's bitter hatred.' 'Tis *plainly* referring to love and marriage."

Her mouth twisting, Juliet sighed. "It describes the requirements to break your curse, although I've not unraveled its exact meaning yet. But I'm certain it doesn't mean literal love and marriage." When he began to argue that, she interjected, "The part about marriage is phrased 'would' not 'will', so 'tis obviously hypothetical. And the part about love doesn't specify 'tis for you."

He suppressed a snort. The entire prophecy was about him, so why wouldn't it be? But Juliet would never concede that, so instead he asked, "Now that you've reviewed the prophecy, what's the next step?"

Juliet drummed her fingers on his desk. "I must learn the details of how Elvaira cast her curse. I'll need some of your hair to cast a scrying spell."

A chill skittered across his skin. Elvaira had used his hair to cast her curse. "No. I can tell you the details you need. I remember that devastating evening well."

Juliet frowned at him. "You telling me isn't enough. I need to *see* how she constructed her curse to best break it."

Oakmoor shook his head. Both clever and knowledgeable,

Juliet was skilled at creating innovative spells and understood magic well enough that she could manage with just his details. "No."

Juliet huffed. "You let the veiled witch use your hair or blood to create that prophecy, didn't you?"

He grimaced but nodded. Only because he'd been desperate, and the veiled witch had needed his blood to create her prophecy. Juliet didn't need a scrying spell; she was simply being overparticular. "That was different."

Her gorgeous eyes sparking, Juliet scowled at him. "Yes, *she* didn't offer to break your curse." Juliet blew a sigh. "Don't be a paranoid idiot, Oakmoor."

Heat flaring at Juliet's insult, he leapt upright. "We've talked enough. Shall we set up your workroom now?"

Juliet exhaled but nodded and collected the prophecy then rose too. After she retrieved an enchanted satchel from her bedchamber that contained her magical supplies, he fetched and carried those as well as the furniture until everything in her workroom was arranged how she wanted it. Then before she could press him about her scrying spell again, he excused himself to cook dinner.

Over the following few days, he continued to refuse to allow Juliet to perform a scrying spell on him, but he recounted the evening Elvaira had cursed him in thorough detail several times. And he described exactly how his body had changed beyond what Juliet could see with him dressed. But despite their lengthy discussions, Juliet made no progress unraveling the prophecy's one sentence about breaking his curse. Perhaps she truly did need that scrying spell.

So at breakfast four days after his natalday, Oakmoor grimaced over his near empty plate and muttered, "Very well, Juliet. You can have some of my hair for your scrying spell."

CHAPTER 18

$\mathcal{A}$t Oakmoor's announcement, Juliet gulped the weak Calatinian kahve she'd been about to sip and burned her mouth. The paranoid idiot had agreed to a scrying spell at last! Now she could finally make progress unraveling his beast curse. She beamed at him. "I'll collect your hair after we handle the dishes and cast my scrying spell this morning. I should have a much better idea how to break your curse by luncheon."

Oakmoor grunted and ate the last of his eggs, bacon, and tubers. "I hope so."

She almost laughed as she finished her breakfast too. How like a man to doubt her. She'd show him. "I know so. Seeing how Elvaira constructed your curse should clarify the meaning of that sentence in the veiled witch's prophecy about breaking it."

Once they'd washed and put away the dishes, she beckoned Oakmoor. "Bend down so I can collect some hair." She smiled when he sighed but bent until his almond-brown mane was within reach. Her pulse stirring at his earthy sandalwood scent, she pinched a lock of his hair and cut it using her will. Then she grinned at him. "All done. And entirely painless."

His gaze on her mouth, Oakmoor grimaced then straightened and stepped back. "I suppose."

Juliet inhaled and resisted the urge to lick her lips. The rake-hell duke was clearly imagining kissing her. He'd probably not been celibate for over a week since he'd first arrived at Calatini's court. And he'd always kissed her whenever they drew so close. Tingling flooded her, and she swallowed. Kissing him as a chimera-like beast should repel her, but it didn't. He was still Oakmoor. Damn his irresistible allure.

She muttered, "I'd best get started." Then she whirled away and swept from the kitchen.

She relaxed and smiled when she strode into the magical workroom Oakmoor had given her. 'Twas truly the most perfect workroom—even better than hers at the palace. This room was around twice as large, and its massive windows filled the room with light and fresh air. Plus, the glass furnace was fascinating and could be used to create some unique spells. Perhaps Oakmoor would use this room as his magical workroom after she left. Without Elvaira's curse, his magic likely wouldn't be erratic, so he'd have no reason to hide it.

Juliet shook her head as she gathered her massive scrying bowl and other spell ingredients from the shelves Oakmoor had arranged for her. Whether he used this workroom later was none of her concern. Breaking his curse was, so she must concentrate on her scrying spell.

Once everything was laid out on the metal table closest to the windows, she poured the unicorn water into her scrying bowl then stirred in eyebright, thyme, powdered moonstone, and colloidal silver while murmuring the scrying incantation. The magical mixture began emitting a redolent icy steam, and she added Oakmoor's hair to set the focus, which made the steam thicken. She swirled her hand over her scrying bowl as she finished the incantation. Then she leaned over and peered into the steaming bowl to see the evening Elvaira had cursed Oakmoor.

Yet the icy steam didn't coalesce into images like it should.

She frowned and directed her will at the steam, but it remained thick and blank. She redoubled her will and belted the scrying incantation twice more while swirling her hand over her scrying bowl. However, the magical mixture continued to show nothing. She nearly swore. No doubt the veiled witch's wards were responsible for this.

She jerked out of the icy steam when Oakmoor cleared his throat behind her and said, "I brought you some tea and rolls stuffed with meat and cheese for luncheon. How's the scrying going?"

Her head whirling from jerking out of her intense spell, Juliet glared at Oakmoor. Luncheon already? That explained her light-headedness and hollow stomach. She huffed but accepted the plate and teacup he offered her. "Terrible. My scrying spell hasn't shown anything. 'Tis all your fault. And the veiled witch's."

Oakmoor frowned. "What do you mean?"

She devoured one of the stuffed rolls then grumbled, "That dratted seer's wards are so incredibly powerful that they're blocking my scrying spell."

Oakmoor frowned harder. "Wards don't usually do that, do they?"

Juliet sipped the tea sweetened with honey Oakmoor had brought. Perfect for helping her recover energy after her spell-work. "Not usually, no." She sighed. "'Tis doubtless a consequence of the power required to prevent *anyone* from entering or leaving the townhouse until your curse is broken. But the veiled witch should have known I'd need to perform scrying spells to understand your curse and taken that into account when creating her wards."

Still frowning, Oakmoor stiffened. "What shall you do now?"

She sighed again. "I'll attempt stronger scrying spells. I began with a basic one, but a stronger one should penetrate the veiled witch's wards." Hopefully. "I'll require more of your hair though."

Oakmoor slowly nodded. "Of course."

After she finished luncheon, she collected another lock from Oakmoor's mane then shooed him from her workroom. She used her will to cast a cleansing spell on the magical mixture to leave behind pure unicorn water in her scrying bowl. She gathered the same spell ingredients from before plus a vial of faedust. Fae created the iridescent powder to enhance their enchantments, and its concentrated power could strengthen any spell.

Yet her scrying spell remained stubbornly blank the entire afternoon. Dratted veiled witch.

Shortly before dinner, Juliet quit attempting her scrying spell. She purified her unicorn water once more then tidied her workroom. She'd attempt an even stronger spell tomorrow.

To cheer herself after her frustrating day, she changed into a modish evening gown in her favorite color. She grinned at the deep-amethyst silk as she applied her gingyr scent. Thank the Goddess she'd used another adapting spell to make her attire vibrant and modish once she'd revealed her identity.

When she joined Oakmoor downstairs, he waved her into the family dining room. "Would you care for a spiritpunch before dinner? I brewed sparkling gingyr this afternoon—quickening the fermentation with magic, obviously—so I could enjoy my favorite spiritpunch tonight."

Juliet smiled but blushed as she sat in her usual seat. Oakmoor truly adored gingyr. No wonder he'd always wanted to kiss her. "I'd enjoy a spiritpunch."

Oakmoor deftly mixed their drinks then handed her a cold copper mug. "A gingyr buck."

She hummed as she sipped the spicy yet sweet and tart spiritpunch. Not surprising Oakmoor adored it. "'Tis delicious."

Oakmoor nodded while he savored a swallow of gingyr buck. "I'm glad you like it." He chuckled. "I should have begun serving spiritpunches before dinner once you revealed your identity. I enjoy them, and you're no innocent young miss who can only drink sparkling wine at most."

Juliet smirked at Oakmoor over her copper mug. "Yet another reason 'tis good I'm not Miss Hawke. I'll enjoy trying your spiritpunch concoctions."

Oakmoor grinned. "Do you have a particular one you prefer?"

She paused for a moment. Her favorite spiritpunch was from Varkhora, although 'twasn't unheard of in Calatini. She inhaled then admitted, "Gingyr-orenge spriss."

Oakmoor's brows arched beneath his goat's horns. "An exotic choice. You must like gingyr too then."

Juliet shrugged. "I'd not wear it as my scent if I didn't." To distract Oakmoor from her favorite spiritpunch, she asked, "Would you mind if we start the first course now? I'm ravenous after all my spellwork today."

Oakmoor rose and gestured for her to remain seated when she moved to follow. "I can fetch everything. You enjoy your gingyr buck." He left then soon returned with whitekrab soup and rolls.

While they ate their soup, she said to keep Oakmoor distracted, "I'd no better success this afternoon with my scrying spells. I must strengthen them more—perhaps a stronger link to you might help. Could I use both your hair and blood tomorrow?"

Oakmoor grimaced. "If you must."

Juliet grimaced as well. "I must. I *need* to see how Elvaira constructed your curse." Too bad the veiled witch had made doing that so complicated.

JULIET COLLECTED Oakmoor's hair and blood after breakfast the following morning then hurried to her workroom to perform another scrying spell. To further strengthen her spell, she added mandrake and bay leaf in addition to his blood. Yet the icy steam remained as blank as ever.

Several hours later, she drummed her fingers on the metal

table as she glowered at her worthless scrying spell. What else could strengthen it and make it work? Maybe if she linked it to Elvaira somehow. She didn't possess anything with a magical link to the dead black witch, but she could add spell ingredients that represented her.

When Oakmoor brought her luncheon, she explained her lack of progress and her plans. After she devoured her meal, he reluctantly allowed her to collect more hair and blood before leaving her to attempt yet another scrying spell.

That afternoon, she added feverfew to represent a gypsy's traveling life, nutmeg to represent a gypsy witch's powers, and powdered black quartz to represent a black witch's evil. But despite the added link to Elvaira, the scrying spell still showed nothing.

An hour before dinner, Juliet purified her unicorn water and tidied everything then paced about her workroom. She'd only one more way to strengthen her scrying spell—Oakmoor's full name. Not that she knew it, and 'twasn't likely to succeed since names possessed less of a magical link than hair or blood. But she had to try it nonetheless.

So when Oakmoor handed her a gingyr-orenge spriss, she described her continued failure then asked, "What's your full name? 'Tis the one thing I've not used in my scrying spells."

Oakmoor tensed. "Mordred Thyme Tremblay."

Fire kindled beneath her skin. Oakmoor had used his *own name* in his deceitful letters? The smug beast. No doubt he'd snickered every time he signed his letters. Making such a fool of the illustrious royal witch he'd once seduced would surely have delighted the insufferable rakehell. Her burning chest constricted. How could she have never realized he was Mordred? The "young witch" from Oakmoor had been too smoothly charming to be anyone else.

Her favorite spiritpunch before her lips untasted, she glared at Oakmoor. "Risky to sign your own name on letters where you were pretending to be someone else, wouldn't you say?"

His ice clinking, Oakmoor swirled his orenge spiritpunch with a wry smile. "Not particularly. I became duke so young that even *I* barely remember my given names, and I certainly never think of myself as them."

Juliet clenched her wine glass. 'Twould be rude to fling her gingyr-orenge spriss in Oakmoor's face. "But why use them at all? To mock me for being deceived?"

Oakmoor winced. "No. I knew I had to approach you as someone else. Even if you'd agreed to instruct me, we'd have ended up quarreling then ravishing each other more than we'd have discussed magic." He shifted in his seat. "But I wanted part of the letters to be true, I suppose."

She snorted as she finally lifted her wine glass to her lips. Men could be so obtuse. Nothing about Oakmoor's letters had been true. Except for his curiosity about everything regarding magic—the reason she'd always enjoyed his letters. Her chest eased. And at least he'd not signed his names to mock her. She sipped her gingyr-orenge spriss then hummed at the bubbly and refreshingly bittersweet yet spicy spiritpunch. "This is excellent." Although 'twould be better with Varkhoran sparkling wine.

Oakmoor relaxed and grinned at her. "It is, isn't it?" Then he asked, "Despite your unsuccessful scrying spells, how do you like your workroom so far?"

Juliet smiled into her gingyr-orenge spriss. "'Tis wonderful. Thanks for letting me use it."

Oakmoor inclined his head. "My pleasure. You're attempting to break my curse, after all."

She and Oakmoor kept their conversation light for the rest of dinner as well as at breakfast the following morning. She'd revealed too much over the past week, and plainly Oakmoor felt the same.

She included Oakmoor's full name in her scrying spell that day, but as she'd feared, it didn't help. However, she still attempted to get her scrying spell to work the entire day. Yet as she left her workroom to dress for dinner, she had to admit defeat.

So over their broiled salmon and creamed spinach, she told Oakmoor, "I can't get my scrying spells to work through the veiled witch's wards." She worried her lip. "You have your linked communication mirror for the council, don't you?" Councilors received one of thirteen linked communication mirrors so they could meet or contact the king and queen when the council wasn't in session.

Oakmoor arched a brow as he cut his salmon. "In my study."

Juliet sighed. "Tomorrow, I'll attempt to use it to call King Devon and Queen Kiera to ask if they can contact the veiled witch." Only the dratted seer could explain how to work around her incredibly powerful wards.

Oakmoor frowned. "Given how your scrying spells failed, shall my communication mirror work?"

She sighed again and lifted a shoulder. "Since your communication mirror is linked to King Devon and Queen Kiera's, I *might* be able to penetrate the wards. And I can better strengthen their enchantment because I created them." 'Twas one of her duties as Calatini's royal witch. She narrowed her eyes at Oakmoor. "But I want you to help me cast the spell. I'll need all the power I can get to penetrate the wards."

After breakfast the following morning, Oakmoor brought his linked communication mirror to her workroom, then she and Oakmoor attempted to call King Devon and Queen Kiera. But like with her scrying spells, his mirror remained white and blank no matter how she strengthened the spell.

When Oakmoor left to prepare luncheon, Juliet paced about her workroom. So even contacting the veiled witch wasn't a possibility. What *else* could she try to see exactly how Elvaira constructed her curse? She must find some way, or she'd never understand it enough to break it, and she'd be trapped here with Oakmoor forever.

She paced and pondered the whole afternoon, reviewing all

the spells she knew to reveal the past. Yet none of them would work since the wards prevented them from contacting anything outside the townhouse. Damn the veiled witch for creating this impossible situation.

Then while talking with Oakmoor at dinner, Juliet froze and scrutinized him. *He'd* seen Elvaira cast the curse. If they shared memories using a mind sharing spell, she could see it too. Although as an untrained witch unaware of his powers, he mightn't have seen all the details she needed. Yet 'twas better than nothing.

She swallowed. Performing such an intimate spell with Oakmoor wouldn't be comfortable. Plus, she'd have to take care to not inadvertently reveal her secrets or pry into his. And a mind sharing spell might inflame their unwanted attraction too. Surely she could find another way.

After dinner, Juliet desperately reviewed all the spells she knew yet again. Maybe, just maybe, she could double the power of her scrying spell if she used both her scrying bowl and her scrying hand mirror. If she included all her other spell enhancements and had Oakmoor help like he had today, it *might* just be enough to penetrate the wards. Please, Goddess.

The following morning, she asked Oakmoor to join her in her workroom to perform the doubled scrying spell. Once she'd collected his hair and blood then laid out the many spell ingredients she'd need, she extracted her scrying hand mirror from her enchanted satchel.

Oakmoor leaned forward, his eyes fixed on the silver hand mirror. "Are those gentians adorning the back?"

Juliet stiffened. Of course Oakmoor recognized the trumpet-shaped alpine flowers even though most in Calatini wouldn't. His duchy contained the start of the D'vark Mountains, and Oakmoor Castle was nestled against them. He'd probably explored the mountains often as a boy.

Oakmoor reached out and caressed the mirror's purple gentians. "Aren't they blue rather than purple?"

She suppressed a wince. Not in Varkhora, they weren't. There, and only there, gentians were a deep purple, the rich color she'd always adored. 'Twas why she rarely let others see the scrying hand mirror Mother had given her. She swallowed and studied Oakmoor. What could she say to conceal her past?

CHAPTER 19

Oakmoor almost frowned at Juliet's unusual still silence. Why had him asking about the purple gentians on her scrying hand mirror upset her? He scrutinized the lovely mirror gripped in her hand. And where had he heard of purple gentians before?

Her face tight, Juliet lifted her chin. "The flowers adorning my mirror are irrelevant."

He studied Juliet and hummed. She'd looked much the same when she'd said leaving her birth kingdom was irrelevant. Clearly, her scrying hand mirror was related to her past before traveling with gypsies that she never mentioned. He arched a brow. "They don't appear irrelevant to you."

Juliet glared at him. "Don't be ridiculous." She pointed at the floor behind her. "Stand there and send me your power like yesterday so I can perform the doubled scrying spell."

Oakmoor sighed as he stood directly behind Juliet. Those purple gentians were definitely important, although 'twas plain she'd no intention of sharing why because she hated discussing private matters as much as he did. He laid his hands on Juliet's shoulders and muttered the power sharing incantation, his body hardening like usual at holding the bewitching witch. Being so close and inhaling her spicy gingyr scent without kissing her was painful.

While he shoved his power through his palms to combine with hers, Juliet added her many spell ingredients to the unicorn water in her scrying bowl and loudly chanted the scrying incantation. The magical mixture began emitting steam that thickened when she set the focus by adding his hair and blood while speaking his full name. Repeating her lengthy incantation, Juliet swirled her scrying hand mirror facedown in the steam, which started shining like the sun through morning mist.

Once she finished her incantation, Juliet flipped her mirror then leaned over and peered into its glowing glass and her steaming scrying bowl. He kept sending her power as she poured her will into the shining steam to make it coalesce into images. Yet it remained thick and blank.

Eventually, Juliet withdrew from the steam and released her scrying spell. She growled, "Damn that dratted seer."

Lightheaded from sending Juliet so much energy, Oakmoor released his power sharing spell then jerked his hands from her shoulders and lurched several paces away. "No success obviously."

Her hands clenched on her hips, Juliet glowered at her no longer steaming scrying bowl and blank scrying hand mirror. "Obviously."

He leaned against the glass furnace and gulped air to help himself recover. "What shall you attempt now that even a doubled scrying spell has failed?"

Juliet snapped her fingers and muttered a cleansing spell to purify the unicorn water. "Not another scrying spell. The veiled witch's wards have made them impossible. We're completely blocked from the outside world until I break your curse."

Oakmoor straightened as his head finally quit whirling. "Perhaps you can unravel how to break my curse without seeing how Elvaira cast it."

Juliet pounded her fist on the metal table beside her scrying bowl. "No. I *need* to see that to truly understand your curse." She whirled to face him, her eyes narrow. "But we've another spell we can attempt that only requires the two of us—a mind sharing spell."

He gaped at Juliet. Was she *mad*? "A mind sharing spell?"

Juliet jerked a nod. "Yes. Since you saw Elvaira cast your curse, if we share your memory of that evening, I should be able to see enough of the details I need."

Oakmoor stalked toward Juliet. Was she purposely being patronizing? "I understand that. I'm not an idiot." He halted before her. "But mind sharing spells are notoriously difficult to cast and require both trust and aligned minds. How do you expect the two of *us* to cast one?" He sneered and gestured at her scrying hand mirror. "You can't even share why purple gentians are important."

Juliet scowled up at him. "What makes you think they are?"

He snorted a sardonic laugh. Juliet must believe him blind as well as stupid. "Your tight face and refusal to discuss them prove they are. Exactly like you refuse to discuss your birth kingdom."

Juliet straightened rigidly upright and thrust up her jaw. "As if you're any better. You use your overly suave charm and empty kisses to avoid discussing matters of any substance. The one part of your past you've shared with me is Elvaira cursing you, but only once you were forced to in order to break it."

Unable to resist, Oakmoor caressed Juliet's set jaw. If he wasn't a beast, he'd kiss her hard disdain into fiery passion. She'd not call his kisses empty then.

Juliet inhaled and shivered, doubtless at his claw grazing her.

He shuddered, yanking his hand from Juliet's soft skin before he succumbed to his primal hunger for her. Even Juliet would scream at a beast kissing her. He swallowed. "I'd be a liar if I denied I was any better about sharing private matters. Which is why us performing a mind sharing spell is mad."

Juliet glared and crossed her arms beneath her chest. "We haven't a choice if I'm to break your curse."

His gaze fixed on Juliet's tempting curves, Oakmoor stepped back until he couldn't touch her. "There's always a choice."

Juliet raised her eyes skyward. "And this one is either perform the mind sharing spell or stay trapped in your townhouse forever with you remaining a beast. Don't you want to be human again?"

He glowered at Juliet. Maddening witch. "Of course I do, but us performing a mind sharing spell is impossible if we can't even discuss private matters."

Juliet huffed. "You want us to discuss private matters? Fine. Purple gentians are important because they're only native to the Varkhora Mountains."

Oakmoor glanced at Juliet's scrying hand mirror on the metal table behind her. Ah yes, the Varkhoran ambassador's wife had mentioned purple gentians at a garden party years ago. *That* was where he'd heard of them before. He turned back to Juliet and drew a sharp breath. She did possess the same olive skin and dark-brown hair and eyes as Ambassador Rossi and his wife. How had he never noticed that before?

He leaned toward Juliet. "You're from Varkhora?" The largest of the twelve kingdoms east of Calatini, Varkhora was a mountain kingdom peopled by fierce warriors known for their protective nature, resilience in battle, and patriarchal society. Their court was also known for its martial pomp and spartan attire as well as the gentlemen always carrying draklizards on their shoulder and ladies faebirds. Very different from Calatini, yet Juliet had fit in here from the first, unlike Ambassador Rossi and his wife who'd lived in Calatini for over four decades but still didn't.

Her lips twisting, Juliet nodded. "Now you know why I'm not my birth kingdom's royal witch despite being cousin to both King Alessandro and Queen Aurora. Women aren't allowed such high positions in Varkhora. Their purpose is to bear children for their husband—preferably sons—and to manage his household. They can't even own property or live independently since they belong to their male relatives. And they must be demure and subservient at all times."

He hummed. How Juliet would have despised all that. She was too strong, driven, and fiercely proud. More like a Varkhoran man was expected to be rather than a woman. His chest squeezed at the oppression Juliet must have suffered growing up. He swallowed and shook his head. "Your birth kingdom may produce Damensea's fiercest warriors, but they're fools to deny women like you the chance to become who they're meant to be."

Juliet relaxed and smiled at him then drawled, "I've always thought so."

Oakmoor grinned back. Despite her subservient upbringing, or possibly because of it, Juliet's delightfully biting tongue and bold spirit had remained indomitable. "I suppose having to be demure and subservient was why you left Varkhora."

Juliet's smile tightened again. "Partly. I was also fleeing the betrothal Father had arranged to advantageously dispose of his otherwise-worthless daughter."

He frowned. What sort of gentleman had Juliet's father chosen for the defiant daughter who'd surely confounded a prominent Varkhoran lord? From her tone, her erstwhile betrothed had been cruel, old, or repulsive... or perhaps all three.

Yet before he could ask, Juliet waved a hand and said, "But enough about that. We should return to our current predicament —breaking your beast curse. Have we discussed enough private matters to attempt a mind sharing spell now?"

Oakmoor snorted and arched his brows. "Not hardly. All you shared was that you're from Varkhora, and not because you wanted to tell me, but to prove a point. And I shared nothing at all." When Juliet scowled at him, he flashed a smooth smile that likely wasn't the least charming on his beast face. "I'd best go prepare our luncheon. Excuse me."

As he turned to leave, Juliet flung at his back, "Coward."

Fire flaring beneath his skin, he whirled to face her again. "*What* did you say?"

Juliet surged toward him. "You heard me." She poked his chest. "You say we must be able to share private matters before we can attempt a mind sharing spell. But you're too scared to share anything, even though you know I need to see your memories of Elvaira cursing you to break your curse."

Burning once more to yank Juliet against him and kiss her to silence that biting disdain of hers, Oakmoor shoved aside her hand instead. "I'm not scared. I'm simply not interested in sharing anything."

Her gorgeous eyes glinting, Juliet smirked. "Because you're scared."

He swallowed a growl. Must Juliet twist his words? "Because I'm a private person."

Juliet smirked harder. "A *scared* person, rather."

Oakmoor growled then snapped, "No, one unaccustomed to sharing private matters. I became the Duke of Oakmoor when I was four, and my elderly guardian barely spoke two words to me every fortnight. The servants who raised me saw me as their duke, so they didn't encourage intimacies. Then when I came to court, everyone was still only interested in the duke, not the man beneath."

Juliet quirked a brow. "Probably because the too suave duke was all you'd let anyone see. All the other dukes in Calatini possess wives, family, and friends who care about them. Even King Devon and Queen Kiera possess that. You don't because you never reveal your true self."

He fisted his hands at his sides. How dare Juliet act so superior? "As if you do. No one in Calatini knows you as anything but our royal witch. I doubt anyone else even knows you're from Varkhora."

Juliet nodded but shrugged. "They don't. I couldn't risk Father or King Cesare finding me."

Oakmoor frowned. Why would the previous Varkhoran king, King Alessandro's elder brother, have pursued their runaway cousin? Unless King Cesare had been the gentleman her father had betrothed her to—an interesting choice for a defiant daughter. And not old or physically repulsive either.

Juliet smiled and leaned toward him. "For two people unaccustomed to sharing, we're making a remarkable start. Maybe a mind sharing spell isn't so impossible after all, hmm?"

He shook his head and sighed. Stubborn witch. If they attempted such a spell, they'd break their minds long before Juliet saw the details she needed. He turned and headed toward the door once more. "I'll return with luncheon shortly."

To PREVENT Juliet from further pressing him about the mind sharing spell, Oakmoor left as soon as he'd brought her luncheon then retreated to his study and locked the door. Not that the lock would halt Juliet if she was truly determined since she could use magic to unlock it, but courtesy would usually make her respect his desire for privacy.

And at dinner that evening, he used all the tricks he'd learned at court as a rakehell duke and the Minister of Foreign Relations—except for flirting which would fail coming from a beast—to keep their conversation away from private matters. He discussed their meal, talked about his mishaps maintaining the townhouse without servants, and told diverting anecdotes about past and present court intrigues. Juliet chuckled throughout dinner, but her lips were pursed when she retired for the evening. Him keeping everything light plainly irritated her, but at least she never mentioned the mind sharing spell.

Over their eggs, bacon, and tubers the following morning, Juliet eyed him and said, "Since your curse has been complete for over a week now, we should test your magical powers to see if they're more reliable."

He sipped his kahve. Having reliable magic he could control would be a relief. And as the most illustrious witch in Calatini, Juliet was the ideal witch to test his magical powers. He smiled at her. "Sounds good."

In her workroom after breakfast, Juliet waved for him to sit on the sofa along the back wall. "I'll start with casting an aura spell to examine the motes in your aura indicating magical powers. You'd a few when I cast one during the Islaye's illusion evening to check you for inactive magic, but they were so faint that I assumed they were a trick of the light. If Elvaira's curse was consuming your powers, they should be brighter now."

Oakmoor slowly nodded. So an aura spell had been the spell she'd cast on him after his first transformation. No wonder she'd looked drained. 'Twas fortunate he'd requested refreshments to help her recover.

Juliet extracted her Varkhoran hand mirror then sat beside him. "I'll transfer my aura spell to my scrying hand mirror so that you can see it too since you aren't a Rhiannon descendant and can't cast your own." She grimaced. "Although even if you were, reading your own aura is challenging, so I might have needed to do so regardless."

He nodded again. Being near blind to your own aura made sense since you viewed the world through it. 'Twas too close to you, and you forgot 'twas there. "Go ahead."

Juliet drew a breath then flicked her fingers and murmured her aura spell, and he shifted in his seat as it pricked his skin like a swarm of inquisitive melissae. Then she humphed, her lips wry. "Elvaira's curse was definitely consuming your magical powers. No way I'd believe your motes a trick of the light now. They're almost as bright as a Rhiannon descendant's." She swirled her hand over her scrying hand mirror and turned it to face him. "See."

Oakmoor peered into the mirror at his glowing yellow aura with many bright ivory motes swirling inside it. 'Twas dazzling. What was Juliet's like? Surely she was skilled enough to read her own. He shifted the scrying mirror until he could see them both, then he inhaled at her rich red aura swirling with twice as many, even brighter ivory motes. As gorgeous as her exotic beauty and powerful air that had bewitched him from the evening they'd met.

Panting, Juliet flicked her fingers again, and the aura spell in her scrying mirror faded. She sagged against the sofa. "Goddess, aura spells are draining. I shouldn't perform more magic today, and I'm ravenous."

He leapt upright. "I'll bring you some food. Rest here." He hurried to the kitchen and fetched a plate of gingyr sweet biscuits. When he returned to her workroom, Juliet was still on the sofa, caressing the purple gentians on the back of her scrying hand mirror. His chest twisting at her obvious nostalgia, he sat beside her and offered her the plate. "I'm surprised you risked keeping that scrying mirror since it betrays you're from Varkhora."

Juliet devoured several gingyr sweet biscuits then sighed. "I couldn't bear leaving it behind." She caressed the purple gentians again. "Mother gave it to me on my sixteenth natalday because I adore purple gentians. Their rich color has always been my favorite—so strong and vibrant. And unlike the amethyst faebird she gave me when I was fourteen, I could actually bring this mirror with me. It could withstand a traveling life and contained no magic that could be used to trace me. I just had to ensure that people rarely saw it. Not that most recognize gentians or know purple ones are only found in Varkhora."

Oakmoor clenched his hands to not pull Juliet into his arms. Despite her fraught relationship with her father, she clearly missed her mother terribly. And her faebird too from the throb in her voice. Instead, he said to comfort her, "You're fortunate to have such a token from one of your parents. I've nothing like that from mine. I only knew them from their moving portrait that Father had commissioned for their wedding and the stories the servants would sometimes tell about them."

Her gaze darkening, Juliet touched his arm. "Your guardian never spoke of them?"

Tingling at Juliet's touch, he nevertheless snorted. That

would have required Bedivere to have spoken to *him*, which his elderly paternal cousin had never liked. "No."

Juliet swallowed and lowered her hand. "Oh." Her gaze fell to the scrying mirror in her lap, and she cleared her throat. "I was thinking that I could instruct you on magic while we're confined together. I'm certain my letters helped, but you need in-person instruction to fully master your magical powers. Besides, other than unraveling your curse, I've little else to do."

Warmth flooded him. The industrious and clever Juliet *would* be bored with so little to occupy her. Yet for her to offer to instruct him after he'd deceived her with his Mordred letters was unexpectedly generous. Without thinking, he pressed a kiss against her palm. "I'll enjoy that. Thank you."

Juliet shivered and snatched free her hand. "Of course you shall. Your desperation for knowledge was why you stooped to writing me those deceitful letters."

Oakmoor winced. He shouldn't have forgotten himself and kissed Juliet. Not only did she despise him for seducing her years ago and deceiving her with those letters, but she also could never desire him as a hideous beast, even against her will. She was only determined to break his curse because she felt 'twas her duty as Calatini's royal witch, not because she wanted or loved him.

CHAPTER 20

After breakfast the following morning, Juliet sat across from Oakmoor with a cool smile. Please let her instructing him on magic encourage him to share further private matters and eventually agree to perform a mind sharing spell. Otherwise, she'd never understand his curse enough to break it. Yet the obstinate man was determined to be unreasonable.

She laced her hands together on the metal table. "To evaluate your current skills, I'll have you cast various spells, beginning with easier ones and getting progressively harder." When Oakmoor nodded, she said, "Start with a light spell."

Nodding again, Oakmoor created a ball of light then kept casting the spells she requested for the entire morning. For someone who'd learned from books and letters alone, he performed remarkably well. But he was panting and his eyes were weary when he finished conjuring faedust several hours later, so she waved for him to relax. He'd drain himself if he cast more spells, although luncheon would help him recover.

She smiled at Oakmoor. "Excellent job. I've a good idea of your skills now, so I can begin your instruction tomorrow."

Oakmoor chuckled and smoothed back his damp mane. "After that grueling evaluation, I'm grateful not to begin today."

Juliet grinned. To continue encouraging Oakmoor to share, she said in a purposely light voice, "I felt much the same after Ceija evaluated my magical powers."

Oakmoor tilted his head. "Ceija?"

Not looking at Oakmoor, Juliet tidied her workroom while she explained, "Ceija Lovari, the head of the gypsy family I traveled with for years. She taught me all the spells the Lovaris knew and greatly broadened my magical education." She grimaced. "Girls with magical powers in Varkhora are only trained as hearth witches, so I'd little knowledge outside that until Ceija. I'm forever grateful to her for her kindness and protection in those rough years after I fled Varkhora."

As they headed to the kitchen to prepare luncheon, Oakmoor rumbled, "How old were you when you fled Varkhora?"

She swallowed but gritted a bright grin. Discussing her past made her stomach quiver, yet unless she did, Oakmoor would never share either. "Almost eighteen."

Oakmoor frowned. "Fleeing your home so young must have been difficult. But traveling with gypsies was doubtless fascinating." At her nod, he sighed and said, "I've always longed to travel. Yet as a duke, I'd too many responsibilities to do so. Becoming the Minister of Foreign Relations was the closest I could manage."

Juliet hummed as she heated water for tea. With his charm and gift for talk, Oakmoor would have made a much better traveler than she had. "If you needed to remain in one kingdom, Calatini is the best you could get. People have more freedom here, and the kingdom is prosperous, peaceful, and open to change."

Oakmoor finished preparing rolls stuffed with meat and cheese. "True, and we've enough foreign visitors, both human and magical creatures, to keep life in Calatini interesting." He studied her as he collected the food tray he'd prepared. "Although I expect what you really appreciate is women being equals to men here like they should be."

She quirked a wry smile while she carried the tea tray from the kitchen. How well Oakmoor already knew her. "Yes."

Once they'd settled in the family dining room, Oakmoor shook his head and said, "The men in Varkhora are truly fools." He grinned at her. "But Calatini is fortunate they are. You've been invaluable here since becoming our royal witch. You're the most skilled witch I've ever met."

A blush heating her cheeks at Oakmoor's compliment, she sipped her tea. "Nonsense. The veiled witch is much more powerful."

Oakmoor shrugged. "Power and skill are different things, and without skill, power is often useless. Plus, the veiled witch is much less straightforward and dedicated to helping Calatini. She never would have helped the kingdom—and me—the way you have."

Warming further at Oakmoor's continued praise, Juliet bit into a stuffed roll to keep herself from asking him why he'd not listen to her and perform a mind sharing spell if he admired her skill and dedication so much. Pressing too hard would only make him retreat behind his charm like he had the other day. Instead, she smiled at him and simply replied, "Thank you. Speaking of being helpful, I'll return to my workroom this afternoon to work on breaking your curse again."

Oakmoor inclined his head. "I'll handle the chores to maintain the townhouse and read in my study until 'tis time to cook dinner. Any special food you'd like?"

She smirked at Oakmoor then drawled to tease him, "I'm still waiting on that pastry-wrapped beefsteak."

Oakmoor laughed, his eyes gleaming. "Demanding witch."

Starting that morning, Juliet and Oakmoor fell into a comfortable routine. She'd instruct him about magic after breakfast. Then she'd work on his curse in the afternoon while he occupied himself elsewhere. They'd enjoy spiritpunch and dinner together before adjourning to the library, gamesroom, garden, or drawing room. Oakmoor remained responsible for cooking their meals, although she helped prepare many of them. Every day, she shared a private matter or two with him, keeping to small ones at first, and he often reciprocated, but she purposely didn't mention the mind sharing spell.

During luncheon after her third morning instructing Oakmoor, she smiled at him over her tea and said, "You're progressing even faster than I'd expected. I'm thoroughly enjoying instructing you." Forcing herself to hold his gaze, she added, "Just like I enjoyed writing those letters to Mordred. Not many share my curiosity about everything regarding magic."

Oakmoor returned her smile. "I enjoyed reading your interesting and insightful replies to my questions. 'Tis why I continued writing after you helped me learn the basics of magic. And why I created those transport boxes. I was greedy for more letters." Looking away, he shifted in his seat. "Although I must apologize for deceiving you about my identity. As you mentioned the other day, I was desperate, and your letters helped me more than I can say."

She blinked. Oakmoor was *apologizing*? He'd seemed unrepentant when she'd confronted him about being Mordred. And he'd been right that their past would have prevented her from openly responding to him as himself. "I do understand why you wrote as another." She narrowed her eyes at him. "But if you *ever* deceive me like that again, I'll curse you worse than Elvaira did."

Oakmoor flashed a wry grin. "I know."

The following evening after a congenial dinner, Juliet readily agreed to Oakmoor's suggestion that they take a turn about the garden. Although not nature witches, they could use some fresh air since they'd been inside for days.

As they strolled through the fragrant garden, Oakmoor studied the flame-like clouds to the west. "What a gorgeous sunset. 'Tis my favorite time of day. So vivid."

She followed Oakmoor's gaze. How like him to favor such

bold colors. "I prefer a clear night when the stars sparkle against the inky sky. Sometimes it can look almost purple."

Oakmoor chuckled. "You do adore the color purple, don't you?" He paused and snapped off a deep-red rose then whispered an adapting spell until it turned a rich purple. He offered it to her. "Here."

Her heart fluttering, Juliet accepted the enchanted rose and inhaled its sweet fragrance. Oakmoor was actually wooing *her* for once. "Thanks." Her face still buried in its rich-purple petals, she glanced at him. "This is the first rose you gave me as myself."

Studying the vivid sky again, Oakmoor shrugged. "I didn't think you'd want roses from me."

She hummed. Astute as ever. "Not if they were simply a rakehell's seductive trick." Yet this rose wasn't that, considering how he'd changed it from the typical romantic token to what she truly loved and the understated way he'd given it to her. She smiled at Oakmoor. "But I like this one." She rubbed the enchanted rose's velvety petals against her cheek, a pang piercing her. "'Tis the same color purple as Gentian was. She was such a sweet faebird."

Oakmoor returned his gaze to her. "You obviously miss Gentian. I understand why you couldn't take her when you fled home, but why did you never get another faebird once you settled in Calatini?"

Juliet blew a sigh. "Because carrying a faebird would betray I was from Varkhora." She swallowed then made herself confess, "Besides, owning another faebird would be a constant reminder of how I abandoned Gentian. And that would hurt too much."

Oakmoor grimaced and rubbed his left horn. "Sometimes our past decisions can hurt us the most. Like succumbing to the seductive wiles of an exotic, older woman thanks to too much wine, a lifetime of isolation, and being independent for the first time. Then fleeing when she revealed her mad obsession with me and flirting with other girls to prove I didn't belong to her, which simply angered her enough to curse me."

Her chest twisting, Juliet touched Oakmoor's arm. "You can't blame yourself for Elvaira cursing you. Yes, you were young and stupid to become embroiled with a madwoman, and you didn't end your affair well, but you didn't deserve to be cursed for those mistakes." She set her jaw. "I'll ensure that you shan't suffer Elvaira's vindictive curse forever."

Oakmoor laid his hand atop hers, his scaled face soft. "Thank you, Juliet." When she shivered as tingling flooded her at his touch like always, he jerked his hand away. "We should return inside; you're cold."

She nodded and sniffed her deep-purple rose again to hide the blush heating her cheeks. She wasn't the least cold, but she couldn't reveal why she'd shivered. Not even to encourage him to perform the mind sharing spell that she needed to understand his curse.

THE DAY after their walk in the garden, neither Juliet nor Oakmoor mentioned private matters, and Oakmoor returned to his overly suave charm. Like her, he probably needed time to recover from their genuine intimacy. Yet by dinner the following evening, she resumed encouraging him to share. If she didn't, they'd be trapped in his townhouse forever.

Since the baked pastry he'd made with their roast beefsteak was a specialty of his duchy, she decided to encourage him to discuss his isolated childhood being raised by servants. "These Oakmoor puddings are delicious. So fluffy and savory."

Oakmoor inclined his shaggy head as he devoured a pudding. "The secret is to use sizzling drippings in the batter. Millie, the head cook at Oakmoor Castle while I was growing up, taught me to make them when I was seven. Although hers were *much* better than mine. And so are her daughter's." When Juliet arched her brows at that, he added, "Martha has been my head cook since her mother died during my first season. And her brother Miles has been my valet since I was fifteen."

She nodded. That matched what the royal agent had said about Oakmoor's servants all being longtime ones from his duchy. "Did you grow up with Martha and Miles?"

Oakmoor lifted a shoulder while he began his roast beefsteak, mashed tubers, gravy, and sauteed peas and carrots. "Not really. They're fifteen or so years older, but growing up, I saw them often since Millie was the first servant to take me under her wing. Within a few months of my parents' deaths, I spent much of my days in the kitchen, although that changed as I grew older. Then I spent more time on my own."

Juliet swallowed a bite of Oakmoor's tender roast beefsteak with a crispy outside and slightly pink center. His years in the kitchen certainly explained his excellent culinary skills. Yet if he'd spent much of his time with servants, how had he developed his suave court charm? She studied him. "Were there other gentry or noble families nearby?"

Oakmoor shrugged again. "Some, although my guardian Bedivere didn't care to entertain. I did visit them once I was older, but I always far outranked them, so they were deferential."

She tilted her head. Doubtless Oakmoor had developed his charm to help him amuse and relax those families to better connect with them. Yet he'd clearly not built any close relationships with those families. Probably because they didn't consider themselves his equal, and he was as particular about whom he trusted as she was. She leaned toward him. "And you'd no other family besides your guardian?"

Oakmoor grimaced as he finished his roast beefsteak. "Merely a few distant paternal cousins who resided in northern Linwick, although now that's dwindled to just a degenerate cousin. The Tremblay family has never been large, and Mother's parents, her only relatives, died shortly after she married Father."

Her heart squeezing, Juliet sipped her red wine. No wonder Oakmoor only kept longtime servants from his duchy. They were the closest he had to family. Plus, he knew he could trust them, and after Elvaira's betrayal, that would have been even more crucial. She offered him a soft smile. "You must have been lonely growing up. I can understand that. I often felt the same."

Oakmoor stilled and eyed her. "Because you'd no family besides your parents and royal cousins?"

She swallowed when her heart squeezed again. She was much more fortunate than Oakmoor had been in that regard. "No, I've plenty of extended family. But I was too driven and outspoken for Varkhoran society. I never fit in with the other ladies, and I angered most gentlemen, particularly Father and King Cesare. The only people I was close with growing up were Mother and my crippled cousin Sandro, now King Alessandro— at least until my brother Giovanni was born when I was sixteen."

Oakmoor frowned as he served her a slice of another specialty of his duchy, an Oakmoor curd tart with currants and spices. "Quite an age difference between you and your brother."

Juliet sighed and toyed with the delectable-looking dessert rather than eating it. "Yes. There were complications during my birth, so Mother suffered many miscarriages after that." She paused then admitted, "When I asked, Mother claimed that Father never forced her to keep attempting to bear a male heir, but that she desperately wanted more children, and that he'd have quit attempting ages ago." She grimaced. "Yet I'm still not certain whether 'twas true. In Varkhora, 'tis a great shame for a family to have no sons, and the wife always bears the blame."

Oakmoor snorted. "How idiotic." He refilled her wine glass. "You must have been terribly jealous when your brother was born."

She pursed her lips. "Because a precious male heir usurped my place after so many years as my parents' sole concern, you mean?" When Oakmoor nodded, she smiled and shook her head. "I wasn't really. While Mother was pregnant, I never believed she'd successfully bear him, and she barely did. Mother was bedridden during the last five months of her pregnancy. Then after Giovanni was born, my parents treated me the same as ever

—Mother still warmly loving, and Father forever berating me to be a demure Varkhoran lady."

Oakmoor's jaw clenched. "Oh, Juliet."

Before Oakmoor could express his pity, she said, "Besides, I was relieved they'd quit risking Mother's health now that they finally had a son." Her voice softened, "And Giovanni was an adorable baby. So even-keeled with the sweetest grins and most delightful giggles. He was just walking on his own and beginning to talk when I fled Varkhora." Her chest tightened. "He's twenty-two now. I wonder what sort of gentleman he grew up to become. Mellow and loving like Mother, or ambitious and censorious like Father."

Oakmoor smiled at her. "Or perhaps your brother is like you. Bold, clever, and industrious."

Her cheeks heating, Juliet ate a bite of her dessert at last. To lighten their conversation, she murmured, "This Oakmoor curd tart is just as delicious as your Oakmoor puddings."

DESPITE THAT INTENSELY INTIMATE CONVERSATION, Oakmoor didn't retreat behind his charm the following day, unlike before. He'd surely agree to a mind sharing spell soon. Thank the Goddess. So while instructing him in her workroom that morning, she described her frustrating lack of progress with his curse and that she truly needed to see Elvaira casting it, but she didn't specifically mention the mind sharing spell. Then for the rest of the day, she waited for Oakmoor to broach it, but the obstinate man never did.

So before dinner the following evening, Juliet smiled at Oakmoor over her gingyr buck and asked, "What shall you do once I eventually break your curse?" Discussing the future should prod him into agreeing to the mind sharing spell.

Oakmoor shrugged. "I'm not certain. Resume my life at court, I suppose."

She arched a sardonic brow. "As a rakehell? Or do you mean

to settle on one of those little girls you were courting and produce an heir?"

His gaze on his gingyr buck, Oakmoor shrugged again but didn't reply.

Juliet scowled at the vexing man. "Do you not want a family?"

Oakmoor exhaled. "No, I do, and not just because I need an heir to prevent my degenerate cousin, who'd ruin my duchy in under a decade, from inheriting. But I don't know the lady I want as a wife or even how to be a father. My guardian Bedivere mostly ignored me."

She swallowed, her scowl fading at Oakmoor's confession. "Why did he?"

Oakmoor grimaced as he sipped his gingyr buck. "Bedivere was too elderly to want to raise another boy not his own, and he resented me. He'd already raised Father and adored him, and he'd never approved of Mother. So when Father committed suicide after Mother died in a carriage accident because he couldn't bear to live without her, Bedivere blamed her and by extension me."

Juliet inhaled. What a heartrending childhood. Given that and Elvaira cursing him, Oakmoor must distrust love and marriage as much as she did. That explained why he could never settle on a lady as his wife. She squeezed his arm. "Goddess, I'm sorry, Oakmoor. But you know how to be a father—just treat your children the opposite of how Bedivere treated you. 'Tis what I intend to do. Unlike Father, I'll love my children, whether girls or boys, for who they are and not attempt to force them into being someone else."

Oakmoor frowned and stared at her. "*You* want a family? You've always seemed too dedicated to being the royal witch to want anything else."

She glared at Oakmoor and jerked her hand from his arm. Must he act so shocked? "Just like *you've* always seemed too dedicated to being the greatest rakehell in Ormas to want one."

His frown becoming a wry smile, Oakmoor laughed. "Fair point."

Juliet sighed then made herself relax and return Oakmoor's wry smile. "Although I'll likely never have those children to love. I've achieved too much to abandon it all for a family, and I was raised to do precisely that, so I doubt I could trust myself or my husband to allow me to have both. And even if I managed to find a husband who'd let me remain myself, I'm turning thirty-nine this autumn, so I'll soon be too old to bear children."

Oakmoor snorted then drained his gingyr buck. "Your husband would be a fool not to be proud of and support such a strong, clever, and illustrious wife."

She warmed, and her heart tingled. Despite Elvaira, Oakmoor truly adored strong ladies. Perhaps 'twas why he attracted her so, even more than his masculine allure. She leaned toward him. "Are you saying only a fool wouldn't listen to a strong, clever, and illustrious lady like me?"

Oakmoor narrowed his eyes at her. "Meaning I'd be a fool for not agreeing to the mind sharing spell that you've been silently pressing for the past nine days?"

Juliet smirked and lifted her chin. Not surprising the astute duke had recognized her plan. "Yes."

Oakmoor grunted then rose to fetch their dinner. "I suppose I'd better agree, else you'll keep prying into my private matters until I go mad."

She stiffened and glowered at Oakmoor. Ungrateful beast. As he strode from the family dining room, she called, "Are you certain you aren't already mad?"

CHAPTER 21

The following morning after breakfast, Oakmoor frowned as he followed Juliet into her workroom. He wasn't looking forward to performing this mind sharing spell—if they could even manage it without breaking their minds. He'd only agreed because Juliet was too determined and wouldn't quit pressing him until they'd at least attempted it. And *if* they managed to succeed, Juliet might see the clues she needed to break his curse.

Juliet waved toward the sofa along the back wall. "Sit there while I brew the mind sharing potion."

He sighed but sat. "What's in this potion?" No doubt 'twould taste terrible.

Juliet collected a silver chalice and several spell ingredients from her shelves. "Unicorn water, thyme, pennyroyal, eyebright, borage leaf, and faedust. Now hush, I need to concentrate."

He sighed again yet remained silent as Juliet poured shimmering unicorn water into the silver chalice and sprinkled in the four herbs, followed by a heaping spoonful of faedust. Chanting a singsong incantation, she cupped the bowl of the chalice in both hands, and the potion began to bubble, hiss, and steam.

When the steam changed from white to an incandescent gold, she quieted then turned and glided toward him.

Juliet settled beside him on the sofa, sitting sideways facing him and holding the bubbling chalice between them. "Turn to face me and cup the chalice too."

Oakmoor swallowed as he did, his heart quickening at their legs touching and Juliet's hands beneath his. How easy 'twould be to kiss her. If he wasn't a beast.

Juliet shivered but lifted her chin. "I'll tell you the mind sharing incantation, then we'll chant it together to begin the spell. We'll drink the potion before taking hands and repeating the incantation to finish setting the spell." Once he nodded, she inhaled and told him the incantation then asked, "Ready?"

He nodded again, and together they chanted in the melodic witch's tongue, "Two minds become one and share all, no secrets shadowing their unity. By the power of our magic, this potion, and the Goddess, let it be so."

Both still holding the chalice, Juliet drank half the bubbling gold potion. They rotated the chalice, and he drank the rest from the same spot she had. The potion tasted medicinal yet sweet— not terrible at all—and made energy surge in his veins. They set aside the chalice then lifted their arms and pressed their palms together. Staring into each other's eyes, they chanted the mind sharing incantation again.

When they finished, his pulse surged, blood roared in his ears, and his vision twisted. Then everything stilled as their minds meshed, her feminine presence entwined with his own pricking and inflaming his senses. He/they blinked at seeing themselves from both views simultaneously.

She/they said, "We should shut our eyes. 'Tis confusing." Once they did, they shuddered at the sandalwood and gingyr scent filling their lungs as well as their palms and legs pressed together. So close to kissing. She/they then said, "Think back to when Elvaira cursed you."

He/they let his memories of that devastating evening flood their minds, and in a dark rolling meadow beneath a moonless sky, the exotically seductive Elvaira pinched off a lock of his hair with her magic then wrenched herself free while the white witchlight above her turned scarlet. Her smile twisting, she said, "Just remember you could have prevented your doom by agreeing to belong to me like you were meant to be."

He frowned and began backing away as Elvaira flung her hands upward and hurled his hair into her scarlet witchlight. She snarled words in the witch's tongue, and a howling wind whipped around them, while black swirled in her scarlet witchlight.

The howling wind trapping him as strongly as any chain, he shouted over its near deafening howl, "Stop this!"

Elvaira cackled, her dark eyes glassy with madness. "No! You had your chance. I told you that you'd regret angering a Rhiannon-descendant witch." Before he could protest, she chanted, "One day a beast you'll be to match your true self. A man-chimera with a goat's lust, a snake's betrayal, and a lion's cruelty. A beast so hideous that no one shall *ever* love you when they see the true self you conceal behind your charming facade. I seal this curse with my magic and heart's blood."

Elvaira flashed a malevolent and terrifying smirk then plunged her lead and ebony dagger into her chest. Scarlet blood, the same shade as her magic, spurted as she crumbled.

He began surging toward the dying Elvaira, but her scarlet and black magic swarmed him like deadly melissae, and boiling agony swamped him. He screamed and collapsed, writhing as his heart raced and scalding tears burned his face.

Juliet/they suddenly said, "That's enough." Her feminine presence increased in their meshed minds like a warm embrace, and the past faded. "Remembering such agony is pointless. I've seen what I needed to."

He/they rumbled and leaned closer. Her presence was as spicy and sweet and hot as her kisses.

She/they inhaled as tingling flooded them and their bodies throbbed. She/they said, "Quit thinking about kisses, you rakehell."

He/they grunted. Impossible when she was so close. He/they replied, "Perhaps we should end the mind sharing spell now."

Nodding with their eyes still closed, she/they said, "Ending the mind sharing spell is simple enough. We just pull our bodies and minds apart while chanting the following incantation." Once she/they shared that, she/they asked, "Ready?"

He/they replied, "Yes." Then they chanted in the witch's tongue, "Let the power of potion and magic fade until meshed minds become two again like the Goddess meant them to be." As they spoke, they attempted to separate their bodies and minds, yet both remained locked together.

After finishing their incantation, he/they jerked back in a desperate attempt to break their connection, but she/they followed like the waves of a rising tide. He/they asked, "Why can't we separate?"

She/they pulled back, and he/they followed. Her/their voice tight, she/they replied, "I don't know. This didn't happen when I performed a mind sharing spell with Ceija. Maybe because she and I were both Rhiannon descendants, so my magical powers didn't overpower hers as much."

He/they grimaced then grumbled, "I never should have let you press me into performing a mind sharing spell. I knew we'd break our minds."

She/they snapped back, "We haven't broken our minds. We just need to forcefully repeat the separating incantation and pull apart harder."

He/they growled. Maddening witch. "Goddess, must you always be so damned stubborn and certain you're right?"

Her/their stomach twisting, she/they winced away from those painfully familiar words, and they plunged into her memories of a stifling summer afternoon in her father's orderly study.

Standing rigid behind his desk, Father slammed his fist on the ebony wood. "Giuliettanna Camilla Sabine, quit being so damned stubborn and certain you're right. Remember your place. You're my daughter, and I say you'll marry him."

Giuliettanna glared, her fists clenched at her sides. "I'll *never* marry Cesare!"

Father stiffened further. "King Cesare, you brazen girl. Although he's your cousin and future husband, he'll beat you if you fail to show the respect due him. No Varkhoran gentleman would placidly accept your insolent tongue."

She defiantly lifted her set chin. "You actually expect me to marry such a cruel bully?"

Father sighed. "You must marry someone, and King Cesare is desperate to marry you. Plus, if you marry him, you'll be queen —the most powerful lady in Varkhora."

She shuddered at suffering Cesare's attentions. "More to the point, *you'll* be father to the queen instead of merely the prominent Duke of Appenninos. 'Tis what you truly want, isn't it, Father?"

Father scowled and leaned toward her. "Enough of this. You'll marry King Cesare next month, even if I must bind you and drag you to the temple. I've promised him your hand, so our family honor depends on it. Now, leave me." Father narrowed his eyes at her. "And *don't* you dare disturb your mother with your defiant whining. She's enough to endure right now."

Giuliettanna whirled and fled Father's study. Why would he *never* listen to her? Life with Cesare would be a ghastly nightmare she couldn't escape. She *had* to flee, but how?

Oakmoor/they interrupted, "Juliet, come back, please." His/their suave voice jolted her/them from the past.

She/they gulped a steadying breath. "Shall we attempt to end the mind sharing spell again?"

They did, but their second attempt succeeded no better than

the first. So after pausing to breathe, they attempted a third time, and she/they desperately flung every bit of her/their will and magical powers into it. Fortunately, their minds slowly separated with an agonizing wrench as their pulse raced, blood burned, and vision blackened.

Drained and panting after all that, Oakmoor sagged against the sofa. Thank the Goddess they'd escaped the mind sharing spell. It had been even more dangerous than he'd expected. Although Juliet's feminine presence no longer being entwined with his own felt oddly empty.

Once his breath calmed, he turned to Juliet slumped on the sofa beside him. She looked utterly drained too. He lurched upright. "I'll fetch us some food to help us recover. Rest here."

He staggered to the kitchen and somehow prepared kahve without falling then grabbed rolls, meat, and cheese. Trembling, he made it back to Juliet's workroom and collapsed on the sofa where she was still resting. Definitely drained, poor witch.

He and Juliet stuffed all the rolls with the meat and cheese then devoured them while downing several bracing cups of kahve sweetened with twice as much sugar as they usually used to help revive them. Thankfully, by the time they finished their early luncheon, his energy had returned somewhat, although he remained tired.

Her face pale and creased, Juliet sighed as she set her empty cup on the tray between them. "I doubt either of us shall be able to perform magic for days. It shall take that long to recharge our magical energy from our surroundings." She tsked. "You're bad for my magic, Oakmoor. This is the second time I've drained myself so in the past month. The first was when I located Miss Hawke and took her place."

He quirked a brow and drawled, "But this time you should recover faster since you're not wearing an illusion spell to deceive me." He forced himself to his feet then drew Juliet upright, leaving the tray on the sofa. "Let's head up to our chambers and rest until we must prepare dinner."

Juliet nodded, and he slowly escorted her upstairs. Having borne the higher cost to end their mind sharing spell, she trembled and clung to him. His body tightened at her soft curves brushing against him and her spicy gingyr scent, and he ached to pull her even closer and trail kisses along her luscious skin.

At her door, Juliet looked as weak as a newborn angelkitten, so he asked, "Do you require help getting into bed?"

Juliet snorted. "How like a rakehell to ask that." She gave him a faint smile and stepped from his arms. "I can manage, thanks."

Once Juliet disappeared into her bedchamber, Oakmoor waited outside her closed door, intently listening for a thump indicating she'd fallen. Yet he heard none, so after several moments, he trudged to his own chambers then fell into bed and sank into slumber.

He awoke an hour before dinner feeling refreshed, even though his magic remained drained. Collecting the luncheon tray from Juliet's workroom on the way, he returned to the kitchen then prepared a simple dinner of gingyr tea, hearty fish stew, rolls he'd baked earlier, and spiced pudding. Fortunately, he'd conjured a week's worth of food before preparing his roast beefsteak dinner the other day, so they'd have enough food to last until he'd magical energy to conjure more.

He'd just finished preparing dinner when Juliet drifted into the kitchen, much less pale than before, although she still looked tired. He smiled at her. "I was about to fetch you. Could you carry the tea and roll tray?"

They devoured their fish stew and rolls in contented silence, but after he returned with their spiced pudding, Oakmoor eyed Juliet. She looked strong enough to talk now. He said, "That mind sharing spell this morning was intense."

Juliet frowned. "Yes, it was, but I think I saw what I needed to break your curse, although I'll require time to reflect on everything first."

He ate half his pudding, continuing to eye Juliet. Would she tell him about that memory of her father? "I saw something unexpected as well."

Juliet winced and stirred her spiced pudding. "You mean that quarrel with Father. Sorry about that."

His pudding finished, Oakmoor leaned toward Juliet. If only he could take her hand to comfort her. "Was he always so censorious toward you?"

Juliet shrugged as she finally ate a spoonful of pudding. "Usually. Father wanted a demure daughter like my gentle cousin Aurora—Varkhora's current queen. Not a driven and outspoken one like me."

He suppressed a growl as he fisted his hands beneath the table. Her fool of a father hadn't deserved an amazing lady like Juliet as his daughter. He inhaled to settle himself. "Given your independent nature, I'm surprised your father thought forcing you to marry someone you clearly loathed would succeed."

Juliet flicked another shrug. "Fathers arranging their daughters' marriages is the way of things in Varkhora. I might have complied if he'd not chosen King Cesare as my husband."

When Juliet shuddered, Oakmoor gripped his knees to avoid pulling her into his arms. "Why did you loathe King Cesare so?"

Juliet set down her spoon, her spiced pudding only half eaten. "Because he was a cruel, condescending bully. I never liked him and wasn't shy about it. Even Mother told me I should conceal that better." She grimaced. "He only wanted to marry me for two reasons. One, because I loathed him and he loved the idea of forcing me. And two, because I was a powerful Rhiannon descendant and he wanted credit for my magical powers since he'd none of his own."

Oakmoor couldn't help his growl this time. How could Juliet's father have expected her to marry such a despicable brute?

Her mouth wry, Juliet shrugged once more. "But I suppose 'tis fortunate Father arranged my betrothal to King Cesare. It goaded me into fleeing Varkhora. I never could have been myself there or achieved all that I have through my own effort like I have in Calatini."

His chest twisted for a heartbeat. And he'd never have met Juliet if she'd not fled Varkhora. Burying that, he arched his brows at her. "You mentioned you were close to King Cesare's brother growing up. Did he help you flee Varkhora?"

Juliet sighed. "I did talk to Sandro once my betrothal preparations began. But as the crippled, younger brother the new king had always despised, he'd little power to help me. In private, he'd attempted to dissuade his brother from the betrothal, but that only made King Cesare more keen. And Sandro couldn't openly defy the crown without risking accusations of treason. In the end, I resolved to flee without Sandro's help to avoid endangering him. To accept his help would have destroyed his and Aurora's future, and they'd been in love for ages. They married two years after I fled Varkhora, and I've heard that they've been blissfully happy together."

Oakmoor inclined his head. He'd heard that as well because King Alessandro's open adoration of his powerful hearth-witch wife had scandalized Varkhora. "Did your mother help you flee then?"

Juliet worried her lip. "No, she was ill that summer. 'Tis what Father meant by her having enough to endure. Thankfully, I'd met Ceija Lovari by chance a month prior, and she'd been so kind that I decided to run away and join her family on their travels." Juliet yawned and rose. "I'm sorry, but I must return to bed now. I'm still exhausted and can barely stay awake."

He leapt upright and escorted Juliet upstairs. Like before, she clung to him, although not as close, much to his body's disappointment. At her door, he couldn't resist pressing a kiss against her brow. "Good night, Juliet."

She shivered but smiled at him. "Good night, Oakmoor." Then she slipped into her bedchamber.

As he cleaned up from dinner, he frowned and reflected on everything Juliet had told him about her past. How could her family, particularly her idiot father, have treated her like they had? She'd been terribly alone when she'd decided she must flee Varkhora. Only a strong and bold lady like Juliet could have ever managed it. She was so amazing and deserved a family who loved and celebrated who she truly was.

He hummed while he settled in his study to read. He couldn't be Juliet's family, but he could surprise her with a special evening to show his gratitude and admiration. Considering all she was doing to help him, she definitely deserved that and more.

So over the following couple days, Oakmoor deftly quizzed Juliet on her favorite foods. Then when she was busy in her workroom attempting to unravel his curse, he prepared for her special evening by researching then conjuring—once his magical powers returned—the recipes, food, and music he needed.

Three days after their mind sharing spell, he spent the afternoon setting up the ballroom and dining room then cooking their special meal. When Juliet joined him to help, he shooed her from the kitchen with a smooth smile before she could see the food. "I'm almost done. Why don't you take a turn about the garden to revive yourself?"

Once he finished dinner, he placed a preservation spell on everything then strode out to the garden to fetch Juliet, who was bending to smell the irises. Of course she'd drifted to the purple flowers in his garden. Juliet was going to adore how he'd decorated the dinner table. He grinned at her. "How was your afternoon?"

Juliet straightened and huffed a sigh. "Frustrating. I know I've everything I need to understand your curse, but how to break it remains just out of reach. Like an illusion spell that hasn't quite taken shape—there but hazy with the pieces not quite fitting yet. So to resolve that, I've begun researching other curses using my tome enchanted with a library spell to display any book I wish from Calatini's witch academies." She pursed her lips. "I was surprised my library spell worked through the veiled witch's dratted wards, although I'm grateful it did."

Oakmoor nodded as they headed back inside. "I've also been able to conjure any food or supplies I needed, even if I'm not familiar with them." Fortunate given the surprise he'd planned.

Her eyes narrowing, Juliet hummed. "Conjuring items you don't know requires knowledge from the outside world, just like my library spell. So we can't contact or see the outside world, but we can access knowledge from it. What a peculiar way for the veiled witch to have constructed her wards."

He shrugged. "No doubt she'd her reasons." Seers always did. "Although I doubt we'll understand them except in retrospect."

Juliet grimaced and sighed again. "Typical when consulting seers. So vexing."

Oakmoor smiled at Juliet. The independent and clever witch would *hate* others limiting her understanding. "Forget about that tonight and enjoy the evening instead." He ushered her into the family dining room.

Juliet stilled on the threshold, her gaze on the floral basket between their plates. "Purple gentians? Those don't grow in your garden here."

He grinned and escorted Juliet to her chair. His secret preparations had genuinely surprised her. And the purple gentians were just the start. "No, I conjured them, among other things. I thought you deserved a special evening after everything you've done to help me."

Juliet blinked at him while he mixed a gingyr-orenge spriss for each of them. "I've not done much of anything yet."

Warmth suffusing his chest, Oakmoor handed Juliet her favorite spiritpunch. Typical of her to be so focused on what she'd yet to do that she forgot what she'd already done. "You will." He toasted Juliet with his wine glass. "To the strong, skilled, and determined lady who shall break my curse."

Hunger flared in his veins at her blush. Goddess, if only he wasn't a beast, he'd thank the bewitching witch in the traditional manner between gentlemen and ladies. And if he was still human, that kiss would have exploded into uncontrollable passion like their kisses always did, so they'd have spent the entire night enjoying each other in his bed. How he needed that. Yet such a wild night would disgust Juliet while he was a hideous beast.

He clenched his free hand beneath the table to not yank her against him. Then he toasted Juliet again. "The only lady who could."

CHAPTER 22

*B*lushing at Oakmoor's toast, Juliet inhaled and eyed him over her untasted gingyr-orenge spriss. From the steady warmth in his gaze and the rough tinge to his usually suave voice, he truly meant everything he'd said. And he'd also conjured those purple gentians and her favorite spiritpunch. 'Twas unexpectedly sweet of him and too sincere to be a rakehell's seductive trick. Since they'd begun sharing private matters and their intense mind sharing spell, Oakmoor had revealed a caring heart he typically kept well hidden. But she'd revealed more of herself too—more than she had with anyone else.

To return to their usual banter, she drawled, "You've even a prophecy from an incredibly powerful seer stating that I'm the only lady who could break your curse. 'Tis fortunate I took Miss Hawke's place, isn't it?"

Oakmoor's lips quirked as he toasted her with his wine glass once more. "Yes, it was. Thank you for trapping yourself with me until you manage to break my curse. I'm incredibly grateful that you'd risk so much to help me. I can't think of another lady who'd do the same. So as a token of my gratitude and admiration, I planned a special evening for you tonight. I hope you enjoy it."

She blushed harder. So much for returning to banter. "I'm certain I shall. You're skilled at knowing how to please ladies... at least initially."

Oakmoor laughed. "I do enjoy that biting tongue of yours. So stimulating and genuine." As her blush deepened even further, he smiled at her over his wine glass. "Although I must admit I've never had to go to such effort to please other ladies. Typically, my charm, wealth, and influence are enough, but *those* simply vex you."

Juliet lifted a shoulder and studied her spiritpunch. "Because you use them to conceal your true self." She'd always recognized that since she did much the same. To distract them, she finally took a sip of her gingyr-orenge spriss then blinked at the bubbly spiritpunch's perfect blend of spice, tang, and sweetness. 'Twas the best she'd tasted in years. "Your gingyr-orenge spriss is even better than last time."

Oakmoor grinned at her. "Not surprising you'd say that. I conjured Varkhoran sparkling wine this time rather than using some from Calatini." He sipped his spiritpunch too then nodded. "It *is* better."

She drank more of her gingyr-orenge spriss. So good. "Varkhoran sparkling wine is fruitier and slightly sweeter than Calatini's, so it better compliments the bittersweet, citrus, and herbal notes of the orenge spriss. And it has lighter bubbles." She sipped again and returned Oakmoor's grin. "Thank you for this. 'Tis lovely, and I've not tasted better in Varkhora."

Oakmoor inclined his shaggy head. "I'm glad you like it." He rose. "I'll fetch our meal." He returned several moments later and set their first course on the table with a flourish.

Juliet blinked at the hearty soup before her. "Is this reboiled soup?" She'd not tasted the Varkhoran soup made from day-old bread, white beans, and vegetables since she'd fled. But 'twas her favorite. It reminded her of cozy winter afternoons with Mother.

Oakmoor hummed as he passed her the plate of crusty bread. "I conjured a book of Varkhoran recipes."

Her chest warmed. To prepare this special meal for her... Oakmoor *had* gone to a lot of effort. She ate a spoonful of reboiled soup then sighed. 'Twas as good as the gingyr-orenge spriss had been. "This is delicious."

Oakmoor nodded before eating a spoonful as well. His brows rose. "No wonder 'tis your favorite. It could almost be a meal on its own."

Juliet tilted her head. "Mother and I often ate it for luncheon, particularly during winter, since 'tis so flavorful and comforting." She smiled at Oakmoor over her bowl. "Is tonight's meal why you've been subtly asking me about my favorite foods the past few days?"

Oakmoor chuckled and devoured more soup. "Guilty." He flashed an impish grin. "Does my skill at knowing how to please ladies still vex you?"

She tsked, her lips twitching. Unrepentant rakehell. "'Tisn't your skill that vexes me, but how you use it on *every* lady you encounter."

Oakmoor waggled his brows. "How else am I to maintain my reputation as the greatest rakehell in Ormas?"

Juliet raised her eyes skyward despite her unwitting smile. Definitely unrepentant.

His scaled face sobering, Oakmoor sighed into his reboiled soup. "You know, I've not had as many lovers as you and court seem to believe. True, I had plenty when I first arrived at court, which built my rakehell reputation, but since I became a councilor, I've been much more particular. Many of my 'lovers' have been mere flirtations that didn't extend past the ballroom, although the ladies claimed we had because they enjoyed the cachet being known as my lover gave them." He grimaced. "As did my actual lovers, so they invariably revealed our affair to all of court. Except for you."

She stirred her half-eaten soup. "Because I want to earn my reputation myself, not through any man. And being known as one of your discarded lovers would make court take me less seriously." Which the astute duke knew since he'd threatened to reveal their affair to make her quit prying.

Oakmoor smiled at her. "I know. I admire your determination to succeed through your own means. And 'twas refreshing to find a lady who appreciated discretion as much as I do and didn't gossip about our private matters."

A blush heating her neck at his warm tone, she smirked at Oakmoor and said to needle him, "Somehow, I can't believe your rakehell reputation is more smoke than fire. You're too lusty a gentleman not to have a lover, and 'tis obvious you change them more frequently than you change your clothes."

His jaw tightening, Oakmoor held her gaze. "Even when I was new to court, I was never *that* inconstant. And I wasn't lying about being particular. I've not taken a lover since I dismissed Lady Aylmer."

Juliet gaped at Oakmoor. But his affair with the widowed baroness had ended last summer. "You can't have been celibate for nearly ten months."

Oakmoor jerked a shrug. "I have. My curse dreams began soon after that, so I knew Elvaira's curse was close to manifesting. Then my responsible cousin who should have inherited died, so I needed to find a wife and produce an heir to prevent his degenerate brother from inheriting instead. And then the Orandians arrived, and I had to escort them about Ormas. So I haven't had time for lovers. And little desire for them too."

She drew a ragged breath. "Impossible." She blushed again. "You've kissed me with plenty of desire in recent months." Desire she'd feverishly returned.

Oakmoor leapt upright and collected their empty bowls. "That's different. The primal desire between us has always been uncontrollable and explosive. We only resisted before because we avoided each other, and since Lady Driscoll and Sir Lorcan arrived, we couldn't do that. Now excuse me, I must fetch our main course."

Juliet sipped her Varkhoran red wine and grimaced.

Oakmoor was right about their irresistible desire. Even with him a beast, she still suffered it. But from how he'd fled, at least it made him as uncomfortable as it did her.

Oakmoor soon returned with braised beefsteak shank, creamy riso, and roasted tomahts and green cucurbit. More of her favorites from Varkhora. And they were just as delicious as everything else he'd prepared tonight. Oakmoor was becoming an excellent cook.

While she was savoring her final bite of the tender beefsteak flavored with cinnaspice, bay leaf, and a zesty green sauce, Oakmoor cleared his throat then asked, "I noticed during that memory of your father that your name is actually Giuliettanna, not Juliet. Would you prefer if I called you Giuliettanna when we're alone?"

She stilled as a pang darted through her. How odd 'twas to hear her birth name aloud. It had been over twenty years since anyone had called her that. She shook her head. "I've been Juliet too long—over half my life now—to think of myself as Giuliettanna. She was the girl I was, not the lady I am today." She swallowed her last forkful of creamy riso. The boiled riso flavored by broth and cheese accompanied the braised beefsteak shank so well. She shrugged. "I shortened my name and changed it from its Varkhoran form as soon as I joined the Lovaris."

Oakmoor nodded while sipping his wine. "To prevent your father or King Cesare from finding you, I presume."

Juliet sighed and ate the rest of her roasted tomahts and green cucurbit sprinkled with hard grated cheese, another ideal accompanying dish for the braised beefsteak shank. She managed a smile and answered Oakmoor, "Yes, I became Juliet to prevent them from finding me. 'Twas also why I disappeared in the middle of the night and met the Lovaris half a day's distance from court, abandoned Gentian and didn't get another faebird, concealed myself with a tracing-ward spell and wore a glamour spell for years, and never returned to Varkhora or dared contact Mother or Giovanni."

Oakmoor's jaw tightened. "You shouldn't have needed to endure all that."

She sighed again. "I had to. No doubt Father and King Cesare pursued revenge since I fled because I'd ruined their plans. I couldn't risk them finding me, particularly King Cesare." Father would have only verbally flayed her, while her bullying cousin would have fetched the knife.

Oakmoor grunted, frowning at his empty plate. "It must have been difficult to act as Calatini's royal witch while constantly maintaining both a tracing-ward spell and a glamour spell. Are you still maintaining them?"

Juliet finished her wine. Thank the Goddess she wasn't. She'd never have managed all the magic she'd performed since helping Oakmoor if those two spells had still been draining her. As he refilled her wine glass, she replied, "No, I dropped the glamour spell when King Cesare died. I'd been established in Calatini for years by then, and the risk of being found wasn't fatal with him dead. Although I waited until after Queen Kiera's coronation to drop the tracing-ward spell, just in case. From what King Sarastor had seen in the Mirror of Wisdom, I wasn't free to leave Calatini until then."

Oakmoor hummed and rubbed his left horn. "'Tis a shame you had to flee your home, abandon your loved ones, and remain so vigilant for so long. But I'm glad you settled in Calatini—and not just because you promised to break my beast curse." He stood. "I'll fetch dessert now."

She inhaled as Oakmoor strode from the family dining room. *Why* was he glad? Because she'd served Calatini well as royal witch? Or for a more personal reason? Unsurprising the warily private duke hadn't specified. Not that she should care about his reasons.

She brightened when Oakmoor returned and set tiny cups of Varkhoran kahve on the table along with dessert. Her mouth watering, she inhaled the concentrated kahve's strong scent while adding sugar to it. She grinned at Oakmoor. "I've not been served proper kahve since fleeing Varkhora, and I've not prepared it since leaving the Lovaris to avoid betraying my heritage. The closest I've gotten has been transforming Calatinian kahve using an adapting spell when alone."

Oakmoor grinned back. "I'd wondered about that. I've heard that Varkhorans are particular about their kahve."

Juliet sipped her Varkhoran kahve and almost purred. So good. "We are." She glanced at the plates of saffron-gingyr cooked cream Oakmoor had brought with the kahve. Although cooked cream was a classic Varkhoran dessert, she'd only enjoyed this version once, but she'd adored its spicy twist. "How did you find a recipe for this? It surely wasn't in your Varkhoran cookbook. I only had it when Father hosted a dinner for the new Tsarkan ambassador when I was seventeen."

Oakmoor shrugged. "'Twas a challenge. I guessed when adding the spices to the cooked cream recipe in my book. Hopefully, I guessed right."

She replied to tease Oakmoor, "Knowing you, you probably added too much gingyr." She ate a spoonful of the sweet and spicy dessert of thickened cream molded into small, fluted domes then sighed. "No, 'tis perfect." She sipped her Varkhoran kahve again. 'Twas even better after the cooked cream's sweetness. "As is the Varkhoran kahve and everything else you prepared tonight."

His eyes crinkling, Oakmoor waved at her plate. "I'm pleased you enjoyed the meal. Now eat your dessert."

She and Oakmoor drank their Varkhoran kahve and devoured their delectable saffron-gingyr cooked cream in silence.

Once she'd drained her tiny cup and scraped her plate clean, Juliet sat back in her chair with a replete sigh. "That meal was amazing, a special evening indeed. Thank you."

Oakmoor smiled then rose and took her hand. He rumbled, "The evening isn't over yet."

A tingle darting up her arm, she allowed Oakmoor to pull her upright. She gestured at their empty dishes as they began leaving the table. "Shouldn't we take the dishes to the kitchen?"

Oakmoor squeezed her arm. "I'll handle them later. Come along."

Juliet nodded and let Oakmoor whisk her down the hall. She studied him through her lashes. What else had he planned? Her brows rose when he ushered her into his dark and still ballroom.

Oakmoor clapped, and countless witchlights burst to life, banishing the darkness and illuminating the ballroom's dazzling stained-glass ceiling. He drew her to the heart of the ballroom then released her. He murmured something, and music began to play from the musician's balcony. Doubtless an enchanted music box.

She blinked as the familiar merry tune echoed through the ballroom. 'Twas half a year out of season. "Is that the reel we danced to at the Duchess of Childes's Longnight ball?"

Oakmoor inclined his head. "You seemed to enjoy the vigorous dance more than ordinary waltzes." He grinned. "Despite us quarreling the entire reel."

Juliet swallowed. She *had* enjoyed their Longnight reel, more than she should have. 'Twas one of the rare occasions they'd danced together. She licked her lips. "You actually remember the song we danced to?"

His gaze fixed on her lips, Oakmoor shrugged. "Just like you do." As she blushed at that, he bowed and asked, "Dance with me, my lady witch?"

Aching to take Oakmoor's outstretched hand, she nevertheless shook her head. "We haven't another couple to form a set with."

Oakmoor grinned. "I'm sure we can manage alone tonight." He slid his hand closer. "And we could use the exercise after our quiet weeks confined in my townhouse."

Juliet exhaled and placed her hand in his, then Oakmoor

swept her into the vigorous Longnight reel full of dizzying spins, bouncing hops, and sprightly steps. When they should have changed partners, he twirled her back into his arms with an overly rakish grin, making her laugh. Ridiculous man. They romped about the ballroom until the Longnight reel faded.

Oakmoor smiled down at her, his gaze warm once more. "Shall we dance again?"

Her blood pounding from their reel and head whirling from his earthy sandalwood scent, she couldn't help swaying closer to Oakmoor. Their wild reel had been such fun, even more than before. Tonight, they were alone and free to be themselves and felt more than just unwanted desire. Returning his smile, she stared into his hazel eyes—the only part of his beast face that remained human. Yet they were the only part that mattered since they revealed his true self when he wasn't hiding behind his charm. Which he wasn't now. He'd plainly loved their reel as much as she had. And the warmth in his gaze was genuine too. After all, he'd planned an entire special evening for her. Her heart swelled as she continued smiling into Oakmoor's alluring eyes. She'd be happy doing that forever. Because... she loved him.

She froze. She *what*?

Shoving that aside, she gritted a bright smile and stepped back from Oakmoor. "Not tonight. I'm tired. Thank you for the special evening. Good night."

Then she fled before Oakmoor could offer to escort her upstairs.

After locking her door behind her, Juliet sank into the bedchamber's plush chair. She loved Oakmoor. How? She'd been determined never to fall in love since that might endanger all she'd achieved. Yet Oakmoor had always allured her despite her good sense, and that desire had grown to love as they openly shared their pasts and true selves. She'd simply been too focused on encouraging him to perform the mind sharing spell and breaking his beast curse to notice.

She shivered. Not that her love changed anything. Oakmoor distrusted love too much—thanks to his father's suicide, isolated childhood, and Elvaira's curse—to ever return her love, no matter how much he desired or liked her. Besides, he didn't want to marry a lady like her, given all those little girls he'd courted when desperately hunting a wife. So she was cursed to remain helplessly in love with a rakehell who could never love or truly want her but merely desired her.

Tears burned her eyes. Yet if Oakmoor *could* return her love and wanted her as his wife, he'd be the one man she could trust to build a life together. He delighted in her biting remarks and genuinely admired her strength and achievements, so he'd never seek to dominate or change her—part of why she loved him. And if they ever had children together, regardless of whether they were girls or boys, he'd love them as fiercely as she would and never attempt to force them into being someone else.

Juliet inhaled then straightened her shoulders. But since Oakmoor couldn't love or want her, she mustn't ever betray her helpless love for him. His pity would corrode her from the inside out like a hydra's deadly spit, and she must remain strong. Somehow, she'd break his beast curse then return to her life as Calatini's royal witch and pretend she didn't love the greatest rakehell in Ormas. And she'd grit a glittering smile to mask her devastation when he eventually chose one of his little girls as his wife.

So the following morning, she began withdrawing from Oakmoor as much as she could while they remained trapped together. She must protect herself from their eventual parting. At breakfast, she told Oakmoor that she'd finished instructing him about magic because developing his skills further simply required study. Then she told him that she must withdraw to finally unravel his curse so they could eventually escape his townhouse and return to their lives. Afterward, she spent the next three days in her workroom, only seeing Oakmoor when he brought her food trays at every meal. Whenever she saw him, her heart twisted, but she forced herself to feign cool indifference.

Her fourth morning in her workroom, Juliet reread the veiled witch's prophecy and her own transcription of how Elvaira had phrased the curse for the thousandth time then gasped as her eyes locked on one word. Despite her saying love couldn't break Oakmoor's curse, it *must* be the answer. Elvaira had said no one could love him if they saw his true self while a hideous beast, but *she* did. And as the veiled witch had prophesied, her love was strong and true enough that she'd agree to marry him even as a beast. Love like that, along with her powerful magic, could reverse his curse by seeing the positives in the creatures Elvaira had cursed him to become and by risking everything to save him.

She leapt upright and began to pace. But *how* exactly? To break the curse, she must completely reverse how Elvaira had cast it. Elvaira had used hatred and death magic, so she must use magic that contained the power of life and love—sex magic. And Elvaira had cast her curse on Oakmoor's natalday, but performing the counter-spell to break it on Summerday should offset that.

She stilled. Performing that counter-spell would truly be risking everything. Pregnancy was a likely consequence of using powerful sex magic because its potent energy would inactivate their strong-magic contraceptive charms, and her counter-spell to break Oakmoor's curse would be similar to a bloodbinding spell. She worried her lip. Pregnancy or a bloodbinding would completely change their lives. She'd might even have to surrender her position as Calatini's royal witch if either happened. She'd never risk as much for anyone else, but she would to save Oakmoor because of how deeply she loved him.

Juliet raced from her workroom to find Oakmoor and tell him how they must break his curse. Somehow, she must explain without betraying that her love enabled her to break his curse and that she was risking everything to save him. She couldn't bear his pity for loving him or his guilty insistence that they marry if she fell pregnant or they became bloodbound. And although she couldn't avoid revealing the risk of bloodbinding because he'd immediately notice that, she could at least not mention the risk of pregnancy since she could conceal that if necessary.

CHAPTER 23

$\mathcal{W}$hen Juliet burst into his study, Oakmoor dropped the cookbook he was scanning for new recipes and gaped at her. The last time she'd burst in like that had been when she'd discovered he was Mordred. Yet she didn't appear infuriated today, but excited—almost glowing with flushed cheeks and bright eyes. He inhaled a ragged breath as hunger surged through him. Goddess, Juliet was even more bewitching than usual. If only he could taste her excitement by capturing her tempting lips in a ravenous kiss. But he was still a hideous beast.

Juliet beamed at him as she sank into the chair before his desk. "I've realized how to break your curse at last."

He straightened as another jolt—this one not from desiring Juliet for once—darted through him. He'd finally be human again! Then they'd be free of the veiled witch's wards and could escape their confinement alone together. The energy darting through him ebbing, he exhaled. No wonder Juliet appeared excited.

Juliet leaned toward him. "I must reverse it using opposing magic and invoking the positives of the creatures Elvaira cursed you to be."

He frowned and drummed his claws on the desk. Opposing

magic? And what positives could Juliet possibly find? "How exactly?"

Juliet leaned closer. "By countering every aspect of Elvaira's curse. Thankfully, she was an ordinary Rhiannon descendant like me, and she cast her curse alone, so I've that part covered." She sighed and straightened. "Elvaira cast her curse on your natalday to bind it to your life force, but performing the spell to break it on Summerday should offset that by invoking the power of the Goddess. Although Longnight or your natalday would be even better."

Oakmoor grunted, his frown fading. Because Longnight celebrated new beginnings rather than courtship like Summerday and his natalday was the same day. "Perhaps we should wait until Longnight or my natalday to attempt breaking my curse."

Juliet grimaced. "I don't think we should. The longer your curse remains, the more ingrained it shall become. And if we wait until your natalday, we'll only have one chance to break your curse since the veiled witch's prophecy states it shall become permanent after that. But if we start our attempts on Summerday, we can attempt again at the other festivals of the Goddess as well as your natalday if needed."

Oakmoor slowly nodded. So they'd have five attempts to break his curse. "Sounds sensible, as long as you can find positives of the creatures I'm cursed to be and can prepare your spell in time. Summerday is just six days away."

Juliet quirked a wry smile. "I'm sure I can. Elvaira cast her curse using her will and an incantation, so all I must prepare in advance is my counter-incantation invoking the positives of goats, snakes, and lions. And writing that shouldn't take long now that I understand what to do."

He exhaled. True, writing a precise and powerful incantation would be nothing to a witch as skilled as Juliet, who was accustomed to creating intricate and innovative spells. Thank the Goddess she was the lady meant to break his curse.

Juliet pursed her lips. "As for the finer details, I'll cast the spell to break your curse around noon in the ballroom. The sun being at its height shall address Elvaira casting her curse under the power of darkness. And your ballroom is the largest open space in Oakmoor House, like the clearing where she cast her curse. The garden, although outside, isn't open enough." She hummed. "Also, I'd rather use your blood to set the focus, instead of hair like Elvaira did, since blood's magical link is a bit stronger."

Oakmoor nodded again. Given all the details Juliet already had settled, she'd certainly be ready by Summerday. He was truly fortunate that she'd chosen to trap herself with him.

A blush darkening her cheeks, Juliet inhaled then said, "Then to seal my spell, I must use sex magic to counter Elvaira using death magic since it contains the power of life."

His blood surging, he gaped at Juliet. He'd *finally* get to make love with her once more. He could sate his primal hunger for the bewitching witch like he'd imagined whenever they drew close, as he had in his carnal dreams for the past fourteen years. His blood cooled. But surely Juliet wouldn't want that now. He shook his head. "You can't possibly be willing to go that far to break my curse."

Still blushing, Juliet lifted her clenched jaw. "Why not? 'Tisn't as if we've not been intimate before."

Their long ago night echoing through him, his body hardened with painful hunger. Dear Goddess, how he burned for Juliet. Yet he was too hideous for any woman to be willing to make love with him. He gripped his knees to remain still, his claws piercing his skin. "Yes, but I wasn't a hideous beast that night or the times we've kissed since."

Juliet shrugged, blushing even darker. "I'm certain we can still manage to make love. We have to—'tis the only way to break your curse. If we don't, the veiled witch's wards shall keep us trapped together forever, and neither of us wants that."

A pang piercing him, Oakmoor charged around the desk and sat beside Juliet. Grasping her chin, he tilted her head until their gazes met, and his heart quickened. He exhaled and forced himself not to caress her soft skin. "Are you *truly* willing to do that for me?"

Her eyes flickering, Juliet stared up at him. Then she twisted her chin free. "I just told you I was, you idiot man. Besides, now that I understand it, the veiled witch's prophecy plainly refers to us making love as part of breaking your curse."

He frowned. So the prophecy's words about love referred to physical love. He never would have realized that. But the prophecy mentioning marriage and her love being strong and true had confused him. Yet doubtless 'twas only referring to Juliet's determination and strength.

Warmth flooded him. Only Juliet would be determined and strong enough to suffer making love to a hideous beast to save someone she felt duty-bound to help. His pulse flaring, he captured her hands and pressed a tender kiss against her palms. "Thank you, Juliet, for risking so much for me."

Juliet jerked her hands free then cleared her throat. "About that... The spell to break your curse shall be similar to a blood-binding spell, so we may end up bloodbound afterward."

Suddenly breathless, Oakmoor inhaled. Being bloodbound would mean his and Juliet's life forces would be bound until death, making intimacy and children with others impossible. He'd *have* to marry her then, and his rakehell days would be over. Although he'd always intended to remain faithful to his wife once he married. And he'd not been much of a rakehell for the past ten months thanks to only wanting Juliet.

Burying that, he flashed a smirk and quipped, "We'd better hope we don't. A renowned rakehell like me being bloodbound would be a tragedy."

Juliet snorted and raised her eyes skyward. "For you. And me, since I'd be bloodbound to you. Everyone else at court would be grateful."

He arched a sardonic brow. "Are you certain about that? I can imagine quite a few other ladies who wouldn't be the least grateful." He laughed when Juliet snorted again, even more disdainfully than before. So delightful. He leaned toward her. "Anything besides bloodbinding that we're risking with your spell to break my curse?"

Juliet stilled. "Death, I suppose, if we expend more magical energy than our bodies can handle. But 'tisn't likely."

Oakmoor studied Juliet's too still face. She was clearly concealing something. "What about pregnancy?"

Juliet drew herself rigidly upright. "Pregnancy isn't a risk you need to concern yourself about."

He grunted. No doubt because the strong-magic contraceptive charms they both wore would prevent that. So *what* was Juliet concealing? He raked her with a narrow glance then almost winced. Probably how disgusting making love to him as a hideous beast would be.

Juliet leapt to her feet. "Now that I've told how we must break your curse, I should begin writing the incantation. Unless you've further questions?"

Oakmoor grimaced and rose as well. Juliet appeared desperate to flee. "Not at the moment."

Juliet nodded then bolted from his study. Yes, she was definitely concealing her disgust at making love to him now. Would she even be able to manage it?

Over the days before Summerday, Oakmoor barely saw Juliet. She spent her days locked in her workroom and only briefly emerged for meals before disappearing again. Ever since the special evening he'd planned, they no longer studied magic together or jointly prepared meals before sharing comfortable evenings talking. Juliet was too focused on breaking his curse for any of that. Which was good because that meant she'd surely break his curse on their first attempt. Then they could resume their normal lives—as long as they didn't become bloodbound. They'd be trapped together forever then. Not a fate either of them wanted, and an unwanted bloodbinding would be painful to endure.

Although her determination to break his curse *was* good, his days were empty with Juliet so busy. He filled his time with chores about the townhouse, preparing more and more complicated dishes, and reading interesting books about magic or distant kingdoms. Yet none of those were as satisfying as talking with Juliet would have been. Not that he missed her specifically—talking with anyone at court would have sufficed. Thankfully, Summerday wasn't far away, so he'd not need to endure this isolation much longer. Unless Juliet failed, which she probably wouldn't.

The evening preceding Summerday, Oakmoor handed Juliet a gingyr-orenge spriss before dinner, and his pulse stirred. Goddess, tomorrow they'd be making love together at last. He could finally kiss and caress her until they both shattered in explosive release, like he'd hungered for since their long ago night. And their coming together would also fuel Juliet's powerful counter-spell that would break Elvaira's vindictive curse, so he'd soon be human once more.

He scrutinized Juliet as she sipped her favorite spiritpunch, and his pulse slowed. She appeared weary—faint lines creased her beautiful face, shadows underscored her dark eyes, and she was somewhat pale. If she didn't rest tonight, she'd never be able to perform her powerful counter-spell tomorrow. And she might hurt herself attempting to do so. But how to convince the stubborn witch she must rest?

After they began their haddock soup, he asked, "Everything prepared for tomorrow?"

Juliet smiled and nodded. "I've my incantation memorized and all the magical accoutrements I need laid out and ready."

He couldn't help his grin at Juliet's calm confidence. "I'm not surprised you're so well prepared." The industrious and skilled royal witch always was. He arched his brows at her. "You said we'll perform the spell around noon?" When Juliet repeated her earlier calm nod, he continued, "I'll prepare an early luncheon for us so we can eat before we start."

Juliet tilted her head as she finished her haddock soup. "Something hardy but not too heavy. We don't wish to fall asleep midway."

While he collected their empty dishes, Oakmoor waggled his brows at her. "I'll have you know, no lady has ever fallen asleep on me midway." When Juliet huffed a disgusted sigh like he'd intended, he chuckled and added, "But I know the perfect luncheon to prepare." One that would nourish her soul as well as her body.

He left then returned moments later with their main course of pastry-wrapped beefsteak, roast tubers, and green beans. "Your pastry-wrapped beefsteak at long last, my demanding witch."

Juliet laughed. "How brave of you to attempt it."

He grinned at Juliet. "After all my practice over the past month, my culinary skills have vastly improved. And I thought you deserved the one special food you'd requested." Plus, with her so busy, he'd plenty of time to figure out how to prepare it.

Juliet's lips quirked as she cut into the flaky pastry wrapped around the slightly pink beefsteak coated with pate and mushroom puree. "Truthfully, although I enjoy pastry-wrapped beefsteak, I only requested the difficult dish to torment you."

Oakmoor chuckled. "I know. But I still thought you deserved it." And tonight would likely be the last dinner he prepared for Juliet, so it had to be memorable.

They both ate a bite of pastry-wrapped beefsteak, then Juliet sighed and said, "Well, your culinary skills didn't fail you. 'Tis excellent."

He smiled into his wine glass. The difficult dish *had* turned out better than he'd expected. "Thanks." Once they'd eaten most of their main course, he arched his brows at Juliet and asked, "Anything besides preparing meals you'll require from me tomorrow?"

Juliet swallowed the last of her roast tubers. "Just to arrive in the ballroom after luncheon in your dressing gown. I can't break your curse without you, and undressing mid-spell shall be difficult."

His pulse stirring once more, Oakmoor nodded. As would making love on the cold, hard ballroom floor. "I'll also steal a mattress from one of the guest bedchambers for us. Much more comfortable, especially at our age."

Juliet blushed as she finished her pastry-wrapped beefsteak. "Good idea."

Reburying his aching desire for Juliet, he waved his final forkful of green beans and asked to shift their discussion from making love, "So what is the incantation you wrote for tomorrow?"

Juliet sipped her red wine. "'Tis best if you don't know so that you're surprised like you were for Elvaira's. Although I did write it in the witch's tongue. The shades of meaning are much more precise."

He nodded again. The complexity of the witch's tongue was why only witches bothered to learn it, but its precision allowed intricate spells that mightn't be possible otherwise.

Juliet grimaced. "I suspect Elvaira only used common tongue to cast your curse so that you'd understand and dread your fate."

Oakmoor sighed as he rose and collected their empty plates. If he'd not known what was coming, Elvaira's curse wouldn't have transformed his entire life like she'd clearly wanted. "Probably."

Juliet flashed a bright smile, no doubt to cheer him. "But since you know the witch's tongue now, I can use it and still have you understand like you must in order for my counter-spell to succeed."

He inclined his head then left and fetched their raspberry tarts along with sparkling wine. He smiled at Juliet as he settled beside her once more. "I thought we could toast tomorrow's success over dessert."

Juliet tsked and eyed her flute of sparkling wine askance. "You know 'tis dangerous to count your faebirds before they hatch."

Still smiling, Oakmoor shrugged. "Not if you're the one hatching them. You always achieve what you set out to do. 'Tis how a powerless Varkhoran girl became the most illustrious witch in Calatini." When Juliet's cheeks darkened at his unplanned praise, he toasted her with his flute. "To another triumph for Calatini's skilled royal witch and life returning to normal."

Her gaze flickering, Juliet echoed his toast. "To escaping the things that trap us. No matter what they are."

He swallowed, almost losing his smile. Juliet *would* be relieved to escape being trapped with the rakehell she'd always hated wanting, who'd become a hideous beast for his sins. He straightened and downed his sparkling wine. He'd be relieved too. Their enforced intimacy had begun to feel dangerously comfortable, and he admired and desired Juliet more than ever now that he'd truly gotten to know her. His jaw tightened. But those mad feelings would surely fade once their enforced intimacy ended and they resumed their normal lives at court.

They devoured their raspberry tarts in silence. After they finished, Juliet rose. "I should return to my workroom."

Rising too, Oakmoor narrowed his eyes at Juliet. And indubitably exhaust herself further. He couldn't let Juliet endanger herself like that. He cocked a brow. "Why? I thought you said everything was prepared for tomorrow."

Juliet shrugged and began toward the door. "It is, but I could review everything again."

He grunted, his mouth firming. "That doesn't seem necessary." Perhaps provoking Juliet's fierce pride would force her to rest. "Unless your true purpose is to avoid me."

Juliet whirled to face him, her set chin high. "As if I'd bother to do that."

Oakmoor smiled and captured Juliet's arm. Thank the

Goddess for her pride. "Then you can't object to playing a few hands of cards before we retire for the evening." Early so she could get enough rest.

Midway through their first hand of ten card in the games-room, Juliet studied him over her cards. "From your toast, it sounds like you're desperate to return to life at court. I suppose being trapped with just one lady *was* impossibly dull for you."

His shoulders stiffening, he kept his gaze on his ten cards. Except being trapped with Juliet hadn't been dull at all, until she became too busy. Not that he could ever admit that aloud. "It was an adjustment."

As he drew a card then discarded one, Juliet tilted her head. "I suppose without Elvaira's curse threatening you, you'll resume your rakehell ways with abandon."

Oakmoor suppressed a grimace. Somehow *that* sounded impossibly dull, unlike his confinement with Juliet. He'd gotten too old to play such empty games. And he did want a family, which meant marriage. While she took her turn, he made himself shrug. "Or I might settle on an eligible lady and start that family we talked about. Like you, I'm not getting any younger." And he'd that degenerate cousin to worry about.

Juliet stilled. "I can't picture you remaining with one lady for the rest of your life."

His jaw clenched and chest twisted. Juliet still only saw him as the greatest rakehell in Ormas. To play the tired, familiar role she obviously expected, he cocked a brow and drawled despite having no intention of taking lovers after he married, "If I marry the right lady—one solely interested in a fashionable alliance—I shan't need to remain with just her."

Juliet shuddered. "Not the most stable home for children. I'll never raise mine that way. People should only marry if they *both* truly love each other." Her voice softened, "For all our battles, Father adored Mother, and I expect my husband to feel the same about me."

Oakmoor swallowed as an ache pierced him, sharper than

any dwarf's dagger. Even though he'd be faithful to his wife, he'd never adore her like Juliet wanted. "You're a romantic."

Her cheeks flushed, Juliet glared at him. "I'm not. Marriage possesses so many disadvantages to an independent lady that only mutual love strong enough to last a lifetime makes it worth the risk. I shan't settle for anything less."

He shifted in his seat and forced himself to play some cards. Juliet deserved the adoring husband she wanted. Which could never be him despite his primal hunger for her. He could never trust a lady or love enough to be such a mad fool. The ache in his chest sharpened.

To distract them both from marriage, he asked while Juliet took her turn, "How shall we handle our return to court?"

Juliet pursed her lips. "I suppose that depends on what happened while we were gone and what King Devon and Queen Kiera told court about our absence."

Oakmoor sighed as he reorganized his cards. "True. But do you think we should return as enemies or friends?" Not that being friends with a former lover you always burned to kiss was truly possible. But they could be friendly at least.

Juliet swallowed and fanned her cards on the table. "I think we should return to avoiding each other while we strive to resume our normal lives."

The curious ache in his chest stabbed him yet again, but he inhaled and made himself shove it aside. While striving to resume his normal life, he'd have no time for the maddening witch anyway. First, he must summon his servants and horses back from Oakmoor, which meant many jump travel spells. Thankfully, he could cast them himself since he could quit concealing his magical powers now that they were no longer erratic. And in addition to reestablishing his household, he must catch up on his ducal and foreign duties, including repairing his relationship with the Orandians. Plus, he must begin his hunt for his future wife, whomever she might be, although she definitely wasn't Juliet. *Fortunately*. He refused to suffer having a wife who wanted an adoring husband.

His teeth tightening, he laid out his cards like Juliet's. "You're right." He studied their cards. Unsurprisingly, Juliet had won. "Six points to you."

They began another hand of ten card and continued playing until she reached a hundred points to win the game. Then he insisted they head to their chambers so she could rest.

After breakfast on Summerday, Oakmoor prevented Juliet's escape to her workroom. She'd only make herself nervous by pondering exactly what they must do to break his curse. And she didn't need to review her doubtless already perfect details. Instead, he occupied her with stories from the recent books he'd read until he left to prepare their luncheon of reboiled soup, crusty rolls, saffron-gingyr cooked cream, and Varkhoran kahve. The ideal hearty meal to nourish them for their difficult spell-work ahead as well as warm Juliet's soul since those favorite dishes reminded her of happy memories from her childhood.

Following luncheon, they changed into their dressing gowns then met in the heart of his ballroom beside the feather mattress he'd brought there earlier. The bright midday sunlight streamed through his dazzling stained-glass ceiling, casting rainbow-hued light about the ballroom, like the golden beam gilding Juliet's exotic olive skin and intense dark-brown hair. Gorgeous. And he was about to make love with her again at long last.

His heart quickening, Oakmoor gave Juliet a smooth grin and drawled, "Ready to break my beast curse and resume our normal lives?"

CHAPTER 24

At Oakmoor's drawled question, Juliet inhaled a steadying breath. "Yes, I'm ready." Even though she'd be risking everything to break his curse and would lose him forever as soon as she did. Plus, somehow she must conceal her love and feign mere desire when they made love. Oakmoor would only pity her if he knew how much she loved him since he could never return it.

She gathered her will and created a blazing white witchlight above her head like Elvaira had. Then she made it turn indigo representing her strong love instead of the scarlet of Elvaira's vindictive hate. She extracted her gold ritual dagger from her dressing gown pocket. "Your hand, Oakmoor."

Once he offered it to her palm up, she slashed his palm and hurled his blood into her witchlight to set her counter-spell's focus before returning her dagger to her pocket and murmuring a weak healing spell to close his wound. Then in the melodic witch's tongue, she chanted, "Oh, mighty wind come and bind this man to me as the sun's healing power fills my magic."

Like when Elvaira began her curse, a howling wind whipped around Juliet and Oakmoor, but sparkling gold rather than the black of death swirled in her indigo witchlight, which soon unraveled into the wind like Elvaira's had. The sunlight and wind swelled her magic's strength and made it glow as bright as the midday sun above the townhouse, binding them together until her counter-spell was complete.

Squinting in the blinding light, she stepped closer to Oakmoor and placed her left hand over his heart and her right on his scaled face. Although Elvaira hadn't touched him when casting her curse, touch would allow her magic to pour directly into him and facilitate her sex magic. Still in the witch's tongue, she belted over the howling wind, "A hideous beast you are, reflecting your first lover's bitter hatred, not your true self. Like a gamboling goat, you are social and suave and filled with determination and desire. Like a supple snake, you are astute and deft with the power of rebirth and fertility. Like a lordly lion, you are influential and masculine and imbued with courage and strength. A man so wonderful that a lady can't help but love you when you finally let her see your true self concealed behind your wary facade. By the power of the Goddess on this Summerday celebrating courtship and the power of life, I seal this counter-curse with my magic, body, and heart."

The howling wind whirling even faster and her magic's blinding light flaring even brighter, Juliet pulled Oakmoor's head down and captured his mouth in a deep kiss while she poured her magic and love into her spell. Returning her kiss with equal hunger, he yanked her against him and slid his hands beneath her dressing gown. As his earthy sandalwood scent surrounded her, she moaned and did likewise. Goddess, she needed him.

Feverish desire consuming them like always, they ripped off their dressing gowns and fell onto the feather mattress beside them. Their mouths and hands desperate, they kissed and caressed each other everywhere before coming together at last. When they shattered in explosive release, she flung all her magic, desire, and love at the vindictive curse trapping Oakmoor.

The howling wind died, and her blinding indigo and gold magic sucked into Oakmoor like oil into a dry wick. Shining with pulsing light, he gasped and stiffened then writhed and screamed as her counter-spell battled the curse inside his body.

Tears scalding her face at his agony, Juliet clung to Oakmoor and kissed him. She whispered against his lips, "Please live, my love, and be free. Please."

Then the light inside Oakmoor exploded and shot skyward, its afterimage dancing before her eyes as it shattered his stained-glass ceiling high above them. She whimpered and buried her face in his chest until her dazzled vision cleared. While colored glass tinkled to the floor but somehow missed them and the mattress, she lifted her head and blinked at him then shuddered a sigh. Oakmoor was human again. Thank the Goddess!

Light bubbling in her veins despite her trembling exhaustion, she placed her palm on Oakmoor's strong jaw, now prickly with a gray-flecked beard. Clearly he'd not needed to shave when he'd a snake's face. Made sense since snakes didn't have hair. She smiled into his dazed eyes. "We broke your beast curse."

Oakmoor tenderly kissed her palm. "No, you did. Thank you, Juliet."

She blushed at the sincere warmth softening Oakmoor's face and roughening his voice. She should really extract herself from their intimate embrace and don her dressing gown. But remaining pressed against him felt so amazing.

Smiling, Oakmoor threaded his hands through her hair and drew her head down. "You're an amazing lady, my royal witch." Then he kissed her.

Giddy with a mixture of exhaustion and desire, she sighed into Oakmoor's soft, lingering kiss. How she loved him. Unable to resist, she opened her mouth and deepened their kiss.

Their mouths never separating, Oakmoor rumbled and flipped her beneath him, his warm hands stroking her and leaving tingling behind.

They made love with sweet and tender passion that was just

as satisfying as their wild and explosive desire earlier. Perhaps Oakmoor *did* love her like she loved him. After their release, they collapsed into slumber with their bodies joined. Both drained from their intense spellwork and passion, they slept entwined for the rest of the afternoon.

When her rumbling stomach finally roused her, Juliet smiled and cuddled closer to Oakmoor, who was still deeply asleep from his slow breathing. If he truly returned her love and wanted her as his wife, she could risk marrying him. Just as well since she was quite possibly pregnant after their passionate afternoon. All that powerful sex magic had definitely inactivated their contraceptive charms, and today was her most fertile time, although pregnancy was somewhat less certain since she was older. But Summerday was the festival of the Goddess that cele-brated fertility, and she *had* invoked the power of the Goddess. Plus, they'd made love not just once but twice.

Somewhat giddy after all that despite her nap, she laid her hand over Oakmoor's heart, and warmth suffused her chest. They could build such a wonderful life and family together. She'd continue serving as Calatini's royal witch, and he'd continue serving as the Minister of Foreign Relations, while they lovingly raised their children and passionately came together at night. They'd be busy and fulfilled but enjoy a life outside their duty. Finally, they'd each have someone they could share secrets with and trust with their entire heart. Something she'd always secretly longed for but never imagined she'd find.

She was about the wake her sleeping love with a deep kiss when Oakmoor suddenly stiffened and his breathing quickened. He cleared his throat. "Well, *that* was intense."

Juliet grinned against Oakmoor's skin then flexed her fingers in the rough hair on his muscular chest. Perhaps they could make love a third time before preparing dinner together. Although she was ravenous and exhausted, food and sleep could wait. She hummed and kissed the hollow of his throat. "Very intense."

Oakmoor swallowed as his body hardened against hers. "Do you feel any different?"

Heat flooding her and her pulse surging once more, she shifted even closer. Oakmoor obviously burned to make love again too. Lovely. She trailed kisses up his neck on her way to his mouth. Between kisses, she murmured, "I feel somewhat hungry and tired, yet remarkably lighthearted and amorous."

Oakmoor jerked back just before she reached his mouth. "Stop that. I can't think when you're kissing me."

Juliet stilled, a faint chill piercing her desire. Why wasn't Oakmoor returning her kisses? "Do you need to?"

Oakmoor frowned at her. "While I'm attempting to determine if we're bloodbound, yes."

She tensed as her chill grew. Them being bloodbound hardly mattered if Oakmoor returned her love. She eyed him. "We're not. Our life forces don't feel joined at all."

Oakmoor blew a loud sigh. "Thank the Goddess for that."

Juliet wrenched herself from Oakmoor's arms, even though her abrupt movement made her head whirl. How dare he sound so relieved? "Excuse me?"

Oakmoor snorted. "Don't act insulted. You don't want to be bloodbound to me any more than I want to be to you." His lips twisted. "We'd be trapped together forever then."

A hollow ache supplanted her earlier desire. Oakmoor considered being bloodbound to her a trap? Then he *mustn't* love her like she loved him. She should have known he couldn't love her or want to marry her. Yet why had he made love to her the second time with such sweet and tender passion? She swallowed. Doubtless to demonstrate his gratitude for breaking his curse. Plus, he *had* been celibate for ten months, an eternity for a rakehell like Oakmoor, and making love once wouldn't have sated him. Surprising he'd not responded to her kisses just now. But he'd probably been too worried about being trapped with her forever.

She flashed a smirk to conceal the ache making her chest as

hollow as her rumbling stomach and drained magical powers. Then she mockingly echoed what he'd said the other day, "And a renowned rakehell like you being trapped by a bloodbinding would be a tragedy. The foolish ladies at court would sob in their cold, empty beds every night that you'd never again seduce then abandon them."

Oakmoor inhaled then yanked her back into his arms and rolled her beneath him. "Speaking from experience?"

Lightheaded from his swift maneuver yet hot and throbbing at their intimate embrace, Juliet shoved his shoulders and winced away from his descending mouth. If Oakmoor kissed her, she'd be lost. She'd let him seduce her once more even though she knew it meant nothing to him. Not only would that further increase her risk of pregnancy, which was already too likely, but succumbing so easily might also make him realize that she loved him.

She huffed. "As if I'd ever sob for a disgusting rakehell like you." She repeated her earlier shove. "Now would you get off me? Your curse is broken, so we've no further need to make love. And your weight is crushing me."

Their gazes locked and her body aching with emptiness, Oakmoor remained motionless above her for several agonizing moments. Then he grunted and rolled off her. "You're the most maddening witch."

Still lightheaded and aching, she gulped a deep breath. 'Twas fortunate Oakmoor had finally moved. She'd not have been able to resist kissing him for much longer. Damn her helpless love for him and his irresistible masculine allure. She drawled, "As you said, thank the Goddess we're not bloodbound. We'd kill each other before the year was through."

Oakmoor grunted again but said nothing.

Juliet swallowed. No reply to that barb, so Oakmoor clearly agreed. Burning to kiss him still, she drew another deep breath. She'd better leave his townhouse before she forgot herself entirely. She hurriedly sat then swayed as her head whirled and vision darkened. Even if Oakmoor had returned her love, making love a third time definitely wouldn't have been wise.

Oakmoor surged upright and gripped her arm with a frown. "Are you all right?"

She shook off Oakmoor's grip despite her lingering dizziness and the tingling filling her at his touch. "I'm fine. Just a bit drained after this afternoon." She managed a dismissive smile. "But nothing to stop me from gathering my belongings so I can return to the palace."

Oakmoor scowled. "Liar. You're so drained you can't even sit without almost fainting. What you need is food and more rest to help you recover. You're going nowhere today."

Juliet grimaced but sighed and nodded. Unfortunately, Oakmoor was right. She'd collapse if she attempted to leave now. Yet remaining would be painful.

His scowl fading at her silent nod, Oakmoor continued, "I'll escort you upstairs then prepare dinner for you. Now, where are our dressing gowns?" He frowned when his gaze halted on their dressing gowns on the floor where they'd dropped them. "They're covered in glass."

She shrugged. Oakmoor must have been too immersed in the magic battling inside him to notice anything else. Not surprising. "When the counter-spell triumphed over your beast curse, it exploded and shattered the ceiling."

Oakmoor glanced upward then frowned fiercer. "Damnation, that stained glass was supposed to be unbreakable."

Juliet followed Oakmoor's gaze. The once-dazzling stained glass was gone, although the steel framework remained. "Not against the amount of magic in that counter-spell." Almost any spell caught in that would have been overpowered and inactivated. Like their contraceptive charms had also been. Somehow she must repair his before he noticed that. He'd wonder about her falling pregnant if he did.

Oakmoor sighed. "I always worried that magic could shatter it. But a shattered ceiling is a small price to break my beast curse." He grimaced. "Although repairing it shall be near impossible. I'll have to summon my duchy's best artisan witches, but none of them have ever created such intricate work."

She hummed as a pang surged through her. "At least they'll have an excellent glass furnace in the townhouse they can use." In her former workroom.

Sighing once more, Oakmoor nodded. "True, but enough about that. 'Tis a problem for another day." He scooped her into his arms and rose.

Her empty stomach fluttering and head giddy again, Juliet squeaked and hit Oakmoor's shoulders. "What are you *doing*?"

Oakmoor arched a brow. "Carrying you upstairs."

She glowered at Oakmoor and squirmed in his arms. Being carried like this was too seductive. "I'm well able to walk."

Oakmoor tsked and shook his head. "Not without cutting your feet on the remains of my stained-glass ceiling."

Juliet sniffed and squirmed harder. Must Oakmoor act so caring toward her? It made feigning indifference painful. "Your feet are as bare as mine."

Oakmoor narrowed his eyes at her. "But *my* magic isn't drained after performing a powerful counter-spell. I can cast a levitation spell to get us safely across. Now quit squirming and hush so I can do so."

She snapped her mouth shut and held herself rigidly still as Oakmoor murmured an incantation to cast his levitation spell then carried her across the ballroom without touching the floor. After he ended the levitation spell in the hall, she began to protest she could walk but fell silent at his glare. He was obviously determined to carry her.

As Oakmoor strode upstairs with her cradled in his arms, she kept herself stiff as a gorgon's stone victim. She daren't relax against him—she might kiss him if she did. Much too revealing. Besides, she should repair his contraceptive charm while he was distracted. She pricked her finger then brushed her blood on the contraceptive charm about his neck to use some of her life force and the very last of her magical energy to re-infuse it with magic. Hopefully, 'twould work since her healing spells weren't powerful enough to create a new one. Blackness danced before her eyes and her dizzy head whirled faster than a dervishwind by the time she finished, so she gulped air to prevent herself from fainting. No matter how distracted, Oakmoor would notice that.

When they finally reached the guest bedchamber, Oakmoor carefully set her on the bed. He wasn't even breathing hard despite carrying her across the townhouse. Unlike her. She sighed as Oakmoor fetched her a nightgown from the wardrobe and tossed it at her. While she donned the nightgown, he rumbled, "Don't you dare leave that bed. I'll return shortly with dinner."

Although she glowered at the overbearing man, Juliet burrowed beneath the covers as soon as he left. Goddess, she was exhausted. And pretending she wasn't in front of Oakmoor, clashing with him, and repairing his contraceptive charm had further exhausted her. She soon sank into slumber despite her empty stomach and only woke when Oakmoor returned with a laden tray.

While he strode to the tea table, she sat up and rubbed the sleep from her eyes. Although she was still ravenous and exhausted with drained magic, at least her head no longer whirled, so feigning normal vigor would be easier. She studied Oakmoor as he set the tray on the tea table. He'd taken time to shave and dress in evening clothes, appearing the suave Duke of Oakmoor once more instead of her intimate companion for the past month. Although he *had* brought her a hearty dinner he knew she'd enjoy—reboiled soup with crusty rolls, beefsteak and mashed tubers, gingyr tea with honey, and fluted domes of saffron-gingyr cooked cream. And he'd decorated the tray with a basket of purple gentians.

Her chest squeezing, she slid from bed and donned a dressing gown. If only Oakmoor's caring was proof that he loved and wanted her. But 'twas mere gratitude and his gift for charming others. To keep her indifferent facade, she arched her brows and murmured, "Isn't this meal practically the same as what you served at luncheon?"

Oakmoor smiled and shrugged as they sat at the tea table. "Yes, except for the gingyr tea, beefsteak, and tubers. I figured we'd need hearty sustenance after attempting to break my curse, so I prepared extra reboiled soup and cooked cream this morning."

Juliet gritted a smirk. "What thoughtful planning." That she'd never enjoy again. Although she could if she revealed her possible pregnancy. Oakmoor would insist they marry out of guilt for her pregnancy being the true price to break his curse as well as to give his child his name. But she couldn't risk marrying him unless he returned her love. Concealing her love for him would be impossible as his wife, and she'd despise his pity about that. Plus, an unrepentant rakehell like Oakmoor would never remain faithful unless he truly loved his wife, and 'twould shatter her when he took other lovers while married to her.

She swallowed and stirred her reboiled soup without tasting it. She definitely daren't share that she could be pregnant. And if she was, she'd have to leave Calatini before her pregnancy showed. Falling pregnant while unwed would destroy her influence at court, and Oakmoor would surely attempt to force their marriage. She sighed. Perhaps she could rejoin the gypsies or settle in Orandia.

Oakmoor frowned and leaned toward her. "Juliet, are you all right? You're not eating."

She tensed then flashed a glittering smile. "I'm fine. Just thinking about returning to our normal lives at court." She forced herself to eat some reboiled soup. "I'm eager to get started."

His eyes narrowing, Oakmoor humphed. "Me too."

She almost winced. No doubt because Oakmoor was desperate to take other lovers again and find that young wife he wanted to bear his children. A wife that would never be her. She made herself finish her reboiled soup and begin her beefsteak and mashed tubers. Not only did she need the food to recover from her intense spellwork, but she might be eating for two.

Smiling anew, Oakmoor cocked a brow once she'd finished the main course. "What changes do you think we'll find at court after our month-long absence?"

Juliet shrugged while devouring her cooked cream. So delicious. She'd miss Oakmoor cooking it for her. "Besides Lord Blaine being wed to Miss Hawke? I'm not certain. Although we'll know soon enough." Once she scraped her plate clean, she rose. "Thank you for dinner, but I should return to bed."

Oakmoor rose as well. "Of course." He swiftly stacked all the dishes on the tray. "I'll see you in the morning."

She swallowed. If only 'twouldn't be their last morning together. She must get Oakmoor to leave before she betrayed that longing. In her haste to open the door, she stumbled on a nearby footstool.

Oakmoor surged over and yanked her against him before she fell.

Their bodies pressed together, Juliet blinked up at Oakmoor and licked her lips as her pulse flared. How she burned for him.

With a groan, Oakmoor seized her mouth in a ravaging kiss.

Feverish emptiness swamping her again, she devoured his mouth and wrenched on his evening clothes. More, more, more.

But just before she reached his skin, Oakmoor jerked back and swore. "What are we *doing*? You need rest, not wild passion." He strode to the tea table and snatched the tray before hurrying toward the door. "Good night, Juliet."

Once Oakmoor left, she staggered to bed and pulled the covers over her head. Goddess, she was too weak where he was concerned. She must leave as soon as she'd rested. She sank into slumber, but despite her exhaustion, her sleep was restless, and she woke not long after dawn.

Her drained magical powers barely recharged, Juliet stumbled from bed and dressed then dragged out her enchanted satchel. Not bothering to pack any clothes—Oakmoor had bought them, so he could keep them—she headed downstairs to her former workroom to collect all her magical supplies. She dumped everything into her satchel, including the gold ritual dagger she'd used when breaking Oakmoor's curse. He must have tidied the ballroom yesterday and returned it here. Then she slipped from the still and silent townhouse to return to her hollow life as the royal witch.

CHAPTER 25

When Juliet didn't join him for breakfast the morning after Summerday, Oakmoor frowned and muttered a preservation spell to keep their eggs, tubers, bacon, and Varkhoran kahve warm before sweeping from the breakfast room to find her. He headed upstairs to her bedchamber first. Perhaps Juliet had been so drained from breaking his curse that she was still sleeping. If so, he'd collect their breakfast and bring it upstairs to eat at her tea table like they had dinner yesterday.

But when he entered her bedchamber, 'twas empty and silent. He exhaled. Juliet mustn't be as drained as he'd feared. Good. He hurried back downstairs. She must be in her workroom, most likely gathering her magical supplies to return to the palace. Why hadn't the stubbornly independent witch waited until after breakfast and asked for his help?

Yet when he stepped inside Juliet's workroom, 'twas as empty and silent as her bedchamber. He scowled and stiffened. Where was she? Perhaps inspecting the ballroom. He hastened there, but it too was empty and silent. His chest tightened. Had Juliet left him without even saying goodbye?

He strode through his townhouse but found no trace of her.

She *had* left him without saying goodbye. For her to be that rude, she'd clearly been desperate to escape the disgusting rakehell she hated wanting. Just as well she'd left though. Their enforced intimacy was too dangerous. He'd begun treating Juliet like an adored wife even though love and sincere commitment weren't for him. Besides, he'd be glad to have Oakmoor House to himself again—other than the servants he'd be fetching back today, of course.

Oakmoor stormed back to the breakfast room and devoured his breakfast then Juliet's, his jaw so clenched he could barely eat. But 'twould be shameful to let the food and Varkhoran kahve he'd prepared go to waste.

Then he went to his study to place another mirror call to Miles at Oakmoor Castle. Yesterday after dinner before cleaning the ballroom, he'd contacted Miles to see which servants would be willing to return today from their paid respites back home. His valet should have a list of other servants ready for him. Please let there be enough to staff the townhouse. Otherwise he might need to hire additional servants from Ormas. And although he no longer needed to worry about people discovering his curse and he could quit hiding his once-erratic magical powers, he still didn't want strangers living inside his home.

Thankfully, Miles said over two-thirds of the other servants were willing to return now, including his sister Martha and the rest of the kitchen servants as well as their cousin and head groom Hunter along with all the other grooms, who'd bring the horses with them. And the remaining servants would be ready to return in another week or two, so no strangers would be necessary.

Oakmoor headed to the ballroom and cast a jump travel spell on an anteroom doorway. He powered it with the sunlight streaming through his missing ceiling then set it to remain open until Miles or Martha said the brief incantation that would activate the closing part of the spell. He smiled as he eyed his deft spellwork. Juliet would be impressed when she saw it and say he'd an excellent teacher. His smile faded. Except she was no longer here. Fortunate because he didn't have time to waste talking with her anyway.

When Miles and Martha stepped through the enchanted anteroom doorway, he welcomed his valet and head cook back with a warm grin. Then he asked them to have Juliet's former bedchamber and workroom cleaned, deflecting them from wondering about the bedchamber by mentioning that the artisan witches who'd be repairing the ballroom's shattered stained-glass ceiling would require the workroom.

After telling Miles and Martha the brief incantation to close his jump travel spell, he left them to oversee the other servants' return. He must visit the palace then Escana House to begin resuming his duties at court. Like Juliet already had. Thrusting the absent royal witch from his mind, he went to the stables then took a carriage to the palace as soon as the first groom with two carriage horses returned.

At the palace, he asked the palace servants about meeting with King Devon and Queen Kiera, and they immediately ushered him up to the private dining room in the royal wing. He blinked at the table already laden with food, including dessert. Obviously, the royal servants had been told to expect him for luncheon.

Shortly after he arrived, King Devon and Queen Kiera bustled into their private dining room. At his polite bow, they gestured for him to sit, then King Devon said, "'Tis good to see you looking so well, your grace. Lady Juliet said you suffered no lingering effects from your beast curse."

Oakmoor inhaled as they all sat about the table. Not surprising that the industrious royal witch had already met with King Devon and Queen Kiera. Juliet despised being idle. He made himself flash a smooth smile. "Not that I can tell, no."

Queen Kiera grinned at him and waved at the food. "When Lady Juliet told us this morning that she'd broken your curse yesterday, we knew you'd be by to meet with us, and we figured a private luncheon would contain the gossip."

King Devon slanted his wife a warm glance while serving her some shredded chicken stew. "And that more food wouldn't go amiss."

As Oakmoor's brows rose at the king's cryptic comment, Queen Kiera grinned brighter and explained, "I've been perpetually ravenous ever since I fell pregnant. Unlike many ladies, I've suffered no nausea."

A pang darted through Oakmoor at the joy lighting King Devon's and Queen Kiera's faces. They were both plainly ecstatic to be starting their family together. Would he and his future wife feel the same? They'd not be in love like the royal couple were. Shoving that aside, he toasted King Devon and Queen Kiera with his teacup. "Congratulations, your majesties. All of Calatini shall rejoice to have an heir to the throne again. Have you announced your happy news to the kingdom yet?"

King Devon shook his head. "We've only told our family, close friends, and the council."

Queen Kiera finished her bowl of shredded chicken stew. "We wanted to wait until I was further along to tell anyone else— probably at our summer masquerade in a month. Fitting given I first appeared at court during the last one." She beamed at her husband while he served her more stew. "Besides, we've some changes to make before the announcement."

Oakmoor studied the royal couple. What did they mean by that? Since Queen Kiera had appeared at court nearly a year ago, she and King Devon had enacted some momentous changes, from her more favorably renegotiating the Nightmara-Calatini Treaty to her education initiative that improved the lives of the poor in Calatini. So what more did they intend to do?

But before he could ask, King Devon said, "Enough about that. We should acquaint you with other developments at court."

As Oakmoor inclined his head, Queen Kiera leaned toward him and said, "After the veiled witch told us you and Lady Juliet were trapped together until you broke your beast curse, we told all of court, including the council, that the two of you were away from Ormas handling a private royal matter for us."

King Devon nodded. "That reduced the gossip about your joint disappearance without disclosing your curse. Only our family knows about that." The king narrowed his eyes at him. "Since you kidnapped my young cousin in your attempt to break it."

Oakmoor shifted in his seat. An innocent girl who never could have saved him. Not like Juliet had with her magical skills and bold determination. And by making love with him. Tingling heat surged in his veins. Their intensely passionate afternoon had been as explosive and satisfying as he'd long dreamt. But dangerous. Burying his mad desire for Juliet, he offered a wry smile as he finished his shredded chicken stew. "A dreadful mistake, your majesty. I was confused about the prophecy the veiled witch gave me."

Queen Kiera patted her husband's hand. "Yes, the veiled witch explained that when she wrote us. Fortunately, Lady Juliet managed to take Pippa's place like she was meant to. And successfully broke your terrible curse in just over a month."

How they'd broken his curse echoing through him once more, Oakmoor swallowed as his body tightened. Never again. He served himself some grilled lamb, roast tubers, and broiled sparrow grass. "Lady Juliet is an amazingly powerful, skilled, and clever witch accustomed to creating intricate and innovative spells. Calatini is fortunate to have her serving as our royal witch. And I'll be forever in her debt."

King Devon and Queen Kiera traded a glance, then King Devon murmured, "True, although I'm shocked to hear you admit it, given the well-known dislike between you."

Queen Kiera smiled over her grilled lamb. "But perhaps that dislike is gone after your month alone together."

Oakmoor froze, his ache for Juliet flaring. Their well-known dislike had never been more than thwarted desire, and his desire for Juliet was stronger than ever. So strong that he'd burned to keep making love with her and never let her go when they'd woken entwined after breaking his curse. Just like they'd been the morning after they'd first made love fourteen years ago, even though he never slept or cuddled with his lovers. Only Juliet. He suppressed a shudder. Such lasting and voracious hunger that felt too right might bewitch him into forgetting that love and sincere commitment were for mad fools. So yesterday he'd buried his obsessive hunger and asked Juliet about being bloodbound instead. Then throughout the day while they were apart, he'd kept reminding himself that their intense intimacy was mad and dangerous and not for him. He nearly grimaced. Yet he'd still almost made love with her after dinner despite her obvious exhaustion, and he'd prepared her beloved Varkhoran kahve this morning and been irritated to find her gone even though he should have been relieved.

Yanking his mind back to his royal meeting, he gritted a smooth grin. He'd no intention of discussing such private matters with anyone, let alone King Devon and Queen Kiera. So in reply to Queen Kiera's comment about his and Juliet's dislike being gone, he simply drawled, "Perhaps." When the king and queen traded another glance, he asked, "Any other developments at court I should know?"

Queen Kiera hummed then replied, "Edouard eloped with Pippa after rescuing her from you. They only returned to Ormas yesterday, and the Duchess of Childes intends to host a fete for them in a week and a half to remove the scandal surrounding their elopement and convince court they simply married quietly."

Oakmoor almost winced. A scandal he'd caused by kidnapping the wrong lady. If 'twas ever discovered, court would never believe Miss Hawke had left his townhouse an innocent—he was the greatest rakehell in Ormas after all—so Lord Blaine had needed to marry Miss Hawke immediately to prevent gossip about her kidnapping from spreading and destroying her reputation. Since their elopement was his fault, he must help the Duchess of Childes remove the scandal surrounding it.

He inclined a nod. "Lord Blaine and the new Lady Blaine are a most devoted couple. I'll do what I can to support them. Now tell me, how did Lady Escana do performing my duties the past month?"

He and the royal couple spent the rest of luncheon discussing how well Lady Escana had handled acting as the Minister of Foreign Relations. Just as he'd expected the poised and diligent countess would.

After luncheon, he bowed to King Devon and Queen Kiera before striding from their private dining room. He stilled as he left the royal wing, his body hardening yet again. Although he'd never visited, the royal witch's wing was nearby. He could easily go see Juliet. And make love with her the entire afternoon... or longer.

He set his jaw. Except Juliet possessed no desire to see him, considering how she'd left him without saying goodbye. Besides, visiting and making love with her would only feed his obsessive hunger for her. He must avoid Juliet like she'd suggested so their lives could return to normal. They *both* wanted that.

Oakmoor turned and rushed from the palace then headed to Escana House. When he arrived, the Escanas' stout butler ushered him out to the garden.

Her and Lord Escana's toddler daughter and two of their hounds gamboling about her skirt, Lady Escana arched her brows at him over the massive stick she was holding. "Back, I see, your grace." The countess hurled her stick across the garden, and her hounds bayed and gave chase with the tiny girl close behind. "Was the private royal matter you and Lady Juliet left Ormas to handle resolved successfully?"

He exhaled. In his letter giving Lady Escana his duties, he'd not explained about his beast curse, so she believed the king and queen's pretense. Not that he was going to correct her. He flashed a charming grin. "Can you doubt it? I just came from meeting with King Devon and Queen Kiera. They said you handled my duties exceptionally well."

Her two hounds returning with the massive stick and her giggling daughter, Lady Escana grinned back at him as she collected the stick. "I enjoyed handling your duties, although Anthony grumbled how busy I was whenever I had to miss outings with the children. He'll be relieved you're back—unlike most gentlemen at court."

Oakmoor couldn't help chuckling. "Because your husband is certain of your devotion to him and that you consider me an annoying older brother." More couples should be like the Escanas. "Now tell me everything that happened while I was gone."

Lady Escana did, mentioning several developments King Devon and Queen Kiera hadn't bothered to discuss. Yet none of his assistant's disclosures were particularly surprising until the final one.

Lady Escana tilted her head as she hurled the massive stick once more. "In addition, a Varkhoran lord arrived in Ormas last week and is staying with his kingdom's ambassador."

Oakmoor stiffened. Varkhoran lords weren't common visitors to Calatini since women being equals here made them uncomfortable. King Devon and Queen Kiera must have forgotten to mention him since they were distracted by her pregnancy. Yet why was this Varkhoran visiting Calatini, and was he a danger to Juliet? He *had* appeared while she was trapped by the veiled witch's incredibly powerful wards. Oakmoor arched his brows at Lady Escana. "Do we know why this Varkhoran lord is visiting?"

Lady Escana sighed as her hounds dropped the massive stick at her feet while her daughter patted their heads and praised them. "No, but Ambassador Rossi fawns on him, so he must be very prominent in Varkhora."

Oakmoor drew a sharp breath. Like Juliet's father, the Duke of Appenninos. Could he and the Varkhoran lord be connected somehow? Then Juliet would definitely be in danger. Oakmoor made himself smile. "I'd best meet our Varkhoran visitor at once. What court event shall he attend tonight?"

Taking her daughter's hand, Lady Escana turned and bustled inside with her hounds racing after them. "The Duchess of Wildewall's ball like most of court. I've your invitation in my study. Since your townhouse was closed while you were away, I had your correspondence directed here. I even sorted it all for you, although I left the many letters from your former lovers unopened."

He nearly grimaced. Lady Escana could have tossed those like he usually did. There was only one former lover's letters he was interested in reading. Dampening his hunger for Juliet yet again, he accepted his correspondence from Lady Escana then returned to Oakmoor House to handle it, which took him barely an hour since Lady Escana had sorted it so well.

Once he finished, he drummed his fingers on his desk. After his month-long absence, he should host a soiree to reestablish himself at court as soon as possible. He reviewed the schedule he'd just created. There were no important court events twenty days from now, so he could make it then. But his stained-glass ceiling must be repaired first. If he paid well enough, surely his duchy's artisan witches could manage that. Although if they couldn't, he could cast an illusion of his renowned ceiling instead. He'd begin arranging everything tomorrow.

That decided, he hastened to the family dining room for his solitary dinner. 'Twas splendid to devour Martha's creations rather than his own, although the meal was too quiet without Juliet across from him. Yet he'd soon become re-accustomed to that. He'd been dining alone for years before their confinement together. And the delightfully biting witch simply provoked and tempted him too much anyway.

After dinner, he headed upstairs to dress for the Duchess of Wildewall's ball. While helping him into his evening clothes, Miles asked him, "We cleaned that guest bedchamber you mentioned. What should we do with the lady's attire in the wardrobe?"

Oakmoor suppressed a grimace, his shoulders tightening. Naturally Juliet hadn't taken the attire he'd purchased when she'd left. She wanted nothing from him. Which was fine. He didn't want anything from her either. He forced a shrug. "Give it to any of the servants who want it. I've no need of it now."

Although clearly curious, his longtime valet simply nodded. As he'd told Juliet, his servants saw him as their duke and didn't pry into his private matters.

When he arrived at Wildewall House, he scanned the crowd for Juliet while greeting his fellow councilor. To avoid Juliet, of course, not because he burned to talk with her. But he didn't spot her, so he began looking for the visiting Varkhoran lord after he left the Duchess of Wildewall. Their Varkhoran visitor should be easy enough to identify—not only would he possess Juliet's exotic coloring, but doubtless he'd openly wear a weapon and have a draklizard on his shoulder.

Yet Oakmoor didn't spot the visiting Varkhoran either, although he did notice Lady Driscoll and Sir Lorcan talking with Lord and Lady Ravenstone along the wall by the garden. He should join them to begin repairing his relationship with the Orandians.

He was about to do so when Lady Georgiana captured his arm and trilled, "Your grace, you're back! Court has been so dull without you."

He swallowed a sigh. Obviously, Lady Georgiana was still determined to become his wife. An even less interesting prospect than before. She was just too young and not biting enough. Although he *should* be seeking an eligible lady he wanted to marry who was willing to become his wife and mother to his children. Not that he must marry immediately with his beast curse broken. Yet he still wanted a family and must ensure his degenerate cousin didn't inherit, so he should begin courting eligible ladies soon.

Lady Georgiana beamed up at him. "You must take my first waltz. That vexing foreigner managed to trick me into promising it to him, but I'd rather dance with you."

Oakmoor frowned and attempted to free his arm. "You gave your first waltz to the visiting Varkhoran lord?" When Lady Georgiana grudgingly nodded, he continued, "Then you must dance with him like you promised."

Lady Georgiana scowled. "He tricked me into promising."

Then the opening strains of the first waltz began, and Lady Georgiana yanked him toward the floor. Not expecting such rude force, he stumbled forward into her arms. And because all of court was watching—closely since 'twas his first appearance in a month—he couldn't reject her without causing gossip.

As they began dancing, he gritted, "You seem quite acquainted with tricks, my lady. Perhaps you and this Varkhoran lord are well-suited."

Lady Georgiana tossed her head. "Nonsense. Now tell me about your time away from court. You were handling a private royal matter?" Her eyes narrowed. "With Lady Juliet, I believe?"

Oakmoor nodded with a smooth smile despite his tight jaw. "Yes, but since 'twas private, I can't discuss it."

Lady Georgiana eased closer to him. "Given how you two despise each other, working with Lady Juliet must have been hard for you."

He firmly shifted Lady Georgiana back to the proper distance. "Not particularly." And definitely not in the way Lady Georgiana meant. "Although whether it was or not is little concern of yours."

Lady Georgiana gasped. "How rude."

Oakmoor arched a brow and drawled, "But much less rude than you tricking me into waltzing, especially when you were promised to another."

Lady Georgiana humphed, and they spent the remainder of their waltz in cold silence. After they'd exchanged a stiff bow and curtsy, he glanced about the ballroom and exhaled. Juliet had finally arrived and was talking to Lady Driscoll and Sir Lorcan. And she no longer appeared drained from breaking his curse, although her magical powers probably wouldn't be fully recharged for days.

Not glancing at Lady Georgiana, he strode across the ballroom. He still must repair his relationship with the Orandians. Even if Juliet was with them.

When he approached, Lady Driscoll was telling Juliet, "I now know I shouldn't have risked using it, but—" She broke off and smiled at him. "Good evening, your grace."

Although his pulse quickened at being so near Juliet, he ignored her and warmly returned the Orandian ambassador's smile. "Good evening, Lady Driscoll. How have you been?"

Sir Lorcan tensing beside her, Lady Driscoll stiffly straightened her long overcoat then murmured, "Well enough."

Oakmoor studied the Orandians. From their tension and what he'd overheard, they were plainly concealing something. But what?

As he opened his mouth to deftly ask, Juliet smirked at him and said, "I see you're already pursuing eligible young ladies again."

He gave Juliet an overly suave smile sure to provoke her. "Actually, Lady Georgiana was pursuing me. *Some* ladies believe I'll make an excellent husband."

Her eyes darkening, Juliet snorted and disdainfully pursed her lips. "Only the foolish ones."

Heat surging through him at her biting barb, Oakmoor eyed Juliet's tempting mouth and drifted closer. How spicy and sweet and hot she'd tasted yesterday.

Lady Driscoll laughed. "I see your time away from Ormas handling a private royal matter together hasn't lessened your truculent flirting at all."

Sir Lorcan smiled and shook his head. "I suspect even marriage couldn't do that, love. They enjoy it too much."

As Juliet flushed and glowered at her friends, Oakmoor

forced his body to settle and managed a smooth smile then replied, "Nonsense. Lady Juliet and I have learned to get along quite well. We'll prove it by dancing the next waltz without a single quarrel." 'Twould also allow him to warn Juliet about the visiting Varkhoran lord. He offered her his hand. "Shall we?"

Juliet sighed but laid her hand in his. As soon as they were twirling about the floor, she frowned up at him and muttered, "I thought we'd agreed to avoid each other."

He drew Juliet slightly closer, until her ruby-red skirt almost brushed his legs. If only he could pull her fully against him. His body aching once more, he smiled into Juliet's eyes. "Smile, else Lady Driscoll and Sir Lorcan shall accuse us of truculent flirting again."

Juliet huffed then produced a glittering grin. "Better?"

Oakmoor rumbled as his blood surged fiercer at Juliet's grin. "Much." He spun her in a complicated twirl then drew her back into his arms, just a shade closer than before. "And I couldn't avoid you when you were talking with the Orandians. After my absence, I must repair my relationship with them." Once Juliet nodded, he added, "Besides, I needed to talk with you."

Her brow furrowing, Juliet tilted her head. "Why?"

Since casting a listening-ward spell or an ignore spell was too much bother, he bent closer to ensure they couldn't be overheard and murmured, "I had to warn you about the Varkhoran lord who recently appeared at court. 'Tis suspicious that he appeared while you were gone. He might be a danger to you."

Juliet blinked. "Unlikely. A Varkhoran lord appearing now is surely a coincidence. Even if he used a caravan travel spell like the affluent often do, 'twould have taken him three months to travel from Varkhora to Calatini. Only a jump travel spell could have managed to get him here in the month we were gone, and one covering that great a distance would require *massive* amounts of power, too much for any human witch." She grimaced. "Although possibly the dratted veiled witch could manage it."

Despite the curious eyes of court on them, Oakmoor drew Juliet even closer. Somehow, he must convince the maddening witch to take care. He grunted. "I still don't trust our Varkhoran visitor's coincidental arrival. What if he was sent by that grasping father of yours to seek revenge?"

When Juliet shivered and swayed toward him, he lowered his bent head until their lips almost met, and his aching body hardened further as her spicy gingyr scent enveloped him. Goddess, how he needed to taste her again. Even though he shouldn't since 'twould only fuel his obsessive hunger for her and destroy any chance of returning to their normal lives. Not even the greatest rakehell in Ormas could kiss a lady before all of court without marrying her.

CHAPTER 26

*T*ingling heat coursing through her, Juliet inhaled Oakmoor's earthy sandalwood scent and lifted her head until their mouths nearly touched. Dear Goddess, how she loved and needed him. And if she kissed him before all of court, he'd *have* to marry her. Even the greatest rakehell in Ormas couldn't evade that.

She froze. Was she *mad*? Marriage to Oakmoor would destroy her. She mustn't let his caring concern and masculine allure make her forget that he didn't love her and never could. And that he'd never truly want to marry *her*. Just moments ago, he'd been pursuing another lady entirely, one who better suited his requirements for a wife. Adoring, young, and *foolish*.

She gasped and jerked back to the proper distance as their waltz ended. "No Varkhoran lord can hurt me now, even if Father did send him." Only Oakmoor possessed that power. She curtsied while he bowed in return. "But thanks for the warning. Please excuse me."

Then she turned and swept out the nearby door to the garden. She required time to settle herself before she rejoined anyone. Damn Oakmoor and his irresistible allure.

She sank onto a stone bench and shivered despite the balmy

summer evening. She was such a fool. If she didn't learn to control herself around Oakmoor, soon all of court would realize she loved him. Then they'd suspect her affair with him, and they'd lose all respect for her and only see her as Oakmoor's discarded lover. She splayed a hand on her still-flat stomach. Like they would if she was pregnant with his child. Which she might be.

She exhaled. But at least no one, including Oakmoor, would suspect her possible pregnancy until she began to show. To prevent other witches from seeing that her contraceptive charm was inactive, she'd soaked it in unicorn water today until she'd left for Wildewall House to give it the semblance of magic. She grimaced. Because she'd completely drained her magical powers yesterday and even used some of her life force to repair Oakmoor's contraceptive charm, she couldn't risk performing further magic until her drained magical powers fully recharged from her surroundings. She could permanently injure herself and her magical powers if she did. Instead, she'd need to soak her contraceptive charm in unicorn water every night while she slept until she could repair it like she had Oakmoor's. But that wouldn't be for half a week at least.

Suddenly, a deep voice called, "Giuliettanna?"

Juliet stiffened at her birth name that only Oakmoor knew in Calatini. Her pulse skittering, she whirled to face the unfamiliar gentleman who'd joined her. He must be the Varkhoran lord whom Oakmoor had mentioned. He wore spartan evening clothes with a bronze-hilted saber on his left hip and a mottled-brown draklizard perched on his right shoulder. Plus, his olive skin and dark eyes matched hers, although his hair and short beard were black not dark brown. She inhaled a sharp breath. Other than the beard and warm smile, he was the image of Father fifty years ago. She exhaled and stepped closer. "G-Giovanni?"

A grin flashed amid Giovanni's beard. "Recognize me all grown up, big sister?"

She couldn't help smiling in response to her brother's grin. He'd often worn that same cheery grin as a toddler—just before he'd perpetrated some mischief or shown sweet affection. She shook her head. "You resemble Father too much not to, little brother."

Giovanni laughed. "Physically at least. Mother always says you're the one who resembles Father in temperament, Giuliettanna. Which is what caused your fierce battles growing up, especially since you're a girl."

Her smile tightened. Yes, girls were worth little in Varkhora. Particularly to Father, even though he adored Mother. Burying that, she murmured, "I go by Juliet now. I've not been Giuliettanna since I fled Varkhora."

Giovanni sobered and inclined his head. "Yes, of course. I should have realized."

To distract her brother, she arched her brows and asked, "So what are you doing in Calatini, Lord Sabine of Appenninos?" As Father's heir, their surname and duchy were Giovanni's full title until he became the next duke, unlike in Calatini where duke's heirs often had courtesy titles.

Giovanni grinned again. "Looking for you, obviously. With Mother's help, I cast a self-renewing continual kin spell to find you when I was thirteen, although it didn't succeed until just after this Plantfete."

Juliet inhaled as tears pricked her eyes. Giovanni and Mother had been actively hunting for her for the past nine years? She swallowed. "Because I concealed myself with a tracing-ward spell until after Queen Kiera's coronation." She lifted her chin. "I suppose since Father possesses no magical powers of his own, he encouraged your attempt to locate his rebellious daughter so you could force me to return and become a proper Varkhoran lady."

Giovanni coughed another laugh. "I doubt anyone could manage that. You're too driven and strong-willed. Just look at all you've achieved here." He smiled. "Father was prouder than a papa roc when he learned you'd become Calatini's royal witch at only twenty-four and remained the kingdom's most illustrious witch for fourteen years. He told everyone at court about your success."

She gaped at her brother. Father had done *what*? But his runaway daughter being the opposite of subservient in a foreign kingdom where women were equals would have been a massive scandal at the Varkhoran court. Proper Varkhoran ladies were never so formidable.

Giovanni smoothed his beard. "Mother was proud too, of course, although she didn't feel compelled to tell everyone since she knew 'twould upset most of them."

Juliet smiled, her chest squeezing. That sounded like Mother. She despised conflict and had always striven to restore harmony following the frequent battles between her husband and daughter. Successfully perhaps half the time.

Giovanni hummed. "Both Father and Mother were overjoyed when my kin spell finally succeeded. Not to force you to return and become a proper Varkhoran lady, but because they missed you and were worried you'd come to harm."

She swallowed as more tears pricked her eyes. If that was true, then Father wouldn't have pursued revenge for ruining his ambition to be the queen's father instead of just a prominent duke. She could have dropped her tracing-ward spell when King Cesare had died and risked contacting her parents and Giovanni. And although she couldn't have left Calatini, she could have spent the last three years getting to know her family again through mirror calls.

Giovanni smiled at her. "When I said I wanted to travel to Calatini to find you, Father and Mother encouraged me to go at once, so I left just over a week later. But even with a caravan travel spell, it still took me three months." He grimaced. "Which was fine, until my kin spell quit working last month."

Juliet winced. Thanks to the veiled witch's wards.

Giovanni shook his head. "Not that I mentioned my kin

spell's sudden failure to our parents. They would have been even more frantic than I was, and they could do nothing to help all the way back in Varkhora." He sighed. "When I arrived in Ormas last week, I asked Ambassador Rossi about you—without revealing why, naturally—and I was almost relieved to learn that you and the Duke of Oakmoor had left to handle a private royal matter around the time my spell failed."

She arched her brows at Giovanni. "*Almost* relieved?"

Giovanni quirked a wry grin. "Yes, I knew you weren't dead like I feared, but you were alone with the greatest rakehell in Ormas. Not exactly comforting news for a brother to hear."

Juliet straightened as a blush warmed her cheeks. Hopefully, the garden was dark enough that her brother couldn't see it. "But I'm certain you also heard about the dislike between myself and the duke. He was no danger to me." Physically at least.

Giovanni smiled. "Your mutual dislike *was* a comfort. Especially once I discovered he was practically betrothed to another."

Her heart stuttered. Oakmoor wasn't practically betrothed yet, although he would be soon. She frowned. "Who told you that false rumor?"

Giovanni's smile twisted. "Lady Georgiana Laurent, the duke's almost betrothed. She's hurled their relationship at me every time we've met, and she jilted me to waltz the first dance with him tonight. Only a betrothed lady, or one as good as, would dare be that rude."

Juliet swallowed to ease her sudden nausea. Perhaps 'twas true after all. Oh, Goddess. She stiffened her spine. Why was she acting so shocked? She'd known yesterday that Oakmoor didn't return her love and would soon marry another. Even though their passionate afternoon could have left her pregnant. She fisted her hands to prevent herself from touching her stomach. Giovanni might suspect such a betraying gesture.

She gritted a glittering smile. "Enough about that rakehell. I can understand why Mother and Father would want to find me, but why did you go to such effort to do so? You were only one-

and-a-half when I fled Varkhora, so you probably didn't even remember me."

Giovanni chuckled. "I didn't, although I almost feel like I do from Mother's many stories. She misses you terribly, but telling stories about you helped ease that. And I loved hearing them as much as she loved telling them. You were my favorite bedtime story as a boy, so I was eager to get to know you in person."

Juliet blinked, warmth flooding her. How sweet. She cleared her throat. "Did Father tell stories about me too?"

Giovanni lifted a shoulder. "Not until my kin spell was successful. Before then, he never spoke of you. Mother said he felt guilty that you'd run away and speaking of you hurt him too much." Giovanni smiled. "Although Father talked about you incessantly in the week before I left Varkhora. He adores you nearly as much as he does Mother—more than me, I think."

She blinked faster as more tears threatened. Father *definitely* hadn't pursued revenge then. If only she'd realized he truly loved her, she never would have run away. But if she hadn't, she'd never have met Oakmoor or achieved all she had in Cala-tini. She inhaled then slanted her brother a sardonic glance. "I doubt Father loves me more than you. You're his precious male heir, Lord Sabine."

Giovanni grinned. "True. I suppose we can say he loves us equally but in different ways. Mother does too."

Juliet nearly touched her stomach again. And she'd love the possible child she carried just as fiercely. Too bad she could only ever bear one since she and Oakmoor would never make love again. She returned Giovanni's grin. "As all good parents should." She arched a brow. "Now tell me, how have you enjoyed your visit to Calatini so far?"

Giovanni hummed, his eyes gleaming. "'Tis been fascinating. I like how outspoken the ladies are here—so refreshing. Perhaps one day ladies in Varkhora shall be like that."

She snorted. Giovanni was an unusual Varkhoran lord to want outspoken ladies. "Unlikely."

Giovanni straightened. "They shall if King Alessandro and I have any success." Before she could quiz him about his intriguing comment, he returned to answering her earlier question, "The Calatinian court is convivial, although 'tis odd to see the gentlemen without weapons as well as no draklizards and faebirds."

Juliet smiled and tilted her head. "When I'd first settled here, I recall thinking that court events felt almost incomplete without draklizards on gentlemen's shoulders and faebirds on ladies'." And thinking that had made her miss her sweet faebird Gentian even more.

Giovanni stroked his draklizard's chest. The mottled-brown draklizard remained still as a statue like any well-trained Varkhoran magical pet, although his iridescent eyes shimmered. Giovanni hummed. "Incomplete, 'tis exactly it."

She stepped forward. "What's his name? May I pet him?" Petting a draklizard wasn't the same as petting Gentian, but 'twas the closest she could get.

Giovanni nodded. "His name is Striker." As she raised her hand to pet Striker, Giovanni began, "But don't touch his—"

Juliet caressed Striker's talons gripping Giovanni's shoulder since Varkhoran draklizards were trained to allow that. But Striker bristled and struck faster than a lightning spell. She jerked back her bleeding hand, her yelp echoing in the quiet garden.

Giovanni continued, "—talons. I've never been able to train him to not s—" Before Giovanni could finish, a strong arm seized her waist and yanked her against a muscular chest. Oakmoor rasped, "Stay away from Lady Juliet, Varkhoran."

Her pulse surging at Oakmoor's protective embrace, she nevertheless twisted her head to glare at him. She mustn't betray her helpless love. "Don't be an idiot, Oakmoor."

He frowned down at her, his hazel eyes dark. "But that Varkhoran attacked you. You screamed, and you're bleeding."

She huffed despite the ravenous tingling filling her. "Giovanni's *draklizard* attacked me, but 'twas my fault. I should have let him finish speaking before petting Striker." She slapped Oakmoor's restraining arms. She must get him to release her before she kissed him. "Now release me."

Oakmoor grunted but kept his arms firmly about her as he glowered at her brother. "Giovanni? As in your brother?"

Glaring back, Giovanni strode forward with his right hand clenched about his saber, obviously about to draw it. "Exactly. Release my sister, you beastly rakehell. You're promised elsewhere, remember?"

Juliet winced at that reminder and slapped Oakmoor's arms harder.

Oakmoor scowled. "Your brother is the idiot here, Lady Juliet, not me."

A gasp pierced the garden, then Lady Georgiana Laurent exclaimed, "Your grace, what are you doing?" She glared at Giovanni. "'Tis your fault, I'm sure."

As Giovanni bristled like his draklizard had earlier, Juliet flushed and slapped Oakmoor's arms yet again. His almost betrothed was the worst person to catch them embracing. Although at least Lady Georgiana hadn't caught them kissing. Juliet shuddered. "Would you release me, Oakmoor?"

While Giovanni and Lady Georgiana began quarreling about him almost drawing his saber on Oakmoor, Oakmoor sighed and pulled Juliet closer against him then said, "After I check your hand. You might still be bleeding."

She shuddered once more, but not from embarrassment this time. "I'm fine. Nothing a minor healing spell can't fix."

Oakmoor grunted. "Then why aren't you holding still so I can heal your hand?"

She struggled in his arms. Because she'd surely betray herself if she did. So although her magical powers had barely recharged yet, she claimed, "I can heal myself. I want you to *release* me. Now."

Oakmoor lowered his head until his lips brushed her ear.

"Liar. Your magical powers surely haven't recharged enough to cast a healing spell. And you rubbing against me only makes me want to release you less, my maddening witch."

Juliet whimpered as Oakmoor pressed his hard body against her. His blatant arousal only made hers harder to resist. But succumbing would eventually destroy her.

Halting his quarrel with Lady Georgiana, Giovanni scowled at Oakmoor and growled, "*What* are you doing to my sister, Oakmoor?"

Without a glance at her furious brother, Oakmoor grasped her wounded hand. "Healing the wound your damned drak-lizard caused, Lord Sabine. If she'd ever *hold still.*"

As Oakmoor crooned a cleansing spell then a healing spell in quick succession, Juliet stiffened and held herself stiller than a gargoyle turned to stone by sunlight to prove to him that she could.

Lady Georgiana gasped like earlier. "You're a witch, your grace?"

Not looking at his almost betrothed, Oakmoor rubbed his thumb against Juliet's healed hand. "It would appear so."

Juliet suppressed a hungry shiver at Oakmoor's caress. He wasn't the least bit affectionate toward Lady Georgiana. Not promising for the success of their future marriage.

His scowl darkening further, Giovanni bristled again and craned toward Oakmoor. "Being a witch *would* explain how you knew my proper title moments ago. You learned it using a scrying spell instead of waiting to be introduced."

Oakmoor's mouth quirked. "I could have."

Juliet flushed. Except Oakmoor hadn't needed to. He'd learned both her birth name and Father's title during their mind sharing spell, and as Calatini's Minister of Foreign Relations, he'd know the rules of Varkhoran titles. She shifted in his arms. "Now that you've performed your healing spell—one I could have easily performed myself—would you release me?"

Oakmoor hummed then drawled, "If I must." He breathed an

incantation that only the two of them could hear, albeit too quietly for her to decipher it, before lowering his arms and stepping back.

Since she couldn't risk casting a probing spell with her still weak magical powers, Juliet scrutinized Oakmoor to guess what spell he'd cast. Her gaze stilling on Oakmoor's tight trousers, she flushed harder. He'd obviously cast an illusion spell to conceal his arousal from holding her. Prudent given how Giovanni had almost attacked him for doing so. Her younger brother was going to erupt like a crazed chimera when she revealed her possible pregnancy. And challenge Oakmoor to a duel for dishonoring her. She shuddered. Somehow she must prevent that.

His eyes narrowing, Oakmoor gestured toward the door. "Shall we return to the ballroom?"

She disregarded the arm Oakmoor offered her and took Giovanni's instead. The only lady that Oakmoor should be escorting from a garden interlude was his almost betrothed. With a grimace, Oakmoor took Lady Georgiana's arm, and the four of them headed inside.

Once they did, Giovanni escorted Juliet to the refreshments table while Oakmoor left Lady Georgiana with her father then strode from the ballroom.

Juliet frowned after Oakmoor over her untasted flute of sparkling wine. The social and suave duke rarely left court events early. And tonight was his first chance to socialize in over a month. Her fingers clenched on her glass flute. No doubt he'd left to find a willing woman to handle the desire she'd aroused. With his curse broken, his future bride chosen, and the Orandians familiar with Ormas, he now had time for lovers once more. And an unrepentant rakehell like Oakmoor wouldn't delay taking a new lover.

Siobhan and Lorcan bustled over, and Juliet swiftly introduced Giovanni as her brother. After some genial conversation, they extracted her from her younger brother's protective hovering, then Siobhan grinned at her and asked, "What was all that about? You flee to the garden after almost kissing the Duke of Oakmoor during your waltz, your secret younger brother follows you, the duke bolts after you both when Lady Georgiana talks with him, she pursues him once she recovers from her shock, the four of you return some time later looking flustered, then the duke immediately leaves."

Juliet lifted a shoulder. "Giovanni wanted to introduce himself in private." Before her friends could probe about Oakmoor and Lady Georgiana's involvement in that, she frowned and asked, "What were you telling me about using the Mirror of Wisdom when the duke joined us earlier?" A perilous risk Siobhan and Lorcan shouldn't have attempted. Her chest tightened. But she'd never gotten to finish warning them about the Mirror of Wisdom before she'd been trapped with Oakmoor.

Paling, Siobhan winced. "Considering how we were interrupted before, a crowded ballroom isn't the best place to discuss it. Could we meet at your workroom tomorrow morning?"

Juliet exhaled but readily agreed then circulated for another hour before returning to the palace. She'd have left sooner, but her leaving couldn't be connected with Oakmoor's.

The following morning not long after breakfast, her maid Lara ushered Siobhan and Lorcan into her bright and airy workroom that now seemed small after using the perfect one Oakmoor had lent her. Once she and her friends settled about her worktable, she frowned and leaned toward them. "Tell me about using the Mirror of Wisdom."

Siobhan shakily smoothed her tan tunic and green overcoat. "I'm surprised King Devon and Queen Kiera didn't tell you when you met with them yesterday morning."

As Lorcan took his wife's hand, Juliet murmured, "They said you'd some trouble involving the Mirror of Wisdom, but they thought you'd prefer to tell me the details yourself." And they'd been more interested in sharing Queen Kiera's recent pregnancy and discussing Oakmoor's broken curse.

Siobhan sighed and gripped Lorcan's hand. "Regardless of the spell, no one could reach you and the Duke of Oakmoor while you were away handling that private royal matter. We mentioned using the Mirror of Wisdom to check on you multiple times, but King Devon and Queen Kiera kept refusing."

Lorcan grimaced. "Which we couldn't understand. Why have a wondrous and powerful enchanted tool if you never use it?" He exhaled. "But we should have listened when you said 'twas no mere tool."

Juliet winced and clenched her fists in her lap. If only she'd warned them better than that.

Siobhan sighed again. "After a month, I was terrified something horrible had happened to you and the duke, and since no one else was bothering to check, Lorcan and I decided we must do it ourselves. We've used enchanted tools before, and we assumed our magical powers could control the Mirror of Wisdom." She shivered. "So a week ago, we snuck into the throne room in the middle of the night, and I asked the mirror to show me how you were."

A chill darting through her, Juliet sharply inhaled. Doubtless even the perilous Mirror of Wisdom couldn't have penetrated the veiled witch's incredibly powerful wards. And asking the mirror a question it couldn't answer was deadly.

Gripping Siobhan's hand tighter, Lorcan shuddered. "The Mirror of Wisdom remained stubbornly blank, but the cursed mirror sucked up Siobhan's magical powers and life force like a starving vampire. She was nearly dead before I managed to break its terrible grip using every bit of my magical powers."

Juliet froze. Exactly as she'd feared. Yet Siobhan seemed in perfect health now.

Siobhan swallowed, her freckles bright in her pallid face. "Thankfully, the veiled witch alerted King Devon, Queen Kiera, and the Ravenstones of my foolishness, so they burst into the throne room just as Lorcan broke the Mirror of Wisdom's grip.

Then Lady Ravenstone soul-healed me so that my death didn't spark a war between our two kingdoms."

Juliet gaped at her friends. Dear Goddess. Her chest eased. But at least Siobhan and Lorcan were both well now, thanks to Lady Ravenstone and the veiled witch.

Lorcan shuddered again. "Siobhan and I owe that soul healer and seer more than we can ever repay. We offered Lady Ravenstone a boon whenever she asks for it, and we've attempted to offer the same to the veiled witch, but we've not be able to meet her."

Juliet frowned. Why was the veiled witch avoiding Siobhan and Lorcan? Not that it mattered at the moment. She reached out and squeezed her friends' linked hands. "I'm so sorry you nearly died trying to help me. Praise the Goddess for Lady Ravenstone and the veiled witch."

Siobhan offered a tremulous smile. "Yes." Her normal color returning, she inhaled then said, "Now, tell us about you and the Duke of Oakmoor handling that private royal matter."

Juliet shifted in her chair. Confessing everything to her friends would be a relief, but she couldn't betray Oakmoor. "We successfully handled it. I'm afraid I can't say more than that. 'Tisn't my secret to share."

Siobhan nodded. "'Tis King Devon and Queen Kiera's."

Juliet swallowed as her neck heated. No, 'twas Oakmoor's, and he was even more important to her than the king and queen she served.

Their brows furrowing, Siobhan and Lorcan traded a swift glance. Then Siobhan asked, "It *is* the king and queen's secret, isn't it?"

Juliet lifted her chin and managed to smile. "They said as much, didn't they?"

Her friends frowned deeper, but then Giovanni bounded into her workroom with her maid Lara protesting behind him. He grinned at her. "Morning, Juliet. Care to go riding?"

She leapt upright. Although she was behind on her duties

following her month-long absence, a ride would allow her to escape her friends' well-meant probing. She returned her brother's grin. "I'd love to." She smiled at Siobhan and Lorcan. "Do you mind if I leave now? Giovanni and I have so much to discuss."

Siobhan and Lorcan traded another glance but rose, and Siobhan replied, "Of course not. We'll see you tonight at the Osteens' rout party. Enjoy your ride."

Juliet gave her friends a final smile before sweeping out to change into a riding habit. Thank the Goddess for long-lost little brothers.

CHAPTER 27

After breakfast the morning following the Duchess of Wildewall's ball, Oakmoor strode straight to his study to arrange the repair of his ballroom's shattered stained-glass ceiling. He chanted a brief spell then waved at his communication mirror to place a mirror call to the largest and best group of glass artisan witches in Oakmoor.

The communication mirror glowed white for nearly ten minutes before a sweating man with soot smeared across his brow finally answered. Four glass furnaces glowing behind him, the glowering man snapped, "What? I'm busy." Then his surly glower smoothed. "Your grace, what an unexpected honor to receive your call."

Oakmoor's mouth twitched. Doubtful, given the artisan witch's earlier glower. "Are you Ferris who runs Lightglass Guild?"

The artisan witch grunted. "I am."

Oakmoor swiftly explained about his shattered stained-glass ceiling and that it must be repaired before his soiree in under three weeks but that they could use Juliet's former workroom in Oakmoor House.

Ferris grunted again. "'Tis a mighty task. I'll have to bring my entire guild to Ormas, and the thirty-six of us'll need to work day and night. Although that still mightn't be enough to finish before your fancy party. Plus, the repairs'll cost a fortune."

Oakmoor shrugged. So he'd expected. "I can afford it. I'll cast a jump travel spell to fetch you and your guild as soon as you're ready."

Ferris jerked a nod. "We'll be ready by luncheon."

After waving a hand to deactivate his communication mirror, Oakmoor left his study then informed Miles and Martha of the artisan witches' arrival, which proceeded smoothly. By the time he left for the Osteens' rout party that evening, noisy industry was spilling from both the ballroom and the workroom. No doubt an incessant din until the ballroom's ceiling was repaired. Sleep would be interesting in the coming weeks.

He grimaced as he headed to Osteen House. Not a problem he could evade. His renowned stained-glass ceiling must be repaired before his soiree to prevent gossip about why it had shattered, which might lead to court discovering his curse. Although gossip about the repairs was probably already rife thanks to the quartz and other materials Ferris and his guild had purchased this afternoon. Fortunately, none of his servants or artisan witches would discuss the repairs with those outside the townhouse, so he could dismiss the repairs as minor ones.

Once he arrived at Osteen House, Oakmoor scoured the crowded drawing room for Juliet while he greeted his fellow councilor and Lady Osteen. He really must avoid Juliet tonight so their lives could return to normal like they both wanted. He suppressed a grimace. Unlike he had yesterday at the Duchess of Wildewall's ball. Then, although he'd told himself to avoid Juliet, he'd done the opposite, largely thanks to his obsessive hunger for her. He'd even nearly seduced her in front of her protective younger brother, Lord Sabine. And he'd been so aroused by their embrace in the garden that he'd left the ball soon after. Otherwise, he might have dragged Juliet into an anteroom and made love with her until neither of them could move. Utter madness, especially since he should be courting an eligible lady he wanted as his wife who was willing to marry him. And Juliet could never be her. She wanted an adoring husband, which could never be *him*. Not that he wanted to be.

When he spotted Juliet and her brother talking with Lady Driscoll and Sir Lorcan near the Osteens' refreshments table, his body tightened with an echo of last night's voracious hunger for her. He yanked his gaze free of the bewitching witch. Yes, avoiding Juliet was a necessity. He must greet the Orandians tonight, but he'd have to wait until she and Lord Sabine were occupied elsewhere.

As soon as he left Lord and Lady Osteen, Lady Georgiana captured his arm. "Good evening, your grace."

Oakmoor immediately slid his arm free and began hunting for Lady Georgiana's father. He wasn't getting caught by another of her tricks. "Lady Georgiana." He exhaled when he found the duke then escorted Lady Georgiana across the drawing room without touching her.

After they'd exchanged greetings, the elderly Duke of Osbourne arched his brows. "I heard you're performing some repairs on Oakmoor House."

Oakmoor flashed a smooth smile. Not surprising his wily fellow councilor had already heard that gossip. The Minister of Intelligence's spies told him everything. Oakmoor shrugged. "Just some minor ones. You'll have to tell me if you notice them at my soiree in a few weeks."

Lady Georgiana fluttered her lashes at him. "And what inspired these repairs?"

His jaw almost tightened at Lady Georgiana's sweetly coy tone. She obviously assumed his repairs were for his future wife, doubtless her. An impossibility. He'd not have such a simpering girl as his wife. Her coy giggles and feigned fragility would drive him mad within a month, even though she simply used them to conceal her steely nature and shrewd wit. He shrugged again. "Mere whim. One of the benefits of being a single gentleman without a wife. I can alter my homes however and whenever I like without enduring endless complaints about dust and noise."

The Duke of Osbourne chuckled. "Still determined to remain unwed, I see."

Oakmoor smiled despite the curious pang darting through him. "Until I begin courting the lady I want to marry."

When Lady Georgiana opened her mouth, probably to protest that he already had, the Duke of Oakmoor interjected, "Speaking of courting—" He inclined his head at Juliet and Lord Sabine. "—it seems that Lady Juliet has an ardent admirer."

Oakmoor followed the other duke's gaze across the drawing room and nearly scowled. "Lord Sabine isn't an admirer. He's her brother."

The Duke of Osbourne blinked then nodded. "That explains their matching coloring. So Lady Juliet is Varkhoran, is she? I always wondered what kingdom she came from, but Varkhora makes sense. Strange that I never considered it until now."

Oakmoor lifted a shoulder. Because Juliet had worn a glamour spell for years preventing such insights.

Lady Georgiana sniffed. "I can't believe you thought Lord Sabine was Lady Juliet's suitor, Father. He must be almost twenty years her junior."

Oakmoor narrowed his eyes at Lady Georgiana. Offensive girl. "Only sixteen. Nearly a decade less than the difference between you and me. And you don't seem to care about that."

Lady Georgiana blushed then lifted her chin. "'Tis different for a gentleman to be older."

Oakmoor held the too young lady's gaze. "A difference by that much is often insurmountable unless genuine love is involved." Which only mad fools would risk. "And even then, 'tis easier if a gentleman is the same generation as his wife." Not that he'd ever enjoy that because most eligible ladies near his age weren't interested in marriage—they'd have already married if they were. Or they were like Juliet and holding out for an adoring husband. Shoving the maddening witch from his mind, he turned from Lady Georgiana before she could reply and nodded at her father. "I should go circulate. Excuse me."

He threaded through the crowd, frequently pausing to talk with various guests. After about an hour, Juliet and her brother left Lady Driscoll and Sir Lorcan to join Lady Ducharme, so he could approach the Orandians at last.

After they'd said good evening, Lady Driscoll twinkled at him. "Interesting timing, your grace. Juliet just left to help her brother procure an invitation to Lady Ducharme's fencing salons. Are you avoiding Juliet and Lord Sabine by chance? *What* happened in the Duchess of Wildewall's garden yesterday?"

Oakmoor managed to keep his charming grin. Why must Lady Driscoll and her husband see so much? "Lady Juliet simply introduced me to her brother, who took an instant dislike of me."

Sir Lorcan chuckled and straightened his overcoat atop his short tunic. "Given your rakehell reputation, I'd take an instant dislike of you too if you'd spent over a month alone with my beloved sister."

Oakmoor's grin twisted. Plus, Lord Sabine had witnessed him embracing Juliet and nearly seducing her. Damn Juliet for being so bewitching that he forgot everything else, including her Varkhoran brother scowling at him like a bellicose dragon protecting his treasure.

Lady Driscoll tilted her head. "Lord Sabine does appear rather protective of Juliet. 'Tis sweet, especially considering they'd not seen each other for over twenty years."

Oakmoor snorted. Lord Sabine's scowl last night hadn't been the least sweet. He'd been fortunate the young Varkhoran lord hadn't challenged him to a duel. He drawled, "Yet Lord Sabine's protectiveness is entirely unnecessary. Lady Juliet is well able to protect herself from my rakehell ways." Except when their uncontrollable hunger overpowered them both. Although *that* was no one's concern but their own. Especially not her protective younger brother's.

Lady Driscoll and her husband traded a glance, then Lady Driscoll asked, "So nothing happened between you while you were handling that private royal matter?"

Oakmoor forced himself to shrug. "Nothing of consequence." Them spending time together, sharing secrets, and making love had only been to break his curse. Juliet wouldn't have left without telling him goodbye if any of that had meant more. Not that he wanted their enforced intimacy to mean more either.

The Orandians exchanged another glance, then Lady Driscoll said, "I'm surprised. I half expected you to be married when you returned. Or at least announce your betrothal."

Oakmoor winced. Juliet would never agree to marry *him*. And even if she did, 'twould be mad. He could never control himself with her. Hence his behavior last night. And after breaking his curse. He gritted a smirk. "Lady Juliet and I both enjoy our independence too much for that." Then he asked to distract Lady Driscoll and Sir Lorcan, "How did Lady Escana treat you during my absence?"

Lady Driscoll hummed. "Very well. Lady Escana arranged several events for all the ambassadors so we could become better acquainted. And even though not a witch herself, she arranged some events for witch families as well." Lady Driscoll slanted her husband a warm glance. "Which Lorcan definitely appreciated."

Oakmoor nearly laughed. Of course the lore witch had. Lady Escana had chosen her events well. She'd truly done an excellent job handling his duties. Having the countess return to his assistant would be a waste.

Lady Driscoll smiled at him. "I'd say we're fully settled in Ormas now thanks to all you and Lady Escana have done over the past months."

Oakmoor returned the Orandian ambassador's smile. "I'm glad." And with Lady Driscoll and Sir Lorcan settled, he'd definitely have more time for private pursuits again, like courting his future wife. He sipped his flute of sparkling wine and began studying the eligible ladies in the crowd.

Then his gaze met Juliet's as she and her brother left Lady Ducharme. His blood heated and breath quickened at the echoing hunger darkening Juliet's gorgeous eyes and flushing her exotic skin. Goddess, he wanted her. And she clearly wanted him just as much.

Their hungry gazes never separating as Juliet glided over with Lord Sabine, Oakmoor fisted his hands to prevent himself from surging forward and yanking her into his arms. He was supposed to be avoiding her, not seducing her. And in front of her protective younger brother once again, along with all of court too. Damn his obsessive hunger for the bewitching witch.

He wrenched his gaze free to glance at Lord Sabine beside Juliet. His beard bristling, the young Varkhoran lord was gripping his saber like he had last night, and the mottled-brown draklizard on his shoulder was stiff and craned forward. Both were ready to attack him for the hungry look he and Juliet had exchanged. If she ever told her brother that they'd been lovers, the boy would surely challenge him to a duel to protect his family honor within the hour.

Oakmoor almost grimaced. And the Minister of Foreign Relations dueling with a prominent foreigner could have disastrous consequences. Yet another reason he should avoid Juliet. He made himself turn to Lady Driscoll and Sir Lorcan with a smooth smile. "I'd best leave before Lady Juliet and her brother return. The boy looks ready to spark a war between our kingdoms. Have a good evening."

He threaded through the crowd like earlier and made himself circulate for another hour, although he didn't bother to flirt with any ladies. He'd begin courting his future wife tomorrow. Tonight, he must focus on avoiding Juliet.

Over the following few days, Oakmoor managed to continue avoiding Juliet, so they only saw each other across crowded court events. Yet he burned whenever their gazes met. Maddening, bewitching witch. He also kept having to evade Lady Georgiana's dogged pursuit. So annoying. And although courting another lady might have curbed Lady Georgiana, he couldn't settle on one since all the eligible ladies were blander than ever, even the flirtatious widows closer to his age.

Yet he still attended court events every afternoon and evening then spent them talking with and entertaining the other guests, although he never bothered to flirt like he had before his curse had begun manifesting. He soon learned all the latest court gossip and smoothly repeated the Duchess of Childes's claim that Lord and Lady Blaine had married quietly rather than eloped to help remove the scandal he'd caused. Then he deftly diverted everyone from his absence with Juliet and his repairs to Oakmoor House by discussing his upcoming soiree, which soon became the most anticipated event of the season before the royal summer masquerade. He even hired a renowned troupe of players from Oakmoor to perform a short play to ensure his guests wouldn't be disappointed.

Despite all his socializing, which he usually enjoyed, a restless ache often filled his chest. Perhaps because he couldn't get proper rest at night or quiet to think thanks to the incessant din at Oakmoor House. Or perhaps because he'd become accustomed to his intimate evenings with Juliet. It had been nice to talk openly with someone he could trust. Not that he missed or needed Juliet specifically. The lady he finally settled on as his future wife would do just as well. He simply needed to find her.

Even though he didn't miss Juliet, his pulse still quickened when he strode into the council room for his first council meeting since their absence. Surely Juliet would attend too, although she didn't always. They'd been gone for over a month after all. And even with her at the opposite end of the table, this would be the closest they'd been since their garden embrace nearly a week ago.

He claimed his usual seat near the foot of the table and talked with Lord Dabar beside him while glancing at every arrival then swallowing a sigh when they weren't Juliet. He almost frowned at her empty seat as King Devon and Queen Kiera opened the council meeting after everyone else had arrived. Apparently Juliet had more important matters to attend than their first council meeting in over a month. Unless she hadn't attended to avoid him. He'd better speak with Juliet at the sirenic play tonight. Gossip would start if they neglected their duties to avoid each other.

King Devon turned to him. "Would you care to speak first, your grace, since 'tis your first council meeting following your return?"

Oakmoor smiled and inclined his head. "Of course, your majesty. Lady Juliet and I successfully handled that private matter thanks to the royal witch's skill. And during our absence, the Orandians finished settling in with Lady Escana's help."

Lady Ducharme leaned forward. "The countess covered your duties extremely well. I'll miss the presence of another lady on the council. We've needed that since we expelled Lady Morwynne for treason last Longnight."

His eyes shadowed like they often were since learning of his mother's treason and assuming her position on the council, young Lord Morwynne murmured with a tight smile, "I apologize for being born a gentleman, Lady Ducharme."

The baroness frowned at the affable young count whom she'd mentored since he'd begun attending her fencing salons years ago. "You know I meant that as no insult toward you."

As Lord Morwynne nodded, Oakmoor sighed. Having a treasonous parent would be a burden to an honorable gentleman like Lord Morwynne. To distract everyone from the ashamed count, he cleared his throat and said, "I'm glad Lady Escana performed so well during my absence. Not that I expected anything less. She's a talented lady." One he must promote from his assistant somehow. Although doing so would require some maneuvering because the only higher position in his ministry was his own.

The council meeting turned to other matters, including the ramifications of Lord Sabine being Juliet's brother and that Lord Farson, the Minister of Internal Relations and councilor for Golddell, would be leaving with his wife the day after the next council meeting, doubtless to return to Golddell even though 'twas the middle of the season.

Once the discussion finally slowed, King Devon and Queen Kiera glanced at each other, then Queen Kiera said, "We've one further matter to discuss. Before we announce my pregnancy to Calatini at our summer masquerade, Devon and I want to alter the royal inheritance laws to allow our firstborn to rule regardless of gender."

As murmurs raced about the table, Oakmoor drummed his fingers against his knee. So *that* had been the changes they'd meant during their luncheon meeting. Not terribly surprising given Queen Kiera's close relationship with the matriarchal nightmara.

Lord Treyvan, on King Devon's right, nodded. "Selena, my parents, and I have been discussing doing the same for the Childes title."

Oakmoor almost smiled. Also not surprising since Lord Treyvan was the king's best friend and his adored firstborn was a daughter.

Lord Osteen humphed with a fierce frown. "But if eldest daughters inherit, our noble surnames shall die."

The Duchess of Wildewall raised her eyes skyward. "Not if her husband takes it. My family has done that since Calatini's founding whenever a daughter is the eldest like me, as have *others* when they've no sons to inherit."

Oakmoor swallowed his chuckle. Including Lord Osteen's several generations ago.

Lady Ducharme tilted her head. "I think 'twould be a positive change—as long as the eldest wants to inherit."

The Duke of Osbourne shrugged. "But if they don't, they only need to abdicate. We could include laws addressing that."

Oakmoor leaned forward. "We should also encourage inheritances across Calatini to work the same." 'Twould prevent fathers in Calatini from acting like Juliet's censorious father. "Although that may cause tension with some foreign kingdoms, particularly Varkhora and the Tsarkan Empire."

Everyone traded glances, then King Devon said, "Think more about this inheritance change, and we'll discuss it again at the next council meeting."

After King Devon and Queen Kiera adjourned the council meeting, Oakmoor talked with his fellow councilors for a while before striding from the palace. If Juliet had skipped today's council meeting to avoid him, she'd missed a chance to support changes she'd love to see in her adopted kingdom. How the devoted royal witch would hate that. He definitely must speak with her at tonight's sirenic play.

CHAPTER 28

The morning of the first council meeting since her return, Juliet joined Giovanni for a walk in the palace gardens rather than attending. Magic wasn't likely to be a focus at today's meeting, and if she attended, the councilors would just ask her and Oakmoor about handling the private "royal" matter as well as scrutinize their interactions. And 'twould be too easy to betray how much she loved and missed him. They'd probably exchange hungry stares across the table for half the council meeting. Since their return nearly a week ago, they'd *both* been guilty of such stares whenever their gazes met, even though they were across crowded rooms and he was often with Lady Georgiana Laurent, who was usually radiant in arachne silk gowns that enhanced her dark beauty.

Her heart twisting like always at Oakmoor's determined courtship of the younger lady, she smiled at Giovanni walking beside her. In any case, she spent her mornings with her brother now. Over the past few days, they'd gone riding, taken long walks, and visited public areas in the palace. They'd also practiced magic in her workroom after her magical powers had finished recharging two days ago. And during all their outings, they'd talked the entire time to get to know each other again.

They'd become as close as they'd been before she'd fled Vark-hora, albeit as peers instead of toddler and much older sister.

Juliet grinned while Giovanni launched Striker into the air to hunt. Her brother was a fascinating young gentleman, particu-larly for a Varkhoran—he was observant, fair-minded, and chival-rous, yet he adored and admired strong ladies. He claimed 'twas because he'd grown up hearing Mother's stories about her. He was even working with Sandro to make women equals in Vark-hora, and perhaps with both the king and the future most prom-inent duke behind that, they might succeed one day. But despite his love of strong ladies, Giovanni was still a fierce Varkhoran warrior. He reveled in sword fighting, hunting with his drak-lizard, and other active pursuits. Although he knew how to use the magical powers they'd inherited from Mother, he didn't enjoy it the way she herself did because 'twasn't physical enough. And like any Varkhoran warrior, Giovanni possessed a deep sense of family honor and was intensely protective of those he loved.

She suppressed a sigh. Her brother had noticed those hungry stares between her and Oakmoor, and they invariably angered him because he felt Oakmoor wasn't treating her with enough respect. Especially since Oakmoor was practically betrothed to another lady. Giovanni was definitely going to erupt if she was pregnant with Oakmoor's child, which she very well might be, although she'd not know for certain for at least another week. A witch healer or a soul healer would be able to tell sooner, but her healing spells weren't powerful enough to reveal pregnancy until she missed her courses. And she couldn't risk anyone else discovering her scandalous pregnancy.

Giovanni grinned at her as he took her arm. "Why so pensive, big sister? 'Tis a lovely summer morning, and you're with the gentleman you love best."

Juliet smiled back despite the hollow ache filling her chest. If only Giovanni *was* the gentleman she loved best. But he wasn't; Oakmoor was. So damned foolish since he'd never return her love. She squeezed her brother's arm. "I was just thinking about all I must do before tonight's sirenic play."

His brow furrowing, Giovanni tsked. "You work too hard, Juliet."

She shrugged as she let her smile turn wry. "Royal witches must in order to fulfill their duties and maintain their position. Besides, I've always enjoyed working hard."

Giovanni sighed and smoothed his beard. "I know, and since it gives you joy, you should. But I worry about you working so hard that you neglect to care for yourself if someone who loves you isn't here to remind you to do it."

Warmed by Giovanni's loving concern, she smiled while squeezing his arm again. "I'll be fine. Don't forget, I've been caring for myself for over twenty years now."

Giovanni frowned down at her. "Yes, but you shouldn't have to. Especially since you've family who love and miss you." He arched his brows. "I mentioned how disappointed Father and Mother were that you were too busy to join my mirror call with them the other day, didn't I?"

Juliet almost winced. She should have agreed to that mirror call, but she'd been too wary. Giovanni had claimed Father had changed after she'd fled Varkhora, yet what if he hadn't? She couldn't handle Father's censure in addition to everything else right now. She made herself nod. "You did, and I'm sorry for disappointing Mother and Father. I'll join you on a mirror call as soon as I finish catching up on my duties." To distract her younger brother from family matters, she smiled at him and said, "Now tell me about Lady Ducharme's fencing salon this morning."

His concerned frown vanishing, Giovanni brightened. "'Twas the best yet. I crossed swords with Lord Ravenstone, and our sword fight was *amazing*. He's the first in Calatini to beat me, although Alex came close the other day using the moves Lord Ravenstone had taught him." Giovanni grinned. "Thanks for helping procure my invitation to Lady Ducharme's fencing salons."

She chuckled. Not many warriors would delight in losing to a superior opponent as much as Giovanni did. Her younger brother was truly a fascinating gentleman. "What else are big sisters for?"

Then Striker returned with a pigeon and presented it to Giovanni, who praised the draklizard before returning it to him to devour. Other than striking when his talons were touched, Striker was a perfectly trained Varkhoran draklizard, although few Varkhoran gentlemen would have kept him with that flaw. Yet another way Giovanni was different.

She and Giovanni walked in the palace gardens for half an hour longer, then she returned to her wing to handle her duties for the day. That evening, Giovanni joined her for dinner before they headed to the sirenic play. He was very excited to attend because sirens rarely visited Varkhora, so tonight would be his first time seeing a sirenic play full of aerial sword fights, glass-shattering arias, and passionate romances. Although 'twas the sword fights which truly interested him.

When she and Giovanni met Siobhan and Lorcan in her box, her friends appeared excited too, although not as much as Giovanni. Orandia was the nearest human kingdom to the countless Sirenuse Isles that sirens called home, so Siobhan and Lorcan had surely seen sirenic plays before, but sirenic plays were invariably both stunning and entertaining. She grinned at her friends. "Anticipating tonight's sirenic play?"

Siobhan and Lorcan returned her grin as Siobhan replied, "Very much. And although 'tisn't how I usually celebrate Neaprevel, I'm certain the Sea God would approve of watching a dramatic play performed by island-dwellers."

Juliet inclined her head. Although they'd not discussed it before, 'twasn't surprising that Siobhan worshipped the Sea God. Many sea witches did, even if they'd been raised as followers of the Goddess or the Twins. And the Sea God likely *would* approve of watching a sirenic play to celebrate his summer festival Neaprevel since he controlled changing influences like passion, storms, earthquakes, and water. Sirenic plays were always exceedingly passionate.

After greeting her friends, Juliet caught King Devon and Queen Kiera's gaze in the royal box beside hers and gave them a respectful nod, but she didn't approach them. Their family and close friends were with them, so they'd not appreciate her intruding. Then her pulse surged as Oakmoor strode into his box, alone for once. Not that she dared look directly at him. They'd exchange hungry glances if she did.

Fortunately, before she could succumb to temptation, Lord and Lady Weston glided into her box with Cassandra and Amaranth, and Juliet beamed at them. Tonight was the first she'd seen Shandor's daughters since her absence. She said, "I wasn't expecting to see you here."

Lord Weston ruffled Amaranth's hair as the little girl bounced between him and Lady Weston. "Unlike most children, Amaranth was wild to attend."

Amaranth grinned. "I've never heard sirens sing before." She bounced again. "So excited!"

Lady Weston slanted her youngest granddaughter a stern look. "Remember, we can only stay for the first half. You're usually already asleep by then."

As Amaranth glumly agreed, Juliet swallowed a laugh. That little girl was undeniably going to be a bard witch like Shandor one day. She smiled at Cassandra, who'd joined her. "And how are you?"

Cassandra smiled back, but her mulberry eyes were probing. "Excited, although not like Amaranth." She scanned the others then asked too quietly for them to overhear, "And how are you after breaking the Duke of Oakmoor's beast curse?"

Juliet clung to her smile. Of course, the veiled witch had told her apprentice about Oakmoor's curse. She murmured back, "I'm fine."

Cassandra glanced toward Oakmoor's box, which was still empty but for him. Unusual. "Because Tihdseare said there'd be consequences for that."

Juliet nearly scowled. The veiled witch had, had she? Dratted seer. Juliet briefly fisted her hands before forcing them flat. Giovanni or Siobhan might notice her anger and question it. She leaned closer to Cassandra. "I promise I'm fine."

Cassandra exhaled. "Good. I was concerned, and not just because I didn't want to be stuck acting for Tihdseare at court forever."

Juliet blinked at Cassandra. Why had the veiled witch had her young apprentice act for her at court? And how exactly? But before she could ask, the witchlights dimmed to indicate the sirenic play was about to begin, and the Westons hurried to their own box.

Once she'd settled in her seat between Siobhan and Giovanni, Siobhan whispered, "What were you and Miss Weston discussing? You appeared upset."

Juliet sighed. She'd not flattened her hands fast enough. "Surprised, not upset. Cassandra just told me that she acted for the veiled witch at court."

Siobhan inclined her head. "I was surprised at first too. Yet Miss Weston possesses a maturity many young ladies her age don't. She performed extremely well when attending court meetings in your stead, providing her own or the veiled witch's advice about magic, and casting spells that King Devon, Queen Kiera, or the council requested. But doubtless the veiled witch knew Miss Weston would. Seers always do."

As the stage curtains glided open, Juliet drummed her fingers on her knee. She really must visit the veiled witch to confront her about her meddling. The veiled witch's incredibly powerful seer vision that included all three types of magical sight—the fairly common nowsight, the less common hindsight, and the very rare foresight—still didn't give her the right to arrange people's lives.

Then the sirenic play began with two burly sirens in silvery armor swooping onstage and crossing swords midair, and Giovanni leaned forward with a cheery grin. She slanted her excited brother a fond smile. Yet as the dramatic and stunning sirenic play continued, her gaze kept flicking from the stage to Oakmoor, and he appeared to be doing likewise. Midway through the first half, their eyes met, and hunger flared inside her like wildfire before she finally wrenched her gaze back to the stage where a female siren was weeping over the slain warrior while the victor sang a sonorous aria of triumph. She gulped a steadying breath. How right she'd been to not attend the council meeting this morning.

Following her and Oakmoor's locked stare, she didn't let her attention drift from the stage for the rest of the first half, which ended with the female siren stabbing the victor on their wedding night as revenge for killing the slain warrior, her secret half-brother. Hence Juliet stiffened when Oakmoor asked from behind her as soon as the witchlights brightened for inter-mission, "Lady Juliet, shall we fetch some refreshments together?"

After she and the others turned to face Oakmoor, Giovanni scowled with Striker on his shoulder craned to attack. He rasped, "Shouldn't you be asking Lady Georgiana that?"

Oakmoor arched a brow. "No. I've a council matter to discuss with your sister." He offered her his arm. "Shall we?"

Juliet huffed. Refusing would only make her brother and friends more suspicious. She rose and smoothed her sapphire skirt. "Very well."

As Giovanni scowled fiercer while Siobhan and Lorcan grinned, she took Oakmoor's arm and inhaled at the usual tingling suffusing her. Please let him and the others not notice.

Once they were in the hall without her brother and friends watching, Oakmoor said in a murmur only she could hear, "You missed an important council meeting today. King Devon and Queen Kiera proposed adjusting the royal inheritance laws so that their firstborn could rule regardless of gender. You of all people should have been there to support that. Why weren't you?"

She pursed her lips. How dare Oakmoor lecture her when 'twas largely his fault she hadn't been there? "I would have if I'd known."

Oakmoor narrowly eyed her. "You didn't decide not to attend to avoid me, did you?"

Juliet glared at the vexingly astute man. "Of course not. I spend the mornings with my brother now, and since magic wasn't a likely topic at today's council meeting, I felt no need to attend."

Oakmoor inclined his head. "Good. Gossip shall start if we neglect our duties to avoid each other. And neither of us wants such gossip."

Despite the truth of that, she barely resisted attacking Oakmoor. Instead, she dulcetly drawled, "Such gossip *would* make your courtship of Lady Georgiana Laurent more difficult. I'm surprised she didn't join you tonight."

Oakmoor grimaced. "Only because I cast a ward on my box preventing anyone from entering."

Juliet gaped at Oakmoor as he ordered their refreshments. He'd done what? Once he handed her an orenge spriss, the closest the theater had to her favorite spiritpunch, its pungent aroma made her stomach shift. The servant wasn't as skilled as Oakmoor at mixing it—too much orenge amaro. She lowered the spiritpunch without tasting it. "You dislike your future wife's company so much? Not promising for the success of your marriage."

Oakmoor snorted into his orenge spriss while they headed back to her box. "True. But Lady Georgiana is determined to ignore that."

Her pulse quickening, Juliet frowned and licked her lips. "As are you since you're still courting her."

Oakmoor hummed, his hungry gaze on her lips. "Am I?"

She swayed closer and lifted her head. Goddess, she needed—

"Juliet, there you are," Giovanni called. "Hurry, the sirenic play is about to resume."

She jerked away from Oakmoor and whirled to face her brother just outside her box. She'd almost kissed Oakmoor in public *again*.

His smile sharp as his saber, Giovanni drew Lady Georgiana Laurent, wearing a deep-lilac arachne silk gown tonight, into the hall. "Lady Georgiana was looking for you, your grace."

Juliet almost winced when the younger lady swept forward and captured Oakmoor's arm with a coy smile. He *must* be courting Lady Georgiana. He'd probably only hinted that he wasn't to seduce her again. How could she love such an unrepentant rakehell?

Not glancing at Oakmoor, she hurried back into her box for the rest of the sirenic play. Perhaps its tangled drama would eclipse that in her own life.

TWO MORNINGS after the sirenic play—which concluded happily with the siren couple falling in love while the warrior recovered from his bride stabbing him then her bearing him a firstborn son whom they named after her slain half-brother—Juliet told Giovanni that she'd some duties to handle and headed across Ormas to Rhiannon's Veils to confront the veiled witch. She strode through the witch shop's weathered red door then grimaced at the dim, hushed chamber heavy with incense and magic. 'Twas eerily mysterious, no doubt by design, but how did the veiled witch stand to work in here? The magical garden where 'twas forever summer, the only part of Rhiannon's Veils she'd seen when helping break the Greysnowe-Ravenstone curse, was *much* nicer than this oppressive chamber.

Seated at the wooden table before cluttered cabinets of spell ingredients and magical accoutrements, the veiled witch waved for her to sit in the chair across the table, jingling bracelets and tiny bells. "Good morning, Lady Juliet."

Inclining her head, Juliet sank into the chair but maintained her elegant posture. She was no supplicant, even though the veiled witch possessed much greater power. "Good morning... what shall I call you? Cassandra calls you Tihdseare, but that simply means 'teacher' in the witch's tongue, and you aren't *my* teacher."

The veiled witch's dark, exotically lined eyes flickered. "Sadly, I no longer possess a name. I had to surrender it many years ago."

Juliet inhaled, a pang echoing through her. How dreadfully lonely. "Why?"

The veiled witch sighed, and her concealing black veils fluttered. "Did you know that in Orandia, the seer's birth name is erased, they're always concealed by white veils, no one ever touches them, and they're only spoken to when requesting a prophecy?"

Juliet couldn't suppress her shudder. "I'd heard the Orandian seer was isolated, but I'd not realized 'twas that extensive."

The veiled witch nodded. "The Orandians do that because relationships cloud the foresight part of a seer's vision. Seers can see everyone's future but their own and those close to them since their lives are intertwined." The veiled witch shook her head. "Yet humans aren't meant to live that isolated, so Orandian seers rarely serve longer than five years, and many go mad from loneliness then fling themselves from the seer's tower."

Juliet shuddered again. Dear Goddess. Perhaps she didn't want to visit that magical island kingdom after all. She swallowed. "What does all that have to do with your name?"

The veiled witch blew another sigh. "Because when I was young, I had a choice. I could keep my name and live a relatively normal life in Orandia's Rathan Forest, providing small prophecies for strangers. Or I could surrender my name and live apart far from home but guide events how they should proceed to prepare for when the Lost Grimoire returns."

Juliet gasped. Shortly before her death, Rhiannon had cast an incredibly powerful spell to conceal the Lost Grimoire, the spellbook she'd written containing the complex and dangerous magic that she couldn't teach the early witches. The Amun Prophecy, given by the first Orandian seer, foretold its return during mankind's greatest need. Hunters of the Lost Grimoire had searched all of Damensea for it with no success since 'twas hidden over two millennia ago. She shivered. She'd never imagined the Lost Grimoire would return in her lifetime. "The Lost Grimoire is about to return?"

Tiny bells jingling once more, the veiled witch tilted her head. "'About' is relative, but as one of the most powerful of Rhiannon's direct descendants, I felt 'twas my duty to prepare for her dangerous spellbook's return."

Juliet gaped at the veiled witch, her head whirling. Rhiannon had supposedly borne a daughter after settling on Orandia, but she'd been well past childbearing years then. "You're a direct Rhiannon descendant? I assumed they were a myth."

The veiled witch chuckled. "No, just extremely wary about revealing ourselves. 'Tis hard enough for ordinary Rhiannon descendants."

Juliet sagged back in her chair. Because the greater powers of ordinary Rhiannon descendants like herself made other witches or humans without magic exploitative or jealous. Yet they were merely descendants of early witches who'd performed a blood-kith ceremony with Rhiannon that had enhanced their magical powers, an enhancement which continued in their bloodline. *Direct* descendants of the founder of human magic must be infinitely more powerful. She sighed. No wonder the veiled witch's powers eclipsed hers like the sun eclipsed the moon. But what a price she'd paid for them.

Juliet straightened and narrowly eyed the veiled witch. "Why are you telling me all this?"

The veiled witch held her gaze. "Because you need to know that I'm not arranging people's lives for my own amusement. Otherwise your blind anger with me would lead you to attempt something foolish, like asking the Mirror of Wisdom about me, even though you normally wouldn't. Not only would you not learn much," the veiled witch's gaze dropped to Juliet's stomach, "but risking that would be deadly for you."

Juliet spread a protective hand over her stomach. The veiled witch's pointed look implied she could see Oakmoor's child growing there. Yet only a powerful witch healer or soul healer might be able to see that so soon. And the veiled witch was neither because she was a seer, and witches couldn't be multiple special witch classes. Surely the veiled witch was just referring to the peril that had nearly killed Siobhan—asking the Mirror of Wisdom a question it couldn't answer.

She lifted her chin. "No matter my anger with you, I'd *never* be so foolish to risk using the Mirror of Wisdom after it nearly killed my friend when she attempted to penetrate your dratted wards." Frowning, she leaned toward the veiled witch. "Why *did* you give Oakmoor wards that completely blocked us from seeing or contacting the outside world until I broke his beast curse?"

The veiled witch arched her brows. "You know why. The two of you needed time alone for love to grow, and love was the only way to break that vindictive curse."

Juliet winced. Yes, she knew that, and she didn't regret risking everything to save Oakmoor, but still... "Yet now I'm helplessly in love with a rakehell determined to marry another." And possibly pregnant by him too.

The veiled witch's eyes crinkled. "I'd not fret about that. Matters shall resolve how they were meant to. They always do."

Juliet huffed and pursed her lips. How like a seer to say that.

The veiled witch chuckled. Then she sobered. "Before you

return to the palace, I must discuss Cassandra with you. Although 'tis irregular, she needs both of us to be her mentors."

Juliet frowned. A seer like the veiled witch should know everything Cassandra needed. "What could I teach her that you can't?"

Her black veils fluttering, the veiled witch sighed. "Plenty, but particularly handling court and performing public magic. I've no experience with either, and Cassandra shall require both in her future."

Juliet blinked and studied the veiled witch. *What* future did she see for Cassandra? Not that the veiled witch would reveal it if anyone asked to avoid changing it. So Juliet asked instead, "Is Cassandra's future why you had her act for you at court?"

The veiled witch lifted a shoulder. "Somewhat. But also because I must remain apart to continue my calling, and being a royal witch, even temporarily, is too public for that. I only agreed to King Devon and Queen Kiera's request so they'd not seek another royal witch before you returned."

Juliet exhaled, her habitual tension with the incredibly powerful seer easing. The veiled witch plainly possessed no desire for the royal position that Juliet had striven so hard to achieve and would never seek to usurp it. Her fingers tightened in her lap. Not that she'd enjoy being Calatini's royal witch for much longer if she was pregnant.

The veiled witch sighed. "Plus, I can't risk meeting the Orandians. They'd recognize me as a fellow Orandian, and word of me might spread to my family back home, making remaining apart impossible."

Juliet grimaced. She understood that loneliness. Thankfully, she no longer needed to hide from her family. She inclined her head. "I'll be glad to mentor Cassandra. She's a delightful girl as well as the daughter of a dear friend."

The veiled witch straightened, her eyes crinkling again. "I knew you'd agree."

Juliet huffed another sigh and rose. Seers. But at least the veiled witch had answered all her questions involving herself. She bid the veiled witch farewell and returned to the palace to handle her duties before Giovanni arrived for dinner and the Campbells' ball afterward. Hopefully, she could keep avoiding Oakmoor there like she had since the sirenic play.

CHAPTER 29

As Oakmoor greeted Sir Ellis and Lady Campbell, he scoured their bustling ballroom for Lady Georgiana. The annoying girl just wouldn't quit her dogged pursuit, so he had to remain on guard to avoid her. Unfortunately, he didn't spot her, although he did see Juliet and her brother with the Orandians near the refreshments table. His pulse quickening, he slipped through the crowd straight toward them. Not to talk with Juliet, whom he'd not been near since the sirenic play, but to avoid Lady Georgiana. The Varkhoran lord vexed the younger lady, so she'd not approach him if he was with Lord Sabine.

Once he joined Juliet and the others, they murmured polite greetings, although only Lady Driscoll and Sir Lorcan seemed pleased to see him. Juliet barely glanced at him before continuing to scan the other guests, while Lord Sabine glowered at him like usual. Disregarding her brother, he asked Juliet, "Who are you looking for?" Not another gentleman surely.

His jaw tightened when Juliet said while still scanning the crowd, "Lord—"

But before Juliet could finish, Lady Georgiana captured his arm and said, "Your grace, finally. I was afraid I'd not find you until after the dancing began."

Juliet and the others eyeing him and Lady Georgiana, Oakmoor stiffened but adroitly freed his arm. Damnation, being near Lord Sabine hadn't helped at all. *What* would get Lady Georgiana to quit? Thanks to her, he didn't know the gentleman Juliet was seeking. One who wasn't him. He gritted a smooth smile at Lady Georgiana. "You really shouldn't waste your dances on an old rakehell like me, my lady."

As Juliet blinked, Lord Sabine glowered fiercer, and the Orandians grinned, Lady Georgiana shifted closer then replied, "Nonsense. You're much too vigorous for anyone to call old."

Lord Sabine snorted and clenched his saber, the draklizard on his shoulder studying Oakmoor with deadly purpose. "*I* would."

Not glancing at Juliet's brother, Lady Georgiana sniffed. "Only because you're a child."

While Lord Sabine glared at Lady Georgiana, Oakmoor scrutinized the young couple. How had he not noticed that their bickering mirrored his and Juliet's? The two were obviously fighting a fierce attraction. Perhaps he could use *that* to deter Lady Georgiana. He drawled, "Aren't you two the same age?"

Although Juliet and the Orandians chuckled, Lord Sabine and Lady Georgiana scowled at him. United, excellent.

He continued, "You're both children to the rest of us." He smiled as the strains of the first waltz began. Perfect. He arched his brows at Lady Georgiana. "I believe you owe Lord Sabine a first dance for the one you missed at the Duchess of Wildewall's ball." When Lord Sabine and Lady Georgiana stared at him, he shooed them toward the gathering dancers. "Go on then."

Lord Sabine narrowly eyed him yet extended a hand toward Lady Georgiana, who pursed her lips but accepted it, and they glided onto the floor.

Lady Driscoll laughed then twinkled at him. "Deftly done, your grace."

As Oakmoor nodded his thanks, Sir Lorcan smiled at his wife and asked, "Shall we follow the *children*'s example, love?"

Grinning, Lady Driscoll smoothed her long tunic and over-coat. "Yes, please."

Once the Orandians joined the other dancers, Oakmoor turned to face Juliet. He offered his arm with a wry smile, his blood surging at holding the bewitching witch once again. "We'd better do likewise to prevent gossip."

Juliet's dark-brown eyes flickered, but she sighed then took his arm. "Very well." As soon as they began twirling about the floor, she frowned up at him. "Why did you shove Lady Georgiana at Giovanni?"

He chuckled and drew Juliet closer. She'd not noticed the obvious yet. "Because they like each other. Why Lady Georgiana is pursuing me when she truly prefers your brother, I don't know."

Juliet glanced at the young couple across the ballroom then hummed. "I should have realized that Giovanni likes Lady Georgiana from how he keeps mentioning her and glowering at you. But I assumed he dislikes you for a... different reason."

Hunger tightening his body as their explosive passion echoed through him once more, Oakmoor pulled Juliet close enough that her topaz-yellow skirt brushed against him then lowered his head to prevent others from overhearing. "You mean because your brother can sense that we burn to ravish each other again?"

Her breath quickening, Juliet stared up at him for several heartbeats. Then she shoved him back to the proper distance. "No, because you're an unrepentant rakehell who can't resist flirting with anyone in a skirt."

He tensed. Except Juliet was the only one he'd bothered to flirt with since their return. But just because the eligible ladies he should be courting were too bland to interest him. And he kept having to evade Lady Georgiana and was busy with his duties. He forced a flippant grin. "Before your brother challenges me to a duel, perhaps you could inform him that Lady Georgiana is safe from me. Despite my unrepentant flirting, I never trifle with innocents."

Juliet narrowed her eyes at him then leaned closer and muttered, "And what was *I* when you first seduced me fourteen years ago?"

Oakmoor almost winced. "That was different. After your years traveling with gypsies, I didn't believe you were still one." Although even if he had, he mightn't have been able to resist Juliet. The primal hunger between them was too voracious.

To distract them both, he spun Juliet in a complicated twirl, and she swayed then stumbled into him. Even though his tight body hardened further at her curves pressing against him, he frowned as he pulled her upright and scrutinized her face. Juliet was never so clumsy. And she appeared somewhat pale. No doubt she was exhausted from struggling to catch up on her duties while getting to know her brother. He should have realized that and fetched her refreshments instead of asking her to dance.

Juliet's palpable exhaustion softening his desire, he scowled and began escorting her from the floor. "Why didn't you say you were too tired to dance, you stubborn witch?"

Juliet glared up at him. "I'm not tired. I was just lightheaded for a moment. That happens when your partner hurls you in a complicated twirl without warning."

He swallowed as his chest twisted. "A twirl you've always managed fine before, so you're plainly exhausted." He pushed Juliet into a chair without anyone nearby not far from the refreshments table. "Sit. I'll fetch you some sparkling wine."

When he returned with a full glass flute, Juliet glowered at him but accepted it. "There's no need for you to be overbearing."

Oakmoor sank into the chair beside Juliet. Fetching her sparkling wine was hardly being overbearing. Her fierce pride was blinding her to sense. To get her to see that, he arched a mocking brow and drawled, "If you persist on working yourself to exhaustion, there is."

Juliet lifted her set chin. "I'm *fine.*"

Oakmoor sighed. Of course Juliet would say that. But for her to have remained seated like he'd ordered meant she must be exhausted. Yet nothing he could say would get the maddening witch to admit it. So instead, he merely nodded at her untasted glass flute and said, "Drink your sparkling wine."

Juliet sniffed her sparkling wine then lowered it with a faint frown, just like she'd done with the orenge spriss at the sirenic play. "I don't want any sparkling wine."

He stiffened. Likely because he'd fetched it. Juliet was blatantly determined to accept nothing from him. 'Twas why she'd left the attire he'd purchased behind at Oakmoor House too. Not that he cared. He was only attempting to prevent the foolish royal witch from fainting at a court event and sparking a scandal she'd despise.

Then the first waltz ended, and Lord Sabine surged over with Lady Georgiana. His beard bristling, the Varkhoran lord glared and demanded, "What have you done to Juliet, Oakmoor?"

Remaining seated in the face of Lord Sabine's protective anger, Oakmoor held the younger lord's gaze. Perhaps Juliet's brother could accomplish what he couldn't. "Nothing. Your sister has been working too hard lately and couldn't finish our dance." At Juliet's sharp inhale, he plucked the glass flute from her fingers then smiled at Lord Sabine, who was frowning at his sister now. "But she didn't want this sparkling wine to help her recover. Perhaps you could fetch her some tea instead?"

As Lord Sabine nodded, Juliet leapt upright and glowered at both of them. "I don't need to recover. Goddess save me from smothering men." When Lord Sabine began to protest, she waved him toward the floor. "Giovanni, go dance with Lady Georgiana again." She scowled at Oakmoor. "You, go irritate another lady." Then she swept over to Lady Driscoll and Sir Lorcan.

As Lord Sabine frowned after Juliet, Lady Georgiana gave Oakmoor a coy smile and said, "How solicitous you are, your grace."

Oakmoor sighed when Lord Sabine turned and glared at him

once more. Goddess save *him* from doggedly persistent ladies. Juliet's brother was undeniably going to challenge him to a duel if Lady Georgiana kept flirting with him. He rose and replied to her, "I'm only solicitous to some." He arched his brows at the young couple. "You'd best do as Lady Juliet commanded. You don't want the most illustrious witch in Calatini angry at you, sister or no."

Lady Georgiana grimacing beside him, Lord Sabine humphed then asked, "And what do *you* intend to do?"

Oakmoor smiled. "Irritate a lady, of course." Just not another one.

His draklizard's iridescent eyes glinting, Lord Sabine humphed again but then turned to Lady Georgiana. "Shall we?"

Lady Georgiana heaved a sigh. "I suppose we might as well. Besides..."

Once the young couple glided back onto the floor, bickering as they twirled, Oakmoor strode to the refreshments table and fetched tea and oatmeal spice sweet biscuits for Juliet. Then he joined her and the Orandians, silently handing her the refreshments, and she accepted them without grumbling, probably to avoid drawing her friends' notice. The fiercely proud royal witch definitely didn't want anyone knowing her duties had exhausted her.

Lady Driscoll and Sir Lorcan grinned at him, then Sir Lorcan said, "I see you convinced Lord Sabine and Lady Georgiana to dance again already."

Oakmoor smiled at the Orandians, although he kept half his gaze on Juliet, only relaxing when she began the refreshments he'd brought. *Finally* she was being sensible. He shrugged. "It didn't require much convincing since Lord Sabine and Lady Georgiana both wanted to, no matter how much they bicker and pretend otherwise."

Lady Driscoll tilted her head and impishly studied Juliet. "A family trait, it seems."

Both Oakmoor and Juliet stiffened at her friend's teasing

comparison, and he was about to protest that their well-known dislike wasn't at all the same when Lord and Lady Farson bustled over and halted his pride-saving lie. Not that his and Juliet's uncontrollable attraction meant anything. She wanted an adoring husband, and he needed a wife willing to bear his children who didn't desire the love he could never give her.

During their greetings, Lady Farson warmly beamed at Juliet but barely offered him a polite smile. Although her husband hadn't behaved differently toward him at the council meeting the other day, Lady Farson clearly disliked him for kidnapping her twin's bride. Unsurprising. She and Lord Blaine were incredibly close, and kidnapping the former Miss Hawke had been a desperate and dishonorable mistake.

Oakmoor swallowed his sigh. Hopefully, Lady Farson could keep her dislike concealed from the rest of court. None of them wanted gossip to start. 'Twould ruin the Duchess of Childes's push to remove the scandal surrounding Lord and Lady Blaine's elopement. To remind Lady Farson about that, he flashed a smooth grin and said, "I'm looking forward to the Duchess of Childes's fete in a few days celebrating your brother's recent marriage, Lady Farson. I've not had a chance to congratulate Lord Blaine and his bride."

Lady Farson's smile tightened before noticeably warming. Good. She'd understood his discreet warning. Lady Farson sipped her sparkling wine. "Edouard and Pippa have only attended family events since they returned to Ormas. At the duchess's instructions, of course. She wants to heighten the impact of her fete."

Oakmoor inclined his head. "The Duchess of Childes has succeeded. 'Tis the most anticipated non-royal event of the season other than my upcoming soiree. But I've the advantage in that because *I'm* still unwed. I do hope you and all your family shall attend."

Lord and Lady Farson traded grins, then Lord Farson replied,

"Edouard and Pippa might attend along with Arvan, but Elise and I shall have left Calatini by then."

As Juliet's eyes widened but the Orandians simply nodded, Oakmoor blinked and studied the Farsons. They weren't just returning to Golddell but leaving the kingdom entirely? Lord Farson hadn't revealed *that* at the council meeting. Yet how could he and his wife leave Calatini? Lord Farson was a councilor with important duties here. And it sounded like they were leaving their teenage ward Arvan, the Duke of Golddell, behind too. Their reason for leaving must be serious.

Lady Farson beamed at Lady Driscoll and Sir Lorcan. "We're visiting Orandia, and we'd like to arrange a meeting to discuss your recommendations for traveling there."

Lady Driscoll smiled. "How about over luncheon the day after tomorrow?"

After the Farsons nodded their agreement, Juliet arched her brows at them. "What made you decide to visit Orandia?"

The Farsons glanced at each other, then Lady Farson shrugged and replied, "The veiled witch advised us to visit Orandia to resolve a problem we're having."

Oakmoor studied Lord and Lady Farson. A serious problem for them to be eager to travel all the way to Orandia when their life and family were in Calatini.

Sir Lorcan grinned and leaned forward. "You received a prophecy from the veiled witch?"

Lord Farson smoothed his beard. "Not a prophecy per se, just advice."

Lady Driscoll sighed and shook her head. "You're fortunate. We *still* haven't been able to meet the veiled witch."

Juliet stilled. "Perhaps you should quit attempting to do so. Seers, especially incredibly powerful ones, are only found when they wish to be."

Oakmoor eyed Juliet. She'd referred to the veiled witch with little of her usual annoyance. Curious. As Lady Driscoll and Sir Lorcan sighed again but nodded, he captured Juliet's arm.

"You've finished your tea and sweet biscuits. Let's fetch some more."

Juliet stiffened but let him escort her from the others, likely to avoid exposing why she'd needed refreshments before.

As soon as they were alone, he asked, "You sounded remarkably mellow about the veiled witch just now. Why?"

Juliet grimaced as he handed her a fresh cup of tea. "This morning, I confronted the veiled witch about her meddling, so she explained her reasons, and they were all extremely necessary."

He hummed. They must have been to convince Juliet. "What *were* her reasons?"

Juliet exhaled into her tea. "'Tisn't my place to disclose that. But the veiled witch must be left alone. And she wants to avoid any Orandians, so we both need to persuade Siobhan and Lorcan to quit attempting to see her."

Oakmoor rubbed his chin. He did owe the veiled witch for her help breaking his beast curse. Besides, Juliet accepted the veiled witch's reasons as necessary, and her insight into magical matters was invariably right. He nodded. "Very well."

Then Juliet straightened and shoved her near-full teacup at him. "I finally see Lord and Lady Weston. I was looking for them earlier. Excuse me."

As Juliet hurried to the older couple, he exhaled and scrutinized her. So Juliet hadn't been seeking another gentleman when he'd first joined her but the Westons. When had she become close with them? And why? She rarely attended their musical evenings, but the Westons and their granddaughters *had* visited Juliet's box at the sirenic play. His eyes narrowed. That surely meant they'd become close somehow. Another secret that she'd not shared with him. His breath stilled. Because their enforced intimacy while trapped alone in his townhouse together hadn't been genuine. He set his jaw. Fortunately. Genuine intimacy was too close to sincere love and commitment, and he wasn't mad enough to want either.

He inhaled then forced himself to quit watching Juliet. Instead, he scanned the ballroom for Lady Escana. They should arrange a meeting to discuss her duties. He soon spotted his assistant and her husband talking with their hosts. When he joined the Escanas and the Campbells, they were discussing yesterday's kelpie race. Not surprising since both couples were sports-mad, although the Escanas preferred hunting with their beloved hounds while the Campbells preferred sword fighting.

Once Sir Ellis and Lady Campbell left to say farewell to the departing Lord and Lady Ravenstone, Oakmoor smiled at his assistant and said, "We should meet to discuss matters sometime soon. When are you free?"

Lady Escana tilted her head. "Tomorrow morning, if you don't mind being overrun with children and hounds." She slanted her husband a laughing glance. "Anthony is abandoning us to attend Lady Ducharme's fencing salon."

Lord Escana grinned back. "I deserve a morning out after you kept abandoning me with them while handling the Duke of Oakmoor's duties. Four children and six hounds who all transformed into little monsters without you were more than a gentleman could handle alone, Eleanor."

Smiling, Lady Escana tsked. "You're the one who insists on riling them up with rowdy horseplay."

Oakmoor chuckled when Lord Escana innocently widened his eyes and replied, "But how else are we to have time alone together at night?"

Lady Escana's lips twitched. "We do have two excellent nursemaids."

Before the Escanas could continue their loving teasing, Oakmoor interjected, "Tomorrow morning should be fine."

When he arrived at Escana House shortly after breakfast the following morning, Lady Escana arched her brows at him. "Mind if we go riding in the nearby park, your grace? That should keep the children occupied while we talk."

He glanced at his morning clothes. He wasn't dressed for

riding, but he could manage, although Miles might grumble when he returned. He shrugged. "As long as you provide a horse. I took my carriage."

Lady Escana smiled. "Of course."

Soon he, Lady Escana, three grooms, and her three older children—a girl and two boys, all under ten—were mounted and riding to the park with her six hounds loping around them. Lady Escana held her youngest daughter before her since the toddler was too little to ride alone. At the park, the older children trotted further from their mother, each of them closely accompanied by a groom and a hound or two.

Her smiling gaze not leaving her children, Lady Escana asked, "So what did you wish to discuss?"

Oakmoor studied Lady Escana's boisterous children as well. Although the countess was his assistant, her life was the opposite of his—full of laughter, family, and love. A pang stabbed him. He turned toward Lady Escana. "About your duties. While I was gone, you performed mine so well that keeping you as my mere assistant would be a waste. Which parts did you enjoy best?"

Lady Escana shrugged. "All of them, really." She urged her mare to ride closer to her children. "Except for missing family outings because I was too busy at court."

He kneed his gelding to remain beside Lady Escana. She'd hinted at that when they'd spoken on his first day back. But that shouldn't be an issue if they were splitting his duties. He nodded. "I can understand that. I'd prefer more time for a family as well."

Lady Escana blinked at him. "You're settling down at last?"

Oakmoor quirked a wry smile. "I've delayed enough, don't you think? I still need to produce an heir to prevent my degenerate cousin from inheriting." And although he'd never love her, he could use a wife he could talk openly with at night.

Lady Escana turned back toward her three older children,

who were now racing against each other. "I assume Lady Geor-giana is the fortunate lady."

He shuddered, making his gelding tense. "Goddess, no. Lady Georgiana is too young for me. And she much prefers another, although she's refusing to admit it."

After answering her toddler daughter who was bouncing in her lap and chattering about her siblings' race, Lady Escana hummed and nodded. "Lord Sabine, no doubt. Well, marrying a gentleman who shall take you from everything you know to a kingdom where women belong to their husbands is a frightening prospect. Especially to a lady accustomed to being more powerful than most of the gentlemen she meets."

Oakmoor drummed his fingers on his thigh. He should have realized those fears were why Lady Georgiana fought her true preference. If only she wasn't pursuing him like a rabid hellhound to escape her fears.

Lady Escana glanced at him again. "So if you aren't marrying Lady Georgiana, who *are* you marrying? Lady Juliet, perhaps? She's the only other unwed lady you've been around lately."

He clenched the reins with a sardonic grin. "Can you see Lady Juliet surrendering her position as royal witch to become my wife?" Even if she loved and wanted to marry him, she'd never do that. And she definitely didn't love and want to marry him. Just like he didn't love and want to marry her.

Lady Escana smiled. "No, I can't see Lady Juliet surrendering her position. But why should she need to? There's no law against the royal witch also being a duchess. And you're not the type of gentleman to demand that his wife have no interests outside the home. I'd not be your assistant if you were."

He shifted in the saddle. They must quit discussing Juliet before he betrayed his uncontrollable hunger for her to his too perceptive assistant. He cleared his throat. "We've digressed. We were supposed to be discussing promoting you from my assistant."

A faint furrow creasing her brow, Lady Escana cheered as her eldest daughter sailed over a log. "How can you promote me? The only higher position in the Ministry of Foreign Relations is yours."

Oakmoor inclined his head. "At the next council meeting, I plan to propose creating the position of deputy minister. Then we can split my duties and find assistants for us both. That way, neither of us would be too busy." He grinned at Lady Escana. "If the rest of the council agrees, would that be of interest to you?"

Lady Escana slanted him a flat glance. "Obviously."

He chuckled. He'd known his future deputy would agree. Now he just needed to convince the council.

Suddenly, Lady Escana's older children galloped toward the park's entrance, shouting, "Papa!"

As Lady Escana beamed at her children mobbing her laughing husband, Oakmoor swiftly bid her farewell so they could enjoy a family outing without him intruding. He returned the gelding to the Escanas' stables before taking his carriage back to his noisy yet empty townhouse. Perhaps one day he'd enjoy similar outings with his own family. Although that meant settling on a wife. He really must do that soon.

After spending the morning with Giovanni, Juliet joined the Westons for luncheon like they'd agreed at the Campbell's ball the evening before. As soon as she glided into the drawing room, Amaranth bounced over and flung herself at Juliet. Embracing Juliet, the little girl caroled, "Lady Juliet, you're here!"

Warmth filling her chest, Juliet returned Amaranth's sweet embrace. If she was truly pregnant, her and Oakmoor's child would one day fling themselves at her with such joy. A wonder she'd begun to believe she'd never have. One that might be worth the pain of loving a rakehell who couldn't return her love and losing everything she'd achieved in Calatini. She smiled and smoothed the little girl's loose curls. "Why so excited?"

Amaranth beamed up at her. "Grandma and Grandpa said you might share more stories about Mama and Papa."

Her and her husband smiling their welcome, Lady Weston tsked and extracted Amaranth from about Juliet. "Not if you demand them like that, you brash child."

Juliet swallowed a laugh when Amaranth heaved a sigh. Young children were so adorably open. She winked at the little girl. "But I might if you ask nicely." While Amaranth brightened again, she turned to Cassandra. "And how are you, Cassandra?"

Her mulberry eyes gleaming, Cassandra smiled. "I'm excited too." She waggled her brows at her much younger sister. "I'm just able to contain it unlike *some*."

Juliet, Cassandra, and the Westons chuckled as Amaranth glowered at Cassandra's teasing.

Lord Weston still chuckling, Lady Weston waved toward the door and asked, "Shall we head to luncheon?"

Like when she'd enjoyed luncheon at Weston House two months ago, Juliet spent much of the lively meal sharing stories about Shandor and Anne, which made Amaranth almost too excited to eat, Cassandra grin, and the Westons exchange bittersweet smiles. Cassandra also replied with related memories from their life in Pruzirias and tales her parents would tell about traveling Damensea.

As the servants were clearing the main course, Cassandra said, "Because of their travels, Mama and Papa acquired some customs from other kingdoms. Mama adored the intricate whitework embroidery from the Tsarkan Empire. She attempted to teach me, but I never possessed the patience. Papa, on the other hand, loved drinking Varkhoran kahve after meals." She grinned and leaned toward Juliet. "He said a close friend of his taught him to make it. Was that friend you?"

Juliet stilled. All of court knew she was from Varkhora now because she and Giovanni had acknowledged they were siblings. Yet she'd concealed her past for so many years that she couldn't help tensing whenever 'twas mentioned. But being known as the Duke of Appenninos's runaway daughter no longer held any danger for her. She inhaled then returned Cassandra's grin. "Yes, I was that friend who taught your father to drink proper kahve. I was disgusted by the pond water he believed was good kahve when I met him."

Lord Weston chuckled and shook his head. "You consider ordinary kahve pond water? How you must have suffered living in Calatini."

She chuckled too. Not having proper kahve was a small price for all she loved about Calatini. "The kahve at court isn't *that* bad. But gypsies can only afford inferior beans. And they even add chicory root to make their kahve supply last longer." She shuddered. "Hideous."

Everyone laughed, even little Amaranth who'd surely never tasted kahve of any kind. Then as the servants returned with dessert, Cassandra said, "I suspected you might be the friend Papa meant, so I asked Grandmother if we could serve a surprise for you at luncheon." Once the servants set bowls of vahnila pudding and tiny cups of Varkhoran kahve on the table, except for Amaranth who received shokolat instead, Cassandra beamed and continued, "Proper Varkhoran kahve with dessert. I had to teach Cook how to make it though. Fortunately, Papa taught me that well before he let me drink it—'twas much more interesting to learn than embroidery."

Light suffusing her, Juliet smiled at the teenage girl while stirring sugar into her kahve. How like Shandor Cassandra was. "Thank you, Cassandra. That was very kind." She lifted her tiny cup but froze when her stomach roiled at the concentrated kahve's strong scent. That had never happened before. Yet she couldn't refuse Cassandra's kindness. She swallowed and tossed back her kahve before managing a grin for Cassandra. "Delicious." Then she hurriedly began her vahnila pudding. Please let it settle her stomach.

Thankfully, it did, so after a few bites, she started sharing about how teaching Shandor to make proper kahve had helped them become dear friends. Yet her mind kept returning to her unexpected nausea. Pregnant women were often sensitive to scents, so that could be a sign of pregnancy. Or it *could* be a sign that she was fretting over being pregnant so much that 'twas making her ill. She'd not know for certain until she missed her courses in a few more days and could perform a healing-sight spell to check for pregnancy.

After everyone finished dessert, Juliet turned to Cassandra. 'Twas time to broach the reason she'd arranged today's luncheon —her becoming Cassandra's second mentor. She smiled and arched her brows at her future apprentice. "Shall we head to your workroom?"

Cassandra leapt to her feet with a grin. "Of course."

Amaranth bounced upright. "I'm coming too."

Lord and Lady Weston, who'd agreed to Juliet's intentions last night, traded a glance. Then Lady Weston rose and wrapped her arm about Amaranth's shoulders. She said, "We've a keyharp lesson directly after luncheon, remember?"

As Amaranth sighed but nodded, Juliet inclined her head to thank the Westons. She and Cassandra should really discuss magic in private. Their discussions would bore Lord and Lady Weston since they weren't witches, and Amaranth was too young. The little girl's magical powers wouldn't likely begin developing for another few years.

Once Juliet and Cassandra settled in Cassandra's large and cluttered workroom, Juliet forced herself to disregard the many piles about the room and smiled at the younger witch instead. "How did you find acting for the veiled witch at court while I was gone?"

Cassandra grimaced and smoothed her brown skirt. "Overwhelming. I'm decades younger than most of the people I needed to interact with, and I don't know court protocol terribly well yet. I only began learning it after Grandmother and Grandfather found us eleven months ago."

Juliet nodded. She'd felt much the same when she'd first joined the Lovaris. A gypsy's life was vastly different from that at court. But Shandor had helped her adjust, and now she could help his daughter do likewise. She smiled at Cassandra to encourage her. "From what I've heard, you performed extremely well. I spoke with the veiled witch, and we agreed that I should become your second mentor even though most apprentices only have one. As long as you're willing, obviously."

Cassandra beamed and leaned forward. "I definitely am. The veiled witch can only teach me a couple times a week, and I can't help her in the witch shop since I'm a noble now and not a seer."

Juliet pursed her lips. "With my duties as Calatini's royal witch, I can probably only teach you a couple times a week as well. Although once you're better trained, I can have you help with those duties." If she was still royal witch by then. She gave Cassandra a narrow glance. "But I must warn you that I'll be a strict taskmaster, and you shan't always enjoy your tasks, like the one I'm about to give you."

Cassandra hummed, tilting her head like an inquisitive moonowl. "Why? What is it?"

Still stern, Juliet waved toward the many piles. "Clean this mess of a workroom. I expect it to be immaculate before your first lesson on the afternoon of your grandparents' musical evening in a few days." Her mouth twitched at Cassandra's groan. She'd known the teenage girl wouldn't enjoy her first task. "I don't know how you can find anything, let alone practice magic, in here."

Cassandra sighed but nodded, exactly like her little sister had with their grandmother earlier. "Yes, Lady Juliet."

HAVING SETTLED BECOMING Cassandra's second mentor, Juliet returned to the palace to handle her other duties before Giovanni joined her for dinner then escorted her to the Nolans' card party. There, she managed not to speak to Oakmoor by partnering Giovanni and remaining across the drawing room. She'd been around Oakmoor too much lately, and that only inflamed her helpless love and desire for him. She also successfully avoided Oakmoor the following evening at the Blackhams' ball. Unfortunately, she didn't manage that the next night at the Duchess of Childes's fete celebrating the new Lord and Lady Blaine.

Thanks to her mirror call checking how the Magehaven ore was doing five months since being neutralized, she and

Giovanni were some of the last people to arrive at Childes House. After briefly greeting their hosts and the Blaines, Giovanni hurried across the ballroom to Lady Georgiana Laurent, who wasn't with Oakmoor for once. Perhaps he wasn't attending tonight to avoid the probable antagonism between him and the Blaines engendered by him kidnapping the erstwhile Miss Hawke. Juliet almost frowned. But Oakmoor missing an important court event would cause gossip, which might lead to people discovering that kidnapping. He really should be here.

She was about to continue past their hosts and the Blaines to find Siobhan and Lorcan when the new Lady Blaine, who was especially radiant in her resplendent arachne silk ballgown glittering with golden suns, captured her hands. Squeezing them, Lady Blaine flashed a glowing smile and said, "Thank you so, so much for taking my place, Lady Juliet. I've no doubt that I'd still be trapped with no chance to escape if you hadn't." She beamed at Lord Blaine, who lovingly grinned back. "And I'd not be the happily married lady I am today."

A pang pierced Juliet's chest. Oakmoor would never regard her with such love, even if they happened to marry. So she wouldn't ever be a happily married lady like Lady Blaine. She made herself return the younger lady's smile as she extracted her hands. "'Twas nothing."

"I'd not say that," Oakmoor suddenly drawled behind her.

Tingling flooding her like always, she inhaled and turned to face Oakmoor. Then her tingling surged at the warm smolder he gave her. If only 'twas because he loved and wanted her like she did him.

Oakmoor continued, "If not for Lady Juliet's powerful magic, clever skills, and bold determination, I'd still be trapped as well."

Lord Blaine narrowed his eyes at Oakmoor. "I'd started to hope you weren't attending tonight."

Oakmoor arched a brow. "'Twould create gossip if I didn't." He grinned at Lord and Lady Blaine. "Besides, I truly wish you both well. I *never* should have attempted to separate such a devoted couple. My deepest apologies."

Juliet scrutinized Oakmoor. From his expression, he sincerely meant his well-wishes and apology. But not because he desired the young lady he'd once kidnapped. His smooth grin was avuncular without a hint of the hunger he'd just showed herself. Good.

Oakmoor leaned toward the Blaines. "I do hope you shall attend my upcoming soiree. I've hired a renowned troupe of players from my duchy to provide entertainment. You and the Duke of Golddell shall enjoy their performance."

Lady Blaine laughed. "Edouard shall definitely enjoy not being one of the players this time, although Arvan shall only enjoy it if it includes horses. But we'll attend regardless. I want to see that magnificent stained-glass ceiling of yours again."

Juliet stilled. Hopefully, Oakmoor's artisan witches would finish repairing his shattered stained-glass ceiling before his soiree. Perhaps she should offer to help him create an illusion of it if they couldn't.

Oakmoor's grin tightened as he replied to Lady Blaine, "I'll look forward to seeing you all there." He slid his arm through Juliet's, and her body quickened again. "Now please excuse us. Lady Juliet has promised me the first dance, and I must fetch her some refreshments beforehand."

Despite visceral attraction coursing through her, Juliet frowned at Oakmoor as he escorted her through the crowded ballroom. Insufferable rakehell. "I never promised you the first dance."

His mouth wry, Oakmoor inclined a nod. "I know. But for your brother's sake, you should pretend you did. Otherwise, Lady Georgiana shall attempt to dance with me."

Juliet grimaced. How true. And Giovanni hated that. She sighed as Oakmoor handed her some tea and apricot pinwheels. "Very well, I'll dance with you." Even though 'twas dangerous to her heart.

Oakmoor clinked his flute of sparkling wine against her

teacup. "Excellent. Now, finish your refreshments before the music starts. I don't want you almost fainting again during our dance."

She glowered and was about to protest when Giovanni and Lady Georgiana sailed over, him glaring and her beaming. Her turquoise arachne silk ballgown shimmering, Lady Georgiana released Giovanni's arm and took Oakmoor's instead. "Good evening, your grace. I'd begun to fear that I'd missed you. Shall we enjoy the first dance together again?"

When Giovanni's glare darkened, Juliet interjected to prevent him from attacking Oakmoor, "The duke and I have already agreed to dance that together."

With the same smooth grin he'd given the Blaines, Oakmoor removed Lady Georgiana's hand from his arm and stepped closer to Juliet. "So you shall have to find another partner, Lady Georgiana."

His glare fierce as ever, Giovanni snapped, "Must you stand so close to my sister, you beastly rakehell?"

Juliet stiffened. Their plan hadn't soothed Giovanni's anger, merely shifted it. Great.

Oakmoor held Giovanni's gaze with a nonchalant smile. "'Tis too crammed tonight to stand further apart. No one dares miss one of the Duchess of Childes's events."

Fortunately, before Giovanni could reply, the opening strains of the first waltz began. Juliet shoved her and Oakmoor's untasted refreshments at the nearest servant then tugged him onto the floor. She must separate him and Giovanni.

As they started to twirl about the floor, she grimaced at Oakmoor. "*That* was a success."

Oakmoor grunted. "I hope your brother and Lady Georgiana settle matters soon. I don't fancy him challenging me to a duel."

She couldn't help her shudder. Goddess, please let that never happen. Especially if she proved to be pregnant with Oakmoor's child. To distract them both, she eased nearer and murmured, "Shall your stained-glass ceiling be repaired by your soiree?"

Oakmoor drew her nearer still, and her pulse surged. He replied, "It should be. An entire guild of artisan witches is working on it day and night." He grimaced. "The incessant din makes thinking or rest impossible."

She swayed toward Oakmoor as his earthy sandalwood scent surrounded her. If only she could kiss him once more.

Oakmoor frowned down at her. "Juliet, are you lightheaded again? I knew you needed those refreshments."

Her cheeks heating, she jerked upright and glared at Oakmoor. Damn him for being so irresistible. "I'm fine. Did you want my help creating an illusion of your stained-glass ceiling if your artisan witches can't finish it before your soiree?" When he narrowly eyed her, she added, "Remember, I don't want gossip about that shattered ceiling any more than you do."

Continuing to scrutinize her, Oakmoor hummed. "I can create one myself if necessary. You're clearly doing too much already."

Juliet scowled. No, she wasn't. "Why do you say that?"

Oakmoor tsked and shook his head. "Because you still look tired, and you keep getting lightheaded during our dances."

She gulped a calming breath. Except she'd not been light-headed today, although she couldn't admit that without betraying her desire for Oakmoor. She pursed her lips. Plus, she'd only been lightheaded during their previous dance because he'd hurled her in a complicated twirl without warning. Not because she was doing too much. True, she'd been lightheaded a few other times recently, but only when leaping upright after sitting for hours. And perhaps she'd begun sleeping a bit more too, but she'd been busy and performing plenty of magic, so she needed more sleep. Neither meant anything.

She sniffed then disdainfully arched her brows. "You're imagining things, Oakmoor. I told you I'm fine." When Oakmoor snorted, she continued, "And if you keep discussing this, I'll shock you with an energy spell again."

Oakmoor glared. "If you do, I'll yank you against me and kiss you in front of court."

Heat flaring in her veins like earlier, Juliet made herself smirk at Oakmoor. "That shan't do your attempts to find a wife any good. Even Lady Georgiana would balk, and the scandal would force you to propose to me instead. Not that I'd ever accept you."

His gaze intent on her mouth, Oakmoor snapped, "Would you silence that biting tongue of yours?"

She inhaled. She'd rather Oakmoor silence it with kisses like he had previously. To avoid licking her lips and betraying that, she flashed a glittering smile. "Gladly."

Hunger still darkening his eyes, Oakmoor shuddered, but he said nothing further, so they danced the remainder of their waltz in silence. As soon as it finished, she hastened to join Siobhan and Lorcan then avoided Oakmoor the rest of the fete. And she continued to do so over the days preceding her first magic lesson with Cassandra.

That morning dawned sunny, but Juliet scowled because her courses hadn't begun like they should have. Should she attempt a healing-sight spell to check for pregnancy? Perhaps she should wait a few days since she'd shown no other signs of pregnancy. Her courses could be delayed just because she'd been so busy lately and was fretting about being pregnant. And her weak healing spell would work better if she waited anyway. Besides, she must hurry to meet Giovanni then handle her usual duties before heading to Weston House to teach Cassandra prior to joining her family for dinner and their musical evening.

CHAPTER 31

Before leaving for the Westons' musical evening, Oakmoor stopped by his ballroom to check on the repairs of his stained-glass ceiling. As always, noisy industry filled the ballroom as nine artisan witches bustled about, most on floating platforms installing new pieces of stained glass. The rest of the laboring artisans were doubtless in Juliet's former work-room creating more of those pieces in the glass furnace. He squinted at the vibrant and intricate stained glass above him. Only around a third in the middle was still missing, so the artisan witches should complete the ceiling before his soiree in another week. Good. Not bothering to disturb the busy witches, he hurried from his ballroom then leapt into his carriage.

He was one of the first guests to arrive at Weston House. Only Juliet, Lord Beza Hawke, and Lady Beza Hawke were already there, talking with the Westons' granddaughters. Juliet had definitely become close to the Westons to be here so early. Interesting that her brother wasn't with her. No doubt Lord Sabine was attending the Dracwyns' ball instead because Lady Georgiana would be there since she much preferred dancing over listening to music. Her absence was why he himself had chosen to attend the Westons' musical evening. He needed a respite from Lady Georgiana's dogged yet misguided pursuit. Please let her not decide to come to Weston House once she realized he wasn't at the Dracwyns' ball.

He greeted Lord and Lady Weston with a charming smile. Attending their musical evening would also allow him to talk with Juliet without her protective younger brother nearby. An unexpected benefit. They'd rarely been able to talk openly since they'd returned to court, and he should check that she was attending tomorrow's council meeting. Then he could resume avoiding her.

Lord and Lady Weston echoed his smile, although their brows were slightly furrowed. Lady Weston said, "How nice to see you tonight, your grace, although we assumed you'd be attending your fellow councilor's ball like most of court."

Oakmoor shrugged with studied nonchalance. No one must suspect the greatest rakehell in Ormas was evading a lady, particularly one over half his age. "I felt like a quieter evening tonight."

Lord Weston chuckled and shook his head. "You might not get that here. Since we knew we'd have few guests, most of them passionate about music, we chose more esoteric songs, including an anvil piece. And that song is clangorous, especially when not performed in a concert hall or outdoors."

Oakmoor arched his brows. "Intriguing." Fortunately he could cast a hearing-ward spell to muffle the ringing anvils. He nodded at the Westons then strode over to Juliet.

Her face tightening, Juliet raked him with a narrow glance, but she simply murmured a polite greeting like the Hawkes and the Weston girls.

He smoothly grinned at the others while he took Juliet's arm, which immediately stiffened. "Please excuse us. I must discuss a council matter with Lady Juliet." Then he began escorting Juliet to the refreshments table. She looked somewhat tired again and probably could use some tea and sweet biscuits.

Once they were away from the others, Juliet sniffed and

asked, "What are you doing here, Oakmoor? You're no music lover."

He quirked his brows at Juliet. That was like a pixie calling a sprite tiny. "Neither are you, yet you're here."

Juliet shrugged. "I recently agreed to become Cassandra's mentor along with the veiled witch."

Oakmoor glanced back toward Miss Weston. The teenage girl being the veiled witch's apprentice clarified why she'd acted for the veiled witch at court while he and Juliet had been gone. And Miss Weston becoming Juliet's apprentice explained Juliet's sudden closeness with the Westons. But a young witch having two mentors at the same time was unusual. He hummed while he handed Juliet some tea and orenge-blossom macaroons. "You agreed to share an apprentice with the veiled witch?"

Juliet glowered at him over her teacup. "It does happen sometimes. Else you never would have claimed as Mordred to have two mentors. Twins, if I recall correctly."

He almost winced at the edge in Juliet's voice. To distract her from his deceit, which clearly still annoyed her, he said, "I'm just surprised you agreed to share *anything* with the veiled witch."

Juliet sipped her tea. "I was glad to become Cassandra's mentor. Her father was a dear friend."

His stomach hardening, Oakmoor eyed Juliet. She'd been dear friends with another gentleman? He made himself smile. "Ah yes, Anne Weston eloped with a gypsy, didn't she? A Lovari, I assume, since you were friends with him."

Juliet nodded as she nibbled on a macaroon. "Ceija Lovari's grandson, Shandor. He was a powerful Rhiannon-descendant bard witch and helped me as much as Ceija to adjust to their traveling life."

Oakmoor's smile tightened. A true paragon, unlike himself. "I'm surprised you never mentioned Shandor when sharing secrets during our confinement."

Her gaze on her tea, Juliet set down her half-eaten macaroon. "I never thought of him while we were trapped together."

He exhaled. So despite being a "dear" friend, this Shandor mustn't have been that important to Juliet. After all, she'd told him all about her family and her subservient upbringing in Varkhora. And those were the secrets that shaped her.

Juliet flicked another light shrug. "And during our confinement, I was more focused on breaking your curse."

Oakmoor grinned at Juliet. As she should have been. "I'm grateful you were. I might still be a beast otherwise."

Juliet snorted into her tea. "You still are. Just a human one, you insufferable rakehell."

He chuckled, his pulse quickening like always at Juliet's delightfully biting barb. "Plenty of ladies like that. Just ask Lady Georgiana." He grimaced. "She's why I'm here tonight. I knew she'd attend the Dracwyns' ball."

Her brow furrowing, Juliet blinked at him. "Yes, 'tis why Giovanni attended that rather than joining me here."

Oakmoor nodded. Exactly as he'd suspected. Hopefully, an evening without him distracting Lady Georgiana would allow Lord Sabine to get her to admit her true feelings. Then she'd quit pursuing him.

But before he could tell Juliet that, the Westons' younger granddaughter bounced over with her older sister close behind. The little girl flung herself at Juliet and said, "Cassie and Miss Wren said I must go to bed, but I wanted to tell you goodbye first."

A warm smile softening her face, Juliet handed her tea and macaroons to a nearby servant to return the little girl's embrace. "I'll see you in a few days after Cassandra's next magic lesson. I promise I'll have more stories to share about your parents then."

While little Amaranth Weston beamed and squeezed Juliet, he swallowed at the pang hollowing his chest. Juliet would make such a loving mother one day. He inhaled as her embracing a little girl and an even littler boy—both with dark-brown hair, light olive skin, and hazel eyes—flashed before him. So right.

Then the Westons' younger granddaughter released Juliet

and bounced from the room, although her sister remained beside Juliet. Miss Weston asked her, "Mind if I sit with you? Wren and Hawke are flirting like mad, Queen Kiera and King Devon aren't attending tonight, and Grandmother and Grandfather must see to their guests."

Juliet smiled. "I'd love to sit with you." She stilled then glanced at him. "Have you officially met the duke?" When Miss Weston shook her head, Juliet continued, "Cassandra, this is the Duke of Oakmoor. He's a notorious rakehell, so ignore his flirting." She turned to him, her gaze fierce and promising a curse if he dared flirt with her apprentice. "Oakmoor, this is Miss Cassandra Weston, a talented Rhiannon-descendant witch."

Another pang bolted through him. Juliet would make such a fiercely protective mother too. Not that he was remotely interesting in flirting with the teenage Miss Weston. And Juliet's skills as a mother didn't matter to him in the slightest since she'd never be *his* wife. Shoving that aside, he gave Juliet's apprentice a smooth yet avuncular smile. "A pleasure, Miss Weston. And congratulations on convincing Lady Juliet and the veiled witch to cooperate."

As Juliet stiffened, Miss Weston blinked and asked, "What do you mean by that?"

Oakmoor smirked at Juliet to tease her. "Only that Lady Juliet dislikes the veiled witch almost as much as she dislikes me, so for her to agree to be your mentor along with the veiled witch is a testament to her regard for you."

Her cheeks darkening, Juliet glared at him with fierce disdain. "Quit talking nonsense. I don't dislike the veiled witch."

He held Juliet's gaze, his blood surging in his veins. "And what about me?"

Still glaring, Juliet lifted her chin. "*You* are irrelevant."

Oakmoor stepped closer until he brushed Juliet's emerald-green skirt. She'd not say that if he kissed her again with all the primal hunger constantly burning inside him. It had been two weeks since he'd last tasted her—an eternity. And she burned for him too, no matter how much she pretended she didn't. They could disappear into the nearby anteroom, lock it with a ward spell, and let their hunger free. Neither of them cared about listening to tonight's music anyway.

He was about to grasp Juliet's arm when Miss Weston cleared her throat and murmured, "Lady Juliet can't dislike you too much, your grace. After all, she broke your beast curse. Tihdseare said 'twas a nasty one, and that there'd be consequences for breaking it. Lady Juliet wouldn't risk that for someone she truly disliked."

He frowned as his neck prickled. No one besides the veiled witch or Juliet could have told Miss Weston about his curse, so Tihdseare—"teacher" in the witch's tongue—must be Miss Weston's name for the veiled witch. But what exactly had the veiled witch meant? He glanced at Juliet. "Consequences? What consequences?"

Her tight smile not reaching her eyes, Juliet inhaled then shrugged like earlier. "Draining my magic for a few days, shattering your stained-glass ceiling, and so on. They were all necessary and could have been much worse."

Oakmoor suppressed a shudder. Yes, being bloodbound forever to the maddening witch he couldn't help but desire who hated that she felt the same would have been wretched. Especially since their intense intimacy always bewitched him into wanting more despite his ingrained beliefs on love and commitment. "True."

Miss Weston waved toward the now filling chairs. "Lady Juliet, shall we go find seats? We may want to sit in the back because of the anvil piece."

When Juliet nodded and began forward, he grasped her arm. He'd never asked his intended question. She'd distracted him too much. Typical. "Before you go... Shall you attend tomorrow's council meeting? You really should be there."

Juliet freed her arm but smiled. "Yes. Although magic shan't be a topic, those changes you mentioned are too important for me to skip the council meeting."

Oakmoor exhaled. Good, Juliet would be there to support both the royal changes he'd told her about as well as promoting Lady Escana.

While Juliet and Miss Weston found seats in the back, he made himself take a chair on the opposite side and not glance at Juliet throughout the evening. As always, the Westons' musical selections were superb—even the clangorous anvil piece, from what he heard through his hearing-ward spell. But not long after that, he stiffened when Lady Georgiana and Lord Sabine arrived. Damnation, could he never escape that annoying girl's pursuit? He swiftly muttered an ignore spell so she'd not spot him. Once Lady Georgiana sat beside Juliet, he rose and slipped from the room. He'd heard enough music, and with Lady Georgiana here, 'twas no reason to stay.

AT THE COUNCIL meeting the following morning, Oakmoor arrived early to talk with all his fellow councilors beforehand and ensure they were receptive to his proposed changes about Lady Escana. He'd talked with everyone but Juliet, who'd probably be more receptive if he *didn't* talk to her, when King Devon and Queen Kiera swept into the council room and opened the council meeting.

King Devon looked about the table. "Thoughts on changing the royal inheritance laws to allow either sons or daughters to rule?"

Juliet leaned forward. "I believe we should, as well as persuade all inheritances in Calatini to do likewise. It may cause some tension with foreign kingdoms like Varkhora and the Tsarkan Empire, but it shall better relations with Orandia and the elves since they already allow firstborn daughters to inherit."

She paused then added, "And it may help fathers value their daughters more, improving family harmony."

The elderly Duke of Osbourne chuckled, his smile wry. "You've obviously been talking with the Duke of Oakmoor. He mentioned your first points at the previous council meeting."

Juliet blinked then glanced at Oakmoor, and his pulse flared when their gazes meshed. After a moment, Juliet wrenched her gaze free and murmured, "We simply happen to agree in this instance."

Queen Kiera smiled at everyone. "Other thoughts?"

The Duchess of Wildewall mentioned some suggestions about abdication, then everyone discussed the details for changing the royal inheritance laws and encouraging similar across Calatini. Once their discussion quieted, King Devon called for a vote on the changes they'd drafted, and everyone but Lord Osteen and Lord Dabar immediately approved them, passing the inheritance changes.

After Queen Kiera asked if anyone had further matters to discuss, Oakmoor cleared his throat then said, "I'd like to create a deputy-minister position in the Ministry of Foreign Relations for Lady Escana. The countess did an excellent job handling my duties while I was absent, so having her perform as my mere assistant would be a waste of her talents. Besides, handling all the duties of being a minister and royal councilor can sometimes consume your entire life... like when new ambassadors arrive do for me. Creating a second in command would help alleviate that."

The studious Lord Islaye nodded. "I agree. Having a deputy minister would have been very helpful during the Magehaven ore crisis. I swear I didn't sleep much the entire three months."

Lord Farson, who was leaving for Orandia with his wife tomorrow, chuckled. "Neither did I when Lady Moonbud and the other nightmara were here to renew the Nightmara-Calatini Treaty. Elise threatened to dose me with a sleep potion at least once a week."

Leaning forward, Oakmoor flashed a smooth grin at the rest of the table. From everyone's smiles or nods, they were receptive to his proposed change for more than just his ministry. "Perhaps we should create deputy-minister positions for all the ministries in Calatini."

King Devon and Queen Kiera exchanged a glance, then Queen Kiera said, "As a relative newcomer to court, that seems sensible to me. But how shall we elect the deputy ministers?"

Not looking at him this time—prudent given their heated stare before—Juliet hummed and said, "Each councilor should probably select theirs. They must collaborate closely with them and, like Oakmoor, probably already have someone they want as their deputy."

Oakmoor hid his smile. He'd known Juliet would support his change even though she gained nothing from it. He was promoting a fellow independent lady after all.

King Devon nodded. "The councilor's selected deputy should be approved by me and Kiera and the rest of the councilors at the start of each term, like we do the councilor's ministries."

Everyone discussed that and further particulars. Then King Devon called for another vote, and unlike earlier, this one was unanimous. Given that, Oakmoor officially nominated Lady Escana as his deputy, and everyone approved her promotion as well.

Following the council meeting, Oakmoor headed to Escana House and told Lady Escana the good news. Over the next few days, he and Lady Escana split his duties between them and found new assistants. He was busy enough that he didn't think about Juliet except for the odd moment or three throughout the day. And whenever they saw each other at evening court events, of course. Yet he never approached Juliet because he kept needing to leave early to avoid Lady Georgiana. He must do something about that annoying girl.

Then the artisan witches finished repairing his ballroom's ceiling the day before his soiree, so he could finally summon the troupe of players to Oakmoor House to practice. By the time he left for Lady Ducharme's ocean feast that evening, everything was prepared for tomorrow night. Thank the Goddess for that. Him hosting a less than polished event wouldn't help reestablish himself at court.

CHAPTER 32

When Giovanni arrived to escort Juliet to Lady Ducharme's ocean feast, he eyed her with a frown while handing her into the carriage. "You appear tired again."

She muffled a sigh as she settled in the forward seat. She appeared tired because she *was* tired. Although she'd denied her fatigue at first, she'd begun taking naps in the afternoons the past few days to stay awake at evening court events. A definite sign of pregnancy. As were her bouts of lightheadedness, sensitivity to strong scents, and nearly week late courses. Yet she'd still not performed the healing-sight spell to check for pregnancy because doing that would make her suspicions reality. And her entire life would change then.

She managed a bright smile for Giovanni, who was still scrutinizing her from across the carriage. Dear Goddess, if her suspicions proved true, how was she to tell Giovanni that she was pregnant without her protective younger brother erupting and challenging Oakmoor to a duel? Giovanni blatantly disliked Oakmoor, and her carrying Oakmoor's child would only inflame that. She murmured, "I'm fine. To catch up with everything from my absence, I've maybe been working a bit too hard recently."

Giovanni frowned fiercer. "I said as much two weeks ago,

didn't I? And your behavior since then has only made me worry further. You clearly need people to remind you to care for yourself." He rubbed his beard. "People like your loving family. Perhaps you should come home with me when I leave." Giovanni leaned forward. "Father and Mother would love having you nearby again. And I'm certain King Alessandro would be glad to appoint you as Varkhora's royal witch. Lord Marcello should have retired years ago anyway."

Her heart twisting, Juliet swallowed. Except if she was truly pregnant, how could she explain her scandalous pregnancy to their parents? Both Mother and Father would be ashamed and probably wouldn't forgive her for bearing a child while unwed. Yet returning to Varkhora might be her best option. If she remained in Calatini, Oakmoor would insist they marry, and she couldn't bear that when he didn't love her like she loved him and didn't truly want her as his wife. She made herself nod at Giovanni. "I suppose I could consider returning with you."

Continuing to scrutinize her, Giovanni petted Striker's upthrust chest. "Are you concerned about seeing Father and Mother again? Don't think I haven't noticed how you've kept being too busy to join me on my mirror calls with them."

She clenched her hands in her lap. Not surprising Giovanni had realized that. Although she couldn't reveal her likely pregnancy yet, she could at least tell him about her concerns regarding their parents. She inhaled. "I'm a bit nervous. 'Tis been so long, and I'm so different now—an adult with a life of my own that's unlike any lady's in Varkhora. Plus, Father and I constantly battled when I was a girl. What if we still do? Mother always hated that, and I don't want to upset her... or Father."

Giovanni tsked and shook his head. "I think you're fretting over nothing. But the only way to know that for certain is to quit avoiding them and to join me on a mirror call."

Juliet nearly grimaced. Giovanni wasn't incorrect, but such advice from her much younger brother was somewhat irritating. "Soon, perhaps."

Giovanni sighed then smiled at her. "So, tell me, what exactly *is* an ocean feast?"

She exhaled at Giovanni's obvious attempt to distract them both. "A lavish dinner where mostly seafood is served, from fish to krab to prawns to scallops to seaweed. And dessert is seafood-themed even though it often contains no actual seafood. Lady Ducharme hosts an ocean feast once a season to honor how her and her husband's families' influence came from the navy. 'Tis part of why Lady Ducharme is Calatini's Minister of Defense."

Giovanni nodded as the carriage halted. "Sounds deliciously exotic. Seafood is rarely served in Varkhora."

Juliet sighed while Giovanni helped her alight. Because the mountainous kingdom was far from any ocean. Seafood would be one of the things she'd miss if she left Calatini. "I remember."

After saying good evening to Lord and Lady Ducharme, who greeted Giovanni warmly since he frequently attended Lady Ducharme's fencing salons, Juliet and Giovanni joined Siobhan and Lorcan at the far end of the drawing room, on the opposite corner from Oakmoor talking with the Duke and Duchess of Childes.

Giovanni glanced about the drawing room, his gaze lingering on Oakmoor then the Duke of Osbourne. "Is Lady Georgiana not here?"

Juliet muffled her grin. Of course Giovanni immediately asked about Lady Georgiana Laurent. He grew more smitten by the day. Understandable. Lady Georgiana was an interesting girl when she wasn't flirting with Oakmoor. Strong, shrewd, and striking—precisely the type Giovanni adored. Juliet murmured, "I believe Lady Georgiana suffers a violent reaction when she eats seafood. The only dinner featuring seafood she's ever attended was the one the Duchess of Childes hosted to celebrate Queen Kiera's arrival at court, although the duchess provided a special meal for Lady Georgiana."

Giovanni slowly nodded. "Lady Georgiana must find remaining alone at home dull. I'm surprised her father is here tonight rather than keeping her company. Someone should join her. The Ducharmes shan't mind if I leave, I'm sure."

Not looking at Siobhan and Lorcan in case that made her grin, Juliet hummed and echoed her brother's nod. "Especially not if you tell them why." When Giovanni nodded again, she continued, "I'll see you tomorrow morning."

As Giovanni strode back to their hosts, Juliet allowed her grin free at last. Yes, her brother was definitely smitten with Lady Georgiana. Now if only he could get Lady Georgiana to quit pursuing Oakmoor.

Siobhan and Lorcan chuckled, then Siobhan said, "That brother of yours is determined to win Lady Georgiana Laurent's hand, Juliet. Think he'll succeed?"

Juliet shrugged and was about to reply when Oakmoor drawled from behind her, "I pray he does. Otherwise, Lord Sabine is going to challenge me to a duel over her flirting one of these days."

Inevitable tingling flooding Juliet, she turned to face Oakmoor. Lady Georgiana soon wouldn't be the only reason Giovanni would challenge him. She forced a smirk. "Lady Georgiana's incessant flirting is no more than you deserve, you rakehell. You've spent three decades at court seducing every lady you meet. Now you know how it feels."

Oakmoor returned her smirk. "Not really. I've never seriously pursued ladies not interested in me."

Her lips tightened at Oakmoor's pointed smirk. Including her, he was silently saying. He wasn't mistaken about her interest, not that she'd ever admit it aloud, especially to him. She lifted her chin. "Have you ever *seriously* pursued any lady? You've never even been betrothed." She sniffed. "Besides, you're only feigning indifference to Lady Georgiana because you don't want my brother to challenge you. If you truly weren't interested, you could make her quit flirting."

Lorcan chuckled and tugged on his long beige overcoat. "Not politely, I'd wager. Lady Georgiana seems most determined."

Oakmoor inclined his head. "And more public attempts would engender gossip, which would lead many to assume I seduced her and moved on but she refuses to accept it. Not ideal."

Arching her brows, Juliet sniffed again. "I doubt the suave Duke of Oakmoor has been outwitted by a girl young enough to be his daughter." No, he must be allowing Lady Georgiana's flirting because he wanted it. He only shoved Lady Georgiana and Giovanni together to appease Giovanni and prevent a duel.

Oakmoor snorted. "Don't forget Lady Georgiana's father is Calatini's wily Minister of Intelligence. The Duke of Osbourne doubtless taught his daughter intrigue before she could talk." He looked at Juliet. "Just like your father taught you politics and your mother taught you magic. Although fortunately neither could teach you to become a properly subservient Varkhoran lady."

Juliet stiffened as Siobhan and Lorcan blinked at her, obviously surprised that she'd told Oakmoor about the childhood she'd never shared with them. Thankfully, Lady Ducharme announcing that 'twas time to proceed to dinner distracted everyone. She sighed but accepted Oakmoor's extended arm. Being so rude as to refuse him would cause talk about them, and she mustn't risk that starting. Particularly while she was likely pregnant with his child whom he knew nothing about.

Once Juliet sat between Oakmoor and Siobhan, Siobhan leaned over and murmured in her ear, "You've shared childhood secrets with the duke?"

Juliet made herself shrug. "'Twas necessary to handle that private matter we resolved during our absence."

Siobhan's brows rose. "Why was telling the duke about your childhood necessary to resolve a private *royal* matter?"

Juliet jerked another shrug. "It just was. Now please quit asking me. You know I'm not free to explain further." She exhaled when the servants brought the first course of rolls and Lady Ducharme's special whitekrab soup, rich with even more krab, butter, heavy cream, and doublewine than ordinary whitekrab soup. She grinned at Siobhan and Lorcan. "You'll love Lady Ducharme's whitekrab soup. 'Tis delicious and always my favorite dish at her ocean feasts."

Yet when Oakmoor served her a full bowl of the thick and velvety whitekrab soup she usually loved, her stomach heaved at its rich scent and bile rose in her throat. Goddess, was she about to vomit before Oakmoor and the rest of court? She snatched a roll and began devouring it to quell her nausea, but her stomach heaved again. She *had* to escape that scent.

Frowning, Oakmoor leaned toward her. "Juliet, are you all right?"

Her eyes narrow, Siobhan grasped Juliet's arm and hauled her upright. "She just needs some air." When Oakmoor and Lorcan began to rise as well, she waved for them to sit. "Stay and enjoy your soup." Once they were a few steps away, she murmured to Juliet, "Where's the nearest refreshing room?"

Still battling not to vomit, Juliet nodded toward the left, and Siobhan bustled her down the hall then into the refreshing room. Once there, Juliet surrendered and wretched until nothing remained. Tears trickling down her cheeks from her violent heaves, she shuddered and sagged after she finally finished.

Siobhan helped her straighten. "All done?" At Juliet's shaky nod, Siobhan flicked her fingers and chanted a cleansing spell, and the sour taste in Juliet's mouth vanished along with her tears. Then Siobhan cast a listening-ward spell on the refreshing room. Leaning toward her, Siobhan asked, "You're pregnant, aren't you? Lately, you've been constantly tired, suffered spells of lightheadedness, and now this. I was the same with all four of mine."

Juliet sighed. Denying it would be pointless, and Siobhan *was* her friend. "Most likely, although I've not performed a healing-sight spell to confirm it yet."

Siobhan hummed and eyed her. "The Duke of Oakmoor's, I'm assuming."

Sighing once more, Juliet nodded. She couldn't deny that either.

Siobhan tilted her head. "Was making love *also* necessary to resolve that private royal matter?"

Her cheeks heating, Juliet smoothed her diamond-white skirt. "We had to perform sex magic to break the c—spell we were resolving."

An impish grin danced across her friend's freckled face. "I see. A hardship for you given how you *dislike* the duke."

Juliet blushed harder. From Siobhan's drawl, her friend knew she didn't truly dislike Oakmoor despite all her fierce claims that she did.

Chuckling, Siobhan shook her head. Then she sobered. "Have you told the Duke of Oakmoor about your suspicions yet?"

Juliet stiffened, her blush cooling. Couldn't Siobhan leave this well enough alone? "No, and I don't intend to."

Siobhan frowned at her. "You can't bear the duke's child without telling him."

Juliet lifted her chin at her friend's shocked scold. "If I tell Oakmoor, he'll insist we marry, and I can't marry him just because I'm pregnant. Perhaps if he loved and truly wanted me, I might consider it."

Still frowning, Siobhan tsked. "You have to tell him, Juliet. At the very least, he has a right to know that he'll be a father."

Juliet winced. A right she'd been refusing to acknowledge because telling Oakmoor was too dangerous. Yet Siobhan wasn't wrong.

Siobhan pursed her lips. "Besides, since you're both free to do so, marriage between you and the Duke of Oakmoor is probably the best option for your child. And as soon-to-be parents, 'tis your duty to put your child first."

Weight crushing her chest, Juliet twisted her hands together in her lap. If she and Oakmoor *did* marry, their child would be legitimate and have both parents raising them. Yet they'd be caught in between parents who never should have married. And marriage to a rakehell who didn't return her love would destroy her, which would distress their child. She set her jaw. "But having miserable, quarreling parents isn't good for any child."

Siobhan snorted. "I doubt you and the duke would be miserable together. You two share an intense attraction and secretly respect each other despite your quarreling. And love can grow from both of those."

Juliet suppressed another wince and studied her tightly interlaced hands. As love had grown for her. But not for Oakmoor. He'd been too hurt by his parents' and Elvaira's obsessive love to let it. And even if he somehow fell in love with her, she still wasn't the type of lady he wanted as his wife from all those little girls he'd courted for months.

Rising, Siobhan drew Juliet to her feet then said, "We should return. Lorcan and the Duke of Oakmoor shall be wondering about our lengthy absence."

Juliet shuddered as her stomach roiled at encountering fish scents again. "I'm not sure that I can."

Siobhan squeezed her hand. "You'll be fine if you cast a nausea-healing spell, although I'd not attempt to eat much of the strong-smelling dishes."

Juliet sighed. Which was unfortunately most of the ocean feast. Yet she flicked her fingers and muttered a nausea-healing spell. Please let hers be powerful enough to curb her nausea throughout the rest of dinner. Then she and Siobhan returned to the dining room.

When they slipped back into their seats, Oakmoor leaned toward her and murmured, "All right?"

She gritted a bright smile. "Of course."

Oakmoor hummed but served her seared scallops, spicy prawns, and grilled broccoli.

Juliet swallowed but made herself eat the scallops and broccoli, although she couldn't manage the prawns, even with her nausea-healing spell. She spent the rest of the ocean feast nibbling on the various courses, avoiding any dishes that were too rich or spicy while feigning calm cheer before Oakmoor. Mercifully, Siobhan and Lorcan helped distract him by asking about his soiree tomorrow.

The following morning, she suffered another bout of nausea until she had Lara bring her mentha tea and dry toast since she remembered that those helped from Mother's many early pregnancies. Then she asked Lara to start bringing her both every morning, which her discreet maid agreed to without giving her a knowing look or comment.

Juliet had just finished dressing when Lara brought her a note from Giovanni stating that he couldn't meet her like usual because he'd business to attend to this morning. Curious. Although his absence *did* allow her time to cast that healing-sight spell she'd been delaying.

She sighed and headed to her workroom, locking the door behind her. To strengthen her spell, she mixed a potion of unicorn water, borage, and eyebright. She waved her hands over the potion while chanting the healing-sight incantation, and the potion exploded into silver mist. She gestured toward her stomach, and the mist settled there as she finished her incantation. Then the mist sank into her body, and her vision followed.

Juliet inhaled at the tiny life growing inside her womb. Her and Oakmoor's child. Warmth expanding in her chest, she swallowed and laid a trembling hand on her stomach. Oh, Goddess. Although bearing their child would completely change her life, somehow she adored him or her already and would do anything to protect them. Tears pricked her eyes. Even sacrifice her pride and ignore her fear of telling Oakmoor about their child. Perhaps even marry him. She'd talk to him tonight at his soiree.

CHAPTER 33

The morning of his soiree, Oakmoor was reviewing his preparations for the evening ahead when Juliet's brother stormed into the ballroom. He suppressed a grimace as he eyed the scowl darkening Lord Sabine's bearded face, the boy's right hand clenched about his saber, and his stiff draklizard craned forward on his shoulder. The young Varkhoran lord appeared burning to challenge him to a duel, likely over Lady Georgiana. But why? He'd not even seen the annoying girl last night because she didn't attend meals featuring seafood thanks to her violent reaction to it. He sighed. Yet somehow he must prevent Lord Sabine from challenging him. Juliet wouldn't like it, and he was too old for senseless duels.

He forced a smooth grin. "Lord Sabine, what a pleasant surprise. Why have you come to visit me rather than attending Lady Ducharme's fencing salon?" 'Twould be a much better outlet for the young Varkhoran's belligerence.

Lord Sabine halted directly before him and glared. "Why have you asked Georgiana to act as your hostess tonight without announcing your betrothal first? Given your rakehell ways, all of court shall assume she's your latest lover."

Oakmoor blinked. Lord Sabine's jealousy was inspiring ridiculous delusions. He'd never ask an innocent young lady to act as his hostess because Lord Sabine was right about the gossip 'twould cause. He'd only risked it with the former Lady Blaine when they'd been courting since she was a widow known for arranging spectacular court events and he'd intended to ask her to marry him soon. And why did Juliet's brother keep mentioning him being betrothed to Lady Georgiana? 'Twas just as ridiculous as him asking her to be his hostess given his lack of interest in Lady Georgiana and her feelings for Lord Sabine. Thankfully, revealing the truth should calm the younger lord.

Maintaining his smooth grin, he arched his brows. "Lady Georgiana isn't acting as my hostess tonight, and we're not betrothed."

Lord Sabine snorted. "Liar. Georgiana frequently told me about your imminent betrothal while you were away with my sister. Then she hurled acting as your hostess at me last night."

Oakmoor inhaled a sharp breath. "Lady Georgiana what?" He stiffened as fire flared inside his chest. That deceitful child. Didn't she realize what damage such lies could do? Lord Sabine might challenge him, and duels could be fatal. Or he and Lady Georgiana might end up being forced to marry, and neither of them actually wanted that. Once she arrived at his soiree tonight, he must get her to quit her misguided pursuit. *Before* she told anyone else she was acting as his hostess.

He made himself drawl, "I'm not the liar here. Lady Georgiana is. I'll admit I courted her briefly months ago, but I decided she was much too young for me. And her misguided lies just prove me right." He shook his head. "In the weeks since we've met, Lord Sabine, have I acted loverlike toward Lady Georgiana at all?"

Lord Sabine frowned and adjusted his saber. "No, you've appeared much more interested in my sister."

Oakmoor nearly winced. Because he was. But admitting his constant primal hunger for Juliet wouldn't calm her protective younger brother. Especially not if Lord Sabine guessed they'd been lovers. He cleared his throat. "Thanks to our shared duties and handling that private matter together, the royal witch and I often have things to discuss. Besides, she's mature enough to not make that 'interest' into something it's not. Unlike your Lady Georgiana."

Lord Sabine flushed then gritted, "Lady Georgiana isn't mine."

Swallowing a chuckle at the young lord's frustrated retort, Oakmoor cocked a brow. "Isn't she? Lady Georgiana is always more alive with you than anyone else. She's only pursuing me to hide her feelings for you." When Lord Sabine gaped at him, he added, "Probably because they and the idea of leaving Calatini frighten her. Especially for a patriarchal kingdom like Varkhora."

His mouth snapping shut, Lord Sabine slowly nodded.

Oakmoor smiled at Juliet's brother. "Arrive early to my soiree tonight. Lady Georgiana shall doubtless do likewise since she told you she's acting as my hostess. Then the two of you can talk and settle matters between you." That should *finally* end Lady Georgiana's misguided pursuit of him.

Lord Sabine smiled back and released his saber at last, his draklizard relaxing as well. "I'll do that. Thank you, your grace."

Once Juliet's brother left, Oakmoor returned to his soiree preparations, which consumed much of the day. But everything was ready to entertain court by the time he went to change for dinner.

During dinner, he was about to begin his triple gingyr fudge when Lady Georgiana swept into the family dining room. He sighed but abandoned his favorite dessert untasted and rose to greet Lady Georgiana. He'd expected her early, although not this early. Please let Lord Sabine arrive soon. He offered Lady Georgiana a cool smile. "Good evening. Where's your father?"

Her lips coy, Lady Georgiana shrugged. "At home eating dinner."

He stiffened. Lady Georgiana was visiting the greatest rakehell in Ormas *alone*? That stupid girl. If anyone discovered her unchaperoned visit, she'd be ruined. And he certainly wasn't marrying her to repair her reputation. He narrowed his eyes at Lady Georgiana. "And where does the Duke of Osbourne think you are? Not here, obviously."

Lady Georgiana shrugged again. "With Grace."

His jaw clenched. His fellow duke wouldn't think to question his youngest daughter visiting one of her elder sisters. Damn Lady Georgiana. Her wily father had taught her intrigue too well. He forced a smooth drawl, "And where does Lady Aynsley think you are?"

Lady Georgiana shrugged a third time. "With Father, of course." She fluttered her lashes at him. "Normally I'd not be so brazen, but I *had* to speak with you alone before your soiree."

Oakmoor inhaled to dampen his irritation with Lady Georgiana. At least with her here alone, he could bluntly reject her without causing gossip. And perhaps that would end her misguided pursuit of him just as well as her and Lord Sabine settling matters between them. He crossed his arms and glared at Lady Georgiana. "I assume you wish to speak with me about the desperate lie you told Lord Sabine about acting as my hostess tonight. Don't fret; I told him you weren't when he visited me this morning."

Her coy look draining from her face, Lady Georgiana paled. "You did?"

He nodded with a coldly sardonic smile. "I told Lord Sabine that imminent betrothal of ours was nonsense as well."

Lady Georgiana paled further. "'Twasn't nonsense."

Oakmoor arched a hard brow. "No? As I recall, I ended our brief courtship months ago once I realized you were much too young for me. Which you later confirmed by pursuing me despite my many polite rejections and truly desiring another gentleman but being too frightened to admit it."

Lady Georgiana winced then lifted her chin. "I don't desire another gentleman."

He tsked at the girl's unconvincing lie. "Anyone with eyes can see that you're in love with Lord Sabine."

A flush supplanted Lady Georgiana's earlier pallor. "I *don't* love Lord Sabine."

Oakmoor couldn't help his laugh. "Right..."

Lady Georgiana bristled. "I don't!"

Before he could so much as breathe, Lady Georgiana hurled herself across the room and smashed her lips against his.

All his skin tightening, he stiffened then shuddered, but not with pleasure like at Juliet's kisses. He'd just grasped Lady Georgiana's arms to thrust her away when the door crashed open. He and Lady Georgiana whirled around.

In the doorway, a white Juliet and a red Lord Sabine stared at him and Lady Georgiana for a silent, pulsing moment. Then Lord Sabine dropped Juliet's arm and burst inside, gripping his saber and his draklizard crouched to attack. Lord Sabine snarled, "I should have realized something like this was behind your *kind* offer to settle matters with Georgiana early at your soiree, you beastly rakehell."

Wrenching her gaze from Lord Sabine, Lady Georgiana whimpered then bolted through the doorway past Juliet, and Lord Sabine raced after her.

Oakmoor pursed a wry smile after the young couple. No doubt their fierce quarrel would soon end in passionate kisses. Which should finally stop Lady Georgiana's pursuit of him, thank the Goddess. He turned to Juliet. "Well, that was dramatic."

Then he frowned. Juliet was still whiter than a banshee mourning a family death. Most unnatural considering her olive skin. She appeared even worse than she had at yesterday's ocean feast. He swallowed. Why had Juliet been so unwell lately? Had breaking his beast curse ruined her health somehow? Was *that* one of the consequences the veiled witch had meant? His chest constricting, he surged toward his too pale witch. "Juliet, are you all right?"

Color flooding her face, Juliet jerked upright and hurried into the family dining room. She flung her hand at the door, and it slammed shut as a listening-ward spell materialized along the walls. "I'm fine. I'm simply furious that I was *foolish* enough to believe your claims that you weren't interested in Lady Georgiana Laurent."

He exhaled. From her vigorous retort and spells, Juliet wasn't unwell at all. Then he tensed as her words brought back his earlier distaste at Lady Georgiana's unexpected kiss. He grimaced. "They weren't claims. I'm not interested in her."

Juliet snorted. "Then why was Lady Georgiana here alone, and why were you kissing her?"

Oakmoor glowered at Juliet. How could she think he was truly interested in that annoying child? "Lady Georgiana invited herself to further her pretense of indifference to your brother. And I wasn't kissing her. She was kissing *me*."

Juliet sniffed and pursed her lips. "'Tis the same thing."

His gaze fixed on Juliet's tempting lips, he shuddered as his blood quickened. It had been ages since their last kiss. He strode toward Juliet. "Not hardly. Allow me to demonstrate the difference."

He yanked Juliet against him and seized her mouth in a ravenous kiss, his aching body hardening further when she kissed him back. As they kissed, their explosive passion consumed them both like it always did, and he pressed her against the wall while they wrenched at each other's evening clothes to reach bare skin. He needed her *now*. They came together like desperate venuses who'd been celibate for years and soon shattered in release.

Panting, Oakmoor buried his face in Juliet's neck and inhaled her spicy gingyr scent. Delicious. His body stirring again despite their recent passion, he nuzzled her and kissed her luscious skin. Goddess, why was Juliet so damned bewitching? They could make love for days, and 'twouldn't be enough. Still kissing her neck, he rumbled, "I want you again."

Her hands fisted in his hair, Juliet purred and arched into his kiss. "Yes, please."

He smiled against Juliet's skin. Perhaps 'twas her equal hunger for him that made her so bewitching. They should determine how many days of making love would sate their hunger for one another. Although they must move to somewhere more private than his family dining room for that. And moving elsewhere required they separate their entwined bodies. How vexing.

He forced himself to withdraw from Juliet then begin straightening his evening clothes. "Shall we head upstairs to my chambers where we shan't be disturbed?"

Her eyes dark and hazy, Juliet stared up at him and licked her swollen lips. As tingling heat flooded him anew, she blinked then stiffened and pressed against the wall behind her. "Oh, dear Goddess, I let you ravage me against your dining room wall."

Oakmoor grunted. From Juliet's tight face, her hunger to make love again had vanished. Unlike his. Inhaling to settle himself, he retied his cravat, which remained crumpled despite his efforts, and arched his brows. "*Let* me? You were just as hungry to make love as I was."

Juliet glared at him while she jerked her deep-amethyst ballgown back into place. "I know—to my deep shame. Moments ago, I caught you kissing another lady."

He set his jaw at Juliet's stubborn misinterpretation. "I told you before, Lady Georgiana was kissing me."

Juliet snorted then muttered a grooming spell and smoothed her rumpled skirt. "You're too experienced to let a young lady kiss you without your consent." Her glare deepened. "No, you're the same disgusting rakehell you always were, eager to seduce anyone in a skirt."

He swallowed a wild laugh while his gaze fell to Juliet's hands on her skirt and lingered. Only if anyone in a skirt meant Juliet. He'd not desired another for months, damn her. Not that he'd ever admit such a helpless obsession aloud. His constant primal hunger for her was more dangerous than his beast curse had been. But surely 'twould fade soon.

Juliet's hands stilled over her stomach. "And to think I was about to—" Her mouth compressing, she inhaled and lifted her chin. "But no matter." She glared at him fiercer than ever. "Don't you have a soiree to host?"

Oakmoor winced then swore beneath his breath. He'd completely forgotten about his soiree as soon as Juliet had arrived. And acting the gracious host would be tortuous while he burned to be upstairs in his chambers making love with Juliet until they finally sated their voracious desire.

Juliet tossed her head then added, "And don't you have a foolish young lady to cozen into marrying you?"

He nearly growled at Juliet referring to him marrying Lady Georgiana yet again. Since clearly nothing would convince her that he'd never marry the annoying girl, he smirked and drawled, "Sadly, our earlier passion foiled that tonight. I couldn't *possibly* approach an innocent like Lady Georgiana while another lady's scent clings to my skin."

Juliet paled then flushed and stalked toward him. "'Tis easy enough to fix with a cleansing spell." She snapped her fingers before his face, and her magic scoured his skin. "Now you no longer smell like me."

Oakmoor captured Juliet's wrist. Maddening witch. How dare she attempt to banish their mutual passion with her magic? He hauled her against him and fiercely kissed her again. Explosive heat flared in his veins when Juliet immediately moaned and returned his kiss. She was his. He began lifting her skirt to bury himself inside her once more.

Juliet gasped and wrenched her mouth free. "No!" She shoved his chest. "I don't want you, Oakmoor."

Fervid desire continuing to course through him, he smiled at Juliet's ridiculous lie. Despite hating that she wanted him, she could never hide that she did. But he couldn't hide that he wanted her either. Not releasing Juliet, he nipped her ear and slid his hand up her leg. "Then why do you keep returning my kisses? And making love with me?"

Shivering, Juliet slapped away his hand. "I only made love with you to break your beast curse."

He chuckled and trailed kisses along Juliet's jaw toward her mouth. His lying wanton. "But I'm not cursed now, and you just made love with me."

Juliet writhed in his embrace. "A mere aftereffect of using sex magic to break your beast curse." She shuddered when he pulled down her bodice and caressed her chest. "And... and... I've been treating you like the gentleman I love every time we've come together."

Oakmoor froze as a hollow ache pierced his chest. "You're in love with someone?"

Juliet swallowed. "Yes, but he doesn't love me and never shall. Now release me." Her voice broke, "Please."

He lurched backward even though his entire body still throbbed for Juliet. He didn't trifle with committed ladies. "Why didn't you mention this gentleman before? I'd never have touched you if I'd known." Hopefully.

Juliet shrugged and smoothed her ballgown with a second grooming spell. "My heart is none of your concern. Now excuse me, I must go find Giovanni."

Oakmoor stared after Juliet while she swept from his family dining room. How could she have concealed such an essential secret from him? Their apparent intimacy during their confinement together *definitely* hadn't been genuine. Nothing more than a mirage that faded when its power broke. His jaw clenched. Not that he cared that Juliet loved another. 'Twasn't as if he loved her. He inhaled to calm his hard and throbbing body. After all, only mad fools fell in love. And he'd never risk being that foolish, not even for the bewitching witch he couldn't help desiring. One who wanted an adoring husband, which he'd never be. He growled. Although the idiot Juliet loved didn't adore her either from what she'd said, so she'd never enjoy the adoring husband she'd always wanted. Yanking his evening clothes straight, he inhaled again then strode to his ballroom to greet the many guests arriving for his soiree.

CHAPTER 34

$\mathcal{C}$linging to a faint smile, Juliet hurried down the hall leading from Oakmoor's family dining room, although she didn't allow herself to run like she ached to do. No one must guess her shattered devastation. Not only did she have her reputation as Calatini's royal witch to maintain, but she also couldn't have gossip about her and Oakmoor starting. Halfway to the ballroom, she slipped into a small drawing room and locked the door behind her while casting a listening-ward spell. Then she covered her face with her hands, sank onto the nearest sofa, and let her trembling and sobs free at last.

Goddess, she was such a weak fool where Oakmoor was concerned. Every time he kissed her, she forgot everything except her helpless love and intense need for him. She forgot her pride and hard-won position, his rakehell ways and inability to return her love or truly want her as his wife, as well as where they were and all her principles. Which was why she'd let him ravage her against his dining room wall, even *after* witnessing him kissing Lady Georgiana Laurent, the innocent young lady he'd clearly chosen as his future bride and mother of his children.

Fresh tears scalding her cheeks, Juliet pressed a hand against her stomach where her and Oakmoor's child grew. A child he'd not want given he'd already chosen another to bear his children. If she told Oakmoor about their child now, he'd be furious that he must marry her instead, although he'd still do so. But he'd likely resent her, and possibly her child as well, for forcing him into a match he'd not chosen. And she had to protect her child and herself from such suffering. Which was why she'd remained silent about their child even though she'd been planning to tell Oakmoor.

She swallowed and caressed her stomach then whispered, "I'm so sorry, little one. I swear I'll tell your father about you once he can no longer hurt us." She'd write Oakmoor soon after she gave birth. Goddess knew where she'd be then, but 'twouldn't be here. She must leave Calatini and surrender her position as royal witch before her pregnancy began to show in a couple months. If she didn't, scandal would shadow her child's birth, destroy her influence at court, and trap Oakmoor if he'd not married Lady Georgiana yet.

Juliet sighed and wiped her damp face. Not that she regretted using sex magic to save Oakmoor and thereby conceive their child, despite all 'twould cost her. No, what she truly regretted was letting him seduce her tonight when she *knew* he'd chosen another. She'd doubtless still succumb to him even after he married, and she despised adultery. Her nausea surging, she shuddered. She mustn't ever allow herself to be alone with Oakmoor again.

She leapt upright and paced about the room. Because Oakmoor was the same rakehell he'd always been and would readily seduce her again given the chance. Although he'd chosen a young lady to be his wife at last, he obviously didn't intend to remain faithful to her, so he mustn't love Lady Georgiana at all. And without love, a rakehell like Oakmoor would never settle on just one lady. Poor Lady Georgiana.

Juliet shivered and fisted her hands at her sides. *How* could she love such an unrepentant rakehell? Yet she did. Because he was strong and bold with an unwavering dedication to his duties along with a caring heart that he revealed to so few. And because he adored strong and biting ladies, he'd never make his wife surrender her identity or ambitions. And because he was astute and could connect with anyone. Not to mention his irresistible masculine allure.

She grimaced. Perhaps she should be grateful to Lady Georgiana for saving her from her helpless love for Oakmoor. Loving him as she did, the fashionable, faithless marriage he intended would *definitely* destroy her. Which was why, along with him having already chosen Lady Georgiana, she'd lied and claimed her desire for him was a mere aftereffect of using sex magic. And why she'd implied that she loved another. But she still could never risk being alone with Oakmoor. Her facade of indifferent dislike would shatter at the slightest word or touch.

Juliet blew a weary exhale as she glanced at the clock on the mantel. Was that really the time? Oakmoor's soiree must be well underway now. She'd better emerge and make an appearance. Although she must repair her face first since 'twas surely red and puffy from her tears. Being pregnant had undeniably made her more emotional. She'd never sobbed like that before, not even as a little girl or when fleeing Varkhora or when first realizing she loved Oakmoor.

She swirled her hand before her face and chanted a brief healing spell. Then she gathered her will and created a mirror of light to check her appearance. No signs of her tears remained, although melancholy made her eyes appear somewhat darker than usual. She gritted a glittering smile. Not entirely convincing, but 'twould do. She sighed and dismissed her mirror of light before removing her listening-ward spell and unlocking the door. Then she inhaled and glided to Oakmoor's main drawing room to join everyone.

Thankfully, when she arrived, Oakmoor was no longer greeting his guests but was along the wall by the garden, talking with the Duke of Osbourne. Probably about his betrothal to the duke's daughter. Her heart twisting, she headed toward the refreshments table across the room. Surprising that Lady Georgiana wasn't with her father and her betrothed. Yet the younger lady was nowhere to be seen—and neither was Giovanni. Their quarrel after Lady Georgiana had fled Oakmoor's family dining room must have been explosive for them both to be missing. Poor Giovanni.

Juliet had just taken a flute of sparkling wine that she didn't truly want when Siobhan and Lorcan swept over to her.

No grin brightening her freckled face for once, Siobhan murmured once they left the bustling refreshments table, "I suppose you've already heard the gossip about the Duke of Oakmoor and Lady Georgiana Laurent."

Juliet managed another glittering smile. Please let it be more convincing than her one earlier. "Heard it? Giovanni and I witnessed it."

Siobhan fingered the edge of her navy overcoat atop her teal tunic, both lustrous arachne silk tonight, likely because 'twas a soiree hosted by Calatini's Minister of Foreign Relations. Siobhan soberly said, "I know. Lady Staghorn and Lady Gilbert overheard Lady Georgiana and Giovanni quarreling over that when they arrived."

Juliet couldn't help her wince. Lady Staghorn and Lady Gilbert were the greatest gossips at court, so no doubt everyone here already knew everything Giovanni and Lady Georgiana had said.

Lorcan shook his head. "Although court can't decide whether the Duke of Oakmoor and Lady Georgiana are simply lovers or actually betrothed."

Twirling her untasted flute before her lips, Juliet managed to shrug. "Betrothed, of course. Despite his rakehell ways, Oakmoor doesn't trifle with innocents." When he knew they were innocents, unlike he had with her all those years ago.

Siobhan frowned. "But what about..." She nodded at Juliet's stomach.

Her chest constricting at Siobhan indicating her pregnancy, Juliet shrugged again and replied, "I didn't tell Oakmoor about that." When her friend's frown deepened, she added, "How could I when he'd already chosen another?"

Lorcan sighing beside her, Siobhan squeezed Juliet's free hand then said, "Oh, Juliet, I'm so sorry."

Fresh tears pricking her eyes, Juliet swallowed and forced herself to smile. She wouldn't cry. She wouldn't. "It doesn't matter." The pricking in her eyes swelled. She must escape before her tears burst free. Considering all the gossip about Oakmoor and Lady Georgiana, no one would notice that she'd left early anyway. She nodded at her friends and handed Lorcan her full flute of sparkling wine. "I must go. I'll see you both later."

She turned and glided from Oakmoor's drawing room, somehow containing her tears until she climbed into the carriage Giovanni had left behind and drew the curtains. Then she let her scalding tears silently pour down her cheeks. Goddess, why must she love Oakmoor so much? And how was she to bear life without him?

THE FOLLOWING morning after a restless night, Juliet awoke late with a roiling stomach. Fortunately, the mentha tea and dry toast Lara brought eased her nausea enough that she didn't vomit, although 'twas a near thing. After settling the worst of her nausea, she whispered the incantation to refresh the nausea-healing charm about her ankle where she'd once worn her contraceptive charm. She'd created it after confirming her pregnancy yesterday, although since she was no healer, she needed to refresh her nausea-healing charm daily, and 'twasn't entirely effective. But she couldn't risk consulting a healer and starting gossip about her pregnancy.

Finally feeling somewhat better, she dragged herself from bed then donned her favorite morning dress of light-amethyst satin with swirling embroidery the rich color of purple gentians.

She must arrange a meeting with King Devon and Queen Kiera before the next council meeting to inform them that she must leave Calatini.

She'd just finished her letter to them and given it to Lara to deliver when Giovanni trudged into her study. His bearded face tight and Striker drooping, Giovanni appeared as upset as she was about the events of last night. Surely because he loved Lady Georgiana Laurent as much as she loved Oakmoor, and like her, knowing his love had chosen another had shattered his heart. But at least *he* wasn't secretly pregnant with his love's child.

Making herself smile, Juliet rose and waved for Lara to head to the royal wing then asked Giovanni, "Have you broken your fast yet?"

His jaw clenching, Giovanni grunted. "No."

She slid her arm through her younger brother's and squeezed it to cheer him. "Neither have I." The tea and toast to control her nausea hardly counted. "Come along."

In her private dining room, she waved her hand at the table to conjure breakfast rather than ringing for servants to fetch some. Lara was busy, and she didn't want the curious eyes and ears of other servants around right now. To comfort herself and Giovanni, she conjured the lighter fare of pastries and Varkhoran kahve typical in Varkhora rather than a full Calatinian breakfast. Although when her stomach quivered at the kahve's strong scent, she swiftly transformed hers into mentha tea. Even with her nausea-healing charm, apparently she'd not be drinking kahve while pregnant. Lovely.

Halfway through their pastries, she said, "I've decided that 'tis time I left Calatini."

Giovanni's mouth twisted. "So have I." He inhaled then smiled at her. "Father, Mother, and I shall be thrilled to have you home again."

A pang darted through Juliet. Not necessarily. They knew nothing of her scandalous pregnancy. "I'm not certain that's a good idea."

Giovanni devoured the last of his breakfast then drew her upright. "Still fretting about our parents? You shouldn't be. You'll see when we call and tell them our news." He swept her back to her study then chanted the brief spell and waved to activate her communication mirror.

While her communication mirror glowed white as it connected with their parents' mirror, she stepped to the side out of its view. Giovanni should prepare their parents before they were faced with their runaway daughter. As Giovanni frowned at her, her communication mirror cleared to reveal Mother and Father, each with their magical pet perched on their right shoulder. Her heart squeezed. Mother and Father appeared so much older than when she'd fled Varkhora twenty-one years ago. Silver gleamed in Mother's dark-brown hair now, and Father's was completely white. Plus, lines fanned from their eyes and around their mouths, particularly for Father, although Mother's were still faint. But Father *was* fifteen years Mother's senior.

Father frowning beside her, Mother leaned forward and asked, "Giovanni? We weren't expecting your call. Is something wrong?"

Giovanni smiled. "No, someone *finally* had a break in her duties." He tugged Juliet into the chair beside him.

Her pulse surging, she offered their frozen parents a weak smile. "Hello, Mother, Father."

Tears shimmering in her dark eyes and her ruby faebird trilling, Mother gripped Father's hands. "Giuliettanna! 'Tis wonderful to see you at long last."

Blinking rapidly with his mottled-green draklizard eyeing the mirror like a plump pigeon, Father gruffly rasped, "Giovanni said you're doing well in Calatini."

Juliet swallowed. Until she'd fallen in love with the greatest rakehell in Ormas. She lifted her chin. "I don't have to be demure or subservient here."

As Mother smiled and wiped away her tears, Father chuckled then replied, "You never were good at either. Much too driven and stubborn. And I suppose your years as Calatini's royal witch have honed that insolent tongue of yours."

Juliet stiffened and fisted her hands in her light-amethyst skirt. So much for Giovanni's claims that Father was proud of everything she'd achieved. He was as censorious as ever. She bared her teeth. "Yes, my insolent tongue is sharper than ever."

Father smiled. "Good. I missed it when you ran away."

As Juliet gaped at Father, Giovanni drawled, "I apologize for not being insolent enough for you, Father."

Father slanted Giovanni a stern glance. "You're insolent enough, just in a different way than Giuliettanna."

Mother caressed her faebird's ruby chest, her eyes crinkling. "Yes, you rarely indulge your father in the explosive battles he so loved with her."

While Mother spoke, Juliet slowly closed her mouth as warmth eased her tight chest. Perhaps Father *hadn't* been being censorious before but expressing his pride and love for her. His demeanor certainly hadn't been harsh. She'd been too quick to react like the powerless, rebellious girl she'd been.

His mouth hardening, Giovanni replied to Mother, "I've become accustomed to explosive battles since visiting Calatini, so maybe I'll indulge Father more often once I return home."

Although their parents traded frowns, Juliet swallowed at Giovanni's bitter reference to Lady Georgiana Laurent. To prevent Mother and Father from asking him to explain, she said, "Giovanni told me you're doing well, although he couldn't tell me much from when he was little. I hope my running away didn't cause you too much trouble at court."

Father grimaced. "No more than I deserved for attempting to betroth you to King Cesare."

As Giovanni nodded beside her, Juliet stared at Father. He was admitting he'd been wrong about that ghastly betrothal?

Sighing, Father shook his head. "But King Cesare was so desperate to marry you that I believed he'd fallen in love with you, and love has redeemed many a gentleman. Plus, being queen would have suited you—you've the strength, intelligence, and drive to excel at it, and as queen, you'd enjoy more power and freedom than any other lady in Varkhora."

Her delicate stomach quivering, Juliet clenched her hands in her lap. Yes, if King Cesare hadn't been such a cruel bully and he'd truly loved her, being queen *would* have suited her. So Father had been considering her when he'd arranged that betrothal, not just his own ambitions. Although he'd still been wrong because he'd misjudged King Cesare.

Father shuddered, his mottled-green draklizard stirring. "Yet King Cesare's violent fury and burning hunger for revenge at your running away proved he didn't love you at all. I was glad you'd fled and that we couldn't find you then, despite our constant worry that you'd come to harm."

Biting her lip, Mother squeezed Father's hand. "Your father wasn't entirely to blame for that mess. I blame myself as well."

Giovanni's frown mirroring her own, Juliet leaned forward and asked, "Why? You were ill that summer." And even if Mother hadn't been, Varkhoran wives couldn't oppose their husbands, so she couldn't have stopped Father from arranging their daughter's betrothal.

Mother sighed. "Yes, but I was ill because I'd ensured that I was with child even though Healer Valerio warned us after Giovanni was born that I mustn't ever fall pregnant again. Always troubled by my miscarriages, your father refused to listen to my pleas that you both needed more siblings. So I sabotaged our contraceptive charms."

Juliet and Giovanni gaped at Mother. She'd done *what*? Given the healer's warning, surely she'd known she was courting death if she risked another pregnancy.

Mother blew another sigh. "'Twas a stupidly mad thing to do, but I'd always desperately wanted at least half a dozen children, and I thought I'd be fine if I used healing magic to maintain my strength. Your father was furious when he discovered what I'd done, then frantic with worry as I became more and more ill during my pregnancy despite using healing magic. He wasn't thinking too clearly that summer, and he kept the betrothal plans from me because I was ill, so I couldn't tell him that no daughter of mine would *ever* marry King Cesare."

Juliet blinked then eyed Mother and Father. Mother's words implied that her opposition would have stopped Father. And although Varkhoran wives didn't usually possess such power, Father adored Mother, so perhaps it might have. Except Mother had been so ill that summer that approaching her for help had been impossible.

Mother suddenly paled, and Father wrapped an arm about her. Leaning against him, Mother continued, "And then the night you fled Varkhora, I suffered a miscarriage and nearly died. It took all of Healer Valerio's healing magic to save me, and your father refused to leave my side. By the time we realized you'd run away, you were impossible to trace. Although your father did try until we realized 'twas better if you remained lost because of King Cesare's hunger for revenge."

Her heart aching, Juliet smiled at Mother and Father. All three of them had made mistakes that summer. "And I was a reckless, desperate child to flee like I did. Although I can't truly regret leaving Varkhora because of everything I achieved here in Calatini." And she'd met Oakmoor and conceived their child. Resisting the betraying urge to touch her stomach, she brightened her smile. "Yet I missed you both and Giovanni terribly the past twenty-one years. I should have contacted you as soon as King Cesare died."

Mother and Father returning her smile, Father replied, "We can understand why you didn't. Besides, you must have been busy with your many duties as Calatini's royal witch."

Juliet inclined her head then grinned at Giovanni, who grinned back. "But thank the Goddess I had a little brother determined to find me and make us a family again. All this," and carrying Oakmoor's child, "has made me reevaluate my life, and I've decided that 'tis time I left Calatini."

Mother and Father both beamed, then Mother exclaimed, "You're returning home? How wonderful!"

While Giovanni smirked at her, Juliet's chest warmed. He'd been right about their parents being thrilled for her to return to Varkhora. Then she almost sighed. Except none of them knew about her scandalous pregnancy yet. And she couldn't shatter their new rapport by telling them now. She made herself smile. "I'm considering it."

Giovanni arched his brows at their parents. "Especially if King Alessandro appoints Juliet as Varkhora's royal witch."

Although Mother's eyes widened, Father straightened and beamed brighter then said, "An ideal solution. I'll arrange a mirror call for Giuliettanna with King Alessandro straightaway."

Juliet leaned forward. "I love you all for your support, but I must speak alone with Sandro." She needed to tell him about her pregnancy before he offered to appoint her.

Father nodded. "Yes, of course. Matters between royal witches and the monarchs they serve should remain private. What's your communication mirror's call signature?" Once she told him, he replied, "I'll contact you once King Alessandro says when he can meet."

Mother smiled at her. "After so many years apart, I can hardly believe that we'll see you in person in just a few months. I can't wait to embrace you again at long last. I'll probably have trouble releasing you."

Juliet swallowed as bittersweet tears pricked her eyes. "Me too."

Father cleared his throat. "We should go and contact King Alessandro, but we'll talk soon."

They all said farewell, then Giovanni waved to deactivate her communication mirror before turning and smiling at her. "I told you that you were fretting over nothing."

Juliet managed a bright smile as they both rose. But she'd yet to share her most scandalous secret. Please let that go as well as today had.

When she and Giovanni left her study, Lara handed her the royal reply to her letter requesting a meeting. She told Giovanni she'd see him later then returned to her study to read it. King Devon and Queen Kiera wrote that they could meet her for luncheon. Juliet pursed her lips. She'd Cassandra's third magic lesson this afternoon, but telling the king and queen that she must leave Calatini was more important. So she swiftly wrote to Cassandra canceling their lesson and arranging to meet in a few days instead. When they did, she'd have to tell the young witch of her decision to leave as well. She sighed then began handling her other duties for the day so that she'd finish them before she met with King Devon and Queen Kiera.

CHAPTER 35

The morning after his soiree, Oakmoor strode into his study then glowered at the pile of letters already awaiting him. No doubt letters inviting him and Lady Georgiana to private events to determine if they were lovers or betrothed when they were neither. He dropped into the chair behind his desk, still glowering at the letters. Last night had been a disaster. Instead of reestablishing him at court, his soiree had made him the cynosure of more gossip than ever. All thanks to Lady Georgiana, although Lord Sabine and Juliet had played their parts as well.

He drummed his fingers on the desk. First, he'd had to endure Lady Georgiana's unexpected and unwanted kiss, which had sparked his explosive quarrel with Juliet. And although their passionate lovemaking had been as wonderful as ever, discovering Juliet loved another hadn't been. Then Lady Georgiana and Lord Sabine had let their fierce quarrel over her kissing him be overheard by the greatest gossips at court just before they'd both stormed home. His jaw clenched. Damn those indiscreet children. Why hadn't they kept their quarrel private like he and Juliet had? Lord Sabine was a witch like his sister, so he could have easily cast the same listening-ward spell she had. Yet Lord Sabine hadn't, so his quarrel with Lady Georgiana might as well have taken place before all of court.

Oakmoor scowled. By the time he'd emerged from his family dining room, every one of his guests had already been gossiping about him and Lady Georgiana. Half believed they were simply lovers while the other half believed them betrothed. And his slightly rumpled attire after making love with Juliet hadn't helped. People could tell he'd been making love with *someone,* so they'd all assumed 'twas Lady Georgiana. Like Juliet, he should have used a grooming spell to repair his attire before joining his soiree, but after she'd swept out, he'd failed to remember to cast one. Although his slightly rumpled attire wouldn't have caused much comment if not for Lady Georgiana. Yet he preferred keeping his private matters discreet, so he really should have cast a grooming spell.

He drummed his fingers faster. Because of Lady Georgiana, Lord Sabine, and Juliet, he'd spent the entire evening deflecting prying about Lady Georgiana while simultaneously scrutinizing all the gentlemen to determine which was the idiot Juliet loved. Yet he'd enjoyed little success with either undertaking. His guests had been so curious about Lady Georgiana that they'd ignored his attempts to divert them, especially once the Duke of Osbourne had approached him to arrange a meeting about Lady Georgiana. After their hushed discussion, even the renowned troupe of players from Oakmoor he'd hired had failed to divert his gossiping guests. A shame because the players' performance had been stellar.

His jaw further tightened. *And* he still had no inkling whom Juliet loved. Although whomever he was, the idiot didn't deserve her since he didn't return her love and would never be the adoring husband she wanted. He narrowed his eyes. As he'd talked with everyone at his soiree, he'd reflected on Juliet's past interactions with each gentlemen guest, but none had seemed suspicious or intimate. And last night, she'd not joined his other guests until he'd been talking with the Duke of Osbourne then left soon after, so the only gentlemen she'd been near yesterday evening had been Lord Sabine, Sir Lorcan, and himself. Yet she wasn't in love with any of them. Lord Sabine was her brother, Sir Lorcan was her friend's husband, and despite making love with him, she'd told him she loved another besides himself.

Oakmoor grunted and forced his fingers still. Not that their passionate lovemaking had been truly making *love*. He certainly wasn't in love with Juliet, and she'd been pretending he was the gentleman she loved. His teeth ground together. No, their love-making had been a mere physical coupling inspired by an uncontrollable hunger neither of them wanted. One that using sex magic to break his beast curse had strengthened according to Juliet. 'Twas good they'd not gone up to his chambers to continue making love—'twould probably have fed their obsessive hunger rather than sated it.

He grimaced. So he'd best avoid being alone with Juliet until that damned hunger finally faded. Unless they'd a private or council matter they must discuss. Which given everything lately was all too likely. Hopefully he could manage to control himself around the bewitching witch, although he'd failed at doing that so far. He sighed and began handling the pile of letters on his desk, mostly by discarding them unanswered. Silence was his best response since nothing he could say would convince court that his relationship with Lady Georgiana didn't exist.

He'd just finished handling the letters when the Duke of Osbourne arrived for their meeting about Lady Georgiana. His gaze narrow, the other duke sat before the desk and said, "Quite a mess we're in. One we could have avoided if you'd not invited Georgiana to visit you alone."

Oakmoor stiffened and glared at his fellow councilor. No, this mess never would have happened if the wily Minister of Intelligence hadn't taught his willful daughter intrigue too well. Oakmoor gritted a tight smile. "I didn't invite Lady Georgiana here. She invited herself." As the older duke's eyes widened, he continued, "Then hurled herself at me after I made my disinterest clear. But her tricks would have come to nothing if Lord Sabine and Lady Juliet hadn't happened to arrive just then."

The Duke of Osbourne winced. "But they did, and now my daughter's name is linked with yours. She'll be ruined if she doesn't marry you, and you'll find it harder to persuade another young lady to marry you with gossip about her hanging over you." He leaned forward. "Georgiana shall make a good wife to you. She's strong and shrewd and understands the duties of dukes and councilors. Plus, she's young enough to provide you plenty of heirs and shall accept your lovers if you decide to take them after your marriage."

A chill skittering across his skin, Oakmoor suppressed a shudder. Yes, Lady Georgiana would doubtless make the perfect fashionable wife he'd first sought when deciding he must marry last season. Yet somehow such a marriage now seemed empty and distasteful. And not just because he wasn't interested in marrying the shrewdly coy Lady Georgiana. His mouth firmed. No matter the scandal, he couldn't ever settle for a mere fashionable alliance. He wanted more. Although he still wasn't risking sincere love and commitment. He held the Duke of Osbourne's gaze. "Thank you for the kind offer, but I can't marry Lady Georgiana."

The elderly duke sagged. "I suppose I can understand your reluctance considering Georgiana's tricks, yet if you don't marry her, she'll be shunned and snickered about at court, and no other gentleman shall ever marry her. I don't want such a life for my daughter."

Oakmoor nearly grimaced. Because thanks to his rakehell reputation, everyone was convinced he'd seduced Lady Georgiana, when the most he'd ever done was endure her unexpected kiss. Although no one would believe that. Even Juliet hadn't, damn her. But he wasn't sacrificing himself to save Lady Georgiana from her folly. He sighed. Yet he couldn't let the foolish girl be ruined because she'd kissed him. Somehow he must resolve this mess.

He drummed his fingers on his desk like earlier. Finding another gentleman to marry Lady Georgiana should work. But not just any gentleman. The one who loved her whom she loved back and who'd witnessed the extent of their involvement. And since the two of them had started the gossip at court in the first place, their marriage would transform it into nothing more than a lover's jealous suspicions. His fingers stilled. Hopefully, Lord Sabine would be easier to convince of the truth than his sister.

Oakmoor smiled and leaned toward the Duke of Osbourne. "There's another gentleman who'd be a better match for Lady Georgiana than I—Lord Sabine. He's the one she truly wants, and he wants her just as much. And their marriage would silence the gossip about her and me that they started."

His brow furrowing, the Duke of Osbourne rubbed his chin. "True, yet how shall you convince Lord Sabine that Georgiana's visit and kiss meant nothing?"

Oakmoor frowned but shrugged. "I'm not certain, although I shall somehow." Perhaps Juliet could help him figure that out. He arched his brows at the Duke of Osbourne. "I'll handle arranging the match between Lady Georgiana and Lord Sabine. You arrange their betrothal ball." He paused as he considered the upcoming court events. "A week after the royal summer masquerade since no events are scheduled that evening. But remain silent about the identity of her future groom." He chuckled. "That worked for the Greysnowes when they announced Lord and Lady Ravenstone's marriage. It encouraged everyone to attend, and the romantic drama was the talk of court for weeks. Just what we need to convince everyone."

The Duke of Osbourne nodded and began to smile. "In the meantime, all of us should say nothing about the gossip linking you and Georgiana. And we'll avoid you as well. Then we shan't have confirmed the rumors, so all of court shall be desperate to learn the truth at Georgiana's betrothal ball in two weeks. I'll speak with Georgiana as soon as I return home." He flashed a wry grin. "Ensuring none of my servants or spies overhear us of course."

Oakmoor returned his fellow duke's grin. An intrigue planned with the Minister of Intelligence was sure to succeed. Thank the Goddess. "Sounds good."

As soon as the Duke of Osbourne said his farewells and left, Oakmoor headed to the palace to visit Juliet. Although she hadn't believed him about Lady Georgiana, she still knew her brother best and would know how to convince Lord Sabine to listen. He swallowed a sigh as he climbed into his carriage. Despite just deciding to avoid being alone with Juliet, resolving this mess with Lady Georgiana was too important not to approach her. Besides, once he'd explained his intentions, Juliet would want to secure her brother's future happiness, so she'd agree to help him regardless of their own issues.

He frowned. And surely if they didn't touch and kept their meeting brief, they'd not succumb to their voracious desire. Shoving that aside, he stared out the carriage window as it rumbled toward the palace. *Why* had a fashionable alliance struck him as wrong when the Duke of Osbourne had proposed it today? He'd been planning one before. He frowned harder. But with his beast curse broken, he no longer needed to marry immediately. Perhaps that was part of it. He snorted. Although even with that pressure, he'd been unable to settle on a young lady, so he'd never truly wanted a fashionable alliance to begin with. He'd simply been desperate. Yet now he wasn't and could afford to wait until he found the right lady for his wife.

He sighed and rubbed his jaw. So what exactly did he want in his marriage? Not love obviously. But he wanted a strong lady he could like, trust, and respect—an equal partner whom he needn't coddle but instead could support, build a life together with, and talk openly with at night. He shifted in his seat. And he wanted to desire his wife too since he'd not be taking lovers after he married and desiring her would make creating their family easier. A family with at least two children so that they'd not be alone like he'd been. He inhaled as a little girl and even littler boy with dark-brown hair, light olive skin, and hazel eyes flashed before him. The children he'd once imagined Juliet embracing. He grimaced. Not that her children would ever be his since she loved another and would never marry him, but maybe she'd instruct his children on magic one day.

At the palace, Oakmoor hurried upstairs to the royal witch's wing and rapped on the door. When a little maid in starched livery opened it, he flashed a charming smile. "Could I speak with Lady Juliet, please?"

The maid blinked up at him. "I believe my lady is preparing to go out, your grace, but allow me to check."

As Juliet's maid left, he followed her inside even though courtesy dictated he should remain in the hall. He'd never visited Juliet before, so he was curious to see where she lived. And she'd certainly seen his townhouse plenty during their confinement together. He glanced about the immaculate and stylish entrance hall decorated with ordinary items rather than enchanted ones. The ambience suited Juliet except for the lack of magic. He flicked his fingers and muttered a probing spell. The bright white glow of magic emanated from a room down the hall —Juliet's workroom, no doubt. How did it compare to the one she'd used at his townhouse?

He was about to go look when Juliet bustled from the room beside her workroom, her study given the desk and bookshelves filling it. She raked him with a narrow glance. "What are *you* doing here?"

His pulse quickening like usual at Juliet's cold disdain, he forced himself to remain still. Why must her biting tongue always make him burn to kiss her? Especially now that he knew she loved another. He didn't pursue or desire committed ladies, even if they loved an undeserving idiot who didn't love them.

Burying his mad desire for Juliet, he quirked his brows and drawled, "I needed to speak with you."

Juliet's tempting lips pursed as she began to sweep past him. "If 'tis about last night, I don't wish to discuss it."

He grasped Juliet's wrist to halt her, and his blood surged. How easy 'twould be to yank his bewitching witch against him and kiss her. Unable to resist, he caressed her wrist with his thumb. "Sadly for you, we must."

Her gorgeous dark-brown eyes turning black, Juliet shivered then wrenched her wrist free and glared at him. "No. Leave, Oakmoor."

He captured Juliet's shoulders before she could move. She obviously still burned for him too despite loving another. How her fierce pride must detest that—no wonder she'd always hated wanting him. But kissing her would drive all that from her mind... and his. He drew her against him. "Not until we talk."

Juliet braced her hands against his chest. "Talk? You're clearly bent on seducing me, you rakehell. Release me. I'm not letting you ravage me against a wall again."

His body hardening further at Juliet's spicy gingyr scent and soft curves, Oakmoor rumbled and wrapped his arms about her. "Then we'll find a bed this time."

As Juliet opened her mouth to protest, he kissed her parted lips. Wild hunger filled him when she fiercely returned his kiss less than a heartbeat later. Not breaking their ravenous kiss, he propelled Juliet down the hall. Her bedchamber was surely the innermost room. Dizzy from kissing her, he steered Juliet into her doorframe like a callow boy, jolting their mouths apart.

Panting, he rasped, "Sorry about that." He began lowering his head again.

Juliet mumbled, "What?" Then just before their lips met, she gasped and shoved his chest. "No!" The blinding white glow of a weak energy spell blazed about her hands.

His chest stinging but not truly injured, he swore and lurched backward, releasing Juliet as she'd plainly intended. He scowled at her. "You shocked me with an energy spell." Just like she'd done the morning after they'd first made love years ago. Hadn't they progressed past such tricks?

Juliet glared back and lifted her chin. "I told you I wouldn't let you ravage me again."

Oakmoor growled as fire, fueled by both desire and fury, flared beneath his skin. Maddening witch. "'Tis no excuse for attacking me with your magic."

Juliet sniffed and smoothed her light-amethyst skirt. "Quit grumbling. A slap would have hurt more and shown on your face later."

He yanked Juliet against him again, securing her wrists so she couldn't slap him like she had in the Duchess of Childes's garden or when he'd kissed her as Miss Hawke. He gritted, "Violence isn't the answer either. Perhaps try saying no and meaning it."

Juliet stiffened in his arms. "I said no. And I'm saying no now."

He lowered his head until his lips brushed hers, wild hunger once more hardening his body until it throbbed in time with his heart. "But you have to mean it, Juliet. Do you?"

Juliet jerked her head backward just before he kissed her. "Damnation, Oakmoor, stop mauling me. I'm supposed to be meeting King Devon and Queen Kiera for luncheon, and I'm already late."

Despite his still hard and throbbing body, he sighed and slowly released Juliet. He mustn't obstruct her royal duties. "Very well, but we *must* talk later." He'd never asked Juliet about her brother, the entire reason he'd visited her.

Juliet glared at him. "No. We've nothing to say to one another." She turned and swept toward the door. "You can show yourself out."

Hungrily eyeing Juliet, Oakmoor strode after her with a wry grimace. He never should have attempted to speak with her alone in her wing. Even though she loved another and he knew that, their explosive passion couldn't help but distract them when they were so alone and near a bed. Yet he still needed Juliet's help convincing Lord Sabine, so he must approach her again tonight at the Islayes' ball. Dancing the first waltz together should hopefully provide them enough privacy to talk.

CHAPTER 36

Trembling and aching from Oakmoor's devouring kisses, Juliet nearly bolted from her wing. If she remained any longer, she'd succumb to his seduction once more, and they'd not leave her bed until morning. She shuddered with throbbing hunger at that tempting image. She'd definitely been right about being alone with Oakmoor. She could never, *ever* risk that again. No matter the reason.

She gulped a deep breath to settle herself. She mustn't let Oakmoor distract her from completing everything she must do to leave Calatini, starting with her luncheon with King Devon and Queen Kiera. 'Twas too important for Calatini, herself, and her unborn child. She couldn't afford to handle it poorly.

When she hurried into the royal wing's private dining room, she offered the waiting King Devon and Queen Kiera a contrite smile. "I apologize, your majesties. I was detained by an unexpected visitor."

As King Devon smiled back and waved for her to sit, Queen Kiera grinned at her and replied, "'Twasn't a problem. I hope you don't mind we already started eating. I'm *ravenous* again." She patted her gently rounded stomach. "I swear this child is part manticore."

Juliet swallowed while she sat across from the royal couple. Too bad her own pregnancy wasn't treating her as well as the queen's. Although thanks to her nausea-healing charm, she should manage to keep luncheon down as long as she avoided rich fare. She made herself beam at King Devon and Queen Kiera. "Of course I don't mind you starting already."

Once she'd filled a plate and begun eating, King Devon arched his brows at her. "Why did you request to meet before the next council meeting, Lady Juliet?"

She sighed and set down her spoon of watercress soup before calmly meeting King Devon's and Queen Kiera's gazes. "Because I've been reconsidering my life since returning to court three weeks ago, and I've decided I must leave Calatini."

King Devon and Queen Kiera traded frowns, then King Devon asked, "Why?"

Juliet clung to her calm smile. To prevent any gossip starting about her pregnancy that might reach Oakmoor, she unfortunately couldn't tell King Devon and Queen Kiera the true reason. She shrugged. "'Tis time, that's all. I'm considering returning to Varkhora with my brother."

Queen Kiera hummed as she finished her watercress soup. "You must miss your family terribly, having been apart... how many years now?"

Her shoulders loosening at the queen's assumption that missing her family was the reason for her leaving, Juliet replied, "Twenty-one years, and I do miss them terribly."

Queen Kiera nodded while King Devon served her roast beefsteak, mashed tubers, and gravy. The queen murmured, "We can understand your need to return home, although we'll be sad to see you leave."

King Devon grimaced over his roast beefsteak. "And replacing you shall be near impossible. You've served Calatini incredibly well."

A pang pierced Juliet. If only she didn't need to leave. "I've enjoyed living in Calatini and shall miss it. As for my replacement, I'm sure the veiled witch shall provide advice about that."

While King Devon blinked at her, Queen Kiera tilted her head and asked, "Would she assume your duties, do you think?"

Juliet finally relaxed enough to resume eating her watercress soup. "No, the veiled witch has other commitments that prevent her from becoming Calatini's royal witch. She only assumed my duties while I was absent with Oakmoor because she knew 'twas temporary. But do you wish for me to contact the veiled witch and request that she advise you on my replacement?"

King Devon smiled at her. "We're visiting the orphanage after the council meeting tomorrow, so we'll meet with the veiled witch then. Her witch shop *is* just down the street."

Studying Juliet, Queen Kiera buttered another roll. "How much longer shall you remain in Calatini? I suspect finding your replacement shan't be quick."

Juliet stilled, not letting herself look at her stomach. "If needed, I could remain for up to two months." After that, her pregnancy would begin to show. "Although I'd prefer to leave earlier if possible."

King Devon and Queen Kiera traded another glance, then King Devon said, "'Tis fortunate we can visit the veiled witch tomorrow then." He sighed. "To avoid causing concern within the council and at court, let's wait to announce your departure until we find your replacement."

Juliet exhaled as she finished her watercress soup. If they kept her departure quiet, then no one, namely Oakmoor, could quiz her about it. She smiled at King Devon and Queen Kiera. "That sounds fine. If you require any assistance finding my replacement, please let me know."

Then she asked King Devon and Queen Kiera about their upcoming visit to Waterstreet Orphanage, and they discussed that and the progress of Queen Kiera's education initiative for the rest of luncheon. When Juliet rose to leave, she swept a deep curtsy. "Thank you for being so understanding about my need to leave Calatini, your majesties."

Queen Kiera embraced her. "Of course. Among everything else, we owe you my life for unearthing the treasonous Lady Morwynne as well as our happiness for providing the tokens for our secret bloodbinding. I hope you find everything you seek back in Varkhora."

Juliet managed a serene smile. Impossible when Oakmoor would remain in Calatini and marry another. "I'm certain I shall. Good day, your majesties."

She returned to her wing and spent the afternoon reading a tome about spirit magic to distract herself from her upcoming departure. Until Father contacted her with word about when Sandro could meet, she couldn't make further plans in any case.

That evening, Giovanni joined her for dinner, appearing just as strained as he had earlier, although he cheered later at the Islayes' ball when young Lord Morwynne and Lord Alexander Greysnowe drew him away as soon as they arrived to discuss Lady Ducharme's fencing salon the following morning.

Juliet smiled after her brother. Hopefully, talking with his friends would distract Giovanni from his shattered heart. She should find Siobhan and Lorcan so that they could do the same for her.

She was glancing about the Islayes' ballroom—which was decorated with dazzling illusions of Calatini's most magical places; the studious Minister of Magic had somehow eclipsed those at his illusion evening nearly three months ago—to find Siobhan and Lorcan when Oakmoor strode over with a cup of tea and a plate of sponge sweet biscuits. He drawled, "Juliet, finally. Have these before we dance the first waltz together. We can't have you almost fainting again."

She stepped backward and refused to accept the refreshments Oakmoor offered, her stomach shifting. "I don't want them. I just ate. And we're not dancing the first waltz together."

Oakmoor narrowed his eyes at her. "We still must talk, and a waltz should allow us some privacy."

Juliet glowered back. Why couldn't Oakmoor just leave her alone? Dancing with him would be painful when he belonged to another. "No, thank you." She waved at Lady Georgiana Laurent along the wall by the garden across the ballroom. "Go dance with your *betrothed*."

His jaw tightening, Oakmoor leaned closer. "I can't. That's part of what we must discuss." He handed the tea and sponge sweet biscuits to a nearby servant then grasped her elbow, making her tingle like always. He continued, "If you'd prefer not to dance, we can talk in an anteroom. 'Twould be more private anyway." His mouth twisted. "Hopefully, we can control ourselves with all of court hovering on the other side of the wall."

She wrenched her arm free. Except 'twould be too easy for either her or Oakmoor to cast wards preventing anyone from entering or overhearing them. Then she'd succumb to her intense need for him as soon as he kissed her, which he'd surely do as soon as they were alone. The rakehell. Her blood quickening, she nearly shivered. "I'm not going *anywhere* with you, Oakmoor."

The same hunger she was suffering turning his hazel eyes black, Oakmoor stepped close enough that his legs brushed her ebony skirt. He rumbled, "And why not, my delightfully wanton witch?"

Juliet stared up at Oakmoor and licked her parted lips. Oh, Goddess, how she burned for him. And she always would. She began to sway toward him.

"What are you doing to my sister, Oakmoor?" Giovanni suddenly gritted behind her.

A chill dousing her, she gasped and jerked backward. She'd been about to let Oakmoor seduce her *in front of* all of court. Even if he wasn't betrothed to another, 'twould have been scandalous. Almost as much as her being pregnant with his child was.

Oakmoor flashed a smooth smile at Giovanni. "Attempting to convince Lady Juliet to talk with me privately in an anteroom. Perhaps you'd care to chaperone us to prevent any gossip from starting?"

His hand clenching his saber and Striker bristling, Giovanni snorted and scowled back at Oakmoor. "Preventing gossip about a beastly rakehell like you is impossible."

Juliet stiffened. Giovanni appeared about to erupt and challenge Oakmoor to a duel. And she loved them both too much to allow that. She slid her arm through her brother's. "The first waltz is about to begin. We should take our places on the floor."

Thankfully, Giovanni allowed her to draw him away from Oakmoor, then she and her brother danced the first waltz together with Oakmoor watching them from the outskirts. Odd that Oakmoor didn't dance with Lady Georgiana, who instead partnered Lord Aynsley, the husband of one of her elder sisters. Maybe Oakmoor and Lady Georgiana were attempting to lessen the scandal surrounding their betrothal by remaining apart.

Tired from her pregnancy and avoiding Oakmoor, who kept watching her and attempting to approach again, Juliet asked Giovanni to escort her back to the palace barely an hour after the first waltz. Wrenching his dark gaze from Lady Georgiana who was smiling and talking with Lord Alexander Greysnowe, Giovanni nodded then whisked Juliet from the Islayes' ballroom.

When she trudged back into her wing, she headed to her study to check if Father had left a message on her communication mirror. He had, stating that Sandro was eager to meet and would call her midmorning tomorrow. Fortunately, she was free other than her usual meeting with Giovanni because she'd not intended to attend tomorrow's council meeting. She exhaled. Her arrangements to leave Calatini were progressing well. She sent a note to Giovanni canceling their morning meeting before crawling into bed and sinking into slumber.

• • •

WHEN HER COMMUNICATION mirror glowed white the following morning, Juliet inhaled then smoothed her sober granite-gray gown before chanting the spell to answer it.

Her communication mirror cleared, revealing Sandro and Aurora holding hands in a cozy study. Like herself, her two cousins closest to her own age had no silver in their dark hair, and their olive skin was still smooth, although they'd both matured since she'd fled Varkhora. His white draklizard on his left shoulder, Sandro was now an adult gentleman rather than a gangly youth and bore a quiet air of wise command. Her diamond faebird on her right shoulder, Aurora was no longer a diffident teenager but a composed lady with a kind and gentle smile.

Juliet smiled at the cousins that she'd grown up with and had always liked, although she'd really only been close to Sandro. Like her, her crippled royal cousin had been a misfit and wanted more, while the one-year-younger Aurora had been too perfect sometimes—the ideal Varkhoran daughter, thanks to her gentle nature and being a powerful hearth witch. Yet Sandro and Aurora had always been the most adorable and loving couple, and reports of their blissful happiness together hadn't been exaggerated since they were clearly still in love as ever. Too bad she'd never enjoy the same with Oakmoor. Shoving that aside, she brightened her smile and said to her cousins, "You're both looking well." She tilted her head. "Although I wasn't expecting to see you, Aurora. Father only mentioned arranging a mirror call with Sandro."

Sandro's and Aurora's eyes crinkled in silent amusement, then Aurora replied, "Arranging things with Sandro nearly always includes me, although no one mentions that to avoid upsetting the more hidebound in Varkhora."

JULIET NODDED, her smile twisting. Goddess forbid that the Varkhoran queen would help her husband rule instead of just bearing his sons. Despite adoring Mother, Father never would have let her help him like that. She suppressed a grimace. "Hidebound gentlemen like Father, you mean."

Sandro arched his brows and chuckled. "Not hardly. The Duke of Appenninos always approved of Aurora being by my side, and his influence and advice helped it be accepted. He's the one who suggested Aurora join me without bothering to mention it. Not surprising given he consults with your mother about everything and has since they married."

Juliet blinked. Father what? But proper Varkhoran gentlemen were supposed to rule over their wives no matter how much they loved them. How had she never noticed that Father didn't?

Aurora hummed and quirked a wry smile. "Not that your parents ever mention that they make their decisions together. The duchess much prefers it to remain secret to avoid conflict."

Blinking again, Juliet inclined her head. Of course Mother did. She inhaled. So Father loved strong ladies as much as Giovanni did and always had. Doubtless her brother's unusual preference hadn't just come from hearing Mother's stories about her, but from Father as well. Yet why had Father been so censorious with *her* for being driven during her childhood?

Sandro squeezed Aurora's hand, his draklizard nuzzling her faebird, who preened. Most unusual behavior between a fierce draklizard and a skittish faebird. Sandro said, "But as king and queen, Aurora and I must challenge conventions if we ever want women to be equals in Varkhora like they should be."

Aurora smiled at Juliet. "Speaking of challenging conventions, your father said you're interested in returning to Varkhora as our royal witch?"

Juliet matched Aurora's smile despite her shifting stomach. "I'm considering it."

Sandro sighed. "We'd love to have you as Varkhora's royal witch, but Lord Marcello isn't ready to retire yet, even though he should because certain tasks are beyond him now."

Juliet pursed her lips. A decade older than Father, Lord

Marcello *was* in his eighth decade, incredibly ancient for even the most powerful witch. Yet Lord Marcello had always been a proud gentleman and wouldn't easily accept surrendering his duties. No more than Father would.

After exchanging a glance with Aurora, Sandro leaned forward and continued, "However, if you're willing to become Lord Marcello's second in command, we could manage that." He grimaced. "'Twould also allow the hidebound time to accept you becoming Varkhora's royal witch."

Juliet smoothed her granite-gray skirt. Plus, having fewer duties would be better for her as a mother raising a child without a husband. She nodded. "I'd not object to becoming Varkhora's deputy royal witch."

Sandro grinning beside her, Aurora beamed and replied, "Deputy royal witch is the perfect title. How did you conceive it?"

An ache squeezing her chest, Juliet managed a bright smile. "I didn't. One of the dukes on Calatini's council recently created a deputy position to promote his assistant." She inhaled and held her cousins' gazes. "But before I accept your kind offer, I must tell you that I'm leaving Calatini because I'm with child and can't marry the father."

His and Aurora's eyes widening, Sandro murmured, "The Duke of Appenninos didn't mention *that*."

Juliet sighed, twisting her hands together in her lap. "Because I've not told my parents or Giovanni yet." Although she must do so soon.

Aurora leaned forward, her brow furrowed but smile soft. "What happened? I can't imagine you accidentally falling pregnant. You've always been so careful and driven."

Her cheeks heating, Juliet swallowed. Around Oakmoor, she wasn't. "I had to use sex magic to save the gentleman I love. But he's now betrothed to another, so I can't marry him."

As Sandro frowned, Aurora bit her lip and said, "Oh, Juliet, I'm terribly sorry."

Juliet made herself smile to reassure her gentle cousin. "I don't regret conceiving my child, but..." She shrugged.

Aurora finished for her, "You wish matters were different." She and Juliet shared a look of feminine understanding.

Sandro cleared his throat, his white draklizard shifting on his shoulder. "It shall be simple enough to tell everyone here that you're a widow. I doubt anyone shall bother to check."

Juliet exhaled. True, especially if Sandro, who rarely dissembled, pretended to believe it. She inclined her head. "Thanks for your warm support, and I accept becoming Varkhora's deputy royal witch."

Sandro and Aurora smiled at her, then Sandro asked, "How long until you arrive in Varkhora?"

Humming, Juliet tapped her knee. "Perhaps almost half a year." There'd definitely be no hiding her pregnancy when she arrived in Varkhora. "I've promised to remain in Calatini for up to two months to give King Devon and Queen Kiera time to find my replacement. And then it shall take three months to reach Varkhora using a caravan travel spell."

Nodding along with Sandro, Aurora said, "We'll ensure Lord Marcello and court are prepared for your arrival. Contact us as matters progress, and we'll do the same."

Juliet echoed Aurora's nod. With her future now settled, they should discuss family matters. She grinned at her cousins. "Tell me about your children. You've two teenage boys, I believe."

Aurora beaming beside him, Sandro flashed a proud grin and replied, "We do. Our eldest Leonardo is clever and steady, so he'll make an excellent future king. Our younger son Marco inherited Aurora's magical powers, but he's restless and has little patience for court intrigues, so he may travel Damensea one day."

Her beam turning wistful, Aurora sighed. "Our boys are wonderful, and I adore them, although I sometimes ache for a little girl to cuddle and giggle with. Boys are so rowdy, and I'm surrounded by them."

Juliet winked to hearten Aurora. "'Tisn't too late—just look at me."

She and her cousins discussed their family for a bit longer before saying farewell. After she waved her hand to deactivate her communication mirror, she sagged back in her chair. Now that her future in Varkhora was settled, all she must do was wait for her replacement here to arrive... and tell her parents and Giovanni about her scandalous pregnancy. Please let them be as supportive as Sandro and Aurora had been.

CHAPTER 37

As soon as King Devon and Queen Kiera adjourned the council meeting, Oakmoor hurried out to prevent anyone from prying further about Lady Georgiana. Lord Dabar beside him had quizzed him unmercifully before the council meeting had begun. Most irritating. He grimaced. Even though court was desperate to determine his intentions toward Lady Georgiana, he'd hoped that his fellow councilors would show better sense and focus on important matters rather than his romantic affairs. And most of them had, but he wasn't lingering in the council room to allow those who hadn't like Lord Dabar the chance to pry.

He sighed as he climbed into his carriage. He'd also hoped that Juliet would attend the council meeting so that he could speak with her about her brother afterward. Yet she hadn't, and he couldn't approach her in her wing again. They'd end up making love rather than talking, and he truly needed her advice about Lord Sabine. Since his soiree, the boy kept glaring at him and clenching his saber, clearly about to challenge him to a duel. Not only that, but the bristling Varkhoran also kept avoiding Lady Georgiana whenever she attempted to join him at every court event, doubtless to explain. Given his continued fury, Lord Sabine would never stop and listen to the truth unless they'd outside help—like his beloved older sister. Oakmoor drummed his fingers on his knee. He could approach Juliet about her brother tonight at the Landrys' ball. His lips twisted. 'Twould enliven the Landrys' otherwise dull event at least.

That evening, the Landrys' ballroom was already bustling by the time he arrived. Despite their dullness, the Landrys' events were invariably well attended because Mr. Landry had amassed a vast fortune in the Tsarkan Empire during his youth and Mrs. Landry was the sister of the Duke of Dracwyn, who served as the Minister of Commerce. When Oakmoor approached them, the Landrys and their coquettish daughter all beamed at him. Considering the current scandal surrounding him, his presence would be the talk of their ball.

After they'd exchanged greetings, Mrs. Landry glanced behind him then asked, "And where's Lady Georgiana Laurent, your grace?"

He arched his brows and brightened his smooth smile. "Arriving with her father, I would imagine. Why ask me?"

Miss Landry cast her mother a smirk. "See, I told you that the Duke of Oakmoor was too cunning to be caught by that desperate spinster."

He almost snorted. Lady Georgiana was a decade or more from being called a spinster by anyone of sense. But the eighteen-year-old Miss Landry possessed much more wealth than sense.

Miss Landry fluttered her lashes at him and grasped his arm. "His grace requires a lady with youthful charm and vivacity."

His smile tightening, he stepped back to free his arm. The callow blonde's flirting was even less appealing than Lady Georgiana's—she, at least, was shrewd behind her coy manner. He said in a deliberately light tone, "I've always preferred ladies sophisticated and strong enough to match me. And at my age, nearly all the eligible ladies seem young, perhaps too young. But

Lady Georgiana is an interesting lady." As long as he wasn't forced to marry her.

While his daughter deflated, Mr. Landry spoke for the first time since greeting Oakmoor, "With a wily father like the Duke of Osbourne, she couldn't fail to be." Then the henpecked gentleman winced as his wife and daughter glared at him.

Excusing himself as Lord and Lady Mythacre arrived, Oakmoor scanned the ballroom for Juliet. He didn't spot her or Lord Sabine, although he did spot the Escanas talking with the Orandians near the refreshments table. Since Juliet was sure to join her friends as soon as she arrived, he slipped through the crowd toward them, pausing to talk with the other guests on his way. Sadly, most of his conversations involved deflecting everyone's prying about Lady Georgiana. All of court was obsessed— no doubt because he was the last unwed duke of marriageable age in Calatini, one who had eluded matrimony for decades and was also the greatest rakehell in Ormas.

When he finally reached the refreshments table, he plucked up a flute of sparkling wine and downed half of it before joining the Escanas and the Orandians. He flashed a charming grin as they all traded good evenings.

His erstwhile assistant scrutinized him, her arm firmly linked with her husband's. She said, "Unusual that you're here so early, your grace. You're typically one of the last guests to arrive at the Landrys' events."

Oakmoor sipped his sparkling wine. Because withstanding their dull events in their entirety was painful. But tonight he was attending with a purpose. He shrugged. "I've a matter to discuss with Lady Juliet."

As Lady Driscoll's and Sir Lorcan's gazes narrowed, Lady Escana hummed then murmured, "Of course you do. Ever since Lady Driscoll and Sir Lorcan arrived, you two have frequently had matters to discuss. Amazing when you consider how assiduously you both avoided each other in the fourteen years prior."

His eyes gleaming, Lord Escana drawled, "Except for Lady

Juliet's first month as our royal witch. Their well-known *dislike* didn't develop until after that."

The Orandians' narrow gazes narrowing further, Oakmoor swallowed a sigh. Why did Lord Escana have to mention that month in front of Juliet's suspicious friends? Most of court failed to remember the month before he and Juliet had made love for the first time and begun avoiding each other. But despite not possessing ambitions beyond ruling his county in Valcrest, Lord Escana was as perceptive as his wife.

Oakmoor shrugged again to feign nonchalance. "Lady Juliet and I didn't know each other well enough to dislike one another then."

As Lord Escana smirked at that, Lady Escana sipped her sparkling wine and asked, "What must you discuss with Lady Juliet? A council matter?"

Oakmoor stilled. If only he could use that excuse again, but he'd used it too often for Juliet's observant friends or his perceptive deputy and her husband to believe it, so he might as well admit the real reason. He sighed. "No, a private matter."

Lady Escana's lips quirked. "And I can guess that matter given what you told me about Lady Georgiana two weeks ago."

While Lady Driscoll and Sir Lorcan glowered at him, Oakmoor suppressed a wince. Although the Orandians had noticed his and Juliet's primal attraction before and attempted to matchmake, now they obviously regarded him as committed to Lady Georgiana and didn't want him near their friend. But if he never spoke with Juliet, he'd never get the mess with Lady Georgiana resolved.

Suddenly, Lady Escana straightened. "Lady Juliet and Lord Sabine are greeting the Landrys now. Anthony and I shall assist you by distracting her brother. Him challenging you to a duel shan't do our relations with Varkhora any good."

As his deputy and her husband swept across the ballroom, Oakmoor turned to the Orandians with a smooth smile. He must convince them to leave him alone with Juliet. But he couldn't admit the actual situation between him and Lady Georgiana where he could be overheard. He held Lady Driscoll's and Sir Lorcan's narrow gazes. "Gossip can be thoroughly misleading, you know."

Juliet retorted while she glided over to Lady Driscoll, "Not when you've witnessed the truth of it."

He glared at Juliet, clenching his flute of sparkling wine. Stubborn witch. "You misinterpreted what you witnessed."

Juliet sniffed. "I doubt it. Now, would you quit pestering me?"

Oakmoor leaned toward Juliet. He could be just as stubborn as she was. "No. I must speak with you. In private where we can't be overheard."

Juliet swallowed and smoothed her silver skirt over her stomach. "We can't. You *know* we can't."

He eyed Juliet's tempting hands like a hungry venus and stepped closer, his pulse surging as their explosive passion echoed through him. Passion she couldn't resist despite loving her undeserving idiot. Not that he should be thinking about their obsessive hunger now. They must talk about her brother. He rumbled, "We have to. I need your help."

Her lips flattening, Juliet lifted her chin. "You've no need for a royal witch. You're not embroiled in troublesome magic now."

At the Orandians' sharp inhales, he and Juliet both stiffened. Engrossed in their quarrel, he'd forgotten about Juliet's friends. Evidently she had too. At least she'd not blurted out more about his beast curse.

Sir Lorcan raking him with a probing glance, Lady Driscoll arched her brows and asked, "Now? His grace was embroiled in troublesome magic before?"

Juliet cleared her throat. "I misspoke. I simply meant that Oakmoor's troubles are ordinary ones, not magical in nature. A royal witch can't provide help for a commonplace betrothal."

As the Orandians nodded, Oakmoor narrowed his eyes at

Juliet. 'Twas *her* help he needed, not that of Calatini's royal witch. He leaned toward her again. "She can if it involves her brother."

Juliet scowled at him. "How is Giovanni involved in your betrothal to Lady Georgiana Laurent?"

He snorted. Was Juliet being purposely obtuse? "His quarrel with Lady Georgiana *is* what started all the gossip."

Juliet scowled fiercer. "No, your private interlude with her did." When he opened his mouth to explain that yet again, she tossed her head and continued, "I'm not arguing further about this. You're absolutely impossible, Oakmoor."

As Juliet swept off and joined the Islayes, he glowered after her. He wasn't the impossible one. Why wouldn't she *listen* to him?

He started when Sir Lorcan murmured, "You and Juliet quarrel like feuding harpies and nagas. So tempestuous."

Oakmoor faced the Orandians he'd forgotten about again, his neck heating. "Only because Lady Juliet refuses to listen." And that wasn't likely to change any time soon. But he or Lady Georgiana must convince Lord Sabine of the truth before her betrothal ball. He suppressed a grimace. Since 'twas just two weeks away, he'd better begin approaching Lord Sabine without Juliet's help, although he'd keep attempting to secure it to facilitate convincing her brother. Without her help, 'twould take even more time to get the boy calm enough to stop and actually listen. He was related to Juliet, after all.

Oakmoor smiled at Lady Driscoll and Sir Lorcan and nodded farewell. "Excuse me, I must speak with Lord Sabine."

He hastened across the ballroom and halted beside the Escanas and Juliet's brother. He gave the young Varkhoran lord a smiling nod. "Good evening, Lord Sabine."

His mottled-brown draklizard bristling on his shoulder, Lord Sabine gripped his saber until his hand turned white. "Why aren't you dancing with Lady Georgiana, Oakmoor? An honorable gentleman doesn't embarrass his betrothed by avoiding her like she carries a virulent strain of wraith flu."

Oakmoor sipped his sparkling wine. Remaining cool in the face of Lord Sabine's belligerence just *might* make the boy listen. He inclined his head. "I agree."

As the Escanas' mouths twitched, obviously understanding his implication that he and Lady Georgiana weren't betrothed, Lord Sabine glared and growled, "Then why are you talking with everyone else at court instead of dancing with Lady Georgiana?"

Oakmoor sighed. Unsurprisingly, remaining cool wasn't enough to get Juliet's brother to listen, but perhaps frank talk might be. Although they must be in private for that. He waved his nearly empty flute of sparkling wine at the anteroom behind Lord Sabine. "I can explain, but not where all of court could overhear. Shall we?"

Lord Sabine's glare darkened. "No. I already know the truth."

As Lord Sabine pushed past him and stalked toward Juliet, Oakmoor bit back a curse. His attempt had accomplished nothing. The boy was definitely as stubborn as his sister. Since staying and attempting to speak with Juliet and her brother tonight would doubtless only worsen matters, he said farewell to the Escanas then left the Landrys' dull ball. He'd try again another evening.

OVER THE FOLLOWING COUPLE EVENINGS, Oakmoor attempted to talk with Juliet and Lord Sabine at every court event they all attended, while Lady Georgiana continued attempting the same with Lord Sabine. Yet he and Lady Georgiana never succeeded. Why must Juliet and her brother be so infernally impossible? The entire mess with Lady Georgiana would be resolved if he or Lady Georgiana could simply manage a frank conversation with the stubborn Varkhoran siblings.

He was in his study attempting to decide how to get Juliet

and Lord Sabine in private at the Serles' rout party that evening when an unexpected letter from Lady Driscoll arrived, inviting him to luncheon in a few hours. He drummed his fingers on his desk. Why had the Orandian ambassador invited him? She and her husband had been chilly toward him since the gossip about him and Lady Georgiana had started.

He hummed. Yet if he could convince Juliet's friends that 'twas imperative he speak with Juliet and Lord Sabine, they could help him arrange a private talk with their friend and her brother. So he swiftly penned his acceptance.

When their butler ushered him into the Orandian embassy's family dining room shortly after noon, Oakmoor blinked at Lady Driscoll being alone at the head of the table. She and her husband were usually together. "Where's Sir Lorcan?"

Lady Driscoll grinned and fingered her overcoat atop her tunic. "In his workroom on a mirror call with the Duke of Wilde-wall. When I went to fetch Lorcan for luncheon, he and the duke were so engrossed in discussing astral projection that I hadn't the heart to disturb them. I had the servants send him a luncheon tray instead."

Oakmoor muffled his laugh as he sat beside Lady Driscoll. The two lore witches would probably discuss the mystical magic of astral projection until they were hoarse. "Kind of you to indulge your husband."

Lady Driscoll lifted a shoulder. "I love him, and I can handle luncheon with you without him."

Oakmoor smiled. True, although another lady arranging a private luncheon would have made him suspect her of attempting to begin an affair with him. And her dismissing the servants and casting a listening-ward spell about the dining room like Lady Driscoll was doing would have made him even more suspicious. Yet Lady Driscoll was too devoted to Sir Lorcan to begin an affair with anyone, so he remained in his seat rather than deftly making his excuses.

He arched his brows as he served Lady Driscoll beetroot

soup. "What inspired your unexpected invitation to luncheon today? Something you wish to remain secret given how you ensured no one can overhear us. Not trouble between Orandia and Calatini, I hope."

Lady Driscoll pursed a grimace. "I didn't invite you here as Orandia's ambassador, but as Juliet's friend." She narrowed her eyes at him. "I want to know why you keep pursuing her when you've chosen another to become your wife."

His jaw tightened. Everyone's assumptions were becoming damned vexing. "As I've said, I've a private matter to discuss with Juliet."

Lady Driscoll snorted into her beetroot soup. "Betrothed gentlemen shouldn't have private matters to discuss with other ladies, *particularly* their past lovers."

Oakmoor stiffened as pain pierced him at Juliet discussing their affair with others. How could she be so indiscreet? He'd always thought she was a likeminded soul about private matters. He rasped, "Juliet told you that we're lovers?"

Lady Driscoll snorted again. "Lorcan and I guessed from how the two of you behave together. *All* she told me when I confronted her about it was that you had to perform sex magic to handle the private royal matter that took you from court."

He inhaled, his body easing. Juliet hadn't talked because she'd wanted to, and she'd only revealed enough to appease her already suspicious friend. She could have revealed so much more. He sipped his fruity red wine. "I see."

Lady Driscoll tilted her head. "Although from what Lord Escana said the other day, I suspect you and Juliet became lovers long ago."

He stilled and forced himself to drawl, "Did we?"

Her lips twisting, Lady Driscoll raised her eyes skyward. "Yes. How most of Calatini's court can be so blind as to not see that, I don't know."

Oakmoor set down his wine glass with a firm clink. He must get Lady Driscoll to quit prying about Juliet. 'Twas more excruciating than court prying about Lady Georgiana. He glowered at Juliet's too curious friend. "Is there a point to this conversation?"

Lady Driscoll glared back. "My point is that you need to leave Juliet alone because you're betrothed to Lady Georgiana."

He hissed a breath then snapped, "For Goddess's sake, I'm *not* betrothed to Lady Georgiana. Juliet and Lord Sabine completely misinterpreted what they witnessed. That's what Lady Georgiana and I have been trying to discuss with them."

Her mouth dropping open, Lady Driscoll stared at him. "But you were kissing Lady Georgiana. Alone in your townhouse."

Oakmoor sighed. Since he'd blurted out part of the truth about Lady Georgiana, he might as well confess the rest. And perhaps 'twould convince Lady Driscoll to help him arrange a private talk with Juliet and Lord Sabine. He held Lady Driscoll's gaze. "Lady Georgiana was kissing me to prove that she didn't love Lord Sabine, which she *does*. And she was only alone in my townhouse to persuade me to let her act as my hostess because she'd told Lord Sabine that she was, a desperate lie on her part." He scowled and clenched his wine glass. "But Lord Sabine's and Lady Georgiana's indiscreet quarrel made court believe that we're involved, so her father and I decided to neither confirm nor deny the gossip while I arrange for a match between Lord Sabine and Lady Georgiana. Their betrothal should resolve the scandalous mess that her folly started."

Lady Driscoll frowned. "But what if Lord Sabine refuses to accept Lady Georgiana?"

Grimacing, Oakmoor sipped his wine. Goddess, please let it not come to that. "*I'm* certainly not marrying her. The Duke of Osbourne shall have to handle the mess then. But at least I'll have attempted to resolve matters."

Lady Driscoll straightened and twinkled at him for the first time in days. "Very noble of you, your grace. Much more than I would have expected from an 'unrepentant rakehell', as Juliet so fondly calls you."

He inclined his head with a wry smile. Fond? Not hardly.

Furious that neither of them could resist their explosive passion, definitely. Particularly since she loved another gentleman. A pang seized him. One who didn't return her love like she deserved. The blind idiot. He fisted his hands beneath the table. Not that Juliet's unrequited love mattered to him. He assuredly wasn't in love with her himself and possessed no desire to be the adoring husband she wanted either. Juliet was simply the bewitching witch he couldn't help desiring thanks to their obsessive, primal hunger. But that would surely fade once he'd found the right lady for his wife. Surely.

Still grinning, Lady Driscoll resumed eating her beetroot soup. "Now that I know your true intentions, I'll help convince Juliet and her brother to speak with you and Lady Georgiana."

Dragging himself back to Juliet's friend, Oakmoor exhaled and made his fists relax. Some progress regarding Lady Georgiana at last. Hopefully, 'twould continue so that he could resume his normal life. Then he could finally begin seeking his future wife. One who wasn't Juliet. Fortunately. Despite the odd stillness in his chest, he warmly smiled at the Orandian ambassador. "Thank you, my lady. I greatly appreciate your help."

CHAPTER 38

Four days after canceling their lesson to meet with King Devon and Queen Kiera, Juliet smiled at Cassandra when Lara ushered the teenage girl into her workroom for their first magic lesson at the palace.

Her mulberry eyes bright, Cassandra glanced about the workroom as she bounded inside. "This workroom is amazing. So full of light."

Still smiling, Juliet swallowed her sigh. Yes, although the workroom Oakmoor had lent her had been even better, her workroom here at the palace *was* amazing, and she'd miss it when she left Calatini. Burying that, she waved for Cassandra to sit at the table beside her.

Cassandra chuckled while she did. "And 'tis so tidy too. No wonder you made me clean mine."

Juliet slanted her apprentice a stern glance. "I hope you're keeping your workroom clean even though we're meeting here today." At Cassandra's grimace and nod, Juliet smiled again. "Good. Now before we begin your lesson today, I've a matter to discuss with you."

Cassandra beamed. "So have I." She extracted a letter from

her reticule and passed it to Juliet. "I *finally* received a reply to the letter I sent Father's family two months ago."

Juliet swiftly read the brief letter from Menowin Lovari, a cousin of Shandor's who'd become the head of the Lovari family after Ceija died. She hummed as she returned the letter to Cassandra. "I remember Menowin. He's a talented witch around my age. A decent man, although a chary one."

Cassandra tilted her head. "I suppose 'tis why he took so long to write and why he wrote they can't contact me using mirror calls or other magic to avoid attracting attention from outside witches. But at least they plan to return to Ormas next summer and are amenable to seeing me and Amaranth then." She grinned at Juliet. "So what did you have to discuss?"

Juliet sighed. Hopefully Cassandra wouldn't be too upset by her news. "I'll be leaving Calatini in the next two months and returning to Varkhora."

Her grin fading, Cassandra stilled and scrutinized Juliet. "This is one of the consequences for breaking the Duke of Oakmoor's beast curse that Tihdseare meant, isn't it?"

Juliet inclined her head with a wry smile. Insightful girl. Cassandra was truly her father's daughter. She might even suspect that becoming pregnant with Oakmoor's child was the main consequence the veiled witch had meant, although Juliet wasn't about to confirm that. She simply replied, "It is. But I don't wish to abandon our magic lessons." Not only did she owe Shandor that, but the veiled witch had said Cassandra needed her as a mentor, and the incredibly powerful seer would know. "I thought that once I leave, we could continue them through mirror calls. Not as good as regular lessons, but we can cover most things."

Cassandra blew a sigh but nodded. "Amaranth and I shall miss seeing you in person, but I'm glad you're willing to mentor me through mirror calls at least."

Juliet squeezed Cassandra's shoulder, her chest aching. "I'll miss seeing you both too." She swallowed then continued briskly, "Now, show me the glamour spell I asked you to create after our last lesson."

Cassandra gathered the spell ingredients and magical accoutrements for her glamour spell. Once she successfully cast it, Juliet quizzed her on why she'd crafted the spell she had, and Cassandra thoroughly answered. She was such an excellent apprentice. Too bad they'd be limited to mirror calls in a couple months. Juliet sighed then began instructing Cassandra on the theory behind divining spells.

Not long after Cassandra left with the task of creating her own divining spell, Giovanni joined her for dinner before they headed to the Serles' rout party. Juliet exhaled as they climbed into the carriage. Since the Serles were from his duchy, perhaps Oakmoor would be too busy with them and the betrothed he'd been neglecting to approach her about speaking with him in private. She grimaced and glowered out the carriage window. Although probably not. Please let her manage to avoid him tonight like she had the previous couple evenings. She'd nearly betrayed her helpless love for Oakmoor the last few times they'd spoken, even when they were in public, so she couldn't even risk that any longer, although she mustn't be rude about it to prevent gossip. She laid a hand on her stomach. No one at court could suspect that they'd been lovers and that she carried his child.

When they arrived at Serle House, Juliet glanced about the lively drawing room for Oakmoor. He was talking with Lord Morwynne and Lord Alexander Greysnowe—Giovanni's friends rather than hers for once—with Lady Georgiana Laurent just steps away talking with the Ducharmes and the Campbells. Juliet's delicate stomach tightened. 'Twas the closest Oakmoor and his betrothed had been in public since his soiree.

Giovanni stiffened and glared at the two cheerfully talking groups. "I swear Oakmoor and Lady Georgiana are monopolizing my friends to annoy me because I keep refusing their attempts at a private conversation."

She frowned and steered Giovanni toward Siobhan and

Lorcan. "Lady Georgiana has been attempting to speak with you?" She'd not noticed that. Oakmoor had been consuming her attention.

Giovanni's jaw clenched. "Ever since our quarrel at Oakmoor's soiree. But I don't wish to hear her excuses for her brazen behavior."

Juliet squeezed her younger brother's arm as they joined Siobhan and Lorcan. No more than she wanted to hear Oakmoor's. "I understand."

Accepting a flute of sparkling wine from Lorcan, Siobhan tilted her head then asked, "Understand what?"

As Juliet grimaced at her friend's well-meant but painful probing, Giovanni scowled and replied, "Why I'm avoiding Lady Georgiana's attempts to talk with me."

Siobhan and Lorcan traded a glance, then Siobhan straightened her cream overcoat and blue-green tunic as she said, "Perhaps you shouldn't. The Goddess greatly approves of forgiveness—even a worshipper of the Sea God like me knows that. Besides, you might like what you hear."

Giovanni snorted. "I doubt it." He dropped Juliet's arm. "I'll fetch us some refreshments."

While her brother left, Juliet narrowed her eyes at her friends. Since Oakmoor's soiree, neither had been sympathetic toward Oakmoor or his betrothed, so what had changed? She arched her brows. "Why suddenly supportive of Lady Georgiana?"

Siobhan sipped her sparkling wine. "I invited the Duke of Oakmoor for luncheon to demand he explain his recent behavior, and what he told me transformed my view of the situation. You need to listen to him too." She glanced at Juliet's stomach. "Remember, you must consider more than just yourself now."

As Lorcan echoed his wife with a stern nod, Juliet stiffened. *What* had Oakmoor told Siobhan? She glanced across the drawing room toward Oakmoor, who was watching her like a starving tygris watched a unicorn. Tingling heat flooded her as their hungry gazes meshed. Unable to look away, she shivered and swayed toward him.

He'd begun to stride toward her when Siobhan gripped her arm, jolting her free from their locked stare. Siobhan murmured, "Juliet, are you feeling well?"

Juliet shuddered as her heart twisted and stomach roiled despite her nausea-healing charm. "No, I'm not. Excuse me."

Extracting her arm, she turned and slipped through the crowd toward the door. She mustn't let Oakmoor reach her. She just wasn't strong enough to withstand another encounter with him. She glanced behind her, and her pulse flared. Oakmoor was much closer now. She gathered her will and flung an ignore spell about herself then bolted from the Serles' drawing room.

AFTER A TORTUOUS NIGHT, Juliet awoke at dawn with a heaving stomach. Not even the tea and toast Lara brought or refreshing her nausea-healing charm helped, so she soon lost everything remaining in her stomach. And she was still suffering dry heaves every quarter hour or so when Giovanni joined her in her study later that morning.

Giovanni frowned at her. "Juliet, you look wretched." He swirled his right hand over his left, and a tiny cup of Varkhoran kahve appeared in his palm. "Drink this."

She retched yet again as the concentrated kahve's strong scent hit her. "Vanish that!"

His frown deepening, Giovanni snapped his fingers, and the kahve vanished. "You're ill."

Juliet sagged in her chair and swallowed to settle her roiling stomach. Goddess, how could she explain without upsetting her protective younger brother? "Not exactly."

Giovanni turned to leave. "Liar. I'm going to fetch a witch healer."

She leapt upright, her delicate stomach heaving once more. Fetching a healer could start gossip about her scandalous pregnancy. "No, don't. I swear I'm not ill." As Giovanni faced her with a black scowl, she blurted, "I'm pregnant."

She winced when Giovanni gaped at her and sputtered, "You're what?!" His skin reddening, he began to vibrate with fury. "That beast Oakmoor is responsible, isn't he?"

Juliet nearly winced again. Blurting her pregnancy like that had been the worst way to tell Giovanni. He was erupting like a crazed chimera as she'd feared. She inhaled then inclined her head while struggling to find the words to calm her furious brother.

Striker about to spring from his shoulder, Giovanni clenched his saber. "I'm going to kill that damned rakehell. How *dare* he dishonor you then become betrothed to another lady. And not just any lady, but the one I—" He halted and whirled toward the door.

Before Giovanni could storm from her study, she snapped, "My pregnancy isn't Oakmoor's fault."

Giovanni surged back around, his beard bristling. "Explain. You just agreed he was responsible."

Juliet hurried across her study even though her haste made her nausea flare. Hopefully, the truth would calm Giovanni. She gripped his arm. "I had to use sex magic to save Oakmoor from a cruel curse cast by a Rhiannon-descendant black witch and conceived his child when doing so. Not that he's aware I did."

Giovanni scowled. "How can Oakmoor not know that? Pregnancy is a likely consequence of using powerful sex magic. And breaking a curse cast by a Rhiannon-descendant black witch would have required powerful magic indeed."

She sighed with a wry grimace. Fortunately Oakmoor didn't realize that. "He assumed our strong-magic contraceptive charms would protect us, and I didn't disabuse him of that."

His scowl becoming puzzled, Giovanni stared at her. "Why not?"

Juliet forced herself to shrug to conceal the ache filling her chest. "Because sex magic was the only way to save him, and I *had* to save him. But I couldn't bear for Oakmoor to insist we marry simply because I fell pregnant."

Giovanni snorted. "He *should* marry the lady carrying his child."

Battling another dry heave, she shivered and gripped Giovanni's arm tighter. Somehow she must make him understand. "No, I could never withstand a marriage to Oakmoor compelled by duty and guilt. He doesn't love me or truly want me as his wife, so he'd soon resent me then take other lovers once our passion waned. And I love him too much for that not to destroy me." She narrowed her eyes at Giovanni. "Imagine the reverse happening between you and Lady Georgiana Laurent."

Paling, Giovanni swallowed. "You actually love that beastly rakehell?"

She managed a trembling smile to convince Giovanni. "If I didn't, I'd not have risked everything to save him, including the royal position I'd striven so hard to achieve." She squeezed her brother's arm. "And I don't regret conceiving Oakmoor's child. Even though he doesn't return my love and shall soon marry another and I must leave Calatini before my pregnancy shows, I'll at least have the child we created together to love."

Giovanni stared down at her, his gaze darkening. "You *do* love Oakmoor, don't you?" He pulled her into a rough embrace. "Goddess, Juliet, I'm sorry."

Tears burning her eyes, she laid her head on her little brother's shoulder. "I love Oakmoor so much that I'd never forgive you if you killed him. So don't even *think* of challenging him to a duel."

Giovanni sighed then squeezed her again. "Although our family honor demands it, I shan't since you don't wish it." He drew back and wiped the tears from her cheeks. "You don't actually wish to return home to Varkhora either, do you? You're just leaving Calatini because of your pregnancy."

She smiled to reassure Giovanni. "Yes, but I'll be glad to live near you and our parents again. I've missed you all so much these past twenty-one years." Then she retched as yet another dry heave swamped her.

Giovanni frowned and eased her into the closest chair. "Your pregnancy is making you ill. You should be resting, not debating with me. Are you certain I shouldn't fetch a witch healer?"

Juliet sagged back in the chair. "I can't risk starting gossip about my scandalous pregnancy." One hand on her roiling stomach, she waved toward her ankle with the other. "And my nausea should soon ease enough that my nausea-healing charm can manage it." Please Goddess. "'Tis always worse in the mornings."

Giovanni hummed. "Then you'd better rest until luncheon. I'll help you to your bedchamber."

She let her brother half-carry her down the hall and ease her into bed. Her head whirling and stomach shifting, she sank into slumber as soon as Giovanni murmured farewell and left. She only roused when he returned several hours later.

Giovanni smiled down at her. "Wake up, big sister. 'Tis time for luncheon, and you're eating for two now."

Juliet nodded but sighed. If only her nausea would let her. She inhaled then sat upright, heaving when her stomach lurched. Luncheon would *not* go well.

Shaking his head, Giovanni offered her a gold anklet that glowed white with powerful magic. "Wear this nausea-healing charm I just purchased from Healer Althea. She's supposedly the best witch healer in Ormas, so her charm should work better than the one you created for yourself. And don't fret; I didn't disclose the identity of the pregnant lady I needed it for."

She smiled at her caring brother then removed her weak charm and donned the witch healer's. She exhaled when her nausea vanished as if it had never been. Grinning, she rose. "Healer Althea's charm definitely works better. Thanks, Giovanni." She flicked her fingers to cast a grooming spell to repair her disheveled appearance. "Shall we head to luncheon?"

Over luncheon, she and Giovanni only broached light

topics until she ate her fill for the first time in days. Then he studied her over his tiny cup of Varkhoran kahve and asked, "When shall you tell Father and Mother about your pregnancy?"

Juliet sipped the concentrated brew she could finally drink again thanks to Healer Althea's charm. "Now that you know, I'll call this afternoon and tell them. I hope they shan't be too furious with me."

Giovanni smiled at her. "Do you want me to join you on the mirror call?"

She smiled back. So caring again. "Thanks, but I should handle that myself." She finished her kahve. "Just like I handled telling Sandro and Aurora myself before accepting their offer to become Varkhora's deputy royal witch."

So once Giovanni left after saying he'd return for dinner before the Greysnowes' ball, Juliet headed to her study to call Mother and Father. She sat then exhaled and smoothed her light-jade skirt before chanting the brief spell and waving to activate her communication mirror.

The communication mirror glowed white then cleared several moments later to reveal her parents smiling at her. Mother said, "Giuliettanna, how lovely. We've the most wonderful news... Violet—Gentian's daughter—is brooding again, so we should have a fledgling amethyst faebird for you when you return home."

Juliet inhaled, a pang darting through her at having one of her sweet Gentian's descendants as her faebird. Yet would Mother and Father be as eager to offer that once they heard *her* news? She clenched her hands together in her lap and made herself return her parents' smiles. "That *is* wonderful news. I've some news to share as well." She inhaled again then confessed, "I'm pregnant. I had to use sex magic to save the gentleman I love from a Rhiannon descendant's curse. Yet he can't marry me because he's since become betrothed to another. 'Tis why I'm leaving Calatini."

Their warm smiles fading, Mother and Father paled and gaped at her.

She swallowed, blinking back the tears pricking her eyes at her parents' shamed shock. "I told Sandro and Aurora when we spoke, and they suggested we tell everyone in Varkhora that I'm a widow, so the scandal shan't follow me or my child."

Mother surged forward, her ruby faebird fluttering on her shoulder. She pressed her hand against the communication mirror's glass. "Dear Goddess, how I wish I could hold you in my arms. You must have been devastated when the gentleman you love abandoned you and your unborn child."

Juliet stared at Mother, who wasn't acting at all ashamed despite her daughter's scandalous pregnancy. "He didn't abandon us. I knew he'd never return my love when I used sex magic to break his curse, and I didn't mention that we were risking pregnancy, so he knows nothing about our child."

His mottled-green draklizard growling, Father grunted as he drew Mother back beside him. "That gentleman you love is a damned fool for choosing another when he could have had you."

Juliet eyed Father like she had Mother. He wasn't acting furious or ashamed either. "Aren't you both upset that I'm pregnant without being married?"

Father coughed. "Such scandals happen in the best families. Your mother was pregnant with you when we married. Fortunately, you were born late enough that everyone thought you were just a couple weeks early."

Her skin heating, Juliet shifted in her chair. She'd never have dreamt her parents had ever behaved so scandalously.

Mother flashed a wry smile. "You're our daughter after all, so your passionate temperament is no surprise. Plus, you've been an independent adult for many years now, and we must support your decisions about your life."

Father grinned at Mother. "Besides which, your mother has been aching for grandchildren to spoil for ages."

Juliet nodded, her blush fading. Doubtless true considering how much Mother adored children.

Mother tsked at Father. "You've wanted grandchildren just as much." She turned and beamed at Juliet. "You shall live with us when you return to Varkhora, shan't you? We'd love to have you. I know that you're accustomed to living alone, but we could tend your child when you've duties to attend to and help you train Gentian's granddaughter as well. Besides, a widow living with her parents would cause less comment."

Warmth suffusing her chest, Juliet smiled back at Mother and Father. "I'd love living with you too."

Father chuckled and shook his head. "I suppose I'd better begin reorganizing our library now. If your child is anything like you, I'll need to hide the more dangerous titles to prevent them from reading those during their midnight forays. And ensure they discover the ones they should read instead."

Juliet blinked at Father's warm amusement. "You knew I used to sneak into the library at night to learn spells beyond hearth magic? And secretly guided what I read?"

Still beaming, Mother inclined her head. "Of course we did. We were always so proud of your fierce drive, particularly your father."

Juliet inhaled and turned toward Father, who'd never once shown her that pride during her childhood. "Then *why* did you constantly censure me for being driven? Our fierce battles about that eventually convinced me I must flee Varkhora."

Paling like earlier, Father winced, and Mother laid a gentle hand over his heart. Father shuddered a sigh then replied, "Because I was terrified how you'd fare in Varkhoran society once you left our household. You refused to conceal your fierce drive behind feminine modesty. Even though I adored you as you were and understood your drive because I share it, I couldn't openly support your bold strength. Your future husband was likely to beat you for your insolent tongue, and other ladies would refuse to befriend you."

Her brow furrowing, Juliet studied Father's tight face. He obviously wasn't lying about his worry for her as a girl. Yet he'd arranged her betrothal to the bullying King Cesare, who would have beaten her for any reason he could imagine—Mother had been right that Father hadn't been thinking clearly that summer.

Father sighed again. "My censure was meant to teach you that you must conform, outwardly at least."

Mother echoed Father's sigh. "Varkhoran ladies must be subtle about their strength. And having a husband like your father who truly wants a strong lady to match him helps. But most gentlemen in Varkhora aren't like that, although that's starting to change thanks to King Alessandro."

Juliet suppressed a grimace. Living in Varkhora would definitely be an adjustment after her many years in Calatini. Yet she must leave to protect her child, and at least she'd be near her family again. A family who'd always loved her as she was even though they'd not shown it well. She met Father's gaze. "I doubt I'll ever truly be a proper Varkhoran lady, but I'll be closer than I was as a tempestuous girl."

Father almost smiled. "You'll be living in our household when you return and a powerful widow with royal support once we're gone, so you don't need to be, thank the Goddess."

As Mother nodded, Juliet blinked back warm tears at her parents' obvious love and support. Maybe that, along with Giovanni's, Sandro's, and Aurora's, would be enough to offset never having Oakmoor's. She straightened then smiled at Mother and Father. "Tell me more about how you guided my reading as a girl. I think you're right that we should begin reorganizing your library now."

When Oakmoor strode into the ballroom at Greysnowe House, he scoured the crowd for Juliet and her brother before greeting their hosts. With Lady Georgiana's betrothal ball in a week and a half, he *had* to get matters settled between the young couple. But Juliet and Lord Sabine weren't among the crowd. Lady Georgiana was talking with Lady Driscoll and Sir Lorcan, likely because Juliet and her brother would join them as soon as they arrived. He'd do the same, except joining Lady Georgiana would convince court of their betrothal. Once he'd finished scouring the crowd, he turned to Lord and Lady Greysnowe with a charming grin, and they traded good evenings.

Afterward, a smiling Lady Greysnowe arched her brows. "Looking for someone, your grace? Your future bride, perhaps?"

He let his grin turn wry. "I might be if I knew who she was." He shrugged. "No, I was looking for Lady Juliet. I've a council matter to discuss with her." Unlike her friends or his deputy, the Greysnowes would think nothing of his too frequent excuse.

As he'd expected, Lord and Lady Greysnowe simply nodded. Then Lady Greysnowe said, "Lady Juliet and Lord Sabine both accepted their invitations, so they should arrive soon."

Lord Greysnowe added dryly, "Although I'd avoid Lord Sabine, if I were you. Since your soiree, he's been scowling at you like we used to scowl at the Ravenstones. A nearly fatal duel waiting to erupt."

Oakmoor almost winced. Too true. Yet he must approach Lord Sabine to convince him of the truth and settle matters. He made himself shrug once more. "Sadly, I fear I shan't be able to avoid Lord Sabine. He and Lady Juliet are rarely apart since she and I returned to court."

After nodding farewell to his hosts, he fetched a flute of sparkling wine then joined young Lord Morwynne and Lord Alexander Greysnowe since he couldn't join the Orandians and Lady Georgiana. Lord Sabine would come talk to his friends after leaving Juliet with hers.

Yet when Juliet and her brother finally arrived, Lord Sabine didn't join his friends after escorting Juliet to Lady Driscoll and Sir Lorcan. Instead, completely ignoring Lady Georgiana beside Lady Driscoll, Lord Sabine fetched Juliet tea and sweet biscuits then hovered over her while she ate. Why was Juliet's brother hovering so? True, Lord Sabine was always protective and caring toward his sister, but not like that. Was Juliet unwell again like she'd often been since their return? Or was her unrequited love for her unknown gentleman upsetting her? Oakmoor's jaw tightened. That undeserving, blind idiot.

Forcing his jaw to loosen, he inclined his head at some quip of Lord Alexander's while continuing to scrutinize Juliet across the ballroom. She didn't appear unwell or upset tonight, merely a little tired. Certainly better than she'd appeared some evenings lately. His chest easing, he exhaled and sipped his sparkling wine. Thank the Goddess for that.

Before he could return his attention to his idle conversation with Lord Morwynne and Lord Alexander, Juliet finished her refreshments then shoved her empty teacup and plate at Lord Sabine while snapping something. A scold for hovering from how Lord Sabine glared before stalking away with Lady Georgiana's frowning eyes fixed on his back. Peculiar that Lord Sabine had left without even glancing at the lady he loved.

Lord Sabine's glare darkened to a scowl when his gaze landed on Oakmoor between Lord Morwynne and Lord Alexander. Lord Sabine thrust Juliet's dishes at the nearest servant before surging through the crowd toward them with his hand clenched on his saber and his mottled-brown draklizard craned to strike.

Oakmoor sighed. Definitely a duel waiting to erupt like Lord Greysnowe had said. Again. Would the boy ever calm down enough to listen and discuss matters sensibly? And Juliet's recent scold wouldn't have improved Lord Sabine's temper, particularly since Lady Georgiana had witnessed it.

Still scowling and ignoring his staring friends, Lord Sabine halted before him. "Oakmoor, I must speak with you. Alone."

Oakmoor muffled another sigh. Although Juliet's brother was clearly fuming, they *did* need to talk, and this was the first Lord Sabine was willing to do so. Surely if he explained the truth about him and Lady Georgiana fast enough, he could cool the boy's belligerence before he challenged him to a duel. After giving Lord Morwynne and Lord Alexander a smooth nod, Oakmoor arched his brows at Lord Sabine and waved toward the nearby garden door. "Shall we?"

As he and Lord Sabine hurried outside, he handed his half-full flute of sparkling wine to a servant by the door. His hands must be free, just in case. At the nearest garden alcove, Lord Sabine halted, and Oakmoor flung a listening-ward spell about the alcove. Anyone overhearing them would ruin his and the Duke of Osbourne's plans. As soon as he finished, he began, "About me and Lady Georgiana—"

His scowl blacker than his beard, Lord Sabine whirled to face him. "This isn't about your betrothed, Oakmoor, but about my sister."

Oakmoor stilled. Then Lord Sabine's fuming and hovering

must be connected somehow. His chest constricted again as he asked, "Is J—Lady Juliet unwell?"

Lord Sabine gripped his saber tighter and snarled, "Yes, your relentless attempts to seduce her have made her so."

Stiffening, Oakmoor eyed Juliet's brother. Had Lord Sabine guessed that he and Juliet were lovers? He must convince the young Varkhoran lord otherwise. The boy would challenge him for certain and *never* listen to him about Lady Georgiana. He gritted a light smile. "I've not been attempting to seduce your sister, merely speak with her."

Lord Sabine sneered, his draklizard hissing on his shoulder. "As if I'd believe such assurances from a beastly rakehell like you. Speaking with ladies doubtless involves kisses for you."

Oakmoor clung to his smile. "Not when I've a serious matter to discuss with them." Usually, at least. With Juliet, their primal desire invariably led to kisses, even though neither of them truly wanted that.

Lord Sabine snorted. "Please, I've seen how you watch Juliet. Like a lusty satyr watching his favorite nymph."

Oakmoor nearly winced. Unfortunately true, no matter how often he told himself not to. Damn his obsessive hunger for Juliet. He lifted his chin. "When she's not feigning disdain, she watches me exactly the same." *Despite* her professed love for another gentleman.

His draklizard launching into the air, Lord Sabine growled and surged forward. "Leave my sister alone, you beast!"

Oakmoor leapt backward to avoid Lord Sabine's fist, but the decades younger Varkhoran with warrior training was too fast for him. Agony exploded in his eye when the boy's forceful punch landed, but he managed to punch Lord Sabine's stomach in return.

Lord Sabine wheezed and bent over but rasped, "Save your attentions for your betrothed."

Fire surging in his veins at that persistent accusation, Oakmoor gritted back, "I'm *not* b—"

"Oakmoor, Giovanni, quit your stupid brawling at once," Juliet snapped before he could finish. He and Lord Sabine wrenched apart and faced Juliet, who was glaring at them from the edge of the garden alcove with her hands fisted on her hips.

As Juliet opened her mouth, doubtless to keep scolding, Lady Georgiana burst into the alcove beside her then gasped and blurted, "Giovanni, did you *punch* his grace's eye? How could you attack the duke like that?"

Lord Sabine scowled back as he jerked upright. "Because I'm a warrior, not some overly charming rakehell."

Even though his swelling eye throbbed, Oakmoor almost laughed at the boy's insult. Lord Sabine hadn't yet learned that charm could be as deadly a weapon as fists or a saber. A much defter one too.

Lady Georgiana huffed. "If you'd just listen to me for once, you'd realize that you've no reason to attack the Duke of Oakmoor."

His draklizard settling on his shoulder again, Lord Sabine sharply retorted, "I've *plenty* of reason to attack that beastly rake-hell. He—"

Juliet surged forward. "Is Calatini's Minister of Foreign Relations, and the two of you shouldn't be brawling. Just imagine the disastrous gossip if anyone else discovered you—even with the listening-ward spell on the alcove."

Oakmoor stiffened and glanced about the otherwise empty garden. Yes, him and Lord Sabine brawling was disastrous, not only for his attempt to explain the truth about him and Lady Georgiana, but also for relations between Calatini and Varkhora. He shouldn't have let the rash boy goad him into it.

Lady Georgiana inhaled. "A listening-ward spell? So *that's* why I couldn't hear them brawling until I entered the alcove." She narrowed her eyes at Lord Sabine. "Your sister's right, you know. You attacking the duke shall simply exacerbate the scandalous mess we're all in."

Lord Sabine glowered back at Lady Georgiana. "Juliet and I

have nothing to do with the mess you and Oakmoor have embroiled yourselves in."

Oakmoor snorted. Lord Sabine was as purposely obtuse as his sister. He couldn't resist murmuring, "Except that your and Lady Georgiana's indiscreet quarrel at my soiree is what started the gossip."

As Lord Sabine turned his fierce glower on Oakmoor, Juliet grasped her brother's arm and said, "Enough, Giovanni. You promised me that you'd not challenge Oakmoor."

Blinking, Oakmoor scrutinized Juliet and her brother. She must have extracted that promise to avoid causing trouble between Calatini and Varkhora. Sensible of her. Not that he'd expect less of the adroit royal witch.

Juliet tugged Lord Sabine toward the ballroom. "Now, I'm tired. Could you escort me back to the palace please?"

His glower softening into a concerned frown like the one he'd worn when hovering over Juliet earlier, Lord Sabine nodded and replied, "Yes, of course."

Oakmoor began to frown too, his chest tightening like before. Juliet's brother was *definitely* worried about her. Lord Sabine admitting Juliet was unwell might have been more than a barb. He inhaled to ease his tight chest. Yet she appeared fine, so surely not.

At the edge of the alcove, Lord Sabine slashed Oakmoor and Lady Georgiana with a disdainful glance worthy of his sister. "I wish you both every happiness. No two people deserve each other more."

While Juliet and her brother swept away, Oakmoor bit back a curse and fingered his throbbing eye. His private talk with Lord Sabine had inflamed matters rather than settling them. Because he'd allowed Juliet to distract him yet again before he could explain about Lady Georgiana.

Her dark gaze on Lord Sabine, Lady Georgiana grimaced. "Obviously you didn't get a chance to tell Giovanni the truth about us before he attacked you."

Oakmoor studied the young lady he'd not spoken with since she'd hurled herself at him before his soiree. Just like after he'd first ended their brief courtship, she'd quit her annoying flirting. She'd clearly realized at last that she didn't truly want to marry him. If only she'd done so *before* her folly caused court to believe they were involved. He sighed. "Lord Sabine wasn't interested in listening."

Lady Georgiana worried her lip, which didn't stir him in the least, unlike when Juliet did so. The young lady replied, "I've noticed. Despite my many attempts, he's not been interested in listening to me either, and he storms away before I can explain anything. What if we can't get Giovanni to listen before my betrothal ball?"

He began repairing the damage Lord Sabine had done to his evening clothes, starting with his cravat. "We must." When Lady Georgiana sagged, he added, "'Tisn't as hopeless as it seems. Lord Sabine and I weren't actually brawling over you."

Lady Georgiana's brows rose. "No?" Then she slowly nodded. "Lady Juliet, of course."

Oakmoor stilled and eyed Lady Georgiana askance. Her tone had been much too knowing. "You don't sound at all surprised."

Shaking her head, Lady Georgiana tsked. "I'm not. You've always treated Lady Juliet differently than other ladies, and the way you watch her..." Her mouth quirked. "All that used to make me frightfully jealous when I was pursuing you."

He winced. Everyone kept remarking on his attraction to Juliet recently. Had he been so obvious? 'Twas remarkable that all of court didn't realize. But thankfully, most saw him only as a rakehell duke who'd desire any lady and were convinced that he and Juliet disliked each other.

Lady Georgiana tsked again. "Besides, who else other than me or his sister would Giovanni attack you about?" She exhaled. "Although if not upset by the supposed betrothal between you and me, I doubt even a protective brother like Giovanni would have attacked you for merely flirting with Lady Juliet. You're a renowned rakehell whose habitual flirting means little, and she's old enough to take care of herself."

Oakmoor suppressed another wince. Except his relationship with Juliet went well beyond flirting. And Lord Sabine *would* attack him for that, even if his sister could take care of herself.

Lady Georgiana inhaled then faced him. "I must apologize for involving you in this scandalous mess. I was a blind fool to visit you alone and kiss you like that, especially considering you were right about me loving Giovanni." She grimaced. "But I was too terrified by the depth of my feelings and the prospect of moving to the patriarchal Varkhora of all kingdoms to allow myself to acknowledge them."

He arched a brow as he drawled his earlier thought, "If only you'd done so before your folly caused court to believe us involved."

Lady Georgiana pursed a wry smile. "Sadly, in addition to being terrified, I'm much too obstinate to have done so. I had to lose Giovanni to be able to let myself see how much I need and love him. And forcing myself to kiss a handsome gentleman like you and feeling nothing more than distaste helped too."

Oakmoor chuckled despite the faint chill prickling his neck at Lady Georgiana's words. He swept a smooth bow. "I'm pleased I could oblige you by returning your kiss so poorly."

Lady Georgiana echoed his laugh. "That wasn't a slight against your skills as a rakehell. You never wanted that kiss and enjoyed it as little as I did." She sobered. "So how are we to resolve this scandalous mess?"

He hummed. They did need to change tactics. "My talking with Lord Sabine only seems to inflame him, so I think you and he must talk instead. He loves *you* after all and should listen to you... eventually. You two simply need time alone where he can't leave until you settle matters."

Frowning, Lady Georgiana sighed. "I suppose, but how? Even if I somehow get Giovanni to listen to me for once, doing that shall take ages, and court shall notice if we disappear together for too long. I only managed it tonight by pretending to leave early, and I can't risk that again before my betrothal ball."

The perfect idea striking him, Oakmoor grinned. "The royal summer masquerade in three days should do nicely. With all the masks, keeping track of everyone is difficult, and scandalous behavior is practically expected." Not to mention that King Devon and Queen Kiera announcing she was carrying Calatini's future monarch would distract everyone. He leaned toward Lady Georgiana. "We should be able to easily rouse Lord Sabine's protective jealousy, which shall compel him into joining us to prevent me from seducing you. Then I can leave you two alone together."

Lady Georgiana pursed her lips. "Rouse Giovanni's jealousy how exactly? I'm not kissing you again."

He flashed a smirk. "By dancing the first waltz together then slipping into the palace gardens." He arched his brows at Lady Georgiana. "I assume you've already chosen your costume." When she nodded, he continued, "You'll have to change it to a nymph of some kind. And I'll dress as a satyr." That would remind Lord Sabine of his derisive barb tonight and undoubtably ensure the boy followed them.

Lady Georgiana raised her eyes skyward then sighed again. "Very well. But what shall prevent Giovanni from leaving before we settle matters?"

Oakmoor wiggled his fingers to indicate magic. How fortunate he'd learned about trap spells to secure the lady meant to break his curse. "Don't fret; I'll handle that. I just need a lock of your hair and Lord Sabine's."

Lady Georgiana began to smile. "This might just succeed. Take whatever hair you need."

He muttered a brief spell to collect a lock of Lady Georgiana's hair then quirked his brows at her. "It shall definitely succeed if you hurl yourself at Lord Sabine like you did at me once you're trapped together."

Their plans decided, he removed his listening-ward spell

from the garden alcove before escorting Lady Georgiana to her carriage without re-entering the ballroom. Then he also left to avoid court gossiping about his lengthy absence after disappearing with Lord Sabine. On his way back to Oakmoor House, he stopped by Healer Althea's to get his still throbbing eye treated. Although he could cast some healing spells, a witch healer would do a much better job healing his injury. And a black eye would create too much gossip.

Over the days before the royal summer masquerade, Oakmoor had a servant steal a lock of Lord Sabine's hair. Thankfully, the boy wasn't as zealous about destroying items that could create a magical link as he himself was. Then he set the trap spell into a charm he could invoke once the young couple was inside an appropriate palace garden. He also purchased an extravagant satyr costume with gold horns, fur, and embroidery. Not his usual taste, but the garish costume was sure to goad Lord Sabine into following. And at evening court events, he quit attempting to speak with Juliet or her brother, and he began joining groups near Lady Georgiana, although he never directly approached her. A couple days of such behavior would inflame Lord Sabine's jealous suspicions into an uncontrollable wildfire.

The evening of the royal summer masquerade, he was one of the first guests to arrive, and after greeting King Devon and Queen Kiera, who were both glowing with excitement at announcing her pregnancy later, he stood beneath a massive chandelier blazing with witchlights so that Juliet and her brother couldn't fail to notice him in his garish satyr costume as soon as they arrived. Which they did given how they stared at him when they entered the palace's rapidly filling ballroom. He concealed his smile behind his flute of sparkling wine. Just as he'd planned.

Pretending not to watch them in return, Oakmoor drifted toward the door to await Lady Georgiana. Juliet and Lord Sabine were striking in their modish costumes of flying magical creatures—she was a topaz-yellow roc, a gargantuan bird of prey known for their fierce family pride and immense strength, while her brother was an ebony dragon in drake form, a rare all-male werebeast known for their physical prowess and powerful magic. Ideal costumes for them both.

Sleek yet coy in her lustrous naiad costume of arachne silk, Lady Georgiana glided into the palace's now teeming ballroom not long before the first waltz. Handing his empty flute to a servant, he strode toward her then kissed her hand with a suave bow. He rose and grinned at her. "A freshwater nymph. The perfect blend of innocence and sensuality, one that lusty satyrs adore to ravish."

Lady Georgiana swallowed with a weak smile. "Shall it be enough, do you think?"

Oakmoor chuckled. 'Twouldn't be surprising if Lord Sabine snatched Lady Georgiana midway through the first waltz, let alone followed them into the palace gardens. "Oh, yes." As the music began, he captured Lady Georgiana's arm and waved toward the floor. "Shall we?"

At her nod, he swept Lady Georgiana to the heart of the palace's ballroom then drew her slightly too close with a smoldering smile. They twirled about the floor in silence and without any complicated moves that would separate them. Yet otherwise, they remained discreet since anything overt like kisses would engender salacious gossip once Lady Georgiana's betrothal to Lord Sabine was announced. Considering the more provocative air at masquerades, only a jealous gentleman in love would suspect them of more than mere flirtation.

He ended their waltz near the garden doors then ushered Lady Georgiana outside into the balmy summer night. Forcing himself to walk slower than usual so Lord Sabine could follow, he led Lady Georgiana to a circular rose garden with high and thick trellises surrounding it. Ideal for his trap spell.

Lord Sabine burst into the rose garden just as Lady Georgiana was settling on the stone bench.

While Lady Georgiana leapt upright again, Oakmoor grinned at the scowling younger gentleman and said, "Good evening,

Lord Sabine. 'Tis about time you arrived." He extracted his trap spell charm from his pocket and waved toward Lady Georgiana. "And about time you and Lady Georgiana settled matters. Her betrothal ball *is* next week."

As Lord Sabine surged toward him, clenching his saber and his draklizard growling, Oakmoor muttered the incantation to activate his trap spell. Still grinning at Juliet's brother, he drawled, "And my trap spell shall ensure you and Lady Georgiana remain here until you do. It shall fade at dawn." He nodded at Lady Georgiana. "Good luck."

Then he turned and hurried from the rose garden before Lord Sabine or Lady Georgiana could reply. The young couple needed privacy, and he must tell Juliet why her brother had disappeared and get her to listen about Lady Georgiana at last.

Back in the palace's ballroom, Oakmoor slipped through the cavorting crowd then fetched tea and shokolat sweet biscuits for Juliet before joining her and the Orandians, who were dressed as mated griffins, beneath the musicians' balcony. His heart quickening, he smiled at Juliet as he offered the refreshments he'd brought her. "Evening, Lady Juliet. We need to talk."

CHAPTER 40

$\mathcal{H}$er stomach and heart twisting, Juliet faced Oakmoor and flared the feathered, topaz-yellow skirt of her roc costume to keep him several steps away. How dare Oakmoor smirk at her and offer her refreshments after he'd danced the first waltz much too close to his young betrothed then slipped out into the garden with her, no doubt with seduction in mind. Oakmoor never openly seduced ladies in public, but he did love doing so in secluded gardens—as she herself remembered quite well. When their explosive kisses in various gardens echoed through her, tingling suffused her in spite of her aching heart. Burying both her visceral desire and helpless love, she narrowed her eyes at Oakmoor. "I don't wish to talk with you."

Oakmoor shrugged then stepped closer and pressed the cup of tea and plate of shokolat sweet biscuits into her hands. "Unfortunate since we've matters to discuss. Now eat your refreshments. I don't want you almost fainting during our private talk."

She stared down at the refreshments Oakmoor had brought, her nausea surging anew despite Healer Althea's effective nausea-healing charm. How could Oakmoor behave so caring toward her when he was betrothed to another? And keep pressing for them to talk alone? They'd never just talk. She shoved the teacup and plate back at Oakmoor. "I'm not hungry, and I've *told* you that we can't risk talking in private."

Oakmoor's smirk tightened into a grimace beneath his gold satyr mask as he forced the refreshments back into her hands. "Eat. You appear pale again."

Both Juliet and Oakmoor started when Siobhan murmured beside them, "The duke is right. You do appear pale, Juliet." Her and her husband wearing matching frowns along with their matching griffin masks, Siobhan leaned forward and added, "You should be eating more right now."

Juliet stiffened and glared at Siobhan and Lorcan. Why had her friend hinted at her being pregnant before Oakmoor?

His gaze narrowing, Oakmoor scrutinized her. "Why should you be eating more right now?"

She made herself shrug then sip the tea Oakmoor had brought. Her stomach shifted, but she thankfully didn't expel its contents. She evaded, "I've been exceedingly busy with my duties," arranging her transition from Calatini's royal witch to Varkhora's deputy one, "so I require more sustenance to fuel me."

Oakmoor hummed. "You're doing too much again, aren't you, my stubborn witch?"

Juliet lifted her chin and devoured a shokolat sweet biscuit, which fortunately settled as well as the tea had. "I'm not *your* witch." Because Oakmoor was betrothed to Lady Georgiana Laurent. Her chest constricting at that, she scowled at the insufferable yet irresistible rakehell she couldn't help loving. "And I'm *not* doing too much."

Snorting, Oakmoor shook his head. "You are. To distract yourself from thinking about a certain undeserving idiot or worrying about your little brother, I suspect." His lips curved in another smirk. "Well, I've news about your brother."

She stilled as a chill skittered along her skin. What had

Oakmoor done to Giovanni? When Oakmoor had taken Lady Georgiana outside, Giovanni had bolted after them, doubtless to stop Oakmoor from seducing the lady he loved even though she'd chosen Oakmoor over him. Juliet swallowed. She should have joined Giovanni to prevent him and Oakmoor from brawling like at Greysnowe House the other day, but she'd been too distressed imagining Oakmoor making love to Lady Georgiana to risk witnessing it in person. She slowly exhaled. Besides, Oakmoor and her brother brawling posed little permanent danger. Giovanni was too fierce a warrior for Oakmoor to best, and Giovanni had promised not to kill Oakmoor. But why had Oakmoor returned while Giovanni hadn't? And where was Lady Georgiana? Had Oakmoor's wild passion scared the young lady into fleeing?

Juliet clenched her teacup and plate then leaned toward Oakmoor. "What do you mean?"

Oakmoor chuckled, his hazel eyes gleaming. "We can't discuss it here."

She jerked backward and glowered at Oakmoor. He was so impossible. "How many times must I tell you that I'm not speaking with you alone?"

When Siobhan touched her arm, she started like she had earlier. She'd forgotten about her friends yet again. Damn Oakmoor. Siobhan said, "You need to listen to what the Duke of Oakmoor has to tell you." Her gaze dropped to Juliet's stomach. "For *everyone's* sake."

Juliet flushed and turned her glower on Siobhan and Lorcan, who were both nodding. Why must Siobhan continue hinting about her pregnancy before Oakmoor? Did Siobhan *want* Oakmoor to discover she was carrying his child? He was betrothed to Lady Georgiana, and she was leaving Calatini in a couple months, so him discovering that would do nothing but complicate matters.

Juliet pursed her lips and held her well-meaning but misguided friend's gaze. "I can't imagine what you mean by that,

Siobhan. The duke's happiness is no concern of mine, and neither is Lady Georgiana Laurent's once she chose him over my brother." Tears suddenly pricked her eyes. If only Lady Georgiana hadn't. If only Oakmoor could love and want *her*. She handed her unfinished refreshments to a nearby servant then inhaled to settle herself. "Now, please excuse me. I find I'm weary after all."

Before Oakmoor or her friends could reply, she whirled and darted through the exuberant and richly costumed crowd. Although she should really stay for King Devon and Queen Kiera's pregnancy announcement, she'd enough of this torturous masquerade. She halted when Oakmoor grasped her wrist moments later, inevitable tingling flooding her like before.

Oakmoor rumbled, "Should you be running if you're weary?"

She wrenched her wrist free and made herself face Oakmoor. "I'm not physically weary, you idiot man. Simply weary of your relentless attempts to speak with me alone."

Oakmoor blew a heavy sigh. "I know us being alone is dangerous, but we *have* to talk, Juliet."

Burning tears pricked her eyes once more. Unlike the roc she'd dressed as tonight, she wasn't strong enough for this. "I can't, Oakmoor, I just can't. Please quit pestering me."

Oakmoor frowned and surged closer, his gold satyr mask glittering in the witchlights. "Are you about to cry?"

She desperately blinked back her tears. Why must pregnancy make ladies so emotional? "Of course not."

Oakmoor's frown darkened. "You are." He flung up a hand and snapped an incantation to hurl a powerful ignore spell about them. Then he yanked her into his arms. "You *must* be weary."

Although she shouldn't, Juliet buried her face in Oakmoor's chest and inhaled his earthy sandalwood scent. Goddess, how she'd missed his arms about her. Soon, he'd be married to Lady Georgiana, and she'd be living halfway across Damensea, and their child would never know him. Her feathered roc mask gouging her face, she pressed closer to Oakmoor and let her scalding tears loose.

Oakmoor rubbed her back and pressed gentle kisses against her hair. "Please don't cry. That blind idiot you love isn't worth it, and I promise your beloved brother shall be fine."

She continued to cry at her blind idiot's futile attempt to comfort her. Perhaps Giovanni might be fine—eventually—but his heart would never be the same. And neither would hers.

Sighing, Oakmoor lifted her head and removed her mask then cupped her face and wiped away her tears with his thumbs. "Enough tears. Please. They corrode my chest like a hydra's deadly spit."

Her entire body aching at Oakmoor's gentle touch, Juliet shivered when he brushed kisses beneath her damp eyes. Why was he comforting her with such tenderness? He was betrothed to Lady Georgiana. She licked her lips. "I can't make myself stop crying, I'm sorry."

His dark gaze locked on her lips, Oakmoor began lowering his head. "Then I must make you."

Oakmoor captured her mouth in a deep kiss. Her tears evaporating, she moaned as heat flared in her veins, and she pressed even closer to fiercely return his kiss. Their intense passion exploded between them like always, and they devoured one another while yanking at the other's costumes. Suddenly, Oakmoor growled and hoisted her in his arms then began carrying her toward the door.

She froze. Goddess, what were they *doing*? And in the middle of the palace's crowded ballroom too. If not for Oakmoor's ignore spell, all of court would be gaping at them. She squirmed in his arms in a futile attempt to free herself. "Oakmoor, stop."

Oakmoor grunted and gripped her tighter. "Once we reach your bedchamber."

Burning hunger throbbing through her at making love with Oakmoor again, Juliet shuddered and shoved at his chest.

"You're never reaching my bedchamber. You're betrothed to another, remember?"

Oakmoor growled. "Not that again. We'll talk about Lady Georgiana later. Much later."

Juliet whimpered as they neared the ballroom door. Once they were alone, she'd be lost. "No!" She gathered her will and flung a jump travel spell about herself, vanishing with a poof.

When she reappeared in her workroom, she sank to her knees and gulped several bracing breaths. Travel spells were incredibly draining, especially jump ones performed with will alone and without using a travel medium like doors, mirrors, bonfires, or pools. Yet she'd another spell to cast.

Gathering her will once more, she cast an impenetrable ward about her wing to prevent anyone from entering. And just in time because moments later, Oakmoor pounded on her front door and shouted, "Juliet, open this door. We must talk."

She staggered upright and glared toward her front door. If she could hear Oakmoor so clearly in her workroom, much of the palace could too—if everyone wasn't engrossed in the royal summer masquerade and the royal couple's happy announcement. Thank the Goddess.

Oakmoor pounded again. "'Tis important. Just open the door, you stubborn witch."

Juliet snorted. If she opened the door, the only talking they'd do would be with their bodies. She shivered as tingling heat surged through her again. How she burned for that. Yet making love with Oakmoor would be wrong. He was betrothed to Lady Georgiana. And even if he wasn't, intimacy with Oakmoor when he didn't return her love and didn't want her forever would eventually destroy her. She must avoid him to remain strong enough to raise their child without him.

Oakmoor pounded even louder than before. "Juliet!"

Instead of shouting back, she used her will to set a hearing-ward spell just outside her ward preventing Oakmoor from entering. He'd comprehend her unspoken reply. She smirked toward the door as Oakmoor's thunderous demands cut off, leaving behind glorious silence. Then she swayed as her head whirled and her vision briefly darkened. Three powerful spells cast using will in the space of a quarter hour hadn't drained her magical powers, but they'd come close. Not ideal when she was already tired from early pregnancy, although draining her magical powers wouldn't harm her unborn child unless she drained her life force as well.

She trudged to the cabinet where she kept some food to help her recover after draining spellwork. She extracted the fruit-nut bars drizzled with ambrosia then devoured them swifter than a starving sprite devoured ripe faeberries. Her head no longer whirling, she headed to her bedchamber to get some sleep. By the morning, her magical energy would have recharged enough to manage most spells.

Yet after she slipped into bed, Juliet couldn't succumb to slumber despite her exhaustion. Her mind kept returning to her latest encounter with Oakmoor. How could she have let him seduce her like that in public? Even the most powerful ignore spell couldn't make them completely invisible. Those already paying attention—like Siobhan and Lorcan—would have noticed her and Oakmoor's feverish kisses. Her friends were sure to lecture her again about telling Oakmoor that she carried his child. But she couldn't.

She buried her face in her pillow. Yet she couldn't withstand Oakmoor either. Whenever he touched her, she forgot everything else and responded like a desperate venus. Unless she stayed far, far away, she'd soon become his lover again. But she mustn't allow that. Somehow she must hasten her departure from Calatini. She'd write to King Devon and Queen Kiera tomorrow and arrange a meeting to request to leave before they found her replacement. Surely the veiled witch could handle her duties until they did.

CHAPTER 41

When the hearing-ward spell appeared outside Juliet's wing, Oakmoor swore and quit pounding on her firmly closed door. He was acting like a mad fool. Upon joining Juliet tonight, he'd simply meant to tell her about her brother and Lady Georgiana. But of course the stubborn witch had refused to speak with him before fleeing, which had goaded him into chasing her. Then her tears, inspired by that undeserving idiot she loved or her beloved brother, had wrecked him. He'd been helpless to resist embracing Juliet to comfort her until she quit crying.

He shuddered. Yet holding Juliet had only inflamed his obsessive hunger for her. Within moments, he was ravishing her in the middle of the palace's ballroom, and he'd completely forgotten about telling her about her brother and Lady Georgiana—and that Juliet loved another gentleman as well as wanted an adoring husband. When she'd vanished from his arms with a jump travel spell, he'd hurtled to her wing then shouted and pounded on her door like a demented minotaur lost in a labyrinth. Ostensibly to tell her about Lord Sabine and Lady Georgiana, but he'd likely have forgotten again as soon as Juliet had opened her door. No doubt he'd have carried her to her bedchamber to make love with her instead.

He groaned as his aching body hardened further at that. Yes, his obsessive hunger for Juliet was truly driving him mad. He never behaved with such indiscreet wildness or forgot all his plans. Considering her professed love for another, Juliet was sensible to have cast wards about her wing to prevent him from reaching or speaking with her. She was just as helpless against their primal desire as he was. And she was stubborn enough to maintain her wards for as long as he remained outside her wing, so he might as well return home. Her brother would simply have to tell Juliet about his betrothal to Lady Georgiana himself.

Oakmoor pivoted then strode from the palace. If *he* was sensible, he'd avoid Juliet and never attempt to speak with her alone again. 'Twas clear he could never control himself around her. He grimaced. Yet somehow making himself avoid Juliet seemed as impossible as controlling himself around the maddening, bewitching witch. Damn his obsessive hunger for her.

As soon as he reached his chambers, he yanked off his garish satyr costume and fell into bed. Yet it took him ages to fall asleep, and when he did, his dreams were all about making love with Juliet, first in her bedchamber then his in Ormas then his at Oakmoor Castle—even though he never allowed, or even imagined, other ladies in his chambers. He awoke not long after dawn hard and throbbing for Juliet, feeling as if he'd barely slept at all. But he managed to calm his aching body with icy ablutions while thinking about the evening Elvaira had cursed him to become a hideous beast.

He was midway through breakfast when his butler Grant, who was another of Miles and Martha's cousins, ushered Lord Sabine and Lady Georgiana into his breakfast room. Smiling, he rose and waved for the young couple to join him. "Please eat if you've yet to break your fast. Or have some kahve or tea if you've already eaten with Lady Juliet."

His draklizard relaxed on his shoulder for once, Lord Sabine smiled back and settled Lady Georgiana into a seat then replied, "Thanks, Oakmoor. We've not eaten yet, and we're ravenous after our eventful night."

Oakmoor swallowed a chuckle and sipped his kahve. While Lord Sabine filled two plates and Lady Georgiana poured them tea, he studied the young couple. Both were glowing despite the shadows beneath their eyes indicating that they'd not gotten much sleep. Doubtless they'd been interested in *other* things once they'd settled matters between them. He drawled, "I can imagine. Yet I'm surprised to see you here so early."

Lady Georgiana beamed at Lord Sabine, who kissed her palm as he sat beside her, making her blush. Not removing her warm gaze from Lord Sabine, she said, "Given how we complicated your life and all your help resolving our ridiculous quarrel, Giovanni and I felt we owed it to you to tell you our news at once. And we knew that once we return to Osbourne House, we'll be involved in making arrangements for much of the day."

Oakmoor's mouth twitched. Lord Sabine and Lady Georgiana had better calm their heated glances before they spoke with her father. He arched a brow as he ate another forkful of bacon and eggs with tubers. "And what arrangements are those exactly?"

Lord Sabine somehow wrested his eyes from Lady Georgiana and faced Oakmoor. "Our swift marriage after our betrothal ball, obviously. I must return to Varkhora soon. I've been gone for four months, and it shall take us three more to travel back using a caravan travel spell."

Oakmoor gave the young couple an avuncular smile over his kahve. "Lady Juliet must have been excited to hear your news, although sad to hear you're leaving her. 'Tis obvious she loves you dearly."

Lord Sabine and Lady Georgiana traded a glance, then Lord Sabine frowned and murmured, "Yes, well, Juliet hasn't heard our news yet. Her wing was surrounded by wards this morning for some reason, so we didn't see her to tell her. I did leave a note with her maid asking her to contact me once she rose."

Oakmoor stilled, his throat tightening. Wards Juliet had cast because of him. To distract Lord Sabine and Lady Georgiana from those wards, he asked, "And what are your plans for your wedding ceremony, other than being soon?"

Lady Georgiana hummed as she buttered some toast. "Nothing elaborate. Just a simple ceremony, at the Great Temple if possible. And no bloodbinding."

He inclined his head with another avuncular smile. Since Lord Sabine was his father's heir, 'twasn't surprising they weren't risking a bloodbinding that would bind their life forces together and make children with others impossible. "I hope I'll receive an invitation to your wedding ceremony."

Lord Sabine and Lady Georgiana glanced at each other again, then Lady Georgiana smiled and replied, "Of course you shall. If not for you, I never would have admitted that I truly loved Giovanni until after he'd left Calatini, and we couldn't have settled matters between us without your matchmaking and magic. Who taught you such an effective trap spell, by the way?"

Oakmoor drained his kahve to avoid shifting in his seat at referring to the secret letters he'd written Juliet for nearly two years. "Lady Juliet."

As Lady Georgiana's brows rose, Lord Sabine narrowly eyed him and muttered, "While you were away from court together, I suppose."

His shoulders tensing, Oakmoor poured himself more kahve. Although Lord Sabine was no longer jealous about Lady Georgiana, Juliet's brother definitely still didn't want him near Juliet. Goddess help him if the young Varkhoran ever discovered they'd done more than discuss magic while confined together. He held Lord Sabine's gaze. "Your sister enjoys instructing others about magic."

Laying her hand on her betrothed's, Lady Georgiana flashed a bright smile. "Now that we're no longer complicating your life, you should consider what *you* truly want. A wife, I assume, given how you were courting young ladies before your absence."

Oakmoor nodded even though he'd no intention of courting countless young ladies again now that he could afford to wait. Too painful and dull. He'd wait until he found the right lady then court her. Although finding her would be near impossible when Juliet kept distracting him. His body aching once more at their explosive passion, he inhaled to calm his mad hunger for her.

Lord Sabine grunted, still narrowly eyeing him. "Given your age, you must be desperate for an heir."

Blinking at Lord Sabine's biting tone, Oakmoor shrugged and shook his head. "I'd like a family one day, yes." The little girl and even littler boy with dark-brown hair, light olive skin, and hazel eyes that he'd imagined with Juliet flashed before him. Why was he picturing her children yet again? They'd never be his, although he'd like some just like them. Burying that, he made himself smile at Lord Sabine. "But children should be more than heirs, and I don't want just any lady to be their mother." He let his smile turn wry. "If I did, I'd have wed long before now."

Lady Georgiana quirked her brows at Lord Sabine before turning back to him. "What kind of lady are you seeking, your grace? Besides a strong one. What you said about them when ending our brief courtship revealed you want one of those." She paused then added, "And perhaps a lady closer to your age? What you said about that when dissuading my blind pursuit indicated you wanted that too."

Oakmoor tensed and set down his cup of kahve with a clink. So he did, but his future wife was no concern of Lord Sabine or Lady Georgiana. He frowned at them. "Why are you quizzing me about this?"

Lord Sabine and Lady Georgiana stilled, then Lady Georgiana smiled and replied, "Now that matters are settled between us, we want everyone we know to experience our joy. Especially someone who's done so much to secure our happiness."

Oakmoor swallowed a groan. He should have realized. He frowned fiercer at the young couple. "I'm old enough to find my own wife without any assistance, thank you."

Lord Sabine snorted. "Can you really? From what Juliet has said, I very much doubt it."

Stiffening, Oakmoor scowled at Lord Sabine. Juliet discussing him with her much younger brother was somehow worse than her discussing him with her friends who'd already guessed they were lovers. And not because the boy would challenge him to a duel if he realized that. He gripped the edge of the table. "And why were you and Lady Juliet discussing me?"

Lord Sabine returned his scowl. "Juliet was reassuring me that you didn't take advantage of her during your absence together and persuading me not to challenge you."

Oakmoor exhaled and released the table. So Juliet had only discussed him to allay her brother's suspicions. Understandable.

Snorting once more, Lord Sabine narrowed his eyes. "Although I'm still not convinced that you didn't take advantage of her."

Oakmoor cocked a brow. Lord Sabine's protective love for Juliet was blinding him to sense. "You don't know your sister very well if you believe that I or anyone else could take advantage of her. She's much too strong and clever for that. Not to mention the most illustrious witch in Calatini who's skilled at powerful and intricate spells. She'd trounce any who tried."

As Lord Sabine frowned at him, Lady Georgiana grinned and said, "How proud of Lady Juliet you sound." She tilted her head. "Do you know, it strikes me that Lady Juliet perfectly matches the kind of wife you're seeking."

He stiffened again as a hollow ache pierced him. Except Juliet loved another and would never marry him. He could never be the adoring husband she wanted. Marriage to the bewitching witch that always made him forget everything but her would be too dangerous anyway. He forced his renowned suave smile. "Don't be ridiculous. Everyone knows that Lady Juliet and I dislike each other too much to become husband and wife. And she's too devoted to being Calatini's royal witch to desire marriage." *Save to that blind idiot she loved.*

Lord Sabine leaned forward, his gaze oddly intent. "It seems that I'm not the only one who doesn't know my sister very well. Juliet has decided 'tis time to change her life, so she's returning to Varkhora with us."

Ice flooding him, Oakmoor froze and stared at Lord Sabine. Juliet was *leaving* Calatini? But she loved it here. Why would she ever leave? His stomach spasmed. That undeserving idiot who didn't return her love was surely responsible. He swallowed. "I'm surprised that Lady Juliet wants to return to a kingdom where she grew up so subservient and powerless."

A sharp smile glinted amid Lord Sabine's beard. "Her entire family is there, and she requires all our love and support right now. And *we* do love her, even more dearly for having lost her for over twenty years."

Oakmoor frowned. What did Juliet's brother mean by her requiring love and support right now? The ice in his chest hardened. Did it involve why she'd been often unwell lately? Or simply her unrequited love for that blind idiot who didn't deserve her?

Lord Sabine smirked at him. "Besides, Juliet shan't be subservient and powerless when she returns to Varkhora. Our cousin King Alessandro has promised to make her Varkhora's deputy royal witch, and she'll become the head royal witch as soon as the current one retires, which shan't be long. Father, Mother, and I are so proud of her, particularly Father—he's been telling everyone about her success here, and he'll brag even more once she returns home." Lord Sabine chuckled while devouring the last of his eggs. "I suspect quite a few unattached gentlemen shall be smitten by Juliet when she returns, so she'll likely have a husband and children soon after."

Oakmoor swallowed again as his stomach spasmed once more. "I see."

Lady Georgiana smiled as she finished her toast. "I'll be grateful for a familiar face when settling in Varkhora, although Calatini and everyone here shall be the poorer for losing Lady Juliet." She turned to her betrothed. "Now that we've eaten, shall we continue to Osbourne House?"

Lord Sabine nodded then rose and drew Lady Georgiana upright, his draklizard blinking lazily. He inclined his head at Oakmoor. "Thanks again for all your help and breakfast. Please remember to attend our betrothal ball next week."

After the glowing young couple swept out, Oakmoor lurched from his seat and strode to the gamesroom for a spiritwine despite the early hour. He needed something to melt the ice still freezing his chest. His hands trembling, he splashed a healthy portion into a snifter then downed it. Yet the ice inside him remained. What was the matter with him?

He scowled and slammed down his snifter. He *wasn't* upset by Juliet's leaving. Merely shocked that she was surrendering the royal position and established influence she'd achieved in Calatini. But perhaps Lord Sabine wished rather than knew that she was leaving. He'd confirm it at today's council meeting. Surely she'd attend to announce her intentions if she was truly leaving Calatini.

Yet when he hurried into the council room later that morning, Juliet wasn't there, and no announcement was made about her leaving. His chest easing at last, he exhaled. Her brother *must* have been mistaken. Thank the Goddess.

Once King Devon adjourned the council meeting, the Duchess of Wildewall paused before Oakmoor as their fellow councilors left, except for Lord Treyvan who was talking with King Devon and Queen Kiera. The duchess scrutinized him and asked, "Are you feeling well, your grace? You were unusually quiet this morning."

He gritted a smooth smile and rose. Of course the observant duchess had noticed that. "I simply didn't have much to say today."

The duchess pursed her lips. "Preoccupied by the mess with young Lady Georgiana Laurent, I suppose."

He clung to his smile. "No, that's been resolved. Please excuse me, I've a matter to discuss with King Devon and Queen Kiera." If they denied Juliet was leaving, he'd know for certain that Lord Sabine was mistaken.

Nodding farewell to the Duchess of Wildewall, he joined King Devon, Queen Kiera, and Lord Treyvan then entered into their talk about yesterday's royal masquerade. After the king's best friend and cousin finally left, Oakmoor smilingly arched his brows at King Devon and Queen Kiera. "Tell me, is it true that Lady Juliet is leaving Calatini?"

King Devon and Queen Kiera exchanged a glance, then King Devon murmured, "Yes, it is, unfortunately."

As Oakmoor froze from the inside out, Queen Kiera added, "She misses her family back in Varkhora. But how did you hear about her leaving? We're waiting until we find her replacement to announce it to avoid causing concern."

Oakmoor managed an insouciant shrug to disguise the ice freezing his chest once again. "Her brother Lord Sabine mentioned it." He allowed himself a wry grimace. "I don't envy your hunt, your majesties. Lady Juliet shall be near impossible to replace, as I've good cause to know."

King Devon and Queen Kiera glanced at each other again, and King Devon replied, "Fortunately, we've the veiled witch to advise us on that."

Oakmoor somehow bid King Devon and Queen Kiera a deft farewell then hastened from the council room and out to his carriage.

Back at Oakmoor House, he snatched the decanter of spiritwine and a snifter from the gamesroom then charged to Juliet's former workroom. Glowering at the glass furnace, he tossed back a snifter of spiritwine and paced between the metal tables. The ice still filling him couldn't be due to mere shock. He *was* upset by Juliet's leaving. No, more than upset. He was... devastated.

He shuddered while pouring himself another spiritwine. But why? Shouldn't he be relieved that the bewitching Juliet would no longer be near, so his obsessive hunger for her could no longer overpower him? He'd be able to resume his normal life then. Find a lady to become his wife then produce a family with her.

Snorting, he downed his spiritwine. Except he'd zero desire to do so. The *only* lady he wanted was Juliet. He clenched his empty snifter. Which was why he kept imagining her children when he thought of his own. Because he wanted that maddening witch as his wife and mother to his children. And no other lady would do. Ever. Because he loved her.

Oakmoor hurled his snifter into the glass furnace. As it shattered with a tinkling crash, he snarled a curse. How could he love Juliet? He'd always sworn never to fall in love. Love and the deep commitment love demanded were for mad fools. He scowled. Yet how could he *not* love Juliet? She was strong and bold and amazing. And her exotic beauty and biting barbs and powerful air never failed to bewitch him.

He shuddered like before. But he'd been too terrified—and too obstinate—to admit that he loved Juliet. So he'd called his love obsessive hunger rather than admitting what it actually was. And he'd feigned indifference then emotionally fled whenever he could, lying to himself that he didn't want love and commitment with her and that he could never be the adoring husband she wanted. Meanwhile, he'd kept providing himself excuses to seek her out every time they saw each other, often for the paltriest reasons. He snorted again. He truly was a mad fool. Definitely in love.

He snarled another curse. Although admitting his love at last didn't help him. He'd already lost Juliet forever. Not only did she love another and saw him as nothing more than the unrepentant rakehell she hated desiring, but she was leaving Calatini entirely.

Halting, Oakmoor clenched his fists at his sides. No. Now that he'd finally admitted he loved Juliet, he wasn't surrendering her without fighting to win her first. After all, he'd triumphed over Elvaira's vindictive beast curse with Juliet's help, so he'd triumph over almost losing Juliet herself with her help as well.

He inhaled a bracing breath. Besides, he and Juliet belonged together. Although he'd constantly told himself he didn't, he *burned* to be the adoring husband she'd always wanted. And despite professing to love another, Juliet could never resist making love with him, so their passion would one day persuade her to love him instead of that undeserving, blind idiot who didn't return her love. But until then, he'd love her enough for both himself and Juliet.

His jaw firmed. Plus, even with her loving family and position as Varkhora's deputy royal witch, Juliet would never be truly happy living in a kingdom that expected women to be subservient. She'd be happier here in Calatini enjoying the influence she'd achieved for herself with a husband who had never wanted her to be anything but her strong and independent self and would adore her even more when her biting tongue broke free. Him. They'd raise that little girl and even littler boy to be strong and independent like their mother while building a happy life together full of tender sharing, fierce quarrels, and passionate lovemaking.

Smiling at that, Oakmoor jerked a nod. He'd speak with Juliet tonight at the Merrileas' ball. Lord Sabine would have shared his news by then, so Juliet would no longer believe him to have stolen the lady her brother loved and would agree to talk with him. Once they were alone, he'd confess his love and beg Juliet to remain in Calatini as his adored wife and equal partner. He grimaced. Although somehow he must wait until *after* she'd accepted his proposal to make love with her again. Their explosive passion would only distract them from the sincere words he must share. Perhaps he should cast a chastity spell on himself.

He shuddered. Or perhaps not. Such spells were said to be excruciating. And surely he could control himself long enough to confess his love and propose.

CHAPTER 42

$\mathscr{W}$hen Juliet finally awoke after a restless night, she slid from bed then dropped the wards about her wing. Yet despite the late hour and having no toast or tea to settle it, her stomach wasn't roiling in the least. Healer Althea's nausea-healing charm was truly amazing.

Lara soon appeared with said toast and tea then handed her a note from Giovanni. Juliet frowned as she read. Apparently, he'd visited shortly after dawn but couldn't reach her due to her wards, so he wanted her to contact him as soon as she rose. She swallowed. Was something wrong? She jotted a swift reply and sent it to her brother with a kin-transportation spell. Moments later, his answer appeared beside her with a poof. She exhaled while reading it. Giovanni would return at luncheon in a couple hours. Whatever had happened mustn't be urgent. And his answer didn't hint at him being upset, so perhaps nothing was wrong. Maybe he'd simply visited to check on her and had been concerned that she'd set wards about her wing.

Since 'twas late morning, she asked Lara to bring a breakfast tray to her study rather than eating in her private dining room. While swiftly devouring that, she wrote King Devon and Queen Kiera to request a meeting about hastening her departure from

Calatini to escape Oakmoor. Then she handled other duties for the rest of the morning to distract herself from their reply and her brother's upcoming visit.

She was composing a letter to the head witch of Glimmerspell Witch Academy in Magehaven when Giovanni asked, "Ready for luncheon, big sister?"

Juliet looked up to smile at her brother then blinked. Lady Georgiana Laurent was nestled beneath Giovanni's arm, and the two of them were glowing. What was going on? Managing a smile, she leapt upright. "Yes, of course. But I must tell Lara to set another place."

Giovanni chuckled as they headed to her private dining room. "You needn't bother. I told her when we arrived—not that she was surprised. Lara had seen me and Georgiana together this morning when we stopped by to visit you. I requested that she not say anything because I wanted us to share our news in person."

Settling across the table from Giovanni and Lady Georgiana, Juliet arched her brows at them. "Let me guess, Lady Georgiana has thrown over the Duke of Oakmoor and agreed to marry you instead?" How wonderful for her brother, although entirely unexpected.

While Giovanni's grin brightened, Lady Georgiana beamed and replied, "Not exactly. I was never betrothed to the Duke of Oakmoor. But please, call me Georgiana since we'll be sisters soon."

Her heart stilling, Juliet gaped at the younger lady. Never betrothed to Oakmoor? When Giovanni served them tuber soup, she snapped her mouth shut and gritted another smile. "And you must call me Juliet. If you weren't betrothed to Oakmoor, why were you two alone and kissing in his family dining room?"

Georgiana blushed and shifted in her seat. "'Twas a remarkably foolish attempt to convince myself that I didn't love Giovanni. One which the duke didn't appreciate in the least as well as created a scandalous mess. Yet his grace spent every day since helping me resolve that mess by striving to bring me and Giovanni together."

Juliet exhaled as her heart resumed its normal beat. No wonder Oakmoor had kept endeavoring to speak with Giovanni. And doubtless his attempts to speak with her had been to secure her assistance with that. Which she'd have provided if Oakmoor had ever fully explained. Why hadn't he? Instead, he'd just hinted at the truth and tried to seduce her. Damned rakehell.

Striker almost purring on his shoulder, Giovanni kissed Georgiana's palm with a heated smile. "And last night, the Duke of Oakmoor finally succeeded—thanks to that powerful trap spell you taught him during your absence. It kept us together until dawn and forced us to settle matters."

Lowering her gaze, Juliet began her tuber soup. Explaining about Oakmoor's letters to her as Mordred would be too complicated and irrelevant to Giovanni and Georgiana's happiness.

Giovanni cleared his throat. When she glanced up, he leaned toward her, his earlier smile for his betrothed supplanted by an intent frown. "Now that matters are settled between me and Georgiana, you must do the same with the Duke of Oakmoor."

Juliet narrowed her eyes at her much younger brother. Although he meant well, her romantic affairs weren't his concern. "There's nothing to settle between me and Oakmoor. I'm leaving Calatini soon."

Georgiana grinned at her while cutting open a roll. "News that clearly upset the duke. And he doesn't even know that you're carrying his child."

Stiffening, Juliet scowled at Giovanni. "You *told* her?"

Giovanni sighed and rubbed his beard. "Of course. I shan't keep secrets from my future wife since doing so would prevent us from being true partners. Besides, Georgiana would have discovered your pregnancy soon enough if you return to Varkhora with us."

Juliet grimaced and echoed Giovanni's sigh. True on both counts, although yet another person knowing about her scandalous pregnancy could lead to Oakmoor or court discovering it too.

Still grinning, Georgiana tilted her head. "Not that you'll be returning to Varkhora. The Duke of Oakmoor shall be ecstatic when you tell him about your pregnancy and marry you as soon as he can find a priest to perform the wedding ceremony."

Her chest twisting, Juliet blinked back the tears pricking her eyes. Oakmoor would, but only out of guilt and to secure his child. Yet he'd resent her and soon take other lovers because he didn't love her and didn't truly want her as his wife. A soul-destroying marriage she could never bear. All of which she'd explained to Giovanni before, and talking about it hurt too much, so she'd not repeat it now. She made herself finish her tuber soup. "Except I'm not telling Oakmoor until after I've settled in Varkhora."

Giovanni frowned while serving her braised chicken and broccoli. "But you love him and don't actually wish to leave Calatini."

Juliet glowered at her younger brother. He'd obviously decided to forget the part about marriage to Oakmoor destroying her. Probably due to his deep sense of family honor. Yet she wasn't sacrificing herself to protect that.

Studying her, Georgiana leaned forward. "Plus, the duke loves you as much as you love him."

Juliet's mouth tightened. If only Oakmoor did. "No, he merely lusts after me, and that shall fade before long. If he loved me, he would have *told* me that you and he weren't betrothed, not just hinted at it."

Giovanni and Georgiana exchanged frowns, and Georgiana began, "But—"

Juliet snapped, "Enough!" She'd begin sobbing if they discussed Oakmoor further. She glared at Giovanni and Georgiana. "Everything is arranged for me to return to Varkhora, and I couldn't possibly disappoint Mother and Father or Sandro and

Aurora by reneging." She inhaled to steady herself. "Let us discuss happier matters. Tell me about your plans."

Giovanni and Georgiana traded another glance, then Giovanni sighed and replied, "Georgiana's father wants me and Georgiana to keep our betrothal secret until our betrothal ball next week to stun court and thereby silence the scandalous gossip. So we sadly must remain apart until then." Giovanni brightened. "Although The Duke of Osbourne has already arranged our wedding ceremony at the Great Temple the following week, making our separation worth the trouble."

Slanting Giovanni a warm smile, Georgiana squeezed his hand. "Priest Melchior Hawke shall officiate our ceremony with his wife Novice Katherine Hawke performing some readings. Quite an honor for us—given his influential family and given she'll be Calatini's high priest one day according to Father's spies."

Juliet inclined her head. Not terribly surprising considering the Goddess had blessed the erstwhile Lady Blaine with that crone illusion. And to think, an unrepentant rakehell like Oakmoor had once seriously courted such a holy lady.

Georgiana smiled at her. "However, our wedding ceremony shall be simple, with just one witness each. We thought you could be mine and the Duke of Oakmoor could be Giovanni's. To keep it to those who know about our secret betrothal."

Juliet hummed. Or to matchmake, more like. Yet she could hardly refuse such a request from her beloved brother's adored future wife. She returned Georgiana's smile. "I'll gladly be your bride witness."

As Georgiana beamed, Giovanni grinned and said, "Good. Then I'll speak with the Duke of Oakmoor at the Merrileas' ball tonight about doing the same for me."

Sighing, Juliet finished her braised chicken. Definitely matchmaking. Yet their attempts would come to nothing. "I must say that I'm relieved you two are marrying so swiftly. That means we can return to Varkhora sooner. The longer we wait, the worse the weather traveling over the mountains shall be. As it is, we shan't reach there until autumn."

Giovanni frowned. "I thought you intended to wait until King Devon and Queen Kiera found your replacement before leaving Calatini."

Juliet managed a light shrug. "I've decided I can't wait for that." Although not because of the weather. "The veiled witch can act as my replacement until the true one arrives."

Giovanni grunted and narrowly eyed her. "I see."

Her gaze probing as well, Georgiana threaded her arm through Giovanni's but only said, "Now that we've told your sister our news, Giovanni, we should leave then avoid each other like Father asked. The longer we're together, the more likely we'll be discovered."

Grimacing, Giovanni rose and drew his betrothed upright. "Very well." He smiled at Juliet. "I'll join you for dinner like usual then escort you to the Merrileas' ball."

After Giovanni and Georgiana left, Juliet returned to her study to resume her duties, and soon Lara brought her King Devon and Queen Kiera's reply to her earlier letter. They wrote that they'd be free to meet with her after the next council meeting. Juliet pursed her lips. Yet since they'd a council meeting this morning, the next one wouldn't be until the day after Giovanni and Georgiana's betrothal ball. Why the delay? She'd prefer to settle her imminent departure now. She exhaled. Even though she'd not settled it with King Devon and Queen Kiera, she could still prepare by creating guidance for her replacement, whomever that might be.

While Giovanni helped her alight at Merrilea House that evening, he muttered in her ear, "Don't fret about my continued belligerence toward the Duke of Oakmoor. I've no intention of challenging him, but I must feign that nothing's changed until the betrothal ball."

Since her brother often forgot to utilize his magic, she muttered back, "To help with that, you should cast an ignore spell or a listening-ward spell about you both when discussing your wedding ceremony."

Giovanni quirked a wry smile. "I should, shouldn't I?"

Once Giovanni left her with Siobhan and Lorcan to fetch her refreshments, he exchanged words with Oakmoor before the refreshments table—"angry" ones by his scowl and hand gripping his saber, although Striker lazily blinking on his shoulder and the listening-ward spell he'd cast about them belied that. No doubt Giovanni was simply saying good evening and asking Oakmoor to be his groom witness. But either way, Oakmoor was responding with his usual suave smile. Yet that had rarely faltered, even when facing the worst of her brother's belligerence.

Siobhan exhaled. "Oh, dear. It seems that the Duke of Oakmoor's plans for the royal summer masquerade failed. We'd such hopes for them too."

Juliet wrenched her gaze from Oakmoor and Giovanni across the ballroom to study her friends. "The Duke of Oakmoor shared his plans with you?" He'd not shared them with her, and Giovanni was *her* brother. Insufferable man.

Lorcan snorting into his sparkling wine beside her, Siobhan fingered her navy tunic and teal overcoat as she replied, "Not exactly. But 'twas obvious from his behavior toward Lady Georgiana Laurent at the masquerade that he must have some."

Lorcan shook his head. "We assumed the duke was attempting to inflame your brother's jealousy enough to goad him into proposing to Lady Georgiana."

Juliet hummed but said nothing. That *did* explain Oakmoor's overfamiliar behavior toward Georgiana yesterday. He'd been goading Giovanni into following them into the palace gardens so he could lock Giovanni and Georgiana together with his trap spell and force them to settle matters. Devious rakehell. Her jaw tensed. Yet she couldn't explain all that to her friends until

Giovanni and Georgiana's secret betrothal was revealed at their betrothal ball next week.

Siobhan sipped her sparkling wine with an impish grin. "The Duke of Oakmoor had already told me that he'd no interest in Lady Georgiana. Which he further proved by joining you as soon as he was free then embracing and kissing you in the middle of the palace's ballroom."

A blush scorching her skin, Juliet winced. Although most of court hadn't noticed that thanks to Oakmoor's ignore spell, of course her friends had. Ignore spells didn't work on those who already knew to watch unless they were particularly persuadable. To distract Siobhan and Lorcan, she murmured, "Enough about that. What did you think of King Devon and Queen Kiera's announcement?"

Although their eyes briefly narrowed at her obvious evasion, both Siobhan and Lorcan smiled as Siobhan replied, "Their joy about their future child was wonderful to see, and 'tis a relief that the Vireni line shall continue to rule Calatini."

Oakmoor glided over with a suave smile. "How true." He offered Juliet some tea and shortbread sweet biscuits. "Good evening, Lady Juliet."

She frowned up at Oakmoor despite her heart quickening like always at his nearness. Even though he wasn't betrothed to Georgiana and never had been, nothing had actually changed. He still didn't return her love or truly want her, and she was a weak fool around him. Yet she must remain strong for both herself and their child. So she daren't betray her helpless love for Oakmoor or ever be alone with him. She narrowed her eyes at him and refused the teacup and plate he offered. "Giovanni is bringing me refreshments."

Oakmoor's eyes crinkled as he continued offering her the tea and sweet biscuits. "He decided he must speak with Lord Morwynne and Lord Alexander Greysnowe."

Juliet sighed. So that Oakmoor must bring her refreshments instead. Damn Giovanni's matchmaking. Swallowing another sigh, she accepted Oakmoor's offerings. She needed the extra sustenance for their unborn child anyway.

Siobhan twinkled at Oakmoor. "How kind of you to offer to bring Juliet her refreshments in her brother's place, your grace. Especially since she needs them so desperately right now."

As Juliet tensed at Siobhan hinting about her pregnancy yet again, Oakmoor smiled and drawled, "Kind? No. Self-indulgent, really."

Juliet blinked and scrutinized Oakmoor while she devoured his delicious tea and shortbread sweet biscuits. Why would he call bringing her refreshments self-indulgent? Her pulse surged. Giovanni hadn't revealed her pregnancy, had he? She exhaled at Oakmoor's light smile. He'd not be so calm if Giovanni had.

Shoving that aside, she sniffed and smirked at Oakmoor over her teacup. "Unrepentant rakehells are always self-indulgent."

Oakmoor chuckled, his gaze gleaming. "Except for all the hours they spend handling their many duties to their duchy and Calatini."

As Siobhan and Lorcan exchanged grins, Juliet forced herself to sniff again and finish her refreshments. Must Oakmoor appear so delighted by her insolent barb? An ache flooded her chest. When she returned to Varkhora, no gentleman would ever appear likewise. Yet she couldn't risk remaining in Calatini.

While she handed her dishes to a nearby servant, the music for the first waltz began, and Oakmoor extended his hand, rumbling, "Shall we?"

Juliet nodded and took Oakmoor's hand. Although she should avoid him, she still must thank him for helping Giovanni where no one could overhear. And doing so during a dance was much safer than adjourning to an anteroom alone together. Once they began twirling, she gathered her will and flung both an ignore spell and a listening-ward spell about them to keep their conversations as private as possible while remaining in the ballroom.

She lifted her chin but kept her eyes fixed on Oakmoor's

cravat. Meeting his gaze would be too dangerous. "I must thank you for helping Giovanni find happiness with his Georgiana, despite all the public embarrassment that him stealing your supposed betrothed shall cause you."

Oakmoor laughed and drew her close enough to crush her diamond-white skirt. "'Tis the third time the lady I was publicly courting found love with another gentleman. The persistent failure of the greatest rakehell in Ormas to secure a wife shall be titillating gossip indeed."

Breathless at Oakmoor's hard body brushing hers and his earthy sandalwood scent, she shivered but managed a faint yet dismissive smile. "The gossip shan't be that bad. Court only knows of two—Georgiana and the erstwhile Lady Blaine. Only us and her family know about you kidnapping the former Miss Hawke."

Oakmoor hummed, his lips quirking. "I wasn't referring to her. I very briefly courted young Lady Ravenstone last autumn. Although since *you* didn't know, I doubt the rest of court does either, so perhaps you're right about the gossip not being too bad."

Juliet blinked then frowned. Oakmoor had wanted to marry the beauteous Lady Ravenstone? But he rarely pursued blondes. No doubt his unusual interest had been due to her potent allure as a soul healer. Not that he knew about Lady Ravenstone's secret powers.

Oakmoor bent and brushed a fleeting kiss against her furrowed brow, and she inhaled as tingling surged through her. He murmured, "Don't frown so. No matter how titillating the gossip, I'd have been glad to help Lord Sabine and Lady Georgiana find happiness together. Not only did that prevent a fashionable alliance I never truly wanted," Oakmoor tilted her chin until their gazes met, "but Lord Sabine is also your brother, and his happiness is dear to you."

Warmth filled her as she stared up at Oakmoor. From the intense yet tender look darkening his eyes, she could almost believe he returned her love and wanted her forever. Yet he didn't. If he did, he'd not have been upset at the idea of being bloodbound to her. That look was most likely a rakehell's seductive trick, just like the deep-red roses he'd given her as Miss Hawke. Her heart twisted. Oakmoor hated being without a lover, and she was ideal since she knew his true situation with Georgiana and always succumbed so easily to his kisses.

She jerked free of Oakmoor's arms with a sharp smile. "Yes, Giovanni's happiness is dear to me, so thank you again, your grace. Now please excuse me, maintaining two spells around us to secure our privacy is fatiguing me after expending so much magical energy last night on that jump travel spell and my powerful wards."

Juliet performed a rigidly perfect curtsy then turned and swept from the Merrileas' ballroom before Oakmoor could reply. Anything he said would be too likely to seduce her. And she daren't succumb. She was leaving Calatini in a few short weeks to protect herself and their unborn child.

CHAPTER 43

*O*akmoor frowned after Juliet as she swept from the Merrileas' ballroom. They'd barely discussed anything during their waltz. He'd not yet confessed his love or even asked her why she was leaving Calatini. He sighed. And was Juliet really fatigued from all her recent spellwork, or did she simply want to escape him? He sighed again then strode to the refreshments table to prevent himself from pursuing her. He must let Juliet rest if she was fatigued like she claimed, and he could speak with her at the Elliots' rout party tomorrow.

Yet over the following few days, Juliet remained stubbornly elusive at court events, even more than she had when she'd assumed him betrothed to Lady Georgiana. Why? Had foresight warned Juliet what he planned to discuss, and she wanted to avoid it because she loved that blind idiot who didn't deserve her? She'd never shown magical insight into the future before. If she had, she'd have discovered his beast curse prior to him trapping them together in Oakmoor House with the veiled witch's wards.

Two mornings before Lord Sabine and Lady Georgiana's betrothal ball, Oakmoor visited Juliet's wing at the palace close to noon. Approaching her so alone was dangerous since their explosive hunger could easily distract them from what he must say, but he *had* to speak with her before matters were publicly settled between her brother and his betrothed. Once they were, Juliet would be too busy with their wedding ceremony the following week and her duties as Calatini's departing royal witch to meet about anything else. And not long after that, Juliet would leave Calatini with Lord Sabine and Lady Georgiana.

When Juliet's little maid in starched livery opened the door, he flashed the charming smile he'd given her on his first visit the day after his soiree. "Could I speak with Lady Juliet, please?"

The maid softly returned his smile. "Allow me to check, your grace."

Unlike last time, he remained in the hall when Juliet's maid disappeared inside her wing. He couldn't begin his all-important discussion with Juliet by riling her.

But moments later, an impenetrable ward and a hearing-ward spell appeared outside Juliet's wing, just like after the royal summer masquerade.

Oakmoor swore and nearly pounded on Juliet's door even though 'twould accomplish nothing. Why must Juliet always be so stubborn and keep refusing to speak with him? Maddening witch. He suddenly exhaled, his lips wry. Yet if Juliet was less stubborn, he'd probably not love her so fiercely. 'Twas simply frustrating when they were at cross purposes.

He frowned as he hurried from the palace. Somehow he must get Juliet to speak with him. But him approaching her at court events and at her wing had both failed. He required help, and fortunately her friends had promised they'd provide it. So he asked his driver to head to the Orandian embassy.

When their butler ushered him into their family dining room, Lady Driscoll and Sir Lorcan studied him with arched brows. Lady Driscoll murmured, "What an unexpected surprise, your grace. Would you care to join us for luncheon?"

Oakmoor inclined his head and sat across from the Orandian couple. "Thank you." Once their servants set him a place and Lady Driscoll dismissed them, he flicked his fingers and cast a listening-ward spell about the dining room. "I've a private favor to ask." When the Orandians nodded, he continued, "Lady Juliet is still refusing to speak with me, and we *must* talk before Lady Georgiana's betrothal ball. Could you help arrange a meeting between us?"

Lady Driscoll and Sir Lorcan exchanged frowns, then Lady Driscoll replied, "How about at luncheon tomorrow? Juliet shan't refuse our invitation—as long as we don't share that you're our other guest."

Oakmoor grinned at Juliet's friends over his fish stew. Thank the Goddess they were more willing to listen than Juliet. "That would do nicely, thank you." He paused and asked, "Any recent news from your children?"

He and the Orandians discussed their four children over the rest of luncheon then he thanked them again and left. At the Mythacres' ball that evening, he studied Juliet across the ballroom but didn't approach her. A private meeting at the Orandian embassy would be better than attempting one here anyway.

The following day, he was purposely several minutes late so Juliet would already have arrived. If she saw his carriage, she'd likely leave without entering her friends' embassy.

While the Orandians' butler led him to the drawing room, Juliet's voice echoed in the hall, "You did *what*?! How could you trick me like this?"

Lady Driscoll calmly replied, "You must speak with the Duke of Oakmoor, Juliet. Regardless of how much you wish to deny it, your lives are entwined now. Avoiding him shan't resolve matters."

Oakmoor smiled. Juliet's friends had obviously guessed he was determined to marry her. Observant as ever. He strode into the drawing room. "I agree."

Juliet whirled to face him, her fists clenched in her aquamarine-blue skirt. "Why can't you quit pestering me?"

As Lady Driscoll and Sir Lorcan slipped out and firmly shut the door behind them, Oakmoor captured Juliet's hands to prevent his bewitching witch from escaping. Unable to resist, he kissed her palms. "Because I need you."

A flush coloring her luscious olive skin, Juliet shivered then wrenched her hands free. "Need a lover, you mean. Well, I refuse to be her. Go proposition another lady."

He wrapped his arms about Juliet when she began toward the door. His proud, stubborn witch. He drew her against his aching body. "Except no other lady would do."

Their primal hunger turning her dark-brown eyes black, Juliet shivered again but shoved his chest. "Don't, Oakmoor. Please, I can't bear it."

He smiled and kissed Juliet's neck, rumbling as her spicy gingyr scent filled his lungs. So delicious. "My lying wanton. As I recall, you bear our lovemaking quite well."

Juliet stiffened in his arms. "And what does an unrepentant rakehell like you know about making *love*?" She shoved his chest once more. "Release me. Now."

Oakmoor sighed. He should. If he didn't release Juliet, he'd soon be making love with her rather than confessing his love and begging her to marry him. And they really must resolve matters before indulging in their voracious desire again. He slowly lowered his arms and stepped back despite his hard and throbbing body. "Very well, we must talk first anyway, and we never manage that when we're wrapped in each other's arms."

Juliet glowered at him. "We've nothing to talk about now that Giovanni and Georgiana are betrothed."

He arched a brow. "We've plenty to discuss, including why your friend considers our lives entwined." When Juliet paled, he frowned and grasped her left arm to steady her. He was rushing her, which might goad her into fleeing. So instead of confessing his love, he asked, "Why are you leaving Calatini?"

Juliet paled even whiter but lifted her chin. "I've decided that 'tis time."

He frowned harder at Juliet's deepening distress, his thumb caressing her arm. "But you love it here and shall never be happy returning to a kingdom where women are expected to be subservient, even if you needn't be as their deputy royal witch." His chest constricting, he leaned toward her. "Are you letting that undeserving idiot who doesn't appreciate your love drive you away?"

Glaring now, Juliet jerked her arm from his grasp. "Don't comment on matters you don't understand, Oakmoor."

His jaw tightened. Juliet *was* running away. But she was so much stronger than that. He echoed her glare. "You're right, I don't understand. That idiot isn't worth surrendering everything you've achieved here in Calatini."

Juliet winced, her mouth trembling and hands clenched before her stomach. "Perhaps not, but 'tis impossible for me to remain now."

He glowered. What had that idiot done to his Juliet to hurt her so? The ungrateful cad should be praising the Goddess that she loved him. Oakmoor took Juliet's hands to comfort her. "You're running away because that blind idiot doesn't return your love? Forget him." Lifting her hands to his lips, he pressed tender kisses against her palms. "Another shall see how amazing you are and love you the way you deserve."

Tears briefly gleamed in Juliet's gorgeous eyes, then she wrested her hands from his and scowled. "How *dare* you keep mentioning love to me? A rakehell who seduces anyone in a skirt then moves on before either can fall in love."

He couldn't help his wince. He'd run away as much as Juliet was running now. Because he'd been terrified to love any lady then too obstinate to admit it once he did. But after almost losing her, he'd learned running away didn't change the truth in his heart. He held Juliet's dark gaze. "I didn't move on from you."

Her lips twisting, Juliet snorted. "You did. After our first time together, you avoided being alone with me for over thirteen years and took countless other lovers."

Oakmoor winced once more, his stomach clenching and heat burning his skin at his empty affairs. Ones that he'd not even enjoyed and had only pursued because he'd been too terrified to pursue Juliet. "Because I was a terrified fool, but I always wanted and needed you. Then after we kissed again in the Duchess of Childes's garden, I couldn't stay away, no matter how much I told myself to."

Juliet sniffed. "Is *that* why you courted all those little girls for months?"

He winced yet again. "I was desperate for an heir before my beast curse manifested, but I couldn't settle on any of those young ladies because they weren't you." Goddess, he'd been such a blind idiot.

Inhaling, Juliet swayed toward him with a faint blush. Then she swallowed and recoiled. "Liar. If you truly wanted me, the idea of us being bloodbound wouldn't have upset you."

Oakmoor grimaced. Except on Summerday, he'd been completely denying his love and panicking at their intense intimacy that felt too right.

While he opened his mouth to say that aloud, Juliet glared at him and continued, "And you stayed away just fine until your beast curse forced us together."

To prove Juliet wrong, he surged forward until their bodies almost touched even though that made talking and not ravishing her senseless much more difficult. Heat coursing through him, he smiled into her eyes and tucked a loose lock of silky dark-brown hair behind her ear. "You broke my beast curse over a month ago, and I still can't stay away."

Juliet swallowed but cocked a disdainful brow, and his heart quickened further. He could easily melt that cold disdain of hers if he kissed her like he burned to. Because *he* was meant to be the adoring husband she'd always wanted, not the undeserving idiot she professed to love.

Juliet sniffed. "You've only been pursuing me because you needed my help with Giovanni and Georgiana."

When Juliet began to shift back, Oakmoor grasped her hips and yanked her fully against him, and they both shuddered. Goddess, so perfect. His body throbbing again, he began lowering his head. He *must* kiss her once more. "Then why have I kept pursuing you even after arranging their betrothal?"

Juliet bent backward, dodging his kiss. "Because you hate being without a lover, and I'm ideal since I know your true situation with Georgiana."

He stilled, his brow furrowing as he studied Juliet. How could she not see how bewitching and amazing she was? Perhaps finally confessing his love would show her. His pulse racing, he swallowed then rasped, "Those aren't why I'm pursuing you at all. Juliet, I—"

Juliet snapped, "Enough! I can't talk about this any longer." Blinding magic flaring about her, she vanished with a poof.

Oakmoor snarled a curse. Why must Juliet keep casting jump travel spells to escape him? And why couldn't she see the love he'd been attempting to confess? He fisted his hands at his sides. Juliet clearly didn't trust him. Both because of his rakehell past as well as her inability to see how amazing she was. Growing up in Varkhora, she'd been raised to believe her bold strength, biting tongue, and clever magical prowess were undesirable in a lady. Then she'd fallen in love with an undeserving, blind idiot who'd hurt her and hadn't returned her love, reinforcing that childhood misbelief. He set his jaw. He *must* win Juliet's trust before she left Calatini forever. Then she'd see his love was sincere and agree to marry him, and his lasting love and their explosive passion would one day win her heart as well.

He hastened from the drawing room to say farewell to Lady Driscoll and Sir Lorcan. Choking down luncheon would be impossible right now.

. . .

EVEN THOUGH THE main court event was a rout party hosted by his deputy Lady Escana and her husband, Oakmoor remained home that evening to plan how to win Juliet's trust. He pondered their encounters over the years, and by morning, he'd devised the perfect plan. One that he must implement tonight at Lord Sabine and Lady Georgiana's betrothal ball. But it could very well eclipse their happy announcement, so he'd better obtain their permission first, although he must approach Lord Sabine since visiting Lady Georgiana would create too much gossip. Hopefully, the protective young Varkhoran wouldn't refuse permission in order to save his beloved sister from a former rakehell. Though having strictly honorably intentions should help with that.

When the Varkhoran embassy's butler showed Oakmoor into the sparring hall where Lord Sabine was practicing sword fighting shortly after breakfast, the younger lord narrowed his eyes but sheathed his saber and dismissed the burly servant opposing him. Once they were alone, Lord Sabine muttered, "What brings you by so early, Oakmoor?"

Oakmoor swiftly cast a listening-ward spell about the sparring hall then flashed a smooth smile. "I require a favor from you and Lady Georgiana. At your betrothal ball tonight, I want to ask Juliet to marry me, but she's being stubborn like usual, so I must be dramatic to make her listen, and that could eclipse your announcement."

Lord Sabine's dark eyes, so like Juliet's, narrowed even further as he drummed his bronze pommel. "Are you requesting *my* permission to marry my sister?"

Oakmoor nearly snorted. Although 'twas common in Varkhora and sometimes Calatini to request permission from a lady's male relatives, Juliet would murder him if he did so. Even if she'd not been independent for over twenty years, she'd never let her family decide such a momentous decision for her. Rightly so—her marriage should be her decision, not her family's. He let his smile turn wry. "Goddess, no. Juliet is the only one I'll be asking to marry her. I'm requesting your permission to create a scandalous scene at your betrothal ball."

Still narrowly eyeing him, Lord Sabine whistled, and his mottled-brown draklizard swooped from a perch near the window to alight on his shoulder. "Can't you ask Juliet to marry you another time?"

Oakmoor shook his head. Tonight was his best and possibly last chance. "Juliet is too determined to avoid me. If we don't speak at your betrothal ball, she'll easily manage to avoid me until she returns to Varkhora with you."

Lord Sabine hummed. "True." His hand gripping his saber, he frowned and leaned toward Oakmoor. "And exactly why are you so desperate to marry my sister?"

His neck heating, Oakmoor shifted but gritted a light smile. "Because I love Juliet and have for ages, although I refused to admit it until you told me she was leaving. That made me realize I couldn't bear life without her."

Lord Sabine grunted, his frown not easing as he continued scrutinizing Oakmoor. "You've no *other* reason for wanting to marry Juliet?"

Oakmoor tensed. Had Lord Sabine finally guessed he and Juliet had been lovers? He wasn't confirming that and risking a duel with her beloved brother. He blandly held the young Varkhoran's gaze. "What other reason could there be?"

Lord Sabine remained silent for a lengthy moment. Then he grinned and clapped Oakmoor's shoulder. "Love *is* the best reason for marriage, and the only one Juliet would be willing to accept." He rubbed his beard. "A double wedding ceremony, perhaps? Our parents are already attending over communication mirror, and you two shouldn't delay marrying."

Oakmoor returned Lord Sabine's grin as his heart surged. Juliet becoming his adored wife in a week sounded almost perfect—if only 'twere yesterday. "I'd like that, and doubtless Juliet shall too."

After exchanging farewells with Juliet's brother, Oakmoor

headed to Bewitching Raiments, a witch shop that specialized in selling enchanted attire and weapons, to purchase the griffin cloak he needed for tonight. Wearing it would remind Juliet how he'd once told her rakehells would never wear them and convince her that his love and proposal were sincere. Plus, griffin cloaks were both extremely expensive and rare, even more than flying carpets in Calatini. Collecting just a pair of feathers from mated griffins—which some couples did to show their ardent devotion—could be deadly, let alone enough fur and feathers for an entire cloak. Hence procuring a griffin cloak would demonstrate how much he adored Juliet. Please let him manage to find one.

Yet the elegant clerks at Bewitching Raiments regretfully told him they'd not had a griffin cloak for over two decades, so he sighed and continued on to Over the Walle, a witch shop that catered to magical creatures, since they sometimes possessed items their patrons had sold them. However, the merlin-garbed wood elf running the exotic witch shop quirked her winged brows when he asked about purchasing a griffin cloak then coolly replied that mated griffins only created those for the unmated they believed desperately needed them and never sold them for any price, so her witch shop had not ever had a griffin cloak to sell.

After that, he directed his carriage across Ormas to visit Rhiannon's Veils. Perhaps the incredibly powerful seer would have seen his need for a griffin cloak and somehow procured one for him.

When he sneezed at her witch shop's pervasive incense, the veiled witch sashayed through the glass beads over the rear door with a linen-wrapped bundle. "Good morning, your grace. About time you arrived. The caravan leaving for Varkhora shall depart in two weeks." She extended the bundle. "But I've the griffin cloak you need."

Oakmoor exhaled and accepted the bundle without bothering to open it. Thank the Goddess for the veiled witch's powerful foresight. He leaned toward her. "Shall it convince Juliet to stay?"

The veiled witch tilted her head, her tiny bells jingling. "It might. No one's future is entirely set until it becomes their past, you know." Her dark eyes narrowed. "And if I share too much of what I see, I'll change their future completely."

He grunted. Juliet had said that about seers, but he'd had to ask. "Which I suppose is why you didn't simply tell me that Juliet was the lady I needed to break my curse."

The veiled witch nodded. "Astute of you to realize that." She sighed, her concealing black veils undulating. "I do hope you convince Juliet tonight, your grace. Matters shall become complicated if you don't."

Oakmoor began to frown. What did the veiled witch mean by that? Although asking her would be futile given what she just said about not sharing too much. Instead, he extracted a bag of gold. "How much do I owe you for the griffin cloak?"

The veiled witch waved a hand, her tiny bells jingling anew. "Nothing. The gold you paid last time covered it."

He swept a deep bow. So doubtless the veiled witch had seen he'd need a griffin cloak when she'd spoken his prophecy. "Thank you, madam witch."

Oakmoor returned home then spent the rest of the day handling his duties to avoid pondering the evening ahead. He ate dinner early but waited to leave for Osbourne House until Lord Sabine and Lady Georgiana's betrothal ball was well underway. They should announce their betrothal before his dramatic attempt to win Juliet stole court's interest.

When his carriage halted at Osbourne House, he opened the linen-wrapped bundle from the veiled witch then inhaled. A few couples at court wore single griffin feathers, but those were nothing compared to an entire cloak. And this one had been created by mated royal griffins since the fabric woven from their fur and the feathers adorning it were a rich gold that glowed even in the carriage's dim light. 'Twas resplendent.

He donned the gold griffin cloak then strode inside to find Juliet. Please, please let this be enough to convince her to listen and agree to become his adored wife and equal partner. His life would be so empty without her.

CHAPTER 44

hen hushed whispers sparked about the ballroom, Juliet was pretending to sip a flute of sparkling wine as she watched a grinning Giovanni dance with a beaming Georgiana, who was remarkably radiant in her silver arachne silk ballgown, for their third consecutive waltz. What scandal was happening now? Surely it couldn't be from her brother and his future wife continuing to dance together. Slightly scandalous behavior was almost expected of a newly betrothed couple. And the last time court had sounded so stunned, King Devon had been introducing then-Lady Kiera to court at his Harvestfete masquerade last year. Not even Giovanni and Georgiana's betrothal announcement half an hour ago had inspired such stunned whispers.

She swallowed a weary sigh. She'd no energy for another scandal. If 'twasn't her younger brother's betrothal ball, she'd already be in bed sleeping. In dreams, she couldn't remember that Oakmoor didn't return her love or truly want her, that she was leaving Calatini soon, and that she must raise their child without him. Besides, although Healer Althea's nausea-healing charm handled that problem, early pregnancy was still draining, so she required additional sleep right now.

Sighing again, she forced herself to turn from her brother and his betrothed then froze at Oakmoor striding across the ballroom straight toward her. Was he wearing a *griffin cloak*? At his soiree for Siobhan and Lorcan just three and a half months ago, he'd sworn that he'd never wear one. Yet the resplendent gold cloak adorned with feathers—which eclipsed Georgiana's arachne silk like the sun did the moon—shone too brightly with griffin magic for it to be anything else. And that magic would force Oakmoor to be true to his heart, likely finding love and commitment, things that he'd always avoided. So *why* was he wearing a griffin cloak? And why was he striding toward *her*?

Juliet gasped, her pulse flaring, when Oakmoor halted before her and swept a deep bow with a blatantly hungry smolder. He was never so indiscreet in public without casting an ignore spell first. Then her pulse raced even more as he plucked her glass flute from her fingers and vanished it before yanking her into his arms and capturing her mouth in a fierce kiss. What was he doing? Even the greatest rakehell in Ormas would have to marry a lady he openly kissed before all of court.

After a timeless moment, Oakmoor lifted his head and rasped, "Juliet, my darling stubborn love, would you make me the happiest of gentlemen and agree at long last to be my adored wife and equal partner? I'll not quit pestering you until you do, you know. I'm quite as stubborn as you once I've decided to do something."

Breathless and aching with desire, she licked her lips and gazed up at Oakmoor as the crowd whispered and giggled about them. "I know you are. But what are you *doing*?"

Oakmoor smiled and caressed her lower lip with his thumb. "Proving how desperately I love you so that you'll take pity on me and agree to marry me. My life would be empty without you."

Her heart surged. Oakmoor loved her? Like she loved him? He couldn't. He'd have told her before now and not pursued other ladies.

She was about to reply when Oakmoor winced at a guffaw from the rapt crowd. He muttered, "Could we perhaps discuss this elsewhere?"

Juliet wobbled a nod. Neither of them enjoyed betraying their feelings in public, particularly Oakmoor. For him to have ignored his habitual discretion with such an intense public display was like a troll leaping into the summer sun in the Tsarkan grasslands, a fatal act given how trolls thrived in arctic climates.

Oakmoor whisked her into the nearest anteroom, and she gathered her will and cast an impenetrable ward and a listening-ward spell about the anteroom to ensure their privacy. As soon as she finished, she turned and faced him then arched her brows and asked, "Well?"

Hungrily eyeing her as she began toward him, Oakmoor nevertheless waved for her to remain across the anteroom. "Stay there. I always forget what I must say when we're close, and we must talk before indulging in our explosive passion."

She stilled. So Oakmoor suffered forgetting everything else as well? And for the ever suave duke to admit it... She crossed her arms over her chest to conceal the light trickling through her veins. Her voice flat, she replied, "I agree. So *when* exactly did you decide that you love me?"

Oakmoor grimaced and blew a sigh. "When your brother told me you were leaving Calatini. I was devastated and could no longer deny that I loved you." He sighed again. "Before then, I called my love obsessive hunger rather than admitting what it actually was—deep, lasting love. Because, like I told you yesterday, I was a terrified fool."

Juliet inhaled and stepped closer to Oakmoor, her heart fluttering. "I thought you were talking about fleeting lust not lasting love."

His hazel eyes darkening, Oakmoor moved toward her. "I know. Because you didn't trust me due to my rakehell past, your childhood misbelief that you're undesirable, and that undeserving idiot you love hurting you."

She stared at Oakmoor. Yes, those reasons were exactly why, although she'd not let herself consciously acknowledge the part about her childhood. He'd understood her better than she had herself. She swallowed. "I suppose winning my trust was what that public display was about."

Oakmoor bridged the final distance between them. "Yes. Because I knew you'd recognize that no one could lie about the truth in their heart when wearing a griffin cloak."

Juliet almost smiled. Vexingly astute of Oakmoor. "And to remind me that you'd said no self-respecting rakehell would ever wear one because they enjoy their freedom."

Oakmoor inhaled and took her hands. "I don't want that any longer. I want to marry you and only make love to you for the rest of our lives." He squeezed her hands. "I want you to be my equal partner whom I can always support and love as well as talk openly with at night. And to raise a couple children to be strong and independent like their amazing mother."

Warmth filled her as sudden tears cascaded down her cheeks at Oakmoor's sincere words echoing her own desires. Tears *again*? Pregnancy was making her as emotional as a newborn nymph.

Oakmoor frowned and tenderly kissed her palms. "Please don't cry, my darling love. I can't bear your tears." He wiped her damp eyes and cheeks. "I know that you love another, but you desire me, and I love you enough for us both, and I burn to be the adoring husband you've always wanted. Please marry me, and we can build such a happy life together full of tender sharing, fierce quarrels, and passionate lovemaking."

Juliet smiled up at Oakmoor. Dear Goddess, how she wanted that too. Yet she asked, "You want to marry me even believing I love another?"

Returning her smile, Oakmoor tucked hair behind her ear.

"My deep love and our primal hunger shall one day make you forget that undeserving, blind idiot."

She laughed as buoyant energy burst through her. Oakmoor *must* be desperately in love for him to risk everything for her. Just like she had when saving him. She grinned into his eyes. "I'm afraid that's quite impossible." When Oakmoor frowned, she cupped his strong face in her hands. "*You're* the undeserving, blind idiot I love. 'Tis why I could break your beast curse."

While Oakmoor began to grin, she pulled his head down and kissed him. She hummed when he drew her even closer and kissed her as if starving.

Eventually, Oakmoor wrested their mouths apart. "So you'll marry me then?"

Giddy from Oakmoor's earthy sandalwood scent and devouring kisses, Juliet laughed like earlier and threaded her fingers through his almond-brown hair. "I think we'd better."

Oakmoor rumbled, "Thank the Goddess." Then he kissed her again, swept her onto the nearby sofa, and tumbled on top of her.

Their hands and mouths wild as ever, she and Oakmoor wrenched off each other's evening clothes then made love like long-separated mated griffins and soon shattered in explosive release. So perfect. Neither moved to separate their entwined bodies while their breath and hearts gradually slowed.

Once those had resumed their usual rhythm, Oakmoor murmured against her skin, "Goddess, I love you, Juliet. So, so much."

Tingling flooding her again, she nuzzled Oakmoor and kissed his chest. "I love you too. More than I ever dreamt I could love any man."

Oakmoor shuddered and slowly began to withdraw. "We'd best separate, or we'll not leave this anteroom for days. And we really should return to your brother and Lady Georgiana's betrothal ball."

Juliet sighed. True, although not separating for days sounded *amazing*. She nodded, and they both rose.

While she was smoothing the wrinkles from her deep-amethyst skirt with a grooming spell and he was tying his cravat, Oakmoor smiled at her and said, "Lord Sabine suggested we have a double wedding ceremony with him and Lady Georgiana. I said we'd like that."

Her hands stilled on her skirt. Giovanni had surely suggested that because he knew she was carrying Oakmoor's child, a secret she must share before they rejoined everyone. Please let Oakmoor be excited that she was pregnant already, not furious that she'd been planning to leave Calatini without telling him. She swallowed but managed a bright smile. "The sooner we marry, the better."

Oakmoor chuckled and arched his brows as he donned his gold griffin cloak once more. "No complaints that I accepted before you agreed to marry me?"

Juliet tensed. She probably *would* have complained about his highhanded acceptance if she wasn't pregnant. Clinging to her smile, she opened her mouth to tell Oakmoor about their child.

Before she could, Oakmoor took her arm with a grin and said, "While you're in an agreeable mood, we should discuss when you want to start our family. Neither of us are getting any younger, so I'd prefer soon."

She inhaled then forced a light tone as she replied, "Fortunate because I fell pregnant on Summerday." When Oakmoor stared at her, she hurriedly added, "Pregnancy is a likely consequence of powerful sex magic because its potent energy overwhelms even strong-magic contraceptive charms, inactivating them."

His brow furrowed, Oakmoor turned her to face him. "Why did you lie and say that pregnancy wasn't a risk I need to concern myself about?"

Juliet winced. "Because I intended to handle any pregnancy without involving you." She worried her lip. "I know I should have told you, but I couldn't let you see that I was risking everything to save you. Even the blindest idiot would have realized that I loved you, and I couldn't bear your pity or guilty insistence we marry."

Oakmoor sighed as he brushed her lip until she quit worrying it. "Oh, Juliet." His eyes narrowed. "Your pregnancy was why you decided to leave Calatini, wasn't it?" When she winced again then nodded, he grunted and leaned toward her. "And not involving me meant you never intended to tell me that we created a child together."

She swallowed then muttered, "I planned to tell you once I returned to Varkhora." When Oakmoor's face tightened, she gripped his evening coat and said, "I was afraid you'd resent me and our child for forcing you into a marriage you'd not chosen. And since I thought you didn't love me, I assumed you'd take other lovers as soon as our passion waned. Loving you as I do, such a marriage would have destroyed me."

Oakmoor exhaled, his face softening. "So if I'd not been too terrified to admit my love, you'd not have been afraid to tell me about our child." He pressed his lips against her brow. "At least we've learned better now." As she sighed and relaxed against him at his understanding, he kissed her hair and laid his hand on her stomach. "In truth, I'm delighted that we've already started our family. A little girl, I think."

Her heart warm, Juliet grinned at Oakmoor. "You sound quite certain of that. Since when did you develop healing sight?" Not that even the strongest witch healer could see their child's gender yet.

Oakmoor chuckled. "I haven't, but I've had recurring visions of you with a little girl and an even littler boy who resemble us both. I think it might be foresight."

Still grinning, she threaded her arms about Oakmoor's neck. Except true foresight was very rare and mostly possessed by seers like the veiled witch. "Or perhaps you simply want a daughter first." Unlike gentlemen back in Varkhora—yet another reason to love him.

Chuckling again, Oakmoor shrugged. "Perhaps." Then he sobered. "I suppose carrying my child is why you've been somewhat unwell and tired lately." His voice tightened, "Your healer says that you're well though, right?"

Juliet stilled. She must phrase this carefully to avoid alarming Oakmoor, who was clearly already worrying. "Other than some nausea, which vanished when Giovanni purchased a nausea-healing charm for me, and slightly less energy, I've been completely fine, so I've not visited a healer yet. But we can visit Healer Althea together soon to check how I'm doing."

Oakmoor squeezed her against him. "How about tomorrow?" When she nodded, he exhaled. "So your brother knows you're pregnant?"

She hummed, her lips quirking at Oakmoor's rueful tone. "As does his betrothed, our parents, our royal cousins, Siobhan and Lorcan, the veiled witch, and my maid. Possibly Cassandra too."

Oakmoor tsked then drawled, "So many for a scandalous, secret pregnancy." When she grimaced, he laughed and drew her toward the door. "Come, we'd better quit talking, or everyone shall have left before we return."

Juliet dropped the wards about the anteroom, and they returned to the ballroom, which was as crowded as when they'd left despite the extremely late hour. Obviously everyone, except King Devon and Queen Kiera who'd been leaving court events even earlier than usual since the queen's pregnancy, had been waiting for them to emerge. Not too surprising.

Oakmoor flashed his suave smile and announced, "Lady Juliet has kindly agreed to become my wife, and we're marrying along with Lord Sabine and Lady Georgiana next week."

The other guests rushed forward, a grinning Lord and Lady Escana the first to reach them. Oakmoor's deputy said, "Our congratulations. Anthony and I wondered how long 'twould be before the two of you made an announcement. We'll ensure everyone moves along after congratulating you so that you can retire at a halfway decent hour."

With Lady Escana and her husband deftly managing the crowd, Juliet and Oakmoor accepted everyone's effusive congratulations and naked curiosity. Most expressed amazement at their betrothal, although a few of the more perceptive at court, like the Duchess of Childes and young Lady Ravenstone, echoed Lady Escana.

When Siobhan and Lorcan finally reached them, Siobhan embraced her while Lorcan shook Oakmoor's hand. Beaming, Siobhan said, "We're so happy for you and relieved you resolved matters before 'twas too late." She turned to Oakmoor. "You better love Juliet like she deserves."

Juliet heated as Oakmoor drew her against him with a laughing leer and replied, "Oh, I do. I promise." His voice lowered to a murmur only the four of them could hear, "And I'll love our children almost as much."

Siobhan and Lorcan exchanged grins then departed. In a remarkably short time thanks to Lady Escana and her husband, Osbourne House's ballroom was empty of everyone except them, the Duke of Osbourne, Giovanni, and Georgiana. After offering his hearty congratulations, the elderly Duke of Osbourne said good night and left too.

Striker dozing on his shoulder and his arm about Georgiana, Giovanni grinned at them and said, "Now I understand why you requested my permission to approach Juliet tonight, Oakmoor. A scandalous scene indeed."

Georgiana laughed. "Yes, you two quite eclipsed us. But we're both so thrilled that you've found happiness together." She winked at Juliet. "'Tis no wonder I could never attract the duke's interest."

Juliet returned her future sister-in-law's grin. To tease Oakmoor, she replied, "Yes, a rakehell like Oakmoor requires the threat of a Rhiannon-descendant's curse to keep him interested."

Oakmoor snorted and squeezed her against him. "After risking everything to save me from one of those, I doubt you'll ever place a vindictive curse on me, my darling witch. Although

I'd love you even if you possessed no magic at all." He arched his brows at Giovanni. "After she agreed to marry me, Juliet told me that other reason you hinted at yesterday. I'm surprised you didn't challenge me to a duel for making your sister pregnant."

His lips wry, Giovanni smoothed his beard. "Juliet loves you, so killing you would have hurt her. Besides, she made me promise not to." Giovanni smiled at her. "I'll arrange mirror calls for tomorrow with our parents and King Alessandro so you can share your news."

Juliet smiled back and inclined her head. Hopefully, their parents and royal cousins wouldn't be too disappointed that she was remaining in Calatini. "Thanks, Giovanni." Then she wobbled as an enormous yawn split her face.

Oakmoor eyed her with a frown. "You're exhausted." He glanced at Giovanni. "Could you escort Juliet back to the palace? I doubt I can trust myself to leave if I do, and she requires decent rest tonight." Before she could protest, he kissed her then withdrew. "I'll collect you tomorrow after breakfast for our visit to Healer Althea. We should have time prior to the council meeting."

Juliet pursed her lips but nodded. Yes, Oakmoor was definitely worrying. Thankfully, their visit to Healer Althea should reassure him. "Until tomorrow, my love."

The following morning, Juliet was just finishing breakfast and instructing Lara about packing her belongings and transporting them to Oakmoor House when Oakmoor arrived. He whisked her to Healer Althea's, where the Rhiannon-descendant witch healer confirmed that both she and their unborn child were healthy, reviewed the upcoming months with them, answered Oakmoor's *many* questions along with her few, then requested they return in four weeks for another visit.

While they returned to the palace for the council meeting, Juliet smiled as she nestled against Oakmoor, who was much more relaxed now. Visiting Healer Althea had reassured him as much as she'd hoped. Good. With him no longer worrying, she shared all the revelations she'd learned since reconnecting with her family to prepare him for their mirror calls later.

Once she finished, Oakmoor hummed then said, "I'm glad your parents loved you like you deserved for your true self, although they didn't always show it well, particularly your father." He sighed. "Not that I was any better."

She grinned and kissed her repentant rakehell's cheek. "You are now, which is the important thing."

Oakmoor rumbled and drew her closer then hungrily kissed her. But he withdrew when their hands began wandering. "Quit tempting me, you bewitching witch. We're due at the council meeting in a quarter hour."

Juliet sighed. Most unfortunate. But at least they'd tonight and the rest of their lives to make love.

At the council meeting, Oakmoor's fellow councilors offered their congratulations once more before King Devon and Queen Kiera arrived. After the royal couple joined everyone, Juliet and Oakmoor reluctantly separated and settled in their usual seats across the room from one another. Following the swift council meeting, they remained behind to speak privately with King Devon and Queen Kiera.

The royal couple grinning, Queen Kiera said once they were alone, "Congratulations to you both. I'm sorry we couldn't remain to congratulate you last night, but late evenings are difficult for me now, so Devon insisted we leave."

King Devon shook his head at his wife. "You need your rest."

Oakmoor gave King Devon a warm smile. "We completely understand, and we'll be leaving court events early too." He grinned. "Juliet is pregnant as well."

Juliet blushed at how proud Oakmoor sounded of that. Their scandalous pregnancy clearly wasn't going to remain secret much longer. Not that court would be particularly shocked by it.

King Devon and Queen Kiera glanced at one another, then Queen Kiera beamed and said, "Congratulations again."

King Devon arched his brows at Juliet. "Since you're remaining in Calatini now, I assume you'll continue as our royal witch?"

She smiled. In many kingdoms, especially Varkhora, the king would assume she'd surrender her hard-won position to raise her family, but not in Calatini. She inclined her head. "Unless you've found a replacement you prefer."

Queen Kiera grinned at her. "No, the veiled witch advised us to wait until after Lady Georgiana Laurent's betrothal ball to hunt for one. And to avoid meeting with you before then too."

Juliet and Oakmoor traded wry glances. Of course the veiled witch had. Seers.

After their meeting with King Devon and Queen Kiera, Juliet and Oakmoor headed to Oakmoor House for luncheon and their mirror calls to Varkhora since her wing at the palace was being packed. While they were eating their reboiled soup, which Oakmoor had requested Martha prepare specially for her, a letter from Giovanni about their mirror calls appeared beside her with a poof. Sandro and Aurora could meet directly after luncheon, while Mother and Father were available all afternoon. So once they finished eating, they adjourned to Oakmoor's study and placed a call to her cousins.

When the communication mirror cleared to reveal Sandro and Aurora holding hands in their cozy study like before, they both blinked at Juliet nestled against Oakmoor. Then Sandro murmured, "I'm guessing your news is that you're remaining in Calatini."

Juliet shifted against Oakmoor but made herself smile. "I hope you're both not too disappointed."

Sandro quirked a grin. "We'll miss having you, but Lord Marcello has been grumbling since we told him about you becoming his deputy. Apparently, he's been grooming his niece to succeed him but has been waiting to secure more favor at court for ladies possessing high positions."

Aurora leaned forward with a gentle smile. "From your glow, I assume this gentleman is the one you love who's responsible for your pregnancy. Please introduce us and tell us what happened to his other betrothed."

Juliet blushed as she introduced Oakmoor and they shared their tempestuous courtship. By the end of their mirror call, Oakmoor had charmed both her cousins with his smooth manner and sincere love for her, so Sandro and Aurora extended their heartfelt well-wishes before saying farewell.

Once their mirror call with her cousins ended, she drummed her fingers on Oakmoor's desk. Sandro and Aurora had been so supportive during all this. She must do something to thank them.

Oakmoor eyed her. "What's troubling you? Calling your parents?"

She grimaced. "I am nervous about that, but 'tisn't what I was thinking about." She explained her earlier thoughts then added, "Aurora longs for a little girl, so I'm going to collaborate with Healer Althea to create a fertility charm that breeds only daughters. If we work at it, I'm sure we can finish it before Giovanni and Georgiana leave for Varkhora."

Oakmoor chuckled and drew her closer. "You truly despise being idle, don't you? Just promise not to work yourself to exhaustion."

Juliet smiled at Oakmoor's loving support and kissed his cheek. "No doubt my caring husband shall ensure that I don't."

Oakmoor rumbled another laugh. "Probably by carrying you to bed and exhausting you another way."

Tingling at his suggestive promise, she nuzzled Oakmoor. "I might just work too hard to provoke that." She moaned when he thoroughly kissed her. After several heartbeats, she forced herself to withdraw before their passion could explode. "We really must call my parents."

Oakmoor sighed but nodded, so they repaired their appearance then called Mother and Father. As soon as the communication mirror cleared, Juliet beamed and waved toward Oakmoor. "Mother, Father, this is the Duke of Oakmoor—the gentleman I love, the father of my child, and my future husband."

Oakmoor offered a warmly smooth smile. "Who adores your daughter and was never betrothed to another even though she assumed I was."

When Mother blinked back tears, Father drew her against him and gruffly rasped, "I'm glad you're less of a fool than I first believed." His mottled-green draklizard echoing his glare, he narrowed his eyes at Oakmoor. "But if you ever distress Giuliettanna like before, I'll make you regret it, despite not possessing magical powers and living across Damensea."

As Juliet sighed at Father's loving yet unnecessary threat, Oakmoor held Father's gaze and replied, "Distressing Juliet wrecks me, so I never shall." He slanted her a laughing glance. "Although I can't promise not to vex her. I adore her biting tongue too much."

Although her parents were watching, Juliet couldn't resist playfully pursing her lips and drawling, "What you adore is kissing me quiet."

Oakmoor eyed her lips like a starving venus. "Almost as much as you adore provoking me into kissing you."

She was about to lean forward to provoke Oakmoor when Father cleared his throat. She blushed as she and Oakmoor turned back toward the communication mirror where Father was watching them with a wry smile and Mother a tremulous one.

Her ruby faebird preening her cheek, Mother sighed and wiped away her tears. "Oh, Giuliettanna, I'm overjoyed you've found love and happiness at last, especially with your child's father, although we'll miss having you living with us again along with our grandchild."

While Juliet swallowed at Mother's loving yet bittersweet sentiment, Oakmoor leaned toward Mother and said, "Although our lives are here, we'll visit Varkhora in a few years after our children are old enough so you can get to know them." He smiled at Juliet. "And by then, Juliet doubtless shall have created a better travel spell that'll shorten the journey to three days rather than three months so we can visit more than once. She's amazing at creating intricate and innovative spells. I'd still be a hideous beast if she wasn't."

Warmed by his praise, Juliet laid her hand over Oakmoor's heart. "Breaking your beast curse took love as much as spell-work." She turned back to her parents, who were both grinning now, even Father. "But creating a better travel spell seems an excellent ambition. And in the meantime, you'll have Giovanni and Georgiana's children to spoil in person and you can meet ours over mirror calls."

Mother brightened. "True enough." She tilted her head. "Although now we must send Gentian's granddaughter to you using a caravan spell. If we cast a sleep spell and a warming spell on her egg once it's laid, we can prevent it from hatching until it reaches Calatini. No faebird, particularly a hatchling, would survive such a journey, but an egg should."

Father nodded as well. "My Skymoss's mate is brooding too, so we can send the Duke of Oakmoor a draklizard egg as well." Father arched his brows at Juliet. "You remember how to train a draklizard to behave properly, don't you? Only us Varkhorans have truly mastered that."

Oakmoor's smile quirking, Juliet grinned and squeezed his knee. He'd enjoy carrying a draklizard on his shoulder once he became accustomed to it. And Father definitely approved of Oakmoor to offer one of his own draklizard's offspring. She replied, "Yes, Father, I remember."

She and Oakmoor spent the rest of the afternoon talking with Mother and Father until Oakmoor insisted she must go eat a hearty dinner for her and their unborn child. Beaming at his solicitude, her parents extended their love then said farewell before ending the mirror call.

After a dinner of braised beefsteak shank and her other Varkhoran favorites, Juliet leaned back with a replete sigh. Oakmoor's caring concern was as wonderful as his loving pride for her and their explosive passion. She studied him beneath her lashes. Passion she was ready to indulge in once more.

Oakmoor exhaled once he finished his cooked cream and Varkhoran kahve. "I suppose we should dress for the Magehavens' rout party. You'll need to conjure one of your evening gowns from the palace so we aren't too late."

She smiled then temptingly licked her lips. "I've no intention of conjuring anything since the only place we'll be heading is your chambers. Earlier you promised to carry me to bed and exhaust me, and I want that."

Her desire reflected in his face, Oakmoor scrutinized her without moving. "Not attending court events after our display yesterday would be scandalous and could tarnish your reputation as Calatini's royal witch. At least until we're properly married."

Juliet tilted her head. "My reputation can handle a bit of scandal, not that I care overmuch. I've more to live for than my royal position now—I've you and the family we'll build together too. A busy and fulfilled life I've always secretly longed for but never imagined I'd enjoy." She slanted Oakmoor a heated glance. "Besides, all of court would be disappointed if the greatest rakehell in Ormas didn't behave scandalously with his betrothed."

Oakmoor laughed and rose. "We can't possibly disappoint all of court." He scooped her into his arms then began carrying her upstairs. "Perhaps we shouldn't emerge until our wedding ceremony. I've missed our days being completely alone together."

She kissed Oakmoor's jaw. She'd missed those days too. "If only we could, but we both have duties to handle, and Giovanni shan't be in Calatini much longer, so we can't. You'll simply have to make do with ravaging me at night instead."

Oakmoor kicked his bedchamber door shut behind them. "Just at night?"

Tingling suffusing her, she grinned at Oakmoor while he tumbled them onto his bed. "Rakehell." She gathered her will and vanished their clothes. "Now would you quit talking and fulfill your promise to exhaust me?"

Oakmoor chuckled against her lips. "Demanding witch."

Juliet purred when Oakmoor kissed her. Her blood surging, she deepened their kiss, and they were soon making love with their usual intense passion. Finally.

WANT MORE?

Sign up for my newsletter for a bonus epilogue to discover if Oakmoor is right about their first child being a girl as well as other exclusive stories and book extras, new book announcements, giveaways, and more.

And order the next book The Lethe Elixir about Elise and Seanian today! Keep reading to learn more about the next book in the Calatini Tales.

LIKE THE BEAST CURSE?

Please consider writing a review. Reviews truly help spread the word about the titles you love.

THE LETHE ELIXIR

The Regency-inspired kingdom of Calatini has witches and seers, enchanted items, and mythical creatures— but nothing is stronger than the bonds of love.

Elise and Seanian have the perfect life together—almost.

After three years of marriage, they're still passionately in love and have a loving extended family. Yet despite many fertility spells, they're still childless, and having children has been Elise's lifelong dream.

So Elise and Seanian leave Calatini's royal court and go on a quest to the magical isle of Orandia to consult a powerful seer about conceiving children. The Orandian seer gives them the lethe elixir, but when they take the perilous potion, it shatters their deep love and happy marriage.

With the help of their nightmara friends and loving family, Elise and Seanian must fight to fall in love all over again and break the lethe elixir's hold on their lives to reclaim their happily-ever-after. But powerful magic is never easy to break...

THIS LOW-STAKES, low-spice, and wonderfully magical second-chance romance ends with a perfect HEA. Fans of the Moon-flower Witches, *Legends and Lattes*, and other sweet, cozy fantasy romance novels will adore The Calatini Tales.

WANT MORE? *Order* **The Lethe Elixir** *today!*

CALATINI TALES

The enchanting Calatini Tales includes...

The Spellbinding Courtship (Book 0.5)
The Enchanted Bird (Book 1)
The Nightmara Affair (Book 2)
The Secret Soulbond (Book 3)
The Goddess's Illusion (Book 4)
The Sun-Nymph Bride (Book 5)
The Beast Curse (Book 6)
The Lethe Elixir (Book 7)

ABOUT KATHERINE

A lifelong creator of her own bedtime stories, **Katherine Dotterer** writes cozy tales of fantasy romance inspired by Regency England. Born and raised in Maryland, she still lives there in an almost cottage surrounded by trees. When not writing, she enjoys reading anything she can find, singing in local choruses, hiking in nearby parks, watching the wildlife outside her windows, and cuddling with her cats. Visit her at Katherine-Dotterer.com to learn about her book releases, read her many book extras, and sign up for her newsletter.